Slowly Charlie Excalibur took his knife from its sheath, stood motionless while he studied the situation. He had long since learned to adapt, his hide thick, his back solid muscles and tendons, passing beyond any concern for comfort to the goal of simple survival which demanded that he pay no attention to whether he was hot or cold, wet or dry...

He moved again, this time to a point within ten feet of the soldier. He could see the soldier's matted black hair plastered against the narrow skull, the contours of the man's back where the rain had molded the shirt against it. No good trying to put a knife in that back, too much chance of the deflection of muscle and bone. A quick and soundless death was mandatory . . .

The Queen's Messenger

ROBERT L. DUNCAN

SPHERE BOOKS LIMITED
30–32 Gray's Inn Road, London WC1X 8JL

First published in Great Britain by
Michael Joseph Ltd 1982 under the authorship of W. R. Duncan
Copyright © 1982 by W. R. Duncan
Published by Sphere Books Ltd 1983
Reprinted 1983

TRADE
MARK

Set in Century Schoolbook

Printed and bound in Great Britain by
Cox & Wyman Ltd, Reading

ACKNOWLEDGMENTS

This book is based on the operation of the Queen's Messengers, a corps of able and dedicated men linking the vast network of British embassies all over the world. A special thanks is due to Lt. Col. E.M.T. Crump, the Superintendent of the Corps, for his invaluable cooperation and to the British Foreign Office, whose News Department reviewed the manuscript for factual error.

Dorothy Goss of Melbourne, Australia, was indispensable as a guide to the Australian spirit. Peter Goodall in Singapore provided insight and guidance into the troubled world of Southeast Asia. To the various members of the Bangkok Metropolitan Police and the Hong Kong Constabulary, who prefer to remain nameless, a special gratitude for their patience and their time.

In London Stuart MacDonald provided contacts; Mike Quinn did yeoman service in tracking down leads; Andrew Nurnberg shared his personal experiences. In Dorking Marjorie and Kenneth Douglass provided indispensable details. Jim Squires of Anaheim, California, spared no effort in providing technical assistance and Tom Pope served as an adviser on Vietnam.

Finally, and most importantly, this book must be dedicated to Lt. Col. John Kimmins, a Queen's Messenger who provided information and hospitality as well as friendship. Without his aid, and the serendipity of a chance meeting in Singapore, this book would never have been written.

PART ONE

PROLOGUE

THAILAND

There were too many ways to die in the jungle.

It had been a ferocious teacher, and in the past six years he had damn near died from snakebite, from a half dozen Asian diseases, from attacks by the CPT, the Khmer Rouge, Pol Pot's bloody sweeps, artillery from various factions lobbing indiscriminate shells into the bush. It had taught him an animal cunning.

As he padded down the narrow trace through the bush, his boots making little noise on the spongy ground, his ears were sorting out the chatter of the monkeys in the trees, the whistling calls of the birds in the multi-tiered foliage overhead. His nose had picked up the faint scent of smoke far off, not the usual burning of rice straw or a fire to drive back the edge of the jungle, but a mixture of smells, including the sweetish, nauseating stink of burning flesh.

He began to trot, the .45 pistol heavy in the holster on the webbed belt around his middle, not a run, no, for the heat would strike down a man who spent too much energy too quickly. A trot, yes, the sweat pouring down over the hard muscles of his bare back, the breath searing in and out of his lungs, his legs hurting after the first mile.

The smell was stronger. He could see the smoke now, a faint haze hanging in the trees, not even a hint of a breeze to dispel it, and he cursed to himself. Goddamn, again. Always again. He slowed down a hundred meters from the clearing, left the path to move into the trees, soundlessly working his way through the underbrush. He unsnapped the holster, lifted the heavy weight of the pistol, heart pounding. He pushed the leaves aside with the back of his left hand, expecting at any moment to hear the thumping explosion of the automatic weapons that would cut him in half. The sound did not come.

He reached the last trees before open ground. Now he could see the fires. The three hooches were burning, the flames leaping straight up from the native houses, disappearing into billows of dense black smoke. He could see the bodies strewn around the camp, the women cut down as they tried to run, bloody piles of flesh and batik, slashed by knives, hit and run, and in the dappled sunlight, a cluster of dead children as if they had been rounded up before their throats were cut. Against a tree were the remains of the one, toothless old man of the village.

Carefully he worked his way around the perimeter of the clearing, the pistol at ready, wanting to kill someone, hoping that the enemy would have left a man or two behind, just in case he showed up. This had all been designed for him, of course, to obliterate Charlie Excalibur, but *by God, King*, he thought, *I'm too smart for that, too cunning.* Still, there was the law of averages, and the attacks had been more frequent lately. They were zeroing in on him, and sooner or later they would snatch one of his men, one of the weaker ones, and commit their multiple atrocities until the pain was too intense for loyalty to survive. He circled the camp, and his rage was frustrated by the marks of cleats where the half-track had stopped to dump its load of killers and pick them up again, once the grisly business was finished.

He moved away from the clearing, remembering now that he was to meet Po, at the river-bank. He wondered if Po had been caught in the massacre. Not likely. Po was a survivor, a goddamned Chinese who had lived through a thousand more terrors than he himself had. He began to trot again, following a narrow trail through groves of bamboo which banked on either side of him like great impenetrable walls, fifteen feet high. He slowed as he neared the river, pulled the pistol again, made his way cautiously. He came to a massive flat rock, the sluggish

4

yellow water just beyond, and he stopped near the gnarled and interwoven trunks of a giant banyan tree. He stood there a long time, listening, afraid that Po had given him up. His nostrils quivered. Cigarette smoke.

He looked around. Po was sitting in a cleft of rocks, not ten feet away, hunkered down with his battered leather bag beside him, a long knife resting across his legs, his pockmarked face expressionless, the cigarette dangling from his thin-lipped mouth.

'Ah, you bastard Chinese,' Charlie Excalibur said with a laugh of relief. He climbed up the rock. 'Give me one of your cigarettes.'

'They got everybody,' Po said.

He smoked in silence for a moment. 'Not everybody. They didn't get me.'

'Only because you have luck. But it's running out.'

'You may be right.' The smoke was strong. 'Can you get to Hong Kong?'

'No,' Po said.

'Singapore?'

'No. I don't know why they're after you, but they're getting too close, and they know I'm running for you. They have the routes covered.'

'Shit,' Charlie Excalibur said. 'I need you to carry for me one more time.'

'One more time may be too many.'

'One more time?'

'One more time only,' Po agreed.

'Time's running out for both of us, and that's the truth.' He thought it through.

Clive, you son of a bitch, you owe me now. I've fed you enough.

This one would be the topper, the big trade in which he would call in the favors due. He fished a writing pad out of the bag, uncapped a ball-point pen. He had to dry the sweat off his hands to keep from ruining the paper. He wrote a few lines on the flimsy sheet, then tore it off, folded it twice, and licked the gummed flap to seal it. On the outside he wrote 'Gordon Clive, Esq. Foreign Office.

5

Whitehall, London.' He handed it to Po, who, his black eyes shining, handed him the blank check from the Hong Kong and Shanghai Bank.

'If you could get across China, how long would it take you to get to Mongolia?'

'A week. Ten days.'

'Can you do it?'

'Sure.'

'Then take this to the Registry at the British Embassy in Ulan Bator. The Queen's Messengers make a regular run up there. How much?'

'Ten thousand Hong Kong dollars.'

'You're a bloody Chink thief.'

'You are a very rich man.'

Charlie Excalibur wrote out the check, signed it with his real name, handed it to him. 'How will you get by once you cross back down to Hong Kong?'

'Everybody will know I have retired. Besides, maybe they already have you by then.'

'I'll survive.'

Po stood up, put the message and the check in his bag, the knife in his belt. 'Your luck's run out, Charlie.' With that he made a formal bow and then, in a moment, dissolved into the jungle.

Charlie Excalibur finished his cigarette, carefully field-stripped it so that a tracker would find evidence that only one man had rested here.

You had better come through for me, Gordon Clive, or the world will cave in on me for good and the senseless killing will just go on.

1

LONDON

Clive came awake with a start, the damn dream again which always vanished just as he came awake and tried to hold onto it. Katherine was lying on her elbow, and she reached out and put her hand onto his hard chest, her fingers soothing.

'The dream again?' she said.

'Yes.'

'Maybe it's better if you don't remember it.'

He came fully awake now, aware of the sunlight streaming through the open window, the sound of the traffic on the street outside. The taxis always seemed to sound their horns when they went down Bedford Place. He thought he heard the sound of boys singing a Scandinavian hiking song in the distance. 'Do you hear that?' he said.

'A busload of Danish schoolboys just unloaded at the B and B down the street,' she said, smiling. 'I watched them for a while, ruddy cheeks, blond. I have a feeling our son is going to look like that when he reaches his teens.'

'Our son?' he said. 'Not even three months along and you've determined the sex?'

'I'm sure it will be a boy,' she said with that radiant smile of hers. She was the loveliest woman he had ever seen, he decided, not the most beautiful, but certainly the sexiest. She leaned down, kissed him on the chest, and he could smell the fresh scent of her long brown hair. 'And he should have your name, love. It's a good combination, don't you think? It's proper Aussie as well as American. Hands across the sea.'

'It's going to be more than hands across the sea if you

don't watch out,' he said. Her mouth was moving across his lean stomach to the thin, puckered line of the scar that traversed his abdomen. She laughed, and he reached down and pulled her up to him, feeling the warmth of her full breasts against his chest, and he kissed her full on the mouth, excited now, his hands caressing her.

The alarm clock went off. With a groan he rolled over and jammed his hand against the button to shut it off. 'That does it,' he said. 'That just really rips it.'

She was already out of bed, slipping into her dressing gown. 'Plenty of time for that, now, isn't there?' She tied the belt. 'What they used to say about you Yanks is true, you know. Oversexed and over here.' She grinned. 'And thank God for that.'

He threw a pillow at her which missed and went wild against the doorjamb just as she was leaving. He took a shower and dressed, then went down the stairs, where she had a piece of warm toast ready for him. He ate it standing up, washed it down with a cup of coffee, pushed by the clock.

'One serious thought,' he said.

'I'm not much for serious thoughts this early in the morning,' she said. 'But what's on your Bostonian mind?'

'Marriage,' he said.

She smiled. 'Why trouble a good arrangement?'

'Our child,' he said. 'Our child is troubling the good arrangement.'

'We'll talk about it tonight.' She glanced up at the electric clock on the wall. 'You have seven minutes to make it to the tube.'

'Jesus.' He grabbed up his attaché case and gave her a quick kiss and was down the street toward High Holborn, cutting across the edge of the park, hitting the mass of people just outside the underground, packed in on the escalator, making his train just in time.

By the time he reached the old building at Queen Anne's Gate and signed in downstairs he was exactly three minutes early. The building was a chaotic one, a massive, sprawling nine-story brownstone, erected, he supposed, somewhere toward the three-quarter mark of the nineteenth century. It contained a rabbit warren of small offices and rich dark paneling, inadequate lifts with cast-iron door gratings, multiple staircases.

Entering it was like moving into a different world, but it was a world he liked, felt comfortable in. He was winded by the time he reached his office, one of the few spacious old Victorian rooms with high ceilings and a partially obscured view of the new Home Office Building to the north. The morning was already becoming steamy, and the air conditioning was functioning fitfully (a power slowdown somewhere, always union trouble), but he did not open the window. He took off his jacket and hung it up, then sat down at the desk to make his morning calls.

One of the pool secretaries brought him tea, and ordinarily, in his set routine, that would have been sufficient to propel him into his work. But something was nagging at him this morning; he was uneasy. His scar was bothering him slightly, as if the skin were pulling, just short of hurting. It had not troubled him for over eight months now. The staff psychiatrist had warned him that it might trouble him from time to time, bringing the past back to haunt him. But the worst of that was past; he had learned to live with pain on his high school football team in Boston, and that ability had seen him through the days of torture which were little more than a red, blurry nightmare to him now.

He could hear Big Ben booming in the distance, and he pushed the uneasiness aside, picked up the red scrambler telephone, and began to run his net of agents. He called Monet in Singapore first. Monet was a compulsive statistician who generally deluged him with numbers. He was currently following up on bank deposits of locally known Russian agents and stringers, but he had nothing to report today except that the weather was bloody hot and that he was going to take a couple of days off in the near future.

After Monet, Clive put in a call to Roberts in Bangkok. Roberts was a new man with little field experience and a low level of tolerance for the antics of Harry Patterson, his superior in Thailand. Roberts was still an unknown quantity to Clive, but his complaints against Patterson were vivid and consistent. Today was no exception.

'The son of a bitch thinks he makes the sun rise and set,' Roberts said. 'He would get himself an elephant and have everybody address him as Rajah if he could get by with it. He wants me to write a report every evening detailing anything I've picked up during the day.'

'Have you picked up anything?'

'Nothing.'

'Then by all means give him his report,' Clive said, amused. 'And stay in there. I'll be shifting you by the end of the week.'

'Thank God for large favors,' Roberts said with a sigh.

It was only when Clive finished the conversation with Roberts that he realized what was making him uneasy. For the past year, ever since he had been out of the cold and on this job, he had been singled out by that unknown stringer in the field, the man who called himself Charlie Excalibur. The messages had come in regular as clockwork, once a month, carried in by Queen's Messenger from Singapore or Hong Kong, once from Saigon. And now Clive realized that there should have been a dispatch from Charlie Excalibur ten days ago.

On a hunch he rang Dunhill in Hong Kong, found him unusually cheerful for having been awakened in the middle of the night.

'You bloody Yanks never did have a sense of proper timing,' Dunhill said with a mock sigh. 'Well, as long as I'm up, how can I enlighten you?'

'Charlie Excalibur.'

'What about him?'

'His dispatch is ten days overdue. What's the name of the Chinese who runs for him?'

'The redoubtable Mr. Po. I've used him myself occasionally.'

'Have you seen him lately?'

'Can't say that I have.'

10

'Keep an eye out for him.'

Clive heard the sound of a yawn. 'Will do, old chap. But I wouldn't fret about your Charlie Excalibur. Whoever he is, he's a resourceful bloke.'

I was also resourceful and they opened me up with a rusty knife.

'Look anyway. I want to know.'

Dunhill was right, of course. Clive knew that as he put down the telephone. There were occasionally odd men out there who joined the net on their own, never revealed themselves, and disappeared eventually without a trace. But he did not want that to happen with Charlie Excalibur.

He picked up the telephone again, resumed his list.

2

HONG KONG

To Major Ashton-Croft's mind, there was no more fascinating run for a Queen's Messenger than Journey 26, which encompassed the trip from Hong Kong to Canton and finally to the Mongolian capital, Ulan Bator. It was the longest journey to the farthest outpost of British diplomacy, and it was made in easy stages, by train from Hong Kong to Canton, by jet from Canton to Peking, and finally by thirty-six hours of rail travel to one of the strangest cities in the world, Ulan Bator, and the embassy at 30 Peace Street.

Ashton-Croft had made the journey many times and had seen the once-continual Chinese and Mongolian harassment of the Queen's Messengers quiet to a wary and sometimes troublesome surveillance. In spite of the occasional discomforts, it was Ashton-Croft's favorite journey.

He looked forward to this one in particular, and it would not be until after it had been made that he would see the sinister pattern to it. As a Queen's Messenger with fifteen years' service he had come to know the other thirty-seven of the Queen's best quite well, and his companion on Journey 26 this time was Bill Marston, an amiable chap with a fine sense of humor.

Sitting in the bar of the Peninsular Hotel on the afternoon before departure, Marston was dutifully taking down the shopping list from Whiting and Merriam, the two Queen's Messengers who had just come down from Ulan Bator. Since the five families which occupied the compound there were so remote from civilization, they were totally dependent upon the Queen's Messengers for

Western-style groceries, headache remedies, film developing, and so forth.

There was a good bit of joking going on, and Marston was making a mock groan over a new request from the ambassador which was going to require some tracking down. The ambassador had continual trouble with his gums and had tried remedies from all over the Far East and had now decided to try an herbal tooth soap he had heard about, available from a Chinese merchant in Hong Kong.

Actually, Ashton-Croft thought, if there was anyone who could find this particular Chinese merchant, it would be Marston. He was a resourceful chap, a retired army captain in his mid-forties, vigorous, athletic. Today, off duty, he was wearing a tropical short-sleeved suit, perfectly pressed, his coarse blond hair had been freshly trimmed, and he glowed with a tan from the tennis courts where he spent his spare time.

As a matter of fact, Ashton-Croft was feeling mellow, for he had a new biography of Churchill tucked away in his personal luggage and there would be plenty of time to read on the long journey across China and Mongolia. Marston would see after most of the details; he enjoyed being efficient.

After the briefing Ashton-Croft did not see Marston again until the next morning at the High Commission Registry, where Marston was joking with the clerks as he and Ashton-Croft were logged out with the white canvas diplomatic pouches and loaded into the minibus for transport to Kowloon Station by the so-called Chinese triplets, Wang, Ling and Fong, the omnipresent Chinese provided by the Hong Kong Diplomatic Service to handle the personal baggage and the driving in this chaotic city.

At Kowloon Station the crowds of travelers and refugees using the terminal as temporary shelter were so thick that the Chinese triplets had to form a flying wedge to get Marston and Ashton-Croft aboard the train to Canton. The trip to Canton was uneventful, full of conversation about little things, many funny stories.

13

Ashton-Croft never had either the opportunity or the desire to crack the new book.

Marston was efficient to the point of cleverness at Canton Airport. There was only one baggage trolley in the whole of the airport, and Ashton-Croft believed that the Chinese officials delighted in hiding it when they knew the Queen's Messengers were coming, so the Brits would have to make the long trek across the airport to the Peking-bound plane burdened down with their cumbersome piles of diplomatic bags, which, by regulation, they could not entrust to a porter. But Marston knew the airport intimately, headed immediately for a small storage compartment beneath a staircase, and *voilà*, there was the baggage cart, one wheel askew but a means of transport, nonetheless. They both laughed all the way to the plane.

Peking was uneventful. Once they had boarded the train from Peking for the thirty-six hour trip along the staggered parallel stretches of track along the Great Wall and then into Mongolia, Ashton-Croft had the chance to read. For he and Marston were housed in separate compartments on this leg of the journey. They took turns stretching their legs at the frequent stops the train made along the way; one would stroll while the other sat with the diplomatic bags.

They crossed the Mongolian border at three-thirty in the morning. The train stopped, and the swaggering little customs official came through the train to make his personal inspection. It was the rule that any foreigner had to be completely and properly dressed for this occasion, no pajamas and dressing robes here. Ashton-Croft was a bit piqued even as he complied, but Marston took it all in great good humor, looking quite natty in his blue blazer, gray trousers, the greyhound tie of the Queen's Messengers perfectly knotted over a pristine white shirt.

At the town of Sair Usu it was Marston's turn to stroll the platform, and when he reentered the train, he had a puzzled expression on his face. Ashton-Croft had just made tea from the boiling water in the Thermos provided for each compartment, and he handed Marston a cup.

'I just had the oddest experience,' Marston said.

'You must have stumbled across a clean water closet.'

'No, I'm serious. This bloody little man comes up to me, Chinese, I think. He looked as if he was frightened half out of his wits. He wanted me to post a letter for him at the Registry in Ulan Bator.'

'You're having me on.' Ashton-Croft sipped his tea. 'You didn't take it, did you?'

'No. I haven't lost my mind altogether.'

Entrapment, Ashton-Croft thought. The bloody Communist countries were always having a go at trying to compromise Western couriers. He could imagine what would have happened if Marston had accepted the letter. At the next stop the police would have come on board and exercised their right to go through Marston's personal effects, leaving the diplomatic bags sacrosanct. He would have to remember to pass on the information during the briefing of the next messengers along this run.

The journey across the plains of Mongolia was fascinating as usual, the train accompanied by Mongolian riders on their wild horses, making relays with red flags on the ends of their lances to make sure the tracks were clear ahead.

The layover in Ulan Bator was uneventful. He and Marston shared the cottage at the rear of the embassy, attended dinner parties, received the undying gratitude of the ambassador for the new tooth soap, which apparently seemed to work.

At one luncheon with the Registry clerks Marston brought up the subject of the little Chinese man who had approached him, telling one of the new men, Treadwell, about the incident.

'Your little Chinese showed up,' Treadwell said as he carefully speared a piece of lettuce with his fork.

'I'll be damned,' Marston said. 'You're saying the message he had was legitimate?'

'Properly addressed to the Foreign Office in London,'

Treadwell said. 'I checked regulations. No reason I could see not to accept it.'

Once they had begun the train trip back down Journey 26, Ashton-Croft finally had the chance to get into the Churchill biography, but he found no new information in it and abandoned it along the way, preferring to chat with Marston, who could always be counted on for conversation.

Marston talked a good bit about the task of rearing a daughter without a mother to see her through all the womanly problems which Marston knew little about. Ashton-Croft was able to share a few insights with him. After all, Ashton-Croft's children were now grown and on their own, and the difficulties which seemed so ominous when a child was in her late teens had a tendency to disappear by the time she was twenty-five.

The train crept along. The stops at the stations seemed to take forever, and Ashton-Croft took his turn at walking the platform just for the exercise. He dozed a lot in between stops, and nothing remarkable happened until they once again reached Sair Usu. Marston poked his head in at the connecting doors, said he was going out for a breath of air, asked if Ashton-Croft wanted any fresh fruit in case there were hawkers on the platform.

'Not with my delicate stomach, old man,' Ashton-Croft said. 'Raw foods have a tendency to do me in.'

'Back in fifteen minutes.'

But Marston was not back in fifteen minutes, and it was only when the train whistle sounded that he suddenly dashed on board. His face was white as a sheet, and his lips were compressed into a tight line.

'What's wrong?' Ashton-Croft said, concerned. 'Are you ill? You look like the wrath of God.'

'No, I'm all right,' Marston said. 'I just need sleep.'

And without a further word he went into his compartment and closed the door. Indeed, something had happened to Marston on that platform, and Ashton-Croft knew it, for from that moment it seemed that Marston had done a complete turnabout. His words had dried up, and he was no longer willing to talk about anything. He continued to look pale, and when they reached Peking, Ashton-Croft suggested that he see a doctor and have a checkup. It was easy to pick up a disease in this part of the world.

Marston refused.

On the flight to Canton some of the urgency had gone out of his manner, but Marston was still silent and moody. They had to stay overnight in Canton, in a seedy, ill-equipped hotel which was the only available accommodation for foreigners. Marston seemed to improve somewhat. He did not comment on what was wrong with him, but when the hotel refused to serve them beer, he went out on his own and with his usual efficiency came back with a pitcher full of lager, from some unknown but ingenious source.

Ashton-Croft found the beer refreshing, but after all the trouble of scrounging it Marston decided he didn't want any. Standing at the screenless window, looking down at the darkened street, Marston finally apologized.

'I'm sorry I've been such poor company,' he said. 'Sometimes I imagine that things are as they used to be, that I'll be going home and Margaret will be waiting for me and Iris will be nervous because she has a violin recital and doesn't know if she can remember the bloody notes.'

'How long has your wife been dead?'

'Two years.'

'It takes time, old man.'

'Yes, I suppose it does.'

By the time the train reached Kowloon Station, Ashton-Croft had come down with a severe case of the trots in which he felt that his insides were constantly on the edge of explosion. He and Marston were met at Kowloon Station by the Chinese triplets, and Marston took care of all the details while Ashton-Croft went to see a doctor, who diagnosed his ailment as diarrhea which he could have picked up anyplace along the line and gave him pills to take and advised him to do nothing for a couple of days so as to allow his system to regulate itself.

Ashton-Croft did not see how he could do that. He was scheduled to continue on Journey 25 almost immediately, to London via Bangkok. He went on to the Registry, where he met Marston, who sympathetically suggested a switch in runs.

'You take the two-day layover and the run to Manila,' Marston said. 'I'll go on back to London.'

'I can't put you out like that,' Ashton-Croft said, secretly hoping that Marston would insist, as he did.

'Nonsense,' Marston said. 'I'll clear with London. You get some rest.'

Ashton-Croft expressed his sincere gratitude, wanting nothing more than an uninterrupted twelve hours of sleep in the air-conditioned comfort of the Hong Kong Hotel. He waited until the signal had been sent to London and the switch approved, endured the obligatory briefing of the two Queen's Messengers who would start the run to Ulan Bator the next day, then retired to his room, took his medication, and fell asleep immediately.

The next morning Ashton-Croft felt better. Marston was scheduled to take a Cathay Pacific flight to Bangkok at shortly after 0900. At the last minute, as Ashton-Croft was going down to breakfast, he remembered something he had forgotten to tell Marston. The ambassador in Ulan Bator, not wishing to put anything on paper, had asked Ashton-Croft to put in an unofficial inquiry at the Foreign Office regarding a new second secretary assigned to Ulan Bator.

It was a matter of some minor urgency. It was too late to call the Registry, but Kai Tak Airport was no more than a few minutes from the Hong Kong Hotel, and Ashton-Croft decided to relay the information to Marston in person. He made it in plenty of time. The Cathay Pacific TriStar was still sitting at the boarding gate and the last of the passengers were just boarding.

It was standard operating procedure, of course, that a Queen's Messenger would be placed aboard the aircraft fifteen minutes in advance of any passengers to settle his packages in the first class seat next to him before the boarding process began. So Ashton-Croft identified himself to emigration and to the uniformed boarding steward, then sauntered on down to the first class boarding door, where he showed his passport to an Oriental stewardess.

She permitted him to pass, and he entered the first class section to find it only partially filled. There was an elderly Chinese gentleman in the second row right, a pair of aging American women tourists in two of the center seats, and two French salesmen poring over fabric samples at the rear of the section.

No Marston.

The stewardess was at his elbow. 'You are looking for the English courier, yes?' she said with a radiant smile.

'Yes. Where is he?'

'He was here,' she said. Marston had been installed in his seat at the proper time, but a man had come on board about ten minutes ago, spoken to him briefly, and they had left the aircraft together.

'They went into the terminal?' Ashton-Croft said sharply.

'Yes, sir. I suppose.'

Damned odd, Ashton-Croft thought. He could think of no circumstances which would pry Marston out of that seat with his diplomatic bags. 'What did the man look like?'

'The courier or the other man?'

'Damn it, the other man,' Ashton-Croft said, losing his patience. 'I know Marston, for God's sake. I know bloody well what he looks like.'

She was not affronted. 'European, I think. He spoke English. He wore a blue suit.'

'Young, old, fat, thin, bald, bearded, what?'

'I'm sorry, sir, I was working. I did not notice.'

Ashton-Croft hustled off the TriStar, the last boarding call sounding, first in English and Chinese, then in Japanese. He queued up at a public telephone and, when his turn came, rang the Hong Kong Registry and asked for Ellison, a bright young man who kept on top of things in dispatch.

Ellison was mystified. 'He's on the jet,' he said. 'Packer put him on board.'

'And where is Packer now?'

'On his way back here, I suppose. He confirmed by telephone.'

'Something's awry,' Ashton-Croft said. He proceeded to tell Ellison what the stewardess had told him. 'So check your bloody staff members. One of them came and got him.'

But of course, Ellison could find no trace. Ashton-Croft left the telephone, braced himself against the wall. He could hear the TriStar's engine in a whining roar as the jet moved out toward the runway. He was indeed sick, not just his innards. It was all planned, for what reason he did not know, the signal flags sticking up in his memory. The beer which Marston found but did not drink. The subsequent stomach cramps. The generous offer to switch the journeys.

He should have caught those signals, put them together with Marston's peculiar behavior, but he had not, and there was no point standing here berating himself. He interrupted the queue, flashing his official papers to a disgruntled Chinese, seized the phone, and dialed the High Commission. He asked for security, identified himself.

'You had better get yourself mobilized immediately,' he said, trying to keep his voice calm. 'I'll meet your men at the departure lounge at Kai Tak.'

'What's going on?' the voice on the line said.

'The impossible, unless, pray God, I'm wrong,' Ashton-Croft said. 'A Queen's Messenger has disappeared.'

3

KOWLOON

At last, Po was safe. Once he reached Kowloon, he went directly to the bank and cashed Charlie Excalibur's check. He folded the money and put it in his pocket; then he found a telephone and rang the British Embassy. He asked for Dunhill, knowing that the line would be tapped, that whatever he said would be all over Hong Kong within a matter of hours. All of the embassies bristled with electronics equipment until the tops of the buildings were forests of metal antennas and grids.

'Dunhill, here.'

'Mr. Dunhill, this is Mr. Po.'

'The prodigal returneth,' Dunhill said with great enthusiasm. 'I'm delighted to hear from you. We've had a lot of interest in what you've been up to. Why don't we get together, say, fifteen, twenty minutes? The usual spot.'

'You don't understand,' Po said. 'I am calling for a different purpose.'

'Are you having difficulties?'

'You don't understand,' Po said, frustrated. 'I am not in business no more, not for you, not for anyone. I have quit business altogether.'

There was a pause on the line. 'Well,' Dunhill said, his voice sober. 'Everybody has to have a little rest sometime. Tell you what, we'll get together anyway and have a little celebration.'

'I am not wanting to see nobody no more,' Po said firmly. 'I am not interested in nobody no more. Nobody should be interested in me. I am out of business.'

'I would give that some thought if I were you. I would –'

Po severed the connection in the middle of his sentence. He had expected this. They would undoubtedly look around for him for a while and try to offer him more money, and other people would do the same thing, but he really was not in business anymore. He was tired of secrets, tired of being watchful all the time, tired of the kind of fright he had suffered in Mongolia.

He had made preparations for this moment. He had kept his room in Kowloon, and all of his possessions were there, his bedding and his clothes, a few phonograph records and some old magazines. But he had also made arrangements for a room in Wanchai, over on the island, and that was where he would stay while the watchers kept an eye on the place in Kowloon, just in the hope that he would come back and allow himself to be persuaded.

He walked down the crowded streets to the shopping complex near the Star Ferry, stopped at a small restaurant, and ate noodles and pork. He felt good. None of the workers on the stools around him knew that they were sitting in the presence of a rich man. He had enough money on the island, in a Chinese bank, to last him for the rest of his life. When things had calmed down some, he would find himself a woman and get married. He would build a small house somewhere in the New Territories and have a son. He was not too old for that. And young women always found an older man attractive if he had money.

He boarded the ferry, went to the upper deck, where there was a cool breeze, watched the boats out in the harbor. It was possible that he would also buy himself a boat, something with a small sail. It was always cool out on the water, and a man in a boat could always see what was around him and be alone if he wished. No more jungles.

He reached the Hong Kong side, moved with the mob of people through the terminal. Suddenly he realized that he was not alone, for there was a tall European on his right. Po picked up his pace, and the man walked faster as well, never looking at him, just staying even with him.

Po walked out of the terminal into the bright sunlight of the street and turned immediately to his left, then stopped short, blinking. For there was another man immediately in front of him, his hand in his jacket pocket, and the man who had been abreast of Po was now at his side. Europeans, Po realized, men with strong bodies and squarish heads.

Po's mouth was very dry. 'You make a big mistake,' he said. 'No more business. Po is retired. No more business for anybody. I called the English. You check and see. Somebody heard the call. I told the English what I am telling you. No more business at all. Retired. Quit. Nothing to say.'

'We have a car at the curb.'

Po shaded his eyes, saw the car, a long black limousine with tinted windows. 'I don't want to go nowhere. I got no business anymore, none. Nothing to say.' He was talking too much, and he knew it, babbling as if enough words would convince them.

The man standing in front of him smiled. 'It is a hot day. We will go somewhere, have something to drink, a little talk.'

Po looked around in desperation. Thousands of people all around, but no police, no hope. The sweat poured down his face. 'If I don't go?' he said, a question.

The man's voice was very reasonable. 'You don't want to find that out, do you, Mr. Po? A few minutes of your time and you can be on your way.'

Po considered running, knew it would do no good. He was too old to be a fast runner, and he was certain they would not hesitate to kill him here if they had to. Too, there was always a chance that they were telling him the truth, that they only wanted to talk, have a drink.

Finally, he nodded, walked toward the car, knowing that his hope was a lie but that sometimes it was necessary to believe in a lie. One of the men opened the back door of the limousine. Po could feel the coolness of the air conditioning. He climbed inside.

Ah, Charlie Excalibur, he thought. *The luck has run out for both of us.*

The men climbed in on either side of him. The doors closed, and the car moved away into the heavy traffic.

4

LONDON

The calls had been packing the switchboard all morning. They were from his marvelous chaps, as Colonel Thomas Evans liked to think of them, calling in from all over the world to express their concern about Bill Marston, to ask if the rumours were true, and finally, Evans told his secretary to take the names of the callers and put through only those calls of a critical nature.

He was superintendent of the Queen's Messengers, a position that involved the complex problems of transportation and communication, keeping the lines open, as it were, to the network of British embassies and high commissions around the world. His thirty-eight men were retired military, all of them sharing a sense of communal pride at being a part of the most élite corps in the United Kingdom.

Their concern about Bill Marston was only natural, Evans thought, because Evans himself was unnerved with the knowledge that Marston was out of pocket and, beyond that, a feeling that the basic orderliness of his universe had been violated.

As he sat in his Spartan office, he found himself hoping each time his secretary appeared through his door that it would be to announce that Bill Marston himself was calling in with that buoyant manner of his to deliver a logical explanation of what had happened to him.

But there was other work to be done. The journeys could not come to a halt just because one man was missing. A list of items demanded his attention; the most important of these, as he glanced at the schedule, was a temporary airport closure in Athens which would require the rerouting of the Queen's Messenger due there this evening.

He made a mental note to send a signal down Journey 12. Commander Pelham would have to hold over until tomorrow morning. There was the chance he could be scheduled out on Swissair before 1100 hours.

The telephone rang. 'A Mr. Gordon Clive for you, sir,' his secretary said. He picked up the telephone, knowing that this Gordon Clive would be MI6.

'Evans here.'

'Good day to you, sir. I'm terribly sorry to trouble you, but I think we should have a bit of a chat. I'm in need of some fresh air. Could you possibly meet me, say, at the steps at the west end of King Charles Street?'

'I'll be there in twenty minutes,' Evans said.

'Very good. I won't keep you long.'

Evans returned the telephone to the cradle, sat motionless, considering his options for the moment. He did not like the idea of the Marston business passing beyond the hands of Foreign Office Security into the shadowy world of MI6.

But then, perhaps they would resolve it quickly, he thought as he walked down the corridor toward the grand staircase, past the great walls of faded murals to the sweep of red-carpeted stairs that led to the foyer below. He had a great affection for the old building with its galleries of marble statues and stone busts of heroes and an omnipresent murky light in its hallways.

He paused to look at the display case of Queen's Messengers' badges, a different one cast for each reign. They stretched back over the centuries, the silver greyhounds modeled after the one King Charles II had broken from a bowl in Belgium four centuries ago as a means to identify a personal messenger. The silver greyhound was now the official symbol of the service. Three hundred years, a long time, and how many couriers had there been since then, no more than a few hundred, and there had never been a breath of scandal or corruption in the corps.

Evans took the time to stop by the outer hall of the

News Department to examine the 'wallpaper,' as the chaps in the department called it, the latest stories from the teletype, tacked up in an overlapping pattern. He flipped through them. Trouble everywhere, but there was no dispatch concerning Marston.

He went out through reception into the cobbled courtyard which now served as a parking lot. Looking through the iron gate to his left, permanently closed to traffic, he could see the black door to Number 10 Downing Street, a guard examining papers. Evans wondered idly how long it would take the Marston business to spread out of this building and take the gigantic leap across the narrow street to a place on Mrs. Thatcher's ordered agenda.

On King Charles Street the parking spaces were filled with motorcycles and mopeds in their racks. High over the parapets of the old buildings, the sun was shining through a few clouds, a warm day. He did not feel warm.

He knew whom he was going to meet, not the individual man perhaps, but one of those polite blokes from MI6 who, in Evans's mind, were all interchangeable, and there would be a little digging chat about Marston, as if a fact were something you defined by filling in all the blanks around it. Evans walked to the base of the statue, looked down the steps toward the full-leafed trees of St. James's Park across the street. A band of tourists ambled past, two men in walking shorts, wives in bright polyester, the men carrying camera bags, the women laden with shopping bags from Harrods.

'Colonel Evans.'

Evans looked around as a man approached, dressed in a rumpled gray suit, carrying an umbrella. Evans knew instantly that this would be Clive from MI6, simply because he looked so ordinary. He was in his mid to late thirties, unruly sandy hair, lean and alert, almost indistinguishable from any of the thousands of men who worked at any of the ministries in Whitehall. But not quite. There was something different about the man. Perhaps it was the piercing skepticism in his brown eyes or the hair falling carelessly over the forehead. He looked American.

Not one of our chaps, Evans thought.

'I'm Gordon Clive,' the man said with a smile, no handshake. 'Warm day, don't you think? Miserable humidity. It might be best if we find a bench in the park.' And he was off down the steps, talking rapidly in an Americanized English accent. 'I don't like London in the summer,' he said as Evans caught up. 'Too many bloody tourists. Trafalgar Square is absolutely packed.' He found a park bench near the lake where he had a good view in every direction. He put his umbrella to one side.

The ritual of identification; Evans produced his Queen's Messenger passport, handed it to Clive, who in turn gave him a black leather identification wallet. Not marked MI6, of course, just general Foreign Office. The picture was nondescript, just an amiable-looking chap.

'Miserable picture, of course,' Clive said with a vague smile, his eyes following a group of middle-aged Japanese led by a young girl tour director who carried a bullhorn and a rising sun flag on a stick. 'Well,' he said finally. 'Your man has put us in the thick of it, hasn't he?'

'Marston, you mean?'

'None other. Would you like a cigarette? American, I'm afraid,' Clive said, removing a pack of Winstons from his pocket. Evans declined and Clive lit one. The smoke poured from his nostrils. His eyes roamed the park. 'Does the name Boris Ludov mean anything to you?'

'Not offhand.'

'Think back to when you were making the journeys yourself. It would have been in Bangkok, Singapore, Hong Kong.'

'Yes,' Evans said, remembering. 'A short little fellow who rather fancied himself. Russian courier, if I remember rightly.' He had not thought of Boris in years, had difficulty seeing the face clearly in his mind. A dandy, a strutting little man who reminded Evans of a peacock, more interested in women than in proper business. 'A funny little man,' Evans said. 'Ineffectual as a courier, I would think, not the right temperament for it.'

'Oh?' Clive said, holding out his cigarette to flip the ashes on the footpath. 'That's your judgment, is it? Ineffectual?'

'That was my impression, yes.'

'He's KGB.'

Evans laughed slightly, despite himself. 'Then they're damned hard up.'

'He's disarming but not ineffective. He was thrown out of India for crashing a debutante's party, but he carried all the details of India's atomic industry off with him. It's a fine cover, I think, the buffoonery, the showy peasant yearning to be an aristocrat. It works for him.'

He pulled a photograph out of his inside jacket pocket, handed it to Evans, who tilted it to one side to reduce the glare of the sun. It was a picture taken on a train platform somewhere in the Orient, the omnipresent swarm of people and a railway coach in the background, awaiting boarding. Marston was there, right enough, standing a full head above the crowd. The picture was slightly blurred, but the shutter had been clicked just as Marston was looking back over his shoulder, an attitude which gave him a slightly furtive air.

'I recognize Marston,' Evans said.

'Look just to Marston's right.' Clive put his index finger on the picture. 'Can you identify your friend Boris? The man with the snap-brim hat.'

Evans squinted, trying to bring the picture into sharp focus. He could see the figure of a man partially obscured by an old woman carrying a bundle of sticks on her back. 'It could be Boris Ludov,' he said. 'I don't know. Where was this picture taken?'

'On Marston's Journey Twenty-six, the run back from Ulan Bator. A Mongolian station platform.'

'Are you suggesting there was an arranged meeting between Marston and Russian intelligence?' Evans said heatedly. 'That's preposterous on the face of it. I met Boris myself. A half dozen of my men have probably had a drink with Boris over the years. That doesn't prove a bloody thing.'

A large woman in a white uniform and starched white nurse's cap pushed a pram past him, one of the wheels squeaking, in need of oil. It brought him up short. He lowered his voice. 'I know a bit about military intelligence,' he said, regaining his composure. 'I know the paranoia that comes when you can't explain an event and yet need to get the facts all tidy.'

Clive sat silent, sucking the last shred of smoke from the cigarette before he stubbed it out against the heel of his shoe. 'Do you know what Marston and Ashton-Croft were carrying out of Ulan Bator?'

'No,' Evans said. 'We're not privy to that kind of information. We make it a point not to be.'

'I understand that's your official line.'

'It's true.'

'But a Queen's Messenger could find out what he was carrying.' Clive said. 'Marston could have found out if he was carrying something hot.'

Evans shook his head. 'I'll send you the history of the Queen's Messengers sometime,' he said. 'Three centuries of service and only two mistakes in all that time. One package was inadvertently left on a plane in Tokyo. The package was recovered. The man was discharged from the service. One other incident in World War Two involved a Queen's Messenger aboard a disabled ship. In the face of certain capture he threw his bags overboard only to discover that they floated long enough for the Germans to retrieve them. I won't permit you to dishonor my service. Until you have hard evidence, sir, you will not start any unfounded rumors or make any innuendos about Captain Marston.'

Clive was unfazed, unaffected. His long hands rested peacefully on his lap. He looked up through the trees at a cloud edging into his field of view, as if gauging the possibilities of imminent rain. 'It's your chaps who aren't making it easy to contain. We're picking up signals from all over the Far East, rumors that a Queen's Messenger defected and took a lot of sensitive material with him.'

'The rumors didn't come from my chaps,' Evans said.

'Nevertheless, I want you to have a press release drafted. Your Captain Marston is ill in hospital in Hong Kong. I would like you to call his daughter, reassure her, and, above all, play it down. We want you to advise your men not to discuss Marston. If the question comes up, they know nothing except that he was taken ill. Can we count on you to do that?'

'Yes.'

'Very good.' Clive hooked his umbrella over one arm. 'I realize this is difficult for you. None of us feels very good about it. I'll let you know what we turn up, and I'll appreciate the same cooperation from your end.' When he walked away, Evans noticed an observable slouch in his posture, a slight bag to the seat of his trousers. Clive was not ex-military, no, nothing spit-and-polish about him.

Definitely not one of our chaps.

Evans heard the sonorous chimes of Big Ben and stood up. He had work to do. He had been a professional soldier, after all, and he would take responsibility for anything that happened. But only after it was proved. He would not allow himself to be upset by possibilities.

He walked back to his office to find that there was nothing new about Marston. Another distracting difficulty had popped up, the delay of flights into Dulles, Washington, a request for rerouting to Washington's National Airport via New York's La Guardia. That could wait.

He called in his secretary, dictated a memo concerning Marston's illness in Hong Kong. Then he looked up Marston's home number in Belgravia and rang it personally only to get a housekeeper on the line. He asked for Miss Iris Marston.

'She's on holiday, sir, on the Continent.'

'For how long?'

'I really can't say because she didn't leave no schedule behind. She's just knocking about, sir, if you get my meaning. Just away until she comes home, would be the way I'd put it.'

'Do you have a number or an address in Europe where I can reach her?'

'She calls home once in a while to inquire about the post. But she's all over, I'm afraid, no one place for very long.'

'When she calls next, have her get in touch with Colonel Evans of the Queen's Messengers.'

'I'll do that, sir.'

Evans rang off, made a mental note to pass the information on to Clive. Then an obvious question struck him, and he wrote it down.

'Who in the hell took that picture of Marston and Boris on the Mongolian train platform?'

He would have to remember to ask.

5

LONDON

Over the next couple of days Clive ran his nets and found them empty. He put in a request for an interview with Ashton-Croft, was informed that the major was back on the Ulan Bator run again, having to fill in since the Queen's Messengers were a man short. But he was sent a written deposition which Ashton-Croft had dictated in Hong Kong, and that helped fill in the blanks.

Occasionally Hubert Ross popped in to see what progress Clive was making, standing in the doorway in an attitude of patrician arrogance, as if there were always something more important waiting for him down the hall and he only had a moment to spare. Ross was deputy director, second only to Sir John himself, and rumor had it that Ross would not be averse to seeing the old man step down and make way for the progress which Ross was certain he represented.

On the third day after his meeting with the superintendent of the Queen's Messengers, Clive received a notice that there would be a meeting at 1300 hours, so he spent his morning running his actives. He spent an hour and a half on the scrambled long line. He had moved Roberts out from under the heavy thumb of Harry Patterson in Bangkok to the more benign atmosphere of Hong Kong, and he rang him first, listening to what Roberts had to say with quiet interest, drumming the eraser of a wooden pencil against the desk top as he listened.

The move had been good for Roberts. He was full of enthusiasm now that no one was breathing over his shoulder, and he had already made considerable progress.

'How much information does the press have about Marston?' Clive said.

'Only what's come out of London,' Roberts said. 'The local scribblers are going absolutely bonkers trying to find which hospital has him. I could give you half a dozen rumors about him. The most common story, of course, is that he disappeared from one of his runs and struck a deal with the Russians, but that's been denied all around.'

'So much for the rumors. What hard information do you have?'

'I questioned the airline stewardess on Cathay Pacific and fixed the time of Marston's departure from the jet at oh-nine-thirty-two hours,' Roberts said. 'Now there were six flights out within the following hour, to Manila, Taiwan, Djakarta, Tokyo, Sydney, and Honolulu. I've covered the personnel connected with all of them in my usual thorough manner, including chief stewardesses, counter personnel. I showed them the standard full-face photo of our phantom messenger. Marston was not on any of those flights. I think he's still in Hong Kong. Furthermore, it's my guess that he walked off that jet of his own volition, not under duress.'

'Your reasoning?'

'Marston has a strong reputation here. During the Chinese Cultural Revolution he was walking across the bridge separating the train in the New Territories from the train on the Chinese side,' Roberts said. 'The Chinese made him run a gauntlet of soldiers, who spat, cursed, poked, kicked him until he had been touched once too often. He put down his bags, doubled up a fist, and bashed an oversized Chinese bugger such a good one that he knocked him flat. The Chinese soldiers were so dumbfounded they just watched him pick up his bags and walk on across the bridge.' Roberts paused. 'So Marston would scarcely allow himself to be herded through the congestion of Kai Tak Airport even on pain of death.'

'What do you have on the other man?' Clive said.

'Nothing. Not even a rumor,' Roberts said, his voice hollow on the scrambler as if he were speaking through a tunnel.

'Has Boris turned up in Hong Kong?'

33

'Ah, Boris,' Roberts said with a chuckle. 'I hear lots of stories about him here, but nobody's seen him of late. Is he involved here?'

'Could be. You put out feelers.'

'I'll do that. But I hear that Boris is not one of your sneakers. No good at that whatsoever. They say he's one of your high-visibility flares, an embarrassment to the KGB. He's getting poor ratings these days because he's not producing. There's no assignment he wouldn't delay if a likely piece of ass came within range, or so the gossip goes.'

'Keep an eye out, nonetheless.'

'Righto.' And Roberts was off.

He's a good man, Clive thought. *Learning fast.*

It was mid-afternoon before the call came from Sir John's office, not from the old man himself but from his secretary, a middle-aged male factotum named Stafford (inevitably nicknamed Staff), who said little, remained impassive, and saw that everything was perfectly aligned in the conference room on the ninth floor, water glasses in place, cups for those who took tea or coffee, three sheets of paper, a ball-point pen in front of each precisely squared-away chair.

Clive was not surprised that Moorhouse and Sampson were already here, the diminutive Sampson scribbling figures on the paper in front of him, continually doing budget analysis, while Moorhouse sat pushed back in his chair, his hands folded over his ample lap. He was the signalman in charge of the physical world net.

Ross arrived late as usual, sat apart at the far end of the table, his perfectly manicured hands packing a briar pipe. He had the look about him of a hunter who had baited a trap a long time ago and had the patience to wait forever to catch his quarry.

Staff came in, pushing a tea cart, and Sir John followed. He was a medium-sized man with gold-rimmed glasses and silver hair cropped close around a shiny bald head. Clive thought he resembled a banker who could pretend pleasantness, feign light conversation, but whose mind was always on the money in the vault. He sat down in the leather chair at the head of the table, smiled, allowed Staff to pour his tea, strong, no milk.

'Well, chaps,' he said, 'we have ourselves an interesting one. It seems that the QM has lost its virginity.'

'Perhaps a case of rape,' Ross said.

'In any event the maidenhead is gone.' He nodded to Clive. 'Background.'

Immediately everything was in order in Clive's mind, but he took out a cigarette and lit it and allowed Staff to pour his tea and move on down the table before he began.

'Captain William Marston, a Queen's Messenger, began a routine run to Ulan Bator in the company of his senior officer, Major Ashton-Croft, on nine June. This run is referred to by the QM as Journey Twenty-six.'

He threaded his way through the facts, avoiding any descriptions, any interpretations, mentioning the approach which had been made to Marston on the station platform at Sair Usu, his denial of the request to carry the letter to Ulan Bator, which the Chinese went ahead and posted anyway. He repeated Ashton-Croft's report of Marston's agitation after walking the same station platform on the way back and mentioned the photograph of Marston on the Mongolian platform as a possible indication of a meeting with Boris Ludov at that time. He went on to describe the change of assignments with Ashton-Croft in Hong Kong, his departure from that flight, his total disappearance.

He paused, sipped the tea, which was unusually strong. A drop of it fell onto his tie. 'The QM superintendent has prepared an illness cover.'

Sir John turned to Moorhouse. 'Can you give me a probability on our friend Boris?'

'There's no doubt at all on that,' Moorhouse said. He fished an enlargement from a canvas case, the area of the photograph which included only the part of the crowd containing Marston and Boris and, in the background, the station sign, written in Cyrillic Mongolian. He pointed out the features of the picture, the indisputable presence of Marston, the points by which he identified Boris, that unmistakable profile, the snap-brim fedora which Boris had worn in the past, embellished by the tip of a peacock feather protruding from the band.

'You know Boris better than the rest of us,' Sir John said to Clive. 'Is that Boris?'

'It's the ornamental rooster himself,' he said.

Sir John sipped at his tea, and Clive changed his image of the man, not a banker at all but a government solicitor looking for weaknesses in a case, probing the soft points. 'We have established identification of the principals. We have established that they were on the same platform at the same time. Is it possible that this is a coincidence, that Boris came in on the same train, took the air at the same scheduled stop? Is it possible that Boris came in from China with no connection to Marston whatsoever?'

'No,' Moorhouse said. 'Boris is persona non grata with the Chinese. They would have picked him up first thing. Besides, our last fix on Boris was in Japan.'

'I see,' Sir John said. 'Where did we get this remarkable photograph?'

Moorhouse shrugged. 'You might call it the free enterprise tourist trade at work. Mongolian photographers generally take pictures of any foreigners crossing the country and then peddle them to any governments which might find them interesting. This came in from Hong Kong.'

'Then Dunhill examined it, recognized Marston?'

'No, he recognized Boris. He identified the Queen's Messenger from the blazer.'

Clive glanced at Ross, who up to this point had not spoken a word, contenting himself with the smoke from his pipe.

Sir John shifted the blank piece of paper on the table absently. 'How many diplomatic pouches was Marston carrying when he disappeared?' he said. 'What was in those pouches?'

'Bad news, I'm afraid,' Moorhouse said, unfolding a typewritten list from his pocket, smoothing it out on the table. 'He had three small bags, an assortment of documents. These were assembled by the Hong Kong Registry from Journeys Twenty-five and Twenty-six. There was a status report on the Tokyo summit, security summaries for Mrs. Thatcher, routed to the permanent undersecretary. From the High Commission in Hong Kong there was a full report on the refugee problem, a detailing of Thai atrocities against two refugee transports. There were sixteen personal letters sent from diplomatic personnel, nondepartmental routing, to be mailed in London.'

He was saving the worst for the last, Clive realized, cantering through the nonessentials. 'Too,' Moorhouse said, 'there was a sealed packet for Clive from Charlie Excalibur via Mr. Po.'

'Ah, our Mr. Po again,' Sir John said. 'Did he contact Dunhill in Hong Kong?'

'Briefly,' Moorhouse said. 'Mr. Po said he was out of business, resisted any contact, and then dropped out of sight.'

Clive was startled. His breath caught in his throat. He looked to Moorhouse. 'Is Ulan Bator absolutely certain that the man who posted the letter was Mr. Po?'

'Affirmative,' Moorhouse said. 'Their description is a perfect match.'

Clive sank back in his chair, aware that the scar was paining him again. Christ, they had wanted the Charlie Excalibur dispatch very badly, and whether Marston had walked away with it or been snatched was suddenly beside the point. Whatever had been in that letter was of sufficient importance that they had gone to great lengths to intercept it.

Watch yourself, Charlie Excalibur, whoever you are, he thought.

'All right, chaps,' Sir John said. 'Now we know what was of value.' He slipped a gold watch from his vest pocket, clicked open the engraved cover. 'What we don't know is how valuable, how they got it, and what price they paid for it.'

He nodded to Staff, who poured him another cup of tea. 'Let's take a look at what we have,' Sir John said. 'Captain Marston walked off that aircraft, carrying diplomatic bags. He may have gone under duress, or he may have gone willingly. If it's the latter case, then we will assume that he was bought and paid for. I shall expect an immediate monitoring of his personal accounts.' Eyes dropping back to the thin tissue of the dossier in front of him. 'That will be your responsibility, Mr. Sampson. Monitor his personal accounts in the Hong Kong and Shanghai Bank and in the Bank of Scotland, new deposits of money, withdrawals, general cash flow. If he's bought a Ferrari lately, we shall want to know it. I want an immediate trace of any new funds.'

Sir John leaned forward. 'A summary of events as they may have happened,' he said. 'On the trip back from Ulan Bator Marston knows there's something important in his bag. At the Mongolian station he is approached by our ubiquitous friend Boris, who also knows there is something of great interest in the bag. He is willing to pay handsomely, and Marston agrees to sell. But it is an impossible situation. The merchandise is sealed in a canvas bag with a crimped metal seal on the top. In addition, it is stowed in the compartment with Senior Officer Ashton-Croft, with absolutely no access to it. So Marston makes plans, pollutes the beer in Canton, takes advantage of Ashton-Croft's resultant indisposition to make the switch in runs. He now has the Charlie Excalibur dispatch in his possession. So he bolts the run in Hong Kong. Boris sends a man aboard the flight to run interference in case Marston has any trouble getting off.'

He glanced around the room. 'Any present questions, any amendments?' There were none. 'On the other hand, if Captain Marston left that aircraft under duress, we have a different problem, don't we?' There was a sudden awkward silence in the room. Sir John looked to Clive. 'What is your opinion, Mr. Clive?'

Clive thought for a moment, then repeated Robert's story of Marston's decking the Chinese soldier on the bridge. 'It's my man's opinion that there's no way Marston would have walked off that aircraft except willingly,' Clive said.

Ross was stirring now, setting his pipe in the crystal ashtray. 'Whether the Russians used force or money, if they've gotten themselves a Queen's Messenger with a vital dispatch, perhaps we need to double the nets in Mongolia and Hong Kong.'

Sampson tapped his pen against the table. 'I must raise a red flag at this point, gentlemen. Our share of the battered budget bag this year has been considerably lessened. Even with the implementation of the search this far, the contingency funds are draining at an alarming rate.'

'We will discuss your proposal later, Mr. Ross,' Sir John said with a tone of finality. He placed both hands flat on the table and pushed himself to his feet effortlessly. Then, almost as an afterthought: 'I would like some of your time, Mr. Clive,' he said. 'You live in Bloomsbury, do you not?'

'Yes, sir.'

'Then, if you will, kindly call your good lady and tell her you will be delayed for an hour or so.'

With that he left the conference room. Staff gathered up the sheets of paper, used or blank, the pencils and the ball-point pens, even sprayed an aerosol mist onto the wood of the conference table and polished it with a cloth to obliterate any possible impressions.

Clive watched them go, sat for a moment in his chair, and then, with a sense of foreboding he could not rationalize, went to call Katy.

6

LONDON

It may be a long night, Clive thought as he found a vacant telephone outside the conference room. He lit himself a cigarette, rang the house, and in a moment Katy was on the line, a little breathless from dashing the stairs again.

'You're going to have to stop that,' he said with mock sternness.

'Stop what?'

'A pregnant lady has no business running the stairs, especially as overweight as you've allowed yourself to become.'

'I've not. I've not gained a pound,' she said indignantly. Then doubt set in. 'Have I? Tell me where.'

'Hush, love, of course, you haven't,' he said. 'But you have to slow down and quit running the stairs or I'll move you to a single-level flat somewhere.'

'You have my word. Listen, I've got news. I had a letter from my father today. He'll be coming in the fall.'

'Good,' he said. 'But we'll have to chat about it later. I have been ordered into the presence for an hour or so, which means closer to three.'

'Damn,' she said. 'I have some fine lamb. Shall I keep it warm?'

'No, I'll pick up something. Now, no more dashes up and down the stairs.'

'Ha,' she said. There was a sound of a kiss on the wire, and she hung up. He was left with a residual contentment from the continuity Katherine was providing them both.

It was rather late in life, to be sure, with her approaching thirty-two. Rather insane, in fact, for they both had decided rationally, intellectually, that this was no safe world for children. But when she had told him, in the middle of one of his tedious telephone chats with old Sampson, while he tried to absorb one of Sampson's interminable budget reports, when she had hung around his neck and bit his free ear and said, 'Now don't you go off your face, but we're about to increase the world population by one,' he slammed down the telephone, gave a whoop and a hug that damn near smothered her. There was never one more word about population statistics or Malthusian principles. By God, they were leaving some unique individual, dimensions and sex unknown, at the moment, to survive them. That was quite good enough.

He snuffed out his cigarette, chagrined that he had taken so long, but he needn't have worried, for there was still a temporary delay in Sir John's anteroom, a room with tasteful but outmoded paneling, a few hunting prints on the wall, one small ormolu desk where Miss Fletcher usually sat but where Staff was now flipping through a leather appointment book, as if people were units to be fitted into Sir John's available time slots.

Finally, Sir John appeared at the door to his inner office, placed his hands on his hips as if he had been doing calisthenics. 'Come in. Do come in and have a drink. We've a lot of ground to cover and very little time to do it in.'

The office was unchanged since Clive had last seen it, the red scrambler phone, a secondary outlet for the electronic transmitting device named Piccolo, and regimental pictures on the wall full of indistinguishable young officers on a polo field, Singapore, perhaps Hong Kong. There was also a wet bar, a glittering and resplendent display of bottles. 'What's your pleasure?' Sir John said.

'Bourbon if you have it.'

'Of course. The national American drink. You spent your childhood in America, did you not?'

'Yes, in Boston as a matter of fact.'

'Your parents are English?'

'English father, American mother. They traveled a lot, business on the Continent, in the States. So I had the best of the boarding schools, the last years in Boston.'

'A broadening experience, I suppose.' Sir John poured bourbon into a glass. 'Ice?'

'And a little water, if you please.' He took the glass, sipped the bourbon, vaguely uncomfortable at revealing himself, at the feelings which had begun to stir within him.

'University?'

'Two years at Stanford and two at Boston University. Always moving around, you see. Nothing quite so unsettling as peripatetic parents, always on the go, a Christmas together here, Thanksgiving there.'

'Where are they now?'

'Both dead.'

Clive drank the bourbon. It burned a path to his stomach. Sir John got nothing for himself but a glass of water with a twist of lemon peel in it. He sat down, crossed his legs. 'Would you say, just offhand, that you were a contented child?'

'You have a complete dossier on me,' Clive said. 'Everything's there.'

'Not quite everything,' Sir John said. 'You must forgive my questions. They do seem impertinent, even as I consider them, but I'm interested, and there is purpose to all this prying.' He sipped the water. 'At your present point in life what is of prime importance to you?'

'The everlasting dailiness,' Clive said. He went to the bar, poured himself another drink. 'The security. The expected.'

Sir John studied him. 'Would you say that you feel a stronger personal loyalty to England or America?'

Clive raised his glass in Sir John's direction, drank. 'England,' he said.

'Why?'

'This is my home. I work for the Crown. I'm a citizen.'

'No deeper than that?'

'I must admit that I'm not much stirred by the banging

of drums and the trooping of the colors, but I like this country very much,' Clive said. 'My child will be born here.'

Sir John lit a cigar. 'Are you bitter?'

'About what?'

'Having been tortured.'

'The scar still pains me now and again.'

'You didn't answer the question. Do you feel bitter that you were not rescued in time? Perhaps you feel that you were abandoned.'

Clive took his time, chose his words carefully. 'I wouldn't call myself bitter about it. It came with the territory.'

'How did you get recruited for this service?'

Clive smiled again, aware for a fleeting moment that he had been singled out for a conversation with an Historic Character, as he and Katy would joke about it later, as if they existed on the outskirts of society and were always surprised when they found themselves included by other people. He was startled by the vague pain he continued to feel, the sense of loss, the reopening of old wounds.

'When my parents died, I came home to take care of business. Of course, there wasn't any to speak of, very little money. Both my parents had expensive tastes. I was twenty-one, no, twenty-two at the time. When I arrived in London, I received a call from this section, as a matter of fact, asking if I would be so kind as to come in for a chat. One thing followed the next, and here I am.'

'When is your child due?'

'Early fall. October, we think.'

'You want a son?'

'I suppose.'

'Pour yourself another drink, old man.'

Clive was surprised to find his glass empty. He poured some more bourbon into it. 'What's the point of all this?' he said abruptly.

'The point? At my asking you in for a chat?'

'More than a chat, I'd call it.' The drink was strong, and Clive felt as if he had crossed some invisible line beyond which he was uncomfortable, but at the same time he would not go back. 'At the risk of being rude, sir, I'd like to know precisely what you want from me.'

'Your opinions,' Sir John said, perfectly relaxed.

'Why mine?'

'You have the reputation of being candid, unintimidated by rank, the American influence, I would guess.'

'What opinions do you want?'

'Let's begin with your view of the service in general.'

'You'll find no better men anywhere in the world,' Clive said. 'But the supporting structure has gone soft, porous, leaky as a sieve. The reputation of M16 is generally gone to pieces, not that I give a damn about reputations except that our present one makes it harder for me to work.'

'Do you believe the state of the service is responsible for the fact that you were not retrieved before you were tortured?'

'Yes, that, too, but I knew the political situation in Thailand. I was the proverbial needle in the haystack.' He paused. 'The risk goes with the job.'

'I understand you talked to the head of the Queen's Messengers this afternoon.'

'Yes. He's genuinely stricken because it seems that one of his men has gone sour, the first in three centuries, no insignificant incident that. And I was building a cover story, sickness, Marston in hospital. But he knew, and I knew, that once the information was loose in MI6, it would be only a matter of time until everything we had leaked out.'

'Yes,' Sir John said. 'The club of gentlemen has been dissolved.'

'Praise be to God for that,' Clive said. 'They almost destroyed the service.'

'And what do you think of this Marston business?'

'No more than I reported in the meeting.'

'No theories? No hunches? Do you think he defected?'

'Not defected, no. The Russians would be crowing about that if he had.'

44

'Had it ever occurred to you ...' Sir John said, pausing for effect, examining the coal from his cigar. 'Is there the most remote possibility that Marston was forced from that flight against his will? In that case, if they wanted something from him he was reluctant to give ...'

Clive shuddered involuntarily, shook his head from side to side, knowing now why he had been called in here, not wanting to accept the knowledge. 'No,' he said flatly.

Sir John ignored the word. 'In the next forty-eight hours I shall expect you to brief yourself on every aspect of the Marston business.' There was a long pause. 'Then I'm going to post you off to Hong Kong.' He picked up a strong manila folder, slid it across the desk to Clive. 'This is every scrap of information we have, all the summaries.'

'No,' Clive said, his palms sweating. 'Absolutely not.'

'You are reluctant. That's entirely natural. Too many things can go awry, is that it?' Sir John relit his cigar, waved out the wooden match, and placed it in a ceramic tray. 'Things can bloody well fly apart and did once before, didn't they? We rattle the dice and we're stuck with the spots.'

'We had a firm agreement when I came in from the field,' Clive said. 'No outside assignments.'

Sir John took the time to put the folder of dispatches in the safe for the moment, then rang security to let it know he was leaving his office. 'Come along, I want you to see something.'

He nodded to the security guard in the corridor and led the way to the elevator, trailing a pall of cigar smoke behind him. There was music playing in the elevator, and Sir John snuffed his cigar before he entered. At the next floor down a pair of secretaries boarded, pretty young girls smelling of perfume. They were on their way out of the building and home, with no real idea of the true nature of the business that went on here.

The secretaries departed at the ground floor, and Sir John pressed the button for the second sub-basement, which housed the chemical analysis laboratories. He led the way down an ancient damp corridor with mosaic tile floors, past doors with frosted glass panes, hatched with wire webbing. There were signs on the pale green walls which advised that this was Section 5/B of the National Health Service Pathological Laboratories.

They came to a pair of opaque swinging doors, and Sir John relit his cigar against the strong smell of formaldehyde. They were met by a tall, cranelike, imperious man wearing white surgical gloves which made it appear that all the skin had been removed from his bony hands. A green badge on his white smock identified him as Mr. Hewitt.

'I want my colleague to have a look,' Sir John said.

Hewitt glanced at Clive, then turned on his heel and led the way down a narrow, chilled corridor and into a larger room which Clive recognized immediately as an autopsy room, six tables with paraphernalia in a long laboratory darkened except for a battery of overhead lights which illuminated a single cadaver.

A nightmare. What lay sprawled on the table in front of him was a collection of colors and layered flesh and putrescent odors, of meat sliced, pulled back from bone. Clive kept his eyes moving, his face impassive. He did not speak. My God, the cadaver had no face. The top of the skull had been removed; the brain currently rested on a weighing scale and the scalp tissue had been pulled down over the front of the cranium.

'Interesting circumstance,' Hewitt said, hovering over the cadaver. 'Quite barbaric.'

'Then he was indeed tortured?' Sir John said.

Clive was short of breath. There was not enough oxygen. He was suddenly in another place. The memory, urgent, vivid, consumed him. *Hustled into the hut, a tin roof overhead, the Thai men reeking with sweat, forcing him onto the slab of wood which served as a table, tying him down with rough hemp rope. 'You won't get a bloody thing out of me.'*

Clive shrugged. 'Who is he?' he said, struggling past memories too painful to endure.

'The redoubtable Mr. Po,' Sir John said quietly. 'Elusive no longer.'

Clive lit a cigarette, hands trembling, breathed the smoke deep, trying to obliterate the smell. *Just tell us what you know, Mr. Clive. The Thai face, six inches from his own, stinking breath. The glitter of the scalpel in the light of the lamp.*

Hewitt was reciting. Mr. Po's fingers had been methodically broken, one at a time, in each of two places, above and below the knuckle joint, with a hammer, probably a ball peen, fingers splayed against a solid wood backing.

It was the dull, broad backside of the machete.

There were still splinters in two fingers of each hand. One eardrum had been ruptured, air forced into the opening, concussive. An electric cathode had been run up Mr. Po's penis, into the bladder, for a series of convulsive shocks. There were other broken bones of a major nature, the collarbone, the pelvis.

The stab of pain, so suddenly unexpected, the sound of his own scream, alien, as if it had not been torn from his throat, the sight of his own flesh violated, blood spurting out, the first incision, the calm voice urging. 'A few words and we patch you up, just a few words.' The keen edge of the scalpel, hovering above his belly, the pain drawing all the breath out of him. 'Otherwise, we are going to have to cut you in two parts, sir.'

'I doubt that he told them what they wanted to know,' Hewitt was saying. 'Otherwise, the torture would have stopped somewhere along the line.'

Sir John scratched his chin. 'Could you say, Mr. Hewitt, that the kind of torture afflicted could give us a clue to the nationality of the torturers?'

'You're asking me if I can say the Kampucheans did this rather than the Russians, the Thais rather than the Chinese?'

Thai ... Thai faces.

'Yes.'

'Interesting. I would have to do some research. I would say, just offhand, that torture methods have become pretty standardized.'

Christ, the babble that was coming out of him, how to

47

stop it, the screams, they were his, he knew they were his, but the pain, my God, waves of pain, and where was the dignity, where was the goddamned training, no training anymore, only that bloody pain and that knife that crept across his belly, hour after hour, an inch at a time. That crazy face peering into his all the while, those black eyes watching his eyes while every word Clive knew poured out in a continuous stream as if the right pattern would make them stop. No, not every word. The important names they wanted, withheld until the very end. And finally, they came, too.

Sir John glanced at Clive, looked back to Mr. Hewitt. 'I think that will be quite enough for the time being, Hewitt.'

Back to the office. How he got there Clive never knew, dazed yet trying to control the rage he felt. He headed straight for the bar, another drink.

'Not a pleasant sight,' Sir John said.

'You bloody bastard,' Clive said. 'You goddamned bloody bastard.' He downed the drink and smashed the glass against the wall. 'He held out and they smashed him to pieces. And I told them what they wanted to know and I'm alive. Is that your bloody point?'

'We all do what we must,' Sir John said. 'We all do what we can.'

Clive slumped in his chair, his head in his hands. Finally, he sat back and stared at Sir John, then leaned forward and slammed his open hand on the desk. 'You looked at that man, what was left of that man, and you tell me we all do what we must. That's damned cold comfort for him. Does he have a son he may never see, a widow? Do you know one goddamned thing about him?'

Sir John waited quietly until Clive had expended his wrath. 'I repeat, we all do what we must. Sometimes it is painful, regrettable.' He lit his cigar. 'Nevertheless, you are still the only man for this job.'

Clive was quiet a long moment. 'Does Dunhill know that Po's dead?'

'Yes.'

'Where was he found?'

'Dumped on a street in Wanchai. But he's dead, out of it now. It's Marston we have to consider.' He opened the safe, removed the manila folder. 'You are the logical man for this assignment, and so you're the one to do it. Remember, all you have to do is find him. You will take no action. When you locate him, you pass the signal and the rest will be taken care of.'

Sir John put the folder in an attaché case, handed it to him.

'I'll think it over,' Clive said.

'Yes, you do that. Think it over carefully.'

Clive picked up the telephone, rang transportation. 'This is Clive, number thirty-seven slash eight. Transportation to Bloomsbury, about ten minutes.'

'Just keep one thing in mind,' Sir John said. 'You will be serving as a pointer, not a retriever.'

Clive left the office in silence.

7

LONDON

There were advantages to the service. Downstairs a black taxi was waiting at the north door, the traditional taxi driven by one of the members of the service with a valid license. Clive gave him the number in Bedford Place and then sat back, the attaché case across his lap.

The night was cool, the traffic incredibly heavy, crowds of tourists around Trafalgar Square and Charing Cross, nothing like what it would be in August, when many of the European countries would close down altogether and there would be no available facilities in London at all. The traffic thinned out near the British Museum, and then, on impulse, he leaned forward and rapped on the glass.

'I want to drive by another address before I go home.'

'Certainly, sir,' the driver said.

Clive went through his pockets, found the memo pad with the preliminary notes for his conference with the superintendent of the Queen's Messengers, found Marston's address in Belgravia, showed it to the driver. 'Do you know this address?'

'Yes, sir.'

'What kind of place?'

'Semi-detached, I believe.'

'Would you call it expensive, astronomical, exorbitant, what?'

The driver pursed his lips, thinking. 'Depends on when he bought it, of course. In the medium range, I'd call it.'

'Let's have a look,' Clive said. He shifted in the seat, trying to get comfortable. The lower part of his abdomen had begun to pain him again. *Absolutely uncanny*, he thought. The scar had not really bothered him for months until this business with Marston. *The power of the mind*, he thought. His stomach was growling as well, and he had told Katy he would be eating out. Well, it would hurt him none to cut down on his calories.

The driver entered a circular street off a main thoroughfare, nice white houses but not elegant, a fringe of trees and small lawns with gardens in back. Ford Escorts, Cortinas, an MG or two. The driver stopped across the street from a house. 'That's it, sir.'

Well, Clive thought. *Comfortable, I'd call it.* He studied the house through the window of the taxi. There was a light in the lounge, and he remembered that Iris Marston was somewhere in Europe. He decided to have a look at the inside of the house. He asked the driver to wait and then crossed the street and went through the cast-iron gate, which had been left ajar. He had no idea what he was going to say or do until he reached the heavy door set between two rounded miniature trees. He rang the bell, heard footsteps from inside. The door opened.

A plump little woman stood there. She was somewhere in her sixties, obviously a housekeeper, and across the sitting room a television was playing, a church choir singing hymns as near as he could tell.

'Yes, sir?' she said. 'Can I help you?'

'I do beg your pardon,' Clive said. 'But I'm Gordon Clive from the Foreign Office. We are quite anxious to get in touch with Miss Marston.'

Her face clouded. 'Would you care to come in, sir? There's a bit of a chill tonight.' And once he was inside, she closed the glass outer door. She shook her head as if preparing herself for the worst. 'I talked to Captain Marston's superintendent earlier. There's nothing's happened to Captain Marston, is there? He hasn't gone down in an air crash, has he? Such terrible accidents they show on the telly.'

'Nothing like that,' Clive said. One glance at the room and he could tell there was no great outlay of money exhibited here, nothing beyond Marston's income. There were some interesting modern paintings on the walls, a largish Oriental carpet on the floor, full of deep reds in a floral design, showing a good bit of wear. The room was sparsely furnished with a few good antique tables interspersed with deep, modern, comfortable chairs.

On the mantel above the fireplace there was a collection of pictures, one of Marston when he was younger, his four-year-old daughter perched on his shoulders, his arm around a woman who displayed a shy smile for the camera, a pretty woman, now dead. And in another photograph Marston was standing with a group of military men in uniform, all of them looking properly somber. The smaller print, which he could not read from this distance, identified the group, and the larger print the place as Suez, the date as 1956. Another picture displayed the daughter, Iris, as she now was, perhaps, a vital-looking girl with long blonde hair and a slight expression of attempted sophistication. Christ, the whole history of the man's adult life was there on that mantelpiece. Not much in the end. He came back to himself, realizing that the housekeeper was waiting for him to go on. 'Is there some young man who might know where she is?' he said, improvising. 'We've had word that she's about to marry.'

'Marry? Her?' the housekeeper said with dumbfounded disbelief. 'Not likely. Not that it wouldn't do her a world of good, settle her down proper. But there's no marriage in the offing for that one, I can promise you that.'

'I'm sure you might, but I do need to have a chat with her. Would you happen to have an address in Europe where I can reach her?'

'She's at an irresponsible age, that's all I can say for her. Hold on.' She went over to a table with one uneven leg which tilted slightly as she rummaged through a pile of cards and envelopes. How had Marston managed, Clive thought, away on extended journeys? The house, which at one time had been so full of life, was now deserted, inhabited by a woman who stacked his mail and his bills and held down the fort. In that moment he realized how empty his life would be without Katy. The housekeeper fetched a picture postcard from a table, handed it to him. 'This came today.'

He examined it thoughtfully. There was a garish picture of the Matterhorn on one side. The other side was postmarked Milano. The message was simple. 'Dear Holly,' it read. 'Europe is a crashing bore. I will be sending my ski things home in a parcel. Have them cleaned. Tell Daddy I shall be needing a hundred pounds directly. I will let him know where to send it.' The card was signed with a letter *I* which trailed off in a squiggle.

'Do you see a "please" or a "thank you" anywhere on that card?' the housekeeper said. 'Do you see a touch of gratitude, even a little whisper of appreciation for what she has?'

'The modern generation,' Clive said, commiserating. 'When she gets in touch, please have her call her father's superintendent.'

'Do you have any idea when Captain Marston will be coming back?' she said.

He may not be coming back at all. It may be at this very moment some son of a bitch is mutilating him, cutting off an ear, snapping a finger. It may be that this empty house will remain that way and the poor bastard will never have a chance to remake his life again. And in that moment, without quite knowing why, he knew he was going after Marston. 'I don't have a copy of his schedule,' Clive said. 'It should be soon.'

'He needs to have a long talk with his daughter,' the housekeeper said. 'A firm hand. A man's hand.'

The night air was refreshing, and as luck would have it, he reached the taxi just as a light rain was beginning to fall. 'Now back to Bloomsbury,' Clive said, settling back with a feeling of some uneasiness, not knowing how he was going to break the news to Katy when he could tell her neither what he had to do nor why.

The driver turned into Bedford Place, just off Blooms-bury Square. Clive signed the mileage chit and then popped up his umbrella and went into the Georgian terrace house, with Katy coming out of the kitchen to give him a kiss, recognizing instantly that something had happened.

'Never believe a man, I say,' she said, leading him into the sitting room. 'If he says two hours which are going to turn into three, it's bound to be four. You haven't had your supper yet, I can tell.'

'A mind reader,' he said with a smile, his arm around her.

'I kept your supper warm, just in case,' she said. 'Now sit down and I'll bring you a drink, love. You look as if you need one.'

He waited for the bourbon and water, sitting in the old chair which had belonged to his father. Outside, the rain was pelting against the windows with a will and the street was alive with taxis. The neighborhood had turned commercial a long time ago, and all the rest of the houses in the block were bed and breakfasts. Noisy until midnight, and then, in the small hours of the mornings, sometimes in the mists and the quiet, the old charm of the street as it once had been came back. And the square itself, the old Bloomsbury, was now more often than not inhabited by drunks, old sailors for the most part, it seemed. Toothless, obscene old men, more of a nuisance than a menace, always looking for a handout. He was not so sure it would be a proper place to wheel a pram.

The future, cloudy at best, and he would have to prepare for it with an attitude of hoping for the best but ensuring against the worst. She came from the kitchen and sat down beside him, resting her hand on his leg. She smelled of baking bread.

'The food will be ten minutes,' she said, kissing him on the cheek. 'Now tell me about your day.'

I saw a man with the flesh pulled down over his face like a grapeskin. I'm considering going back. He tucked the errant thoughts away for the moment. 'I have made a decision, dear heart,' he said. 'You will listen to what I have to say, and you will not interrupt until I've finished.'

'That depends on what you have to say,' she said.

'You're doing it already,' he said with a smile, putting

54

his fingers to her mouth. 'Just be quiet and listen. I have decided that we are going to be married.'

She broke out with a delighted laugh. 'That's it?' she said. 'That's the large decision you've made, is it? You're determined to make an honest woman out of me, are you?'

'Not that at all,' he said. 'I've loved you for a long time and I have always been one for permanence, you know that.'

Her eyes searched his face. 'You're not just teasing about it this time, are you?'

'Never more serious.'

'I don't know whether you can understand this, love,' she said, 'but it has meant a great deal to me that you have stayed with me when there was nothing to tie you down, when you've always been free to make that choice. I couldn't bear it if I thought, even for a moment, that you were marrying me from a sense of obligation, not even the tiniest wee sense of it.'

He took her hand in his. 'I want this, Katy. It means a great deal to me.'

She was silent a moment. 'All right then,' she said. 'We'll plan to get get married when my father comes in the fall.'

'No.'

'What do you mean, "no"? I should have some say.'

'Oh, you'll have some say, of course, about where the ceremony will be held, whether you want a vicar or a civil servant. But your decision is going to have to be a swift one because I intend to marry you on Friday morning.'

'Friday?' she said, startled. 'The day after tomorrow?'

'Exactly. Ten o'clock in the morning. That will give us the weekend for a short honeymoon to decide what kind of larger honeymoon we want to take.'

She laughed, threw her arms around his neck. 'You are totally daft. All right then, if it means so much to you, Friday it is.'

He kissed her lovingly. 'I love you,' he said. He patted her leg. 'Now, can you hurry the dinner along?' he said. 'I'm famished.'

'Five minutes, love, and it's done.'

He watched her go and then fetched the attaché case up from the floor, not opening it but comforted by its heaviness, all those papers, the background on Marston, the thousands of little pieces. There would be time to go through these files later, when he was on his own and out in the field where he had to go. But for now, he would not think about Marston. He would enjoy this woman while he had her, knowing that the present was all he had for certain and perhaps all he would ever have.

8

THAILAND

Charlie Excalibur's legs were like rubber, threatening to give way at any time. His eyes burned, and he wanted nothing more than to sink down by the side of the trail and sleep. He fell into an old trick he had learned at boot camp and later used on the long forced marches through the jungle, counting the steps that he took, conning himself into believing that once he had taken a hundred steps, he could rest if he wished.

Ninety-seven, ninety-eight, ninety-nine ...

At a hundred he started again. He crossed a stream, splashed through it, and abandoned the counting, for all at once the terrain came into focus and he knew where he was, no more than a mile now from the small compound of houses next to a rice field. Epstein would be there, and Epstein would want to know everything that had happened, for he was a part of this plan, too. And Charlie Excalibur could sleep soundly, knowing that Epstein, with his skeptical eyes and his arsenal of weapons, would stand watch.

Charlie Excalibur reached the broader road, paused in the shade of some trees. Across the flooded field he could see the wall around the houses, the peaked roofs protruding above it like resting birds. To reach the gate, Charlie Excalibur would have to move into the open, and he took his time, scouting the road, which he could see for a mile in either direction before it curved and disappeared into the trees. He was going to have to run three hundred yards, and he did not know whether his legs were going to put up with that. But at the end he could count on a cool drink, and then Epstein's Thai woman would cook him some food, and after he had eaten and told Epstein everything, he would allow himself sleep, blessed sleep.

He took a deep breath of the hot morning air and then pushed himself into a run, his ankles hurting with every jolt of a booted foot against the ground. The length of three football fields. He could do that. Count, you bastard, and keep pumping away. One, two, three, four. One, two, three, four. A musical cadence, his lungs protesting, his muscles yelling at him. He saw the gate, broken in one hinge, sagging, and he pushed through it, closed it behind him, and then leaned against the inside surface of the wall. He had made it.

He started to light a cigarette, stopped short. There had been a vegetable garden here when he left, perfectly tended with rows of flowers near the house. Now the whole area was a jungle of weeds. He expected the door to the first wooden house to open and Epstein's woman to come out to greet him, bowing, pressing her hands together. But the door did not open and the weeds stood tall and he was suddenly awake and wary.

He pulled his pistol, moved up the walk to the wooden steps of the first house; his eyes moved from the bamboo blinds covering the first window to the blinds on the next. They were on the west side of the house and should have been up to allow the air to circulate until the sun flooded in and made the shade imperative.

At the top of the steps he paused, listening. The door was slightly ajar, and he could hear the drone of a voice, a chant of some sort. He pushed the door open with his elbow, stepped inside, keeping the pistol in front of him. The room was dim, empty. It smelled musty, and the heat was ovenlike. There had been furniture in this room before, old carved teak which belonged to the parents of Epstein's girl, but it was gone now.

The droning came from the next room, and he moved toward it, paused to one side, and looked in. Epstein was sitting in the middle of the room, cross-legged, wearing the fatigue jacket from his old marine company, 'The

58

Walking Dead,' an élite unit which wore a shoulder patch of a white skull superimposed on an ace of spades. It had been noted for its ruthlessness, specializing in the complete annihilation of entire villages, and the men of Lima Company were noted for their coolness. But Epstein was not cool now. His long hair fell in tangles about his neck, and his lean face was covered with patches of unkempt beard. In the dim light Charlie Excalibur could see a patch of black cloth attached to the top of Epstein's mangy head, and Epstein rocking back and forth, chanting away in a language Charlie Excalibur did not understand.

Charlie Excalibur put the pistol back in his holster, and in that moment, no more than the blink of an eye, Epstein had grabbed up a revolver, which was instantly pointed at Charlie Excalibur's midsection. There was a wild expression in his eyes, nothing of the here and now, and Charlie Excalibur realized he was a blink away from death.

'Shit, man,' he said. 'It's me, Epstein. Put that goddamned thing down.'

But Epstein had him fixed, did not move, continued to glare with wild, bloodshot eyes.

'Charlie Excalibur, remember? I got great news. Everything's moving, and we're going to get out of here. We're going home.'

Epstein said nothing, but there was a squint to his eyes now, a touch of some rationality that Charlie Excalibur could see and use. 'It's burning up in here,' Charlie Excalibur said, and he moved to one of the glassless windows and raised the blind, the fresh air rushing in. Only in the light could he see the bad shape that Epstein was in. His face was gaunt, skull-like, the wild hair plastered against his sweat-soaked skin, a starved look about him, as if he had not eaten for days. Epstein lowered the revolver. Breathing a sigh of relief, Charlie Excalibur opened the rest of the blinds and then hunkered down beside him in the center of the bare room. He lit a cigarette and offered it to Epstein, who ignored it.

'I sent the message,' Charlie Excalibur said. 'You were supposed to monitor the radio, remember?' He inhaled the cigarette, expelled the smoke wearily. 'This was a two-man deal, remember?'

'They came,' Epstein said.

'What does that mean?'

Epstein shrugged. 'Whoever,' he said.

'You mean soldiers, troops?'

Epstein sighed. 'I told the girl to take her parents and go and she did. But I hid out, and they came and stripped the house and lived in it a couple of days and then moved on. So I came back in.'

'The radio.'

'Gone.'

Charlie Excalibur nodded. 'All right, we find another way, buddy. We move on and get closer to point zero and hole up. Jesus, I can see why you'd go wacko sitting here by yourself. We got to get some food into you and some water, maybe some salt tablets. You're dehydrated, that's what's wrong with you.'

'Two out of three,' Epstein said.

'Two out of three what?'

'I just woke up and there was this Vietcong standing over me and the point of his bayonet was on my chest. And he said to me, "Tell me that you're not such hot shit after all."'

The past, yes. Epstein had flipped back and was repeating a story Charlie Excalibur had heard him tell a dozen times, whenever he was distressed, upset. The Vietcong had infiltrated the lines, murdered 'The Walking Dead,' leaving every third man alive. Epstein had been a third man.

'Sure,' Charlie Excalibur said. He stood up, still sucking on the cigarette. There was going to be no sleep today. 'I'm going to find you something to drink, maybe a little food. We got a long way to go, and you sure as hell aren't in any shape for a walk now. I'll be right back.'

'Wait,' Epstein said in a voice with no force behind it. 'I got something to tell you.' Charlie Excalibur waited while

Epstein searched for whatever it was, his face showing an awful distress at the effort.

'What's that goddamned thing on your head?'

'My head should be covered.'

'Covered for what?'

Again Epstein could not tell him.

'Something religious then.' Charlie Excalibur moved for the outside door. 'I'll get the water and see if I can find some food.'

He was no farther than the yard before he heard the explosion. He ran back into the house, and when he came into the room, he stopped dead in his tracks. Epstein had put the muzzle of the revolver to his chest and pulled the trigger.

The force of the blast sent him sprawling backward. Charlie Excalibur sat down by Epstein and watched while the tortured lines faded slowly away. Epstein lifted a hand, touched him on the arm, and, with the fresh, sweet smile of innocence restored, relaxed in death. Charlie Excalibur's breath caught in his throat, too painful for tears. Epstein had been special, and here he had gone and done what all his enemies had not been able to do.

Epstein, why did you have to go and do that? We would have made it out together, and after a while you would have forgotten all this.

Dead was dead. He straightened Epstein's legs, crossed his arms over his chest.

He walked back outside into the sunlight. He should dig a grave, give Epstein a proper burial, but there was no time for that, and he did not have the energy. He would not leave him here to rot in the jungle heat. He piled up some wood at the corner of the house, twigs at the base, and then struck a match and held it beneath the pile. The kindling smouldered, caught, and a shoot of flame licked up the side of the building.

By the time Charlie Excalibur reached the trees the black smoke from the compound was boiling into the sky like a beacon and a memorial. He turned his back on the burning buildings and disappeared into the brush.

LONDON

Boris, you little ferret, where are you? Sir John thought as he studied the Southeast Asia wall map in the chart room. Each flagged pin in the map represented a Russian agent or control, and there were clusters in Hong Kong and Saigon, a few in Tokyo, a scattering of others in a dozen places. It was kept up-to-date by the analysts, and he could see at a glance any major shift by the Soviets.

The pin with the yellow flag was Boris, and it had been moved temporarily from Mongolia to a section off the map marked 'Whereabouts presently unknown.' The Russians had pulled him out of the general Ulan Bator area right enough, but to where?

A young signalman handed him the telephone, and he found Sampson on the line, his accountant's voice precise. 'Marston's accounts are all in order,' Sampson said. 'No income except salary, dividends on a small savings plan, an inheritance of fifteen hundred pounds from his wife's estate. No large outlays. Funeral expenses, of course, during the first quarter of last year. Two hundred pounds for his daughter's trip to Europe. Nothing remarkable.'

'I expected that would be the case.'

'If you want a detailed statement ...'

'That won't be necessary.' He handed the telephone back to the signalman just as Ross came into the chart room, nattily dressed as usual in his vested dark suit, his glossy black hair perfectly groomed as if he were perpetually ready to have his photograph taken. Sir John frowned, tapped the yellow flagged pin with the tip of his forefinger. 'Where have they moved the little bastard? That's the question.'

'Not the main question, I would say,' Ross said, glancing around the room. It was a familiar gesture, Sir John realized, with Ross always surveying the territory when he was about to make a stand. 'Do you have a few minutes?'

Sir John consulted his watch. 'No, as a matter of fact, I don't. I'm going to Clive's wedding.'

'Then I will cut this short,' Ross said. He sat down, adjusted the creases in his trousers before he crossed his legs. 'I believe Clive is the wrong man to be sending out.'

'Oh?'

'He's been burned. There's no possible cover for him that will be credible. I'm in favor of leaving this in the hands of the special team we have in Hong Kong.'

'So,' Sir John said, keeping his eyes on the map, his hands clasped behind him. 'Then you've turned up something after all with those electronic seismographs of yours, have you?'

'Not yet,' Ross said with slight discomfort. 'But I'm convinced that we will.'

'Exactly what hard news do you bring me?'

Ross was good at summaries. He ran down the list in less than three minutes. If the Russians had Marston, there was no reflection of it from the Moscow listening posts. The Special Section in Hong Kong had turned up some leads, but as yet there was nothing definite. 'I believe, however, that it's only a matter of time before they find something.'

Sir John tapped the yellow flag again. 'It's highly significant, don't you think, that we have absolutely no idea where Boris is? He always stands out like a beacon, makes no real pretense of cover. Yet there's not a hint of where he's stashed for the moment. He's our key here.' He turned to face Ross, looked at his watch again. 'I'm running late. Now, as to Clive, I'm sending him because he knows Boris and Boris knows him. Clive also knows the territory like the back of his hand. He speaks three Oriental languages. He is the one man Charlie Excalibur chose to receive his dispatches.' He turned, took one last look at the map. 'For the next forty-eight hours see what you can find on our friend Boris.'

Ross watched him go, stared at the map, thinking not so

much of Boris but of the congestion of pins and Sir John himself. *Really too single-minded for the job*, he thought, not so much a criticism as a description of what he considered to be fact. The time would come, of course, and soon, when it would become evident that even teams of men could neither process nor interpret the significance of these multiple shifting agents and controls, and leadership would pass to the man properly prepared to lead the firm into the electronic age. And that man, of course, would be Hubert Ross.

Sir John used one of the firm's taxis to go to the little chapel near Westminster and for all his hurry arrived in mid-ceremony, taking a seat at the back just as the vicar in the robes was going through the changing of the rings. There were few people here, mostly friends of the bride, Sir John supposed, and the fact of this rather hurried wedding disturbed him. He could remember quite clearly the hurried weddings of the past, officers in his regiment posting their nuptials before they went off to battle, just in case, and he did not want that attitude present in Clive.

The girl was a pretty one, the white dress, the long brown hair, Clive in a suit. He could not hear the vicar distinctly, but finally, there was a chord from the wheezing organ, and Clive was kissing his bride and walking down the center aisle, his radiant bride on his arm.

Outside, there was the usual throwing of rice, and Sir John stood to one side, knowing that Clive had seen him. After all of the laughing and the hugs of congratulation Clive brought his bride over and introduced her. Sir John shook her hand and wished her luck. In a moment or so she was back with her bridesmaids, and Clive walked over to him, looking rather solemn.

'I'm honored that you could take the time, Sir John,' Clive said.

'You haven't told her yet?'

'No. We're off to Brighton for a day or two. I'll have the time then.'

'It's always hardest on the women,' Sir John said, reflectively. 'Have you had second thoughts about the assignment?'

'I have, yes,' Clive said. 'Of course, I have.'

'I'm here to give you the chance to reconsider. If you decide to turn it down, I'll accept your decision with out prejudice.'

Clive looked toward his bride. The decorated car had just been wheeled up next to the curb. He was tempted. He looked back over the hours of briefing with Sir John and the others. His routes were established, his contact points set up all along the way. It had all been set in motion. When he turned back to Sir John, there was a certain unyielding hardness in his face. 'I've accepted the assignment. I'll be in touch.'

He walked toward the car. *Then so be it,* Sir John thought to himself, and summoned the taxi to take him back to Queen Anne's Gate.

BRIGHTON

'Would you like to go pub-crawling tonight?' he said, sitting by the window, looking out at the pebbled beaches and the sea. 'Or I'll take you to Wheeler's for dinner, if you like.'

She smiled from the bed, where she lay naked, flesh glowing in the sunlight. She raised a languid hand. 'Are you printing pound notes on the side, love?'

He came to her, sat down beside her on the bed, put his large hand on her naked stomach, just beginning to swell. 'We'll go out and look at the sunset directly, and then we'll celebrate our last night in Brighton. But you'll have to put on your clothes for a change.'

She reached up, pulled his head down to hers, kissed him. She smelled of perfume and lovemaking. 'Whether it bankrupts us or not, I've loved being here,' she said. 'I'll hate to leave.'

He stood up, forced a smile, knowing that the time was

at hand. He would try to make what he had to say as casual as possible. 'Oh, this is just the beginning,' he said. 'We start our real honeymoon tomorrow. I've saved the best to last. What would you say if I told you that it's off to Australia tomorrow? A month dodging the chill in Melbourne, maybe a week in Brisbane to take the sun.'

'I'd say you're around the bend,' she said with a laugh. 'Delusions of grandeur. We're going to be pinched as it is. Leftovers for weeks.'

He turned his smile toward her. 'No, it's all set, won't cost us a cent. All courtesy of Her Majesty's government.'

It seemed as if, while he looked at her, she withdrew into herself, the terrible suspicions there which even his smile could not dispel. 'That bloody little man,' she said.

'What bloody little man?'

'At our wedding. I should have known.' She got up from the bed, slipped into her dressing gown, joined him at the window. He turned his face away. 'Melbourne, is it?'

'Yes.'

'For both of us, the two of us on the same plane, a clear, unencumbered holiday.'

'Not exactly,' he said. He shook his head, put his hand on her arm. They stared at each other.

'Why haven't you told me straight out?' she said, her bewildered anger rising. 'No, let me tell it to you. You're half Yank, but you're more of a bloody pom than you know. We're not going on the same plane at all, are we? I'm going straight to Melbourne, I am, but you're going in a different direction. A spot of work to do, nothing dangerous, just routine, and then you pop into Australia and we're off on our honeymoon.'

'You knew my job when we moved in together.'

'Then it's true. I've struck the vein of what you intend to do exactly, haven't I?'

'Yes. I'll be a week in Hong Kong.'

She tossed her head, her anger fading into a terrible sorrow. 'You told them you weren't going back out again. You came close to dying the last time. Do you have no memory at all?'

With a hand on each of her shoulders he turned her toward him. 'Look at me, Katy,' he said. 'Don't turn away.' Her eyes met his, stricken. 'I have never lied to you, and I won't begin now. There is a man missing, and it is my job to find him. I won't tell you his name because I don't want you to know it, but it's possible he's in the same bloody fix I was in. No one found me. I don't intend to let that happen to him.'

'I don't care about him, whoever he is; you're my husband.'

'I'm not finished,' he said firmly. 'I have the best chance of finding him, and that's all I'm doing, by the way. No heroics, no derring-do; just a routine investigative procedure and then I'm through. A minimum of risk.'

'A minimum,' she said, angry. 'Damn your minimums. If there were no risk, you would have told me when it first came up.'

'There are no guarantees in anything,' he said. 'But that's the way it's going to be.'

There were tears in her eyes now, but she did not turn away. 'One honest answer, if you have it in you: If there's no risk, then why did you rush the marriage? If you're so damn sure, then why do I feel that you married me just in time to make me a widow, to give the child a name?' She began to weep with a will now, unable to speak, and he gathered her to him, running his hand over her hair, the truth of things so rawly exposed that it gave him physical pain.

The bastards, all of them. Sir John in particular, moving him into a position from which there was no turning back. And he never should have gone to Marston's house. The man should have remained abstract, not a human being with a house and a daughter and the terror of his own death following so close on the loss of his wife. A bloody shambles.

Clive smoothed her hair and with great effort summoned forth the lie. 'Hush,' he said. 'I should have told you sooner, and that's the truth. But I wanted to surprise you with the trip to Melbourne. You'll have a week with your family to prepare them for the shock of me. And then I'll come down from Hong Kong, and that will be that. And as for marrying you so quickly, it may not be romantic, but I have a bit of Scot's blood in me somewhere. Her Majesty's government frowns on paying the expenses of a civil servant's unmarried lady, no matter how loved or pregnant she happens to be.'

She was quiet against him. The crying subsided. 'Scot's blood, is it?' she said finally.

'We could never have afforded it on our own.'

'Yes,' she said. She pulled away, reached for a tissue, blew her nose, getting herself together. 'Well, then, if that's the way it is, we'll make the best of it.'

'Yes.' He saw her face, a momentary glimpse as she turned, half lighted from the window, and in that unguarded moment recognized that she knew the lie but would accept it in the face of a possible truth so painful as to be unbearable.

'When does my plane leave?' she said.

'Tomorrow evening. I'll see you off and then catch the Hong Kong flight an hour later. And in exactly one week we will be in Melbourne together and all this will be behind us.'

'A week is not so long,' she said. She sighed, the last audible doubt she would express. He sensed the fierce support in her, the strength she would display not only for herself but for his sake as well. 'In that case, we should have a final night on the town, love, while I'm still able to fit into a fancy dress.' She raised her toes, gave him a brief kiss, and was off to sort through the wardrobe, clucking over her limited choice while he stood at the window, finding himself braced against an inner pain that would not go away.

9

HONG KONG

Clive came awake with a jolt, and it took him a moment to realize where he was, to accustom himself to the position of the seat which had held him cramped for so many hours. The roar of the jets was a steady, distant whine. He stopped the stewardess as she passed and asked for a glass of water. His mouth was dry.

'How long until we reach Hong Kong?' he said.

'About thirty minutes, sir.'

'Thank you.'

He had been awake to see the green jungled strip of Vietnam slide by far below, with its snaking, slugging yellow rivers, and then the port of Danang and the bank of clouds which lay just offshore, over the South China Sea. Then he had gone to sleep again.

He checked his watch, trying to reckon where Katy would be at this moment, over the Indian Ocean someplace, perhaps over the continent of Australia itself. He was grateful that the day of departure had been so hectic, the hurried trip from Brighton to the house, the preparation, with Katy placing her plants in the tender care of the widow who lived next door. Katy had made three attempts to call Australia, reaching her sister Emily, only to be cut off twice. On the third try she was finally able to relay her flight number and the time of her arrival. Then she had to pack her winter things in a pair of suitcases, and it was off to Gatwick, the bother of reaching that remote and inconvenient airport. She stayed beyond the reach of emigration until the last moment; then he caught her up in his arms and soundly kissed her, and she was off, passing through the electronic security booth, turning to wave at him once more before she was lost in the crowd. His own apprehension had passed as well. He could handle whatever happened, one moment at a time.

He decided to stretch his legs. He got up and walked down the long aisle of the 747 back into the economy section. And there his first challenge was awaiting him, a voice from a seat near the window.

'Clive, old man.'

He recognized the man from the past but could not place him at first. The man was smooth, handsome, with the smile of an aging movie star, a slightly florid face with bright eyes which implied he knew great secrets he could not divulge. He sat with a cigarette squeezed between thumb and forefinger, grinned at Clive across a vacant seat as if they were old friends.

Cavendish, that was the man's name, Clive remembered. Cavendish of the *Straits Times* in Singapore, Earl Cavendish, who, when he was drunk, called himself the Earl of Cavendish and mimicked a British accent. Cavendish was Australian. He had no love for the British.

'You don't recognize me,' Cavendish said.

'How could I forget the Earl of Cavendish?' Clive said with a smile he did not feel. He shook the man's hand. 'Do you mind if I join you? Is this seat taken? I could use a beer.'

Cavendish snapped his fingers at the stewardess, ordered a beer for Clive and a gin and tonic for himself. 'I must say I didn't expect to see you in this part of the world again.'

'One never knows, does one?' Clive said. He nodded at the stewardess, who poured his beer for him and handed Cavendish the tray of small bottles and the ice.

'As long as fate has thrown you my way,' Cavendish said, 'I could always use a rousing story about how martyred you feel, and I assume you do, and about how you hate the bloody Asians with a passion or how you feel you were betrayed by your own country. Something like that. Bitterness always draws readers. Former spies always have a built-in attraction.'

'That's old news.'

'Oh, come now, old man,' Cavendish said with a mock British accent. 'The word's circulated that you've been sent to look for Marston.'

'Who?' Clive said.

'The errant Queen's Messenger.'

'Ah, the Queen's Messenger. The current hot rumor.'

Cavendish chuckled. 'Everybody knows about the QM who took French leave from Hong Kong. You're such a bloody good faker I'm almost tempted to believe you.'

'And you're just a suspicious son of a bitch who has made a reputation of sorts for your gossipmongering journalism,' Clive said pleasantly. 'You're still in Singapore, I take it?'

'Yes. On my way home from holiday.'

'I won't be surprised if you end up with some paper in Hong Kong one of these days.'

'Why Hong Kong?'

'Your Chinese genius prime minister has cleaned up Singapore,' Clive said. 'How can you flourish with your drama in a country where the big issue is to get everybody to smile and be courteous to each other? No dope rackets because Dr. Lee executes dope dealers, and if you're caught littering, it costs you five hundred Singapore dollars.'

'Are you being critical of Singapore?' Cavendish said, fishing.

'There you go again,' Clive said. 'For the record, I love Singapore and clean streets and courtesy and an Asian city where it's safe to walk after dark.' He drank the beer. 'I should be getting back. We're due to land shortly.'

'Maybe we could have a drink. I have a few hours before I go down to Singapore.'

'Sorry. All tied up.'

'I take it you will be seeing your old flame?' Cavendish said, trying to raise something to hold him.

'My what?'

'The marvelous Liz. It was widely known that you had a thing going before your spy business folded.'

'I like Liz Sullivan,' Clive said. 'Is she still with the *Asian Wall Street Journal?*'

'She's shifted to the *Far Eastern Economic Review*. You're sure you won't have an extra hour?'

'Some other time. Thanks for the beer.'

Clive went back to his seat. He lit a cigarette, responded to the seat belt sign, watched the dramatic approach to Hong Kong, the green islands in the blue sea far below, the hilly edge of the mainland off in the distance, the occasional freighters and junks leaving wakes on the calm surface of the water. He thought about Marston. The news was out then, as he suspected it would be by this time, not all of it but enough. Cavendish was far down the journalistic line.

He put out his cigarette as the 747 made its dramatic drop, seeming to skim the tops of the hills, and there was Hong Kong below, an island of Victoria with its green peaks and dramatic monoliths of modern buildings flanking the harbor, with the congestion of Kowloon just across the gap of water. The jet banked, seemed destined to hit the high buildings on the Kowloon side, then turned and slid into the pattern to touch down on the runway of Kai Tak, an airport built on fill land extended like a large, flat rectangle into the water.

When he left the jet, he went immediately to the men's room, bought a disposable razor from the Chinese porter, and shaved, making himself presentable. The men's room was a bedlam. Down the line of lavatory basins a Malaysian was washing his hair. In one of the toilet stalls a Japanese businessman was changing into a fresh suit, hanging his wrinkled clothes on the stall door.

The shave refreshed him, and he went through customs, spotted Dunhill waiting for him. Dunhill was an efficient little man in his late forties, slightly overweight, hair thinning, possessed of a marvelously placid disposition. Clive liked Dunhill because it was quite obvious Dunhill liked himself and his life here. He met Clive with a broad smile and a firm handshake.

'Good flight, I hope?' he said. 'Grand to see you. I have things all set for you, such as they are. Not perfect, of course, but I have three lined up, unless you'd rather rest a while.'

'I'd like to get right down to it.'

The terminal was crowded with people, the waiting areas and the lounges filled with scores of refugees, gathered around their belongings wrapped in piles of cloth. Despite the air conditioning, there was a stench to the place. Clive would not have been surprised to see them setting up their own bazaars or cooking fish on open braziers.

'Poor devils,' Dunhill said, leading the way through them, a comment rather than an expression of sympathy. 'They're not in for an easy time of it, now are they? But that's the price of modern politics.'

They reached a small office in the British Airways section which had been vacated for their use. An electric wall fan was humming across a steel desk bare except for a telephone on it. The wall was dominated by a colorful poster advertising holidays in London.

'A safe room,' Dunhill said with a sigh. 'Your cover's blown, of course, just being seen with me. But then you really don't need cover, do you?' He sat down, clipped the end off a cigar. 'Would you care for a drink, tea, anything?'

'Nothing,' Clive said. 'Who are the Watchers?'

'No idea,' Dunhill said, puffing the cigar into life. 'Probably a mixed bag. I'm watched by all of them. The popularity doesn't go to my head.' He smiled at his own humor. 'But they will be far more interested in you.'

'Who do you have for me?'

'Three of them. The first is Loretta Wang, the stewardess who saw Marston leave the plane.'

'Wang? Ashton-Croft's report said she was Thai.'

'Ashton-Croft wouldn't know a Balinese from a Burmese.'

'Who else?'

'P.J.C. Daniels, security officer for the departure area that day. And one other stewardess, from economy. Gloria Brightwell.'

'English?'

'Yes.'

'What do you have from these people in preliminaries?'

'You have the statements. Miss Wang saw him leave, has no idea what the visitor actually looked like.'

'And Daniels?'

'No Queen's Messenger went past him.'

'Finally, Miss Brightwell.'

'Nothing. She was not even in first class on that flight. But you asked for any crew who worked the flight that day. Sorry I couldn't put together more of a selection.'

'We'll see what we can do.' Clive sat down, opened his attaché case, took out the folder pictures of Marston, the full-face shots in his blazer, his hair gleaming almost golden, a very handsome man. 'Give me Daniels for a start.'

Daniels turned out to be retired military, a rawboned, sharp-eyed man in his early forties who took his job very seriously. He sat down across the table from Clive, declined a cigarette, reiterated his earlier statement: No one had passed him.

'Where were you at the time of the loading of the Bangkok flight?'

'At the terminal end of the corridor, sir, near the security gate. I was the one who directed Mr. Ashton-Croft to the aircraft in the first place.'

Clive showed him the photographs. 'And you did not see this man come back down the corridor and go into the terminal?'

'He did not go back into the terminal,' Daniels said with great determination. 'Nobody did. That's not quite accurate. One small Vietnamese boy wandered up that way, came back to the transit lounge. But no adults, not until Ashton-Croft came back through.'

'Perhaps you might have been distracted by Ashton-Croft. He was upset, after all. How did he get to the head of airport security?'

'I directed him to the office,' Daniels said. 'I did not leave my post. I was there for a full hour before the Bangkok flight and three hours afterward. I will stake my reputation on it. Captain Marston did not go into the terminal.'

'Thank you very much,' Clive said, rising, shaking his hand. 'You've been most helpful.'

Clive lifted the telephone, informed Dunhill he wanted to see the first class stewardess next. And would Dunhill please send in some soft drinks?

In a moment there was a light tap on the door and Loretta Wang came in, a beautiful girl, no more than twenty-two, wearing a batik dress. He stood up, smiled.

'Do sit down, Miss Wang. I'm sorry to put you to all this bother. You must be tired of questions. Would you care for a cigarette?'

'Please.'

She accepted the cigarette and the light, sat down, very much at ease. 'Do you speak Chinese as well as you speak English?' Clive said, chatting.

'Not quite as well,' she said. 'My mother is English and my father is Chinese. We speak English at home. But I can make our Chinese passengers feel at ease.'

'I'm sure you can,' Clive said. A girl brought in a tray with two bottles of Coca-Cola, two glasses, and a small bucket of ice. Clive watched as she left the room; then he took the ice tongs. placed cubes in both glasses.

'None for me, please,' she said. 'I'm counting calories.'

He filled his own glass. 'Now, if you don't mind, perhaps you could go through this business one more time.'

'There's really nothing to tell,' she said apologetically. 'Captain Marston came aboard fifteen minutes before the other passengers boarded. He put two small dispatch bags in the seat next to him. Another man came aboard, spoke to him, and they left together. That's all I know.'

'In your original statement you said the man was European,' Clive said with a smile. 'What made you think so? How did you come to that conclusion?'

She frowned, puffed on the cigarette. 'When he passed me in the aisle, we almost collided. I'm not sure, but I think he said, "Excuse me."'

'Then you did hear his voice?'

'I feel very foolish,' she said. 'I really can't remember if he spoke to me or not. But I think he must have done so. I remember making a mental note that he would be picking a meal from the Western menu rather than the Oriental.'

'I'm sure you were very busy.'

'I'm glad you understand. Most people don't know how busy we are.'

'The galley is in the center of that aircraft, isn't it? So you were busy serving drinks before takeoff, moving up and down the aisle.'

'Yes.'

'So you moved past the man as he was talking to Marston.'

'I must have. I really don't remember.'

Clive slowed the pace. He was used to debriefing agents, and an inquisitorial tone would be inappropriate here. 'What I'm getting at ...' he began, then paused. 'Is it possible he wasn't standing in the aisle when he talked to Marston, that he wasn't in your way at all? I'm suggesting that perhaps he sat down, that Marston moved over in the seat, held the bags in his lap perhaps to make room for his visitor.'

'Yes,' she said brightly. 'Of course. He wasn't standing in the aisle.'

A small feeling of well-being passed through Clive. It was a pleasure questioning the bright mind of someone trying to be helpful, nondefensive. 'You've flown other flights when a Queen's Messenger was on board?'

'Several.'

'Enough to be familiar with their regulations?'

'Yes.'

'One of which is that a Queen's Messenger always takes two seats, one for himself, one for his bags. No one is allowed to occupy that other seat, to get even semiclose to those sacred bags.' He shook a cigarette from his pack, lit it. 'What disturbs me is this: If this visitor had information urgent enough to persuade him to leave the aircraft, why didn't he just lean over and say it? Why did he have to sit down?'

She adjusted the batik skirt over her bare knees. 'They were looking at something together. I remember that. When I passed them, Captain Marston was looking at something.'

'That makes sense.' He leaned back in his chair, allowing her time to think. 'Was it papers of any sort, say, something large, like a map?'

'I honestly don't remember,' she said, frustrated. 'I don't think it was anything large or I would have remembered it.'

'Was either of the serving tables on the backs of the seats in front of them pulled down?'

'No.'

'You're sure of that, are you?'

She smoothed her hair away from her forehead. 'No, I'm not sure. I think one of them was down, as a matter of fact. The orange juice glass was still in the holder. It must have been half full or I would have picked it up.'

'The folding table in front of Marston?'

She nodded. Her cigarette lay on the groove of the ashtray, smoldering, the ash long. 'The man had put something, a packet, I think, on the folding table and Captain Marston was examining them.'

'Them? More than one item?' He was sweating. He stood up to catch the breeze of the electric fan.

'Pictures,' she said, with a sudden delighted smile. 'They were looking at pictures.'

'Photographs?'

'Yes.'

'Large? Small?'

'Snapshots, I believe.'

He followed up on the photographs, urging, suggesting, yet leaving her room to think, to consider, for inside that pretty, bright head of hers were all the details, many of them mixed with other flights, other passengers. The art

77

of debriefing lay in seizing on one detail and using it to prompt another. He exhausted the pictures, moved on to the man himself. And from her clouded memory he extracted small items. The man had a bald spot on top of his head, a monk's cap across which lay wisped strands of gray hair. That led to the dandruff on a black jacket he wore, too heavy for the climate, and then the color of his skin. His ears were a brownish color (from either the sun or racial origin, she did not know), and the ears led to a partial memory of glasses frames looped over them, old-fashioned (no memory of the color).

Was Marston agitated? She did not know.

Was the black jacket a tweedy or smooth material? She did not know.

The ears of the visitor. Was there anything else unusual about them, prominent lobes perhaps? She did not know.

Finally, he knew he had gone as far as he could go in one sitting. There was beginning to form in his mind the basic idea which, if correct, would make any further information from her unnecessary. 'Just one last thing,' he said. 'The man when he passed you in the aisle said, "Excuse me." He didn't say, "Sorry." Correct?'

'Yes.'

'How can you be sure?'

She smiled. 'I'm engaged to an English boy. He says, "Sorry," all the time, and I kid him about it. So I would have remembered that.'

He returned her smile. 'Thank you for your help.'

'I'm sorry I can't do more,' she said. 'I do hope Captain Marston will be all right.'

'I'm sure he will.' He saw her out of the office and then called in his last interview. Miss Brightwell was another cup of tea, a honey blonde in her late thirties, hanging on to her figure and her position. He had the impression as she entered the room that she scanned him as a possibility of reprieve, in search of the right man who could take her away from the eternal round of flights. But by the time she sat down, crossed her legs, leaned forward to accept a light for her cigarette the impression was gone.

'Actually,' she said, 'I don't think I can be of much use to you. I was never even close to the first class section that day. I was working economy.'

'Still, I would like to have you look at these pictures,' Clive said. 'One never knows.'

She shrugged, accepted the glossies, went through them, stopped for a brief moment, puzzled, then shrugged it off, went through the rest, and handed them back to him. 'I recognize none of them. As I say, I wasn't even close to first class.'

He isolated the photograph which had disturbed her temporarily. It was Marston, full face, a close-up, his hair gleaming like a torch in bright sunlight. He handed it back to her. She held it with her scarlet fingernails shining against the white back of the photograph.

'This one seems to have puzzled you briefly,' he said. 'Why?'

'A coincidence,' she said, squinting at the picture.

'Do you use reading glasses ordinarily?'

'Yes, but I can see quite well without them.'

Vanity, Clive thought. 'If you wouldn't mind using them, I would appreciate it.'

She removed the half-moon glasses from her purse, held them up to her eyes.

'Now,' he said, 'even if it seems totally unimportant to you, I'd like to know what you're thinking.'

'It just strikes me as odd,' she said, folding the glasses, putting them away. 'I had a passenger on economy that flight who bears a resemblance to this man.'

'Oh?' Clive said, restraining his excitement. 'How did your passenger differ? How was he similar?'

'Mine was not nearly so handsome. Mine had black hair, very ill-kempt. His clothes were dreadful, didn't fit him.'

'Do you remember what he was wearing?'

'No.'

'But the face?'

'Similar,' she said. 'Quite.'

'Was he alone?'

'Nobody's alone in economy.'

'I mean by that, did he board alone?'

'Sorry, I really can't say.'

'Who was seated next to him?'

'I don't know. I really don't.'

'Could it have been an older man, black suit, balding head, glasses?'

'There were so many passengers. It was a full flight. I really can't remember.'

Clive leaned back in his chair. Of course, she would not remember, this woman with the scanning eyes, looking for possibles. The visitor would not have been a possible; therefore, he would have gone unnoticed, if indeed he had been there at all.

'Can you remember the man's seat number?'

'That's impossible. So many flights since then.'

'Did you work both aisles?'

'No, the starboard side.'

'Then he was on the starboard side.'

'He would have had to be, wouldn't he?'

'Quite. Now, was he toward the front of the section or the rear?'

'I honestly don't know.'

'Think, please. This could be very important.' But he could tell from the expression on her face that she had gone as far as she could go. She would have no more information for him.

'Sorry,' she said.

'I appreciate your time.' He saw her out of the office and then collapsed on a chair in front of the electric fan, absolutely drained, saturated with sweat, fetching out another cigarette as Dunhill came in, stood waiting for some indication of how things had gone.

Clive put the cigarette in the ashtray without lighting it. 'Let's take a look at the departure gate.'

'Certainly,' Dunhill said, still openly curious, deciding not to push it. He led the way through the terminal to departure, where an official from Hong Kong emigration bypassed the inspection booths. Clive looked down the long corridor from the position where Daniels must have been standing. An international flight was boarding. Over the loudspeaker he could hear the multilingual calls for boarding a Cathay Pacific flight to Tokyo, and one part of the corridor was an almost solid mass of people with duty-free shopping bags lined up in front of the door for boarding the economy section and a smaller line in front of the door for first class passengers ten feet farther down the corridor. Clive watched the boarding procedure for a while, the pursers checking tickets, issuing boarding passes; then he went past the group to a point almost at the end of the long corridor and a similar pair of doors.

'Was this the departure gate for the Bangkok flight?' he said.

'That's correct,' Dunhill said. 'Marston came out this door here in the company of his visitor, went down the hallway toward the terminal. That was the last anyone ever saw of him.'

Clive paused at another door marked 'STAFF ONLY. NO EXIT.' 'Where does this lead?' he said.

'Down to the tarmac. But he didn't go that route. There was a baggage handlers' dispute that day and the field was swarming with security people in case there was outside interference.'

Clive nodded, wiped his perspiring neck with his handkerchief. 'How about a loo?' he said. 'Can I reach one without going through those damned security barriers again?'

'Righto,' Dunhill said. He led the way to a men's room halfway down the corridor just opposite the diminishing mass of people assembled for the Tokyo flight. Again it was bedlam, this time lacking a Chinese porter, lavatory sinks lined up like army barracks, rows of urinals, equally long rows of closed toilet stalls. Clive went into one of the stalls, closed the door, locked it, observing the panels which came to within six inches of the floor on either side. When he emerged, he washed his hands next to a man with sleepless, bloodshot eyes whose chin and jowls were covered with shaving cream. Clive dried his hands on paper towels, pushed them into the door of a wastebin which closed when the pressure against it was released.

When he came out, the corridor had begun to fill again for another flight, hand luggage propped against the wall, masses of what appeared to be Filipinos crowded around one of the economy doors. Dunhill was patiently waiting. He fell in step with Clive toward the central part of the terminal.

'You can see the difficulties here, old chap,' Dunhill said, making way for a small pregnant Filipino woman carrying a baby in one arm and a large cloth-tied bundle in the other. 'Utter mass confusion.'

They walked out of the terminal to an area where a car was waiting. 'I took the liberty of having your bags picked up. I've booked you into the Furama if you have no objection. The Peninsular was full.'

'That's very thoughtful of you,' Clive said offhandedly. The car carried them through the tunnel from Kowloon to the island.

'Damn it all,' Dunhill said with a frowning smile. 'I'm trying to be politic, old chap, but I'm fairly bursting with impatience. What did you find out? What are you thinking?'

'First contact Roberts for me and put him on hold. And you can call off your special team here. Marston did not defect. He was grabbed. He is not in Hong Kong.'

'We have reason to believe he is,' Dunhill said. 'A man of his description was spotted in the New Territories, in a Fiat, up near the Chinese border.'

'If he had defected, he would be out of the country by now. If he were being held captive here and they were transporting him from one place to another, they would blindfold him, tape his mouth, and stuff him in the boot of a car or the back of a lorry. In neither case would he be visible.'

'You've been in this business long enough to know that the illogical is often commonplace.'

'Your chaps are on the wrong track,' Clive said. He realized he was being querulous, abrupt, but he felt irritable that so much time had passed and none of the examiners had picked up on the truly important pieces of information. 'Have you had any signals on Marston's daughter? Has she been located?'

'Nothing definite. Still knocking about Europe. Why?'

'Unless I'm wrong, she's at the center of what happened to Marston.'

The car had come to a stop in front of the Furama Hotel, and Clive did not pursue his explanation until after he had been checked in and reached his room on the fifth floor. Then he located a small bottle of bourbon in the minifridge, mixed it with water, and dropped in a single cube of ice. Dunhill slumped down in a chair, watching, just waiting for Clive to pick up his narrative.

'I will give you my scenario,' Clive said, sitting down on the edge of the bed, kicking off his shoes. 'I want you to play the devil's advocate. Knock holes in it if you can.'

'That goes without saying. Continue.'

'The train platform in Mongolia. Marston gets off the train feeling quite cheerful, comes back looking like the wrath of God. We know he met Boris there. In that conversation Boris informs Marston that they have his daughter, that terrible things will happen to her if he doesn't cooperate with them in handing over the Charlie Excalibur dispatch. Marston doesn't believe him and refuses to cooperate, but Boris insists that Marston set up the run to London so he will be carrying the dispatch. Further proof will be provided later. If Marston doesn't go along, they will send him some part of her on down the line.'

'Pure conjecture,' Dunhill said.

'So far. But it all fits. Marston does as he's been told. He really has nothing to lose. If the proof is not forthcoming, he simply makes the run to London and everything is fine. When he reaches Hong Kong he makes a frantic attempt to reach his daughter in Europe but fails. So Marston boards the jet to Bangkok.

'Now we have a stranger who comes on board that flight to see Marston. But we have to characterize him first, determine how he arranges that. He's a man in his mid-fifties, nondescript, balding, wearing glasses and a black suit. How did he get past security in the first place? He didn't have the diplomatic papers Ashton-Croft carried. No one at security even remembered him. Conclusion: He had to be a ticketed passenger.'

Dunhill pursed his lips. 'You got that description from the Wang girl?'

'Yes.'

'Perhaps you had better give my chaps a good course in interrogation techniques one of these days. Go on.'

'The visitor waits until the stewardess is occupied, slips past her into the first class cabin. We can imagine Marston's feelings because this is bound to be the man Boris said would have the proof about his daughter. Marston is sufficiently jolted to suspend one of the cardinal rules of the Queen's Messengers and allows the stranger to occupy one of the sacred seats.'

'How do you know the man sat down? That's in none of the depositions.'

'The stewardess remembered.' Clive sipped his dri..k. The jet lag was beginning to catch up with him. 'The man showed Marston photographs of his daughter, some rather lurid, threatening ones I'm sure, sufficiently convincing to make Marston get up and leave the aircraft.'

'Intriguing,' Dunhill said, rubbing the cleft of his chin with an index finger. 'But you're making a broad leap to a conclusion. After all, we do have some evidence the daughter is in Italy.'

'Was in Italy,' Clive corrected. 'A hundred to one says she's not there now.'

'I won't concede that without evidence. But continue.'

'They left the aircraft together, but they did not leave the corridor. I have Daniel's word for that, and I believe him. No, they were seen disappearing into a cluster of people waiting down the corridor for another aircraft. But they went into the men's room, after the man with Marston had retrieved a couple of bags he had left propped up against the wall in the corridor. Marston was given another set of clothes, went into a toilet stall to change. He was forced to put his dispatch bags into a larger bag, probably nylon, which his escort provided. Then, dressed in these ill-fitting clothes, he was forced to rinse his hair with black dye. You've seen the toilets. Such an extraordinary act anywhere else would pass there without notice.'

'So where did they go from there?' Dunhill said, fascinated.

'The man had a passport for Marston under a different name. He also had a pair of tickets in the economy section of the same flight to Bangkok. They simply went back down the corridor and boarded through the economy door.'

'Proof?'

'A bit of luck. Our economy stewardess with her sharp eye for the eligible men spotted a likely one. Except that his hair was black, unkempt, and his clothes didn't fit him. But she recognized Marston's face.'

'Damned clever of them,' Dunhill said with a grudging admiration. 'Same flight, different section. Damned clever.'

'Have your chaps try to track down a pair of seats on that flight, European names, booked shortly after Boris had his conversation with Marston in Mongolia. Also, check the inbound flights from Europe for the forty-eight hours after the conversation. We might get lucky and find a match. The pair of seats will be on the starboard side of economy. Also, book me a flight to Bangkok in the morning, if you will.'

'Righto,' Dunhill said. 'I'll let you get some well-deserved sleep.' He stood up. 'By the way, I had a call from Elizabeth Sullivan, the *Far Eastern Economic Review*.'

'I know her,' Clive said. 'What does she want?'

'An interview. She said she would be in the Furama bar at six o'clock tonight if you wish to meet her. If you don't show up, she said to let you know she understands.'

'I'll see her.'

Dunhill cleared his throat, a mannerism which indicated that he was about to approach a sensitive subject. Clive lighted a cigarette, looked at Dunhill's reluctant expression. 'Out with it, man,' he said. 'It's obvious you have something to say.'

'You're right, of course,' Dunhill said. 'Best to put it on the table. I've been requested by members of the special team here ...' He paused, sweating. 'If you need them in Bangkok, they would prefer to be requested through Patterson and through me.'

Clive understood instantly. For a moment he felt as if he could not breathe. He forced himself to inhale the cigarette. 'You can tell them for me that if I wanted their bloody names, Sir John would have them on the wire tomorrow.'

'Personally I would trust you with my life,' Dunhill said, doing his best to make amends. 'It's just that after the business last time ... You know what I'm trying to say.'

'Twist old Clive and he cracks wide open, is that it?' Clive said. 'You can reassure your chaps that they will be protected. I'm here strictly as a pointer, not a retriever.' He paused for a moment. 'Now let's get on with the business at hand.'

'Portia is going to be very put out that she didn't snag you for a dinner party,' Dunhill said, trying to restore a sense of normalcy.

'Some other time perhaps.'

'Yes,' Dunhill said, 'some other time. If you need anything, let it be known.'

And he left the room.

10

HONG KONG

Clive slept until four-thirty, then shaved, showered, and put on a fresh suit. Still early, he poured himself a short drink, sat down by the window, and watched the boat traffic in the bay, the Star Ferry just leaving the Kowloon side. He thought of Katy and wondered why he had never told her about Liz, but then there had never been a reason for such revelation; Liz belonged to the past, and he had been certain he would never see her again.

At half past five he went down to the bar, intending to leave a message for her with the bartender and then to absent himself from the hotel for the evening. He was startled to see that Liz was already there, sitting at a low table against the backdrop of a carved teak wall, and it seemed to him she had not changed at all in the year since he had seen her. Indeed, for one brief moment time collapsed and he was in the past, meeting her here at the end of a long and grueling day at the High Commission, and they would have a drink and dinner and finally share the brass bed in her flat, for sleeping or talking or making love, or perhaps all three.

She smiled as he approached the table, raising her hand to be taken in both of his, and only now could he see the changes in her. Her formerly long blonde hair had been cropped into short curls now, she was perhaps a bit thinner, but those pale blue eyes were still the same, reflecting that combination of shrewdness and warmth which had attracted him in the first place. Her hand was soft, nails unpolished. She was wearing a perfume he remembered from the past, a white linen suit, as she had the last time he had seen her. He was certain that neither

87

the perfume nor the suit was coincidental. She intended to evoke the past.

'Well,' he said, a single word, and let it rest. He sat down, feeling somewhat awkward, snapped his fingers at the waiter, ordered a bourbon for himself and a refill of her glass.

'You're looking well and fit,' she said. 'I'm glad you agreed to meet me.'

'Why wouldn't I?' he said. The waiter served the drinks, departed. 'Why shouldn't I see an old friend?'

She laughed, genuinely amused. 'We were always more than that,' she said. 'Lovers, adversaries, companions, adjacent stones in a wall, a thousand things.' She touched his hand, fleetingly, the smile turning serious. 'More than friends.'

He sipped his drink. 'I almost didn't show,' he said. 'I'm half angry without knowing why, and the rest is a mixture of apprehension and untempered delight. Why in the hell didn't you call?'

'When?'

'After that bloody business in Bangkok. They hauled me back to Brixton for debriefing. They didn't allow me any outbound messages, but I kept waiting for some word from you.' He shrugged. 'I don't blame you, not really. A scandal tends to taint anyone connected with it.'

'If it's of any interest to you, I tried to call,' she said. 'I was informed that you didn't want any calls from anyone. I didn't realize until much later that they probably had you hidden away.'

'Thank you for that. It's really water under the bridge,' he said. 'Why did you call Dunhill? What are you doing here?'

'You're newsworthy,' she said. 'Henry came into my office this morning and clapped his pale little hands together. He's always gleeful when he thinks he's creating a dilemma. Anyway, he popped in and said, "Guess what? Your precious spy has turned up again. Do you want to cover it?"'

'Then you're here on business.'

'I'm here because I wanted to see you again,' she said softly. 'I'm not so sure that was a good idea, but here I am anyway.'

'I'm not so sure it's a good idea either,' he said. 'But I'm glad you're here. There are so many bits of unfinished business in my life. I'm not very highly regarded in this part of the world.'

'Everything passes,' she said. 'You were a sensational story for a while, but there was always an undertone of sympathy to it. You just had too much, that's all. There's nobody who works out here who couldn't understand what happened.'

'What's been happening with you?' he said, deliberately changing the subject. 'You're not with the *Journal* anymore.'

'No. My prose was a bit too flamboyant and chatty for a financial paper, I think. Not that they were displeased, but the *Review* offered me more money and more freedom. I really didn't care much about anything after you left, so I went to Japan for a while, found that didn't help, and finally decided I had better get on with it. So I came back here and took the offer and settled in.'

'Are you married? Involved?'

'No,' she said. 'But I know you are. You're living with an Australian girl named Katherine Haskins, nicknamed Katy, currently pregnant.'

'How do you know that?'

'Hong Kong isn't the end of the world. Reporters come through here all the time. We gossip about everything. You're a prime topic as far as I'm concerned. I've kept track of you as best I could.'

'I married her before I came out here.'

'I guess I should have expected that,' she said, a wistful tone to her voice. 'I'm sorry, but I don't like your Katy. I don't like the fact that she's pregnant and you're married, and I'm sitting here feeling miserable for lost chances.'

'I'm not,' he said, touched by her candor. 'We had some fine times together.'

'Past tense.'

'Yes. Past tense.'

'No sparks left?'

'Plenty of sparks, but nothing I can't handle. You're still the most alive woman I've ever known, the most exciting. If things had gone differently, we would have made a permanent life together, I think.'

'But?'

'Everything got turned upside down. And I'm settled in now, quite content on the whole.'

'And that, as the saying goes, is that.'

'Yes. That is that.'

She drank her drink straight down. 'Then we'll get to the other,' she said. 'It makes it more difficult, but it's my assignment.'

'What's your assignment?'

'You are.'

He smiled. 'You were never any good at being oblique,' he said. 'You could never get by with telling me half of anything. Your neck flushes when you're being devious.'

'Other people aren't so astute, thank God, or I'd be out of business.'

'What's your full assignment?'

'The biggest story around. Marston. Do you know that the Hong Kong gamblers are making a book on him? Even money that he's defected. Five to one that he's been snatched. Ten to one that he won't be found alive. But it's more than that. He represents the incorruptible part of England. So what has happened to him is of very keen interest in Hong Kong. He's become a symbol and a bloody good story in the process.'

'And what makes you think I'm here on the Marston business?'

'It's obvious, darling,' she said. 'You forget the reputation you had before the fall. You were the greatest puzzle solver of all time. And now that there's a rather grand puzzle on hand, they've dispatched you to solve it.'

He fell silent, aware of the people in the room, the dozens of ways his conversation could be recorded, deciphered, understood. 'I think we should go to my room,' he said.

'Am I being propositioned?'

'Long beyond that, old girl,' he said. He settled the check. They made innocuous conversation in the mirrored elevator, and once they were in his room, he turned on the television set, not for the picture but for the sound, to fuzz up any recording devices, if they had gone to that trouble. He pulled the drapes while she searched through the minifridge, came up with a small bottle of bourbon for him and a cognac for herself. She checked the price list atop the minifridge.

'Outrageous prices for drinks,' she said.

'It's all courtesy of Her Majesty's Foreign Office,' he said.

She put ice cubes in his drink, then kicked off her shoes and sat down on the bed, tucking her feet beneath her. 'To the old times,' she said.

'We did have some bloody good ones,' he said. 'I'll drink to that.' He sipped his drink, sat down in a leather chair, the television chattering Chinese in his ear. 'We need an agreement,' he said.

'On what?'

'I will give you a story on Marston. And you print it exactly as you get it from me, no more, no less. Then, when the rest of the story breaks, you can have an exclusive on the whole thing.'

'Without going through the Foreign Office?'

'They'll clap a D Notice on it, first thing. You'll have it straight from me.'

'Agreed,' she said with a toss of her head. 'You know what happened to Marston then?'

'To a degree. You will attribute the story to a reliable source, a highly placed official in the British government. He waited while she drank the cognac. 'Shouldn't you be taking notes? Pencils, paper, that sort of thing?'

'I don't need them. I can remember word for word.'

'You'd better,' he said. 'You are to say in your story, according to this highly placed source, that it has been determined by the authorities that Marston did not defect but was snatched. You can also say that he was taken by intelligence agents to another country, that he's no longer in Hong Kong. Also add that the British government is determined to have him back.'

'My God, is that true?'

'Yes.'

'There must be more.'

'Off the record.'

'All right then, off the record. I have a thousand questions. Who snatched him? What country? How did they manage it? How do you know all this?'

'I think it was a Soviet operation. It's typical of their style. I can't tell you how they forced him into it because that might jeopardise another person.' The Chinese commentary in his ear had changed to discordant music now. Why do you want this story published?'

'It's my way of letting them know that I'm willing to do business, if he's still alive.' The whiskey was beginning to relax him. 'If they've gotten what they want from Marston, they may want to trade him for a number of minor characters we've bagged.' He shook his glass. The ice had dissolved. The glass was empty. 'The poor bastard,' he said almost to himself.

'Are you well?' she said, quietly concerned. 'Did you heal?'

'I'm quite fit,' he said. 'Anyway, that's as much as I can explain at the moment. I'm here to find what pieces are left, to pick them up, if possible.'

'Where do you go from here?'

'Bangkok. In the morning.'

'Is there anything else I can do for you aside from the story.'

'Not that I can think of.'

She took a business card from her purse, wrote on it. 'I have a new home number. If I'm not there, I have an amah who'll take the message. You can trust her.'

He took the card, noticed her glass was empty. 'Would you like another cognac?'

'No,' she said. 'But before I go, I'd like to see the view from your window.'

'Certainly.' He opened the drapes and dimmed the lamp. She stood by the window, almost luminous in her white suit, looking very fragile. He was engulfed by a profound sadness, remembering the nights he had shared with her, a whole part of his life which had receded into a dreamlike memory. Beyond her the lights of the harbor were reflected in the water and Kowloon was garishly ablaze across the way. A party boat passed down the harbor, colored lights strung from bow to stern.

'God, it never fails to take my breath away,' she said.

He stood beside her, and, quite without knowing how it happened, he was kissing her with incredible fervor. And then he just stood and held her to him, one hand caressing her hair.

'I've never been indirect,' she said, her voice muffled against his chest. 'It's up to you.'

'Yes,' he said. He held her for a moment longer and then released her. There was no room for further complications in his life now. 'Christ, it's a bloody jolt to be here with you, to have to tell you to go home.'

She smiled that knowing smile of hers. 'I'm very pleased to be able to shake you up,' she said. She put on her shoes. 'Will you be coming back through Hong Kong?'

'I don't know.'

'See if you can arrange it. We'll be in touch.' She kissed him lightly on the lips. He stood at the door of his room and watched her as she walked toward the elevator. She smiled at him once before the elevator swallowed her up, and he felt a sharp yearning, a keen desire, for he could remember every detail of her body, the direct and unabashed savagery of their lovemaking.

He went back into his room to prepare his notes for his meeting with Patterson.

THAILAND

Charlie Excalibur was hungry. His stomach ached with it. There was fruit on the trees, a dozen varieties of strange shapes and tastes. He had learned about jungle fruit. One time, a thousand years ago, shortly after he had entered the jungle, he had appeased his hunger with fruit until he was bloated with it. And within twenty-four hours he was so doubled up with pain that he lay in the concealment of the sawtooth grass and prayed to die. He scoured for a full six days afterward. He ran in semi-exhaustion for two weeks.

Now he knew better. The myth of the jungle paradise, living off the natural plants, was all shit, unless you were a gook. Rice, meat, fish. That was what he wanted. He would have given a hundred dollars for a loaf of bread.

He heard a rumble of thunder, and the daily monsoon rain began, with no spattering of isolated drops to announce it, just a sudden drenching dump of water roaring through the trees. The tiers of leaves overhead offered little protection against it; however, the rain did not slow him down. He continued to pad along the trail, the ground turning spongy under his boots.

The rag which formed a headband around his forehead kept the wet hair from his face, but he had to squint against the downpour to be able to see the trail three feet ahead of him. He was suddenly aware of another sound, dimly audible through the roar of the rain. Music. Tinny, distant. He followed the trail until he could see its termination in a muddy road which cut across it, and he slowed down, turning cautious, melding into the brush until he could view the road without being seen himself.

About twenty meters to his left an old truck sat squarely in the middle of the muddy track, an antique American military troop carrier, a six-by, its canvas top rotting and patched over the arced metal frames of the truck bed. The rear of the truck had been jacked up and a wheel was missing. Near the open front door on the passenger side a small canvas tarp on wooden poles had been slanted to shelter a small fire from the downpour. Squatting beside it was a bony Oriental soldier dressed in a ragged uniform, his back to Charlie Excalibur. His thin arm made a circular motion as he stirred something in a round cook pot with a wooden stick.

The music was coming out of the open truck door, Thai music. Against the side of the truck was propped an American M-16 rifle.

Charlie Excalibur stayed where he was a long time and then began to move parallel to the road, keeping his eyes open for a second man. There was none. Obviously two vehicles had been traveling together, and when a tire on this one blew, the other vehicle had taken it to a village to be fixed, leaving this poor bastard behind to stand guard. As he edged closer, he recognized the man and remembered him from one of the CPT camps, a guerrilla from the Communist Party of Thailand who had once tested a captured weapon in Charlie Excalibur's presence by shooting a prisoner, literally cutting him in two with the spray of bullets from an automatic weapon.

No powerful hero now, just a dumb gook squatting in the mud. Charlie Excalibur did not underestimate him. The bastard would cut his throat if he had the chance.

Slowly Charlie Excalibur took his knife from its sheath, stood motionless while he studied the situation. He had long since learned to adapt, his hide thick, his back solid muscles and tendons, passing beyond any concern for comfort to the goal of simple survival which demanded that he pay no attention to whether he was hot or cold, wet or dry.

He moved again, this time to a point within ten feet of the soldier. He could see the soldier's matted black hair plastered against the narrow skull, the contours of the man's back where the rain had molded the shirt against it. No good trying to put a knife in that back, too much chance of the deflection of muscle and bone. A quick and soundless death was mandatory.

He walked out into the mud of the road, every movement smooth and practiced, threw his left arm around the man's throat, cutting off the air, yanked him backward, and in the same moment drove the knife home into the man's chest, in the vulnerable point immediately below the sternum. The man thrashed around, scrambled away even as he was dying, not a sound coming out of him. He crawled as far as the front wheel of the truck, grabbed the tire with both hands like a helmsman wrestling with a ship's wheel, and tried to pull himself erect. He fell backward into the mud. Charlie Excalibur wiped the knife blade against the tattered edge of the truck seat, put it back into its sheath.

He turned off the truck radio, the better to hear any alien sound through the rain. He examined the contents of the pot. Rice, a kind of saffron curry, small pieces of gray meat, probably dog. He did not care. He held his hands up to the rain to wash the blood off his fingers, then dipped them into the pot. The food was lukewarm. He pressed it into his mouth, ignoring the sour, spiced taste. He ate until he was full.

He went through the truck in search of anything he could use, but the vehicle was a shambles. The springs poked through the worn-out front seat and were kept down by a rattan pad which served as a seat cover. There was no cargo in the back, and the wooden troop benches had long since rotted out. He slogged through the mud, rolled the dead soldier over with his foot, went through his pockets. He found no money, nothing but a pocket compass, which he added to his small pack.

As he went back to the truck and sat down on the edge of the frayed seat, he was aware that he was being watched. He extracted a cigarette from his dwindling supply, unsnapped the holster, and held the pistol across his lap. If it were the enemy out there, assuming that his adversary had the means to do it, he knew he would already be dead by now. In the protection of the cab he lit the cigarette and waited and in a moment saw the shape of the man in the brush at the side of the road. Casually he raised the pistol, pointed it.

'Come on out,' he said in English, having to yell against the sound of the rain. 'Come on out or you're a dead man.'

The man separated himself from the brush, came into the clear. 'Hey, man,' he said in a litany, as if his words would keep him alive. 'Hey, man. It's okay.' Another grunt, a tall, broad-shouldered American wearing a fatigue jacket with the arms cut out, heavy-muscled biceps, tattooed, a mass of long red hair and beard covering his head. His fatigue pants had been cut off into shorts, and he had sandals on his feet made from tire tread. 'I'm not armed, man,' he said.

'Come on over here,' Charlie Excalibur said. He did not lower the pistol. 'You try to shit me and I'll blow your head off.'

'I wouldn't shit you,' the man said. He came through the mud, and his eyes fell on the food in the pot. 'You mind if I eat some of that?'

'What's your name?'

'I call myself Utah Red.'

'Go ahead. Eat.'

Utah Red fell to with a will, dipping his large, thick hands into the pot, filling his mouth, the saffron-colored mixture staining his beard. Charlie Excalibur could see no sign of a weapon on him, not even a knife.

'How long you been out?' Charlie Excalibur said.

'Over four years.'

'How have you stayed alive?'

'Not easy,' Utah Red said. 'One village after another. You know how it goes. Man, this ain't no life.' He said nothing more until he was full; then he wiped his hands on his shirt. There was less desperation in his eyes now. 'You got an extra smoke?'

Charlie Excalibur moved over in the truck cab, made room for him, still keeping the pistol across his lap. He gave Utah Red a cigarette, watched him light it. 'I just had enough of the army. That wasn't no life either,' he said, pausing to inhale the smoke. 'Couldn't win. No way.'

As Utah Red began to talk, Charlie Excalibur's mind shifted into a different mode, storing away the facts and the details of the story he had heard a dozen times before. Utah Red had been a sergeant with Search and Destroy, on some really big strikes, well planned, backed by air cover, out to destroy a unit of the Vietcong only to move into an area and find no enemy concentration there at all.

Invariably, when the operation dissolved, there would be a counter-attack and Utah Red's unit would lose a dozen men or so.

'Hell, I used to go to my unit commander and tell the son of a bitch to get with it or I wasn't going to take my boys out there. We weren't going out on any more hunts when the enemy knew what we were going to do before we did it.' He inhaled the cigarette again. 'The son of a bitch said he was going to court-martial my ass or shoot me, one of the two, so I just took off.' He shook his head. 'That's been four fucking years, and I still can't get it out of my mind.'

'How have you gotten by without a weapon?'

Utah Red grinned. His teeth were bad, and his breath was foul. 'Hell, I was a walking arsenal when I left. For all the goddamn good it done me. I fell in with a CPT guerrilla unit, and they grilled me and took my rifle away from me, some grenades. But they didn't kill me. They just interrogated me every day, and as long as I would say things about how wrong I thought we were to be in Vietnam and how wonderful the world was going to be under communism, they fed me good. I even had a woman for a while, lived in a hooch. But then they wanted me to do some radio monitoring for them, translate the army slang, that sort of thing. So I said sure, and first chance I had, I just wandered off.'

He looked at Charlie Excalibur sharply. Then he began to laugh. 'Jesus Christ, man, why am I telling you?' he said. 'You know how it was. Shit, you're Charlie Excalibur, right? I heard about you all over everywhere.' He sucked the last smoke out of the cigarette, flipped the butt out into the rain. 'Hell, I knew it was you when I watched you stalking this gook.'

'What do you hear about me?'

'The CPT is burning about you, man. They'd really like to have your ass. They offered me lots of money to tell them anything I knew about you, but I didn't know nothing. What'd you do to them?'

Charlie Excalibur shrugged. 'Where you headed now?'

'I don't know. I been thinking about heading to the

coast someplace, maybe down into Malaysia.' His forehead wrinkled. 'You got any use for that M-16 out there? If you don't, I'd buy it off you, except I got no money.'

'You can have it,' Charlie Excalibur said. 'It's too heavy for me to carry. But don't try to cash me in. I don't kill people of my own kind if I can help it.'

'Shit,' Utah Red said. 'I don't know nothing. Besides, the minute any of these gooks catch me with the rifle they're going to figure I killed that man out there in the mud. No, I'm heading south. All the way to Singapore if I can make it.'

Charlie Excalibur nodded, said nothing more. Utah Red climbed out of the truck into the rain, picked up the M-16 with an expert hand, examined the magazine. 'Hell, I'm in business,' he said. 'I'm much obliged to you. I wish you luck.'

Charlie Excalibur nodded. He watched Utah Red move through the mud to the edge of the jungle and raise the rifle as if in a salute before he disappeared into the undergrowth. Charlie Excalibur took the time to take the small notebook out of his pack, peeling back the layers of waxed paper which kept it dry. With a stub of a pencil, he added all the details of Utah Red's story and then, with the same care, rewrapped the notebook and put it away. The notebook would be his passport home when the time came.

He had stayed here long enough. It might be hours before the other truck came back, but he couldn't chance it. He stepped out into the rain, then leveled the pocket compass in his hand until the needle stopped moving and gave him directions. He would continue west northwest for a while, find a neutral village, and hope that his luck held.

He walked past the body of the Oriental soldier. The blood had spread into the pools of water now.

If Charlie Excalibur's luck did not hold, then he could go mad, like Epstein. Or this was another alternative, to rot on some road like this in a jungle where no one would ever know his real name.

He moved on, toward Laos. To wait.

CLASSIFICATION 1/1/1. 07309/A-B. MILANO-BARCLAY TO LONDON/ROSS. CODED/BOCCA 0064. DECODED/POWELL 9144. 6/8/79 OPEN.

IRIS MARSTON WAS IN MILAN ON 5 JUNE 1979, STAYING AT THE PENSION IL TRATTORIO. THERE SHE RECEIVED A TELEPHONE CALL AT 1032 HOURS, 5 JUNE, STATING THAT HER FATHER HAD SUFFERED MAJOR INJURIES IN AN AUTOMOBILE ACCIDENT AND WAS IN AN HOSPITAL IN VIENNA.

SHE BOOKED THE NEXT FLIGHT TO VIENNA, ARRIVING IN VIENNA AT 0936 HOURS ON 6 JUNE. SHE WAS MET AT THE AIRPORT BY A MAN WHO CALLED HIMSELF DUPREZ. PHYSICAL DESCRIPTION: APPROXIMATE AGE 56, BALDING, 12 STONE, MEDIUM HEIGHT, HEAVY MID-EUROPEAN ACCENT. DUPREZ PICKED HER UP IN A BLACK 1975 SEL MERCEDES, AUSTRIAN LICENSE PLATE, NUMBER UNKNOWN. THEY CROSSED THE BORDER INTO CZECHOSLOVAKIA, DESTINATION PRAGUE.

PARTIAL REPORTS FROM PRAGUE INDICATE THAT A WOMAN ANSWERING IRIS MARSTON'S DESCRIPTION WAS PLACED ABOARD A PRIVATE AEROFLOT VASLIV JET-RANGE 6342 KM- AT APPROXIMATELY 2230 HOURS, 6 JUNE. SHE WAS DESCRIBED BY OUR AIRPORT WATCHER AS A HOSPITAL PATIENT, HEAVILY SEDATED. POSSIBLE BUT UNCONFIRMED CHOICE OF DESTINATIONS: BOMBAY, DJAKATA, VIENTIANE, BANGKOK. JET CARRIED FULL FUEL. DO YOU WISH MY PERSON CONTINUED FOLLOWUP? RESPOND TO VIENNA. BARCLAY. CLOSE.

CLASSIFICATION 1/1/1. 97436/A-B. LONDON-ROSS TO VIENNA-BARCLAY. CODED/POWELL 0144. DECODED HAMPSHIRE/0939. OPEN.

YOUR SIGNAL DISTRIBUTED DOWN THE LINE. PROCEED BY ALL MEANS. WE HAVE NO INFORMATION ON DUPREZ, BUT WE ARE PROCESSING HIM THROUGH THE COMPUTERS. CONCENTRATE ON THE DESTINATION. VITAL. ROSS. CLOSE.

PART TWO

11

BANGKOK

The seat belt sign flickered on to announce the descent into Bangkok, and Clive came instantly awake, nerves taut. He peered out the window. The same flat country, incredibly so, and the jet had banked to make its approach from the west, allowing him a glimpse of the bank of monsoon clouds off to the north. He felt the remembered fear. If he could have done it, he would have ordered the pilot to make his turn and head back to Hong Kong, where he would catch the next connection to London and Katy.

No, Katy was in Australia and this was something which he had to face. It had been put off long enough. He turned back to the window, Bangkok spread out below him. As he spotted the airport, he could see the changes that had taken place in the past year. The last time he had been here, the airport was crowded with American traffic, rows of helicopters, banks of giant C-130 transports, which even from a distance looked like giant freight cars with wings, and now they were all gone, and with them, the American presence.

In the end that American presence seemed to have been assimilated. Thailand had an infinite capacity to absorb foreign cultures. The Japanese Army had been here with a collaborative Thai government during World War II, and their occupation had ended with little changed. The Americans had used Thailand as one massive supply base in the Vietnam disaster, and now they were gone and the airport looked as seedy as ever.

One runway was torn up, in the process of being replaced, with giant craters and matching jumbled piles

103

of smashed concrete. As his flight landed, Clive could see the heavy equipment idle with at least one bulldozer and one earthmover broken down. Swarms of men stood around doing nothing as if waiting for some magic to occur, some miracle of modern technology which would suddenly heal the machines and set the engines to running again.

He went through customs and immigration without incident. He had a dim memory of the last time he had been through this airport, when he had been taken out on a stretcher. Shaking off the past, he reclaimed his bag and stood a moment in the fetid lounge with dirty floors while he watched the people around him. He smoked a cigarette and made himself visible. He wanted the Russians to know he was in Bangkok.

Years ago the Russians had developed a system which they still followed in the Far East. They hired locals, a student, an old man, a pregnant woman, literally anybody with the ability to remember faces. Then a KGB agent would show them no more than a half dozen photographs of faces and place them in an airport where they watched the passengers from incoming flights. These people were called Watchers in the trade, and they were paid an hourly wage with a sizable, indeed an overwhelming bonus if they spotted one of those faces and reported it. The Watchers were almost impossible to single out.

There was an old man leaning against the wall opposite Clive, dirty, his Nehru jacket disheveled, alternately dozing and coming awake with a start, never looking directly at Clive but certainly aware of him. A more likely candidate was a Thai student in his twenties on the bench to Clive's right, a young man with thick glasses and a less-than-absorbed interest in the book he was reading.

Clive dropped the cigarette on the floor, squashed it out with the sole of his shoe. His instincts told him that the Watcher would be that single-minded student who seemed to pay no attention to Clive at all. Clive went toward the exit doors, stopped in the shelter of a column, and waited. Almost momentarily the student snapped the book shut and headed for the bank of telephone booths on the far side of the lounge. The message would be passed immediately. Clive had arrived.

He went outside into the blast furnace of the day, caught an air-conditioned taxi for the long ride into town. The boulevard was treeless and dusty, despite the daily monsoon rains. When he reached the Siam Intercontinental, the taxi turned into the U-shaped drive. He saw the great curved roof of the hotel designed after the pattern of an ancient Thai warrior's helmet, but it had always seemed more like a bird's wing to him. He was entering a Western enclave which was in Bangkok and yet not of it, a vast walled compound with tennis courts and acres of lawns. There was the obligatory swimming pool and one area of carefully landscaped forest with a private zoo for the enjoyment of the guests. Everything was a pastiche of luxury with a Thai motif. The compound exuded a sense of security against the poor, noisy, festering city which lay outside the walls. Clive was not deceived. He had every reason to know that there was no real security in the whole of Thailand.

He checked in, was shown to a room in the garden wing next to the pool. He ignored the temptation to rest in the air-conditioned privacy. Instead, he went through the mental checklist which was a part of his discipline. He had left the clearest trail possible. He had registered under his own name. He unpacked the minimum clothing he carried, hung the wrinkled suit until he could have the valet service pick it up. He opened a bottle of mineral water from the minifridge, drank it in a single draught. He lifted the telephone and asked the operator to call the British Embassy, well aware that this was an insecure line.

He asked for Harry Patterson, knew he would have to wait. Patterson was everything Roberts said he was and more, a roguish, mercurial man who did damn well what he pleased. Finally, Patterson's voice came on the line, clipped, efficient.

'Patterson here,' he said. 'When did you get in?'

'I've just arrived.'

'We had better arrange a meeting first off,' Patterson said matter-of-factly. 'Hold on, I'll check my schedule.' There was a pause, and Clive could hear the deliberate turning of pages. 'The ambassador is holding a garden party tonight. It might be a good idea if you attended. We'll have a chance to chat.'

'I'm not carrying a dinner jacket.'

'Anything conservative,' Patterson said. 'It's a rag-bag group, but you know the structures, visiting Indonesians, Malaysians, a trade delegation, I believe. About eight o'clock. I'll see that a car is sent around. You may find it interesting. Boris will be there.'

'Ludov?' Clive said, startled. 'Where in the bloody hell did he come from?'

'Flew in this morning from Manila, I believe. He's the new cultural attaché as of this week. Interesting possibilities, what?'

'Very. Another matter. I'm expecting some responses to queries. They may be routed through you.'

'Yes. We'll discuss them tonight.'

Clive summoned a valet, sent the suit to be pressed, the shoes to be shined, and only when he realized that for the moment he had gone as far as he could go did he allow himself the luxury of a nap.

At the garden party Clive was amused to find that though many of the faces had changed since he was here last, the atmosphere was exactly the same. Somewhere in the manuals of protocol were rules governing such affairs which made them all identical. There was a large striped canopy tent covering the small orchestra. A long table did duty as an open bar. Hosts of uniformed local waiters passed drinks to the clusters of people that dotted the open lawn.

The monsoon rain had stopped less than an hour ago. The torrent had come straight down to rattle against the plastic sheeting with which the lawn had been covered.

The moment the rain stopped, the Thai boys scampered to roll up the plastic, leaving the grass damp but not soggy.

Clive felt very much at home from the moment he arrived at the gracious compound of the embassy buildings built on the edge of a filled-in canal off Wireless Road. The orchestra was alternately playing classical music and Indonesian melodies which did not translate well on Western instruments.

Patterson was not there to meet him and Clive had already made his way to the bar and ordered a bourbon and water before he heard Patterson's voice saying, 'There you are.' Clive accepted the drink with his left hand, shook Patterson's wiry brown paw with his right. He was a tall, lean man with a perfect military bearing, looking quite at home in a white dinner jacket crossed by a multicolored sash representing some high Thai honor which had been bestowed upon him. His face was leonine with that long Roman nose of his fringed by a disciplined line of mustache on his upper lip. The hair on his scalp was clipped short, now turned iron gray. As Patterson moved, he was partially backlit by one of the decorative torches staked around the grounds.

'Have you met the new ambassador?' Patterson said.

Clive peered through the crowd toward the reception line. He saw an elderly man with white hair, a pained expression on his face which was meant to convey great pleasure as he shook the hand of a short Indonesian gentleman. The ambassador was properly sashed and medaled, and next to him stood his wife, a short, plump woman in a frilly organdy gown and floppy hat. Apparently she had modeled herself after the queen mother. 'I don't recognize him,' Clive said.

'Sir George Ormsby-Fletcher, Kindly Call Me God,' Patterson said with a hint of derision. 'He's been here six months from Djakarta, is applying himself to learning Thai, for which he has no gift, and speaks atrociously. He was moved here for his ability in economics, but so far he has demonstrated no grasp of Thai business. I'll introduce you to him, and then we can chat.'

'I'll finish my drink first,' Clive said. 'Has Boris Ludov shown yet?'

'The buffoon is never on time,' Patterson said. 'He will be late and in his cups by the time he gets here.'

'Don't underestimate him.' Clive finished the drink, dried his hands of the condensed moisture on a napkin. A flying shape swooped near the flame of the torch. Ah, the bats, he had forgotten the omnipresent bats, drawn by the insects. How could he have forgotten that in all the pain, lying on the hard table while they cut him open inch by inch, he had kept his sanity by watching the bats darting past the kerosene lanterns. He sighed, relaxed. *Thank God for small things like bats,* he thought. 'All right,' he said. 'Lead on.'

Patterson led the way across the springy turf. Patterson was always wound tightly, Clive realized, always at a bounce on the balls of his feet as he walked, as if there were no way he could spend all his energies, the unused parts of him continually building pressure within him.

Sir George was standing on the edge of a marble terrace which on occasion was used for dancing. His eyes were glazed, his starched collar slightly wilted under the high humidity. The hand he presented to Clive was competently firm. It was immediately obvious to Clive that Patterson's reservations about the man were misplaced. Sir George was simply old, probably at his last post before retirement, but his voice was steady, his mind sharp. The moment he heard Clive's name, his eyes snapped brightly, an instant recall of the name, the man, the past situation.

'Mr. Clive,' he said. 'I'm indeed pleased to meet you.'

'Thank you, sir.'

'I hope you will be in Bangkok long enough to dine with me one night. I should be quite interested to hear your views on the turbulent days here.'

'That would please me very much.'

'Then I shall have my secretary call you.'

Clive moved on to Lady Ormsby-Fletcher, a deceptively gentle woman, he decided, who could make pleasantries and imply a kind of soft and shallow charm while providing her husband the steel devotion which had seen him through a long career in strange and foreign cultures. They talked climate and horticulture for a moment; then Clive headed back for the bar to get himself another drink while Patterson requested a glass of mineral water, no ice.

'You've joined the temperance league,' Clive said.

'Only when I'm on duty. By the way, Clive, do you remember the snake trick?' Patterson said, leading the way to a pair of lawn chairs away from the orchestra.

'A fantastic show of reflexes, that,' Clive said.

'The Thais do it all the time. It's a matter of conditioning.'

'Could you still do it?' Clive sat down, sipped his drink.

'Certainly,' Patterson said. 'As a matter of fact, I'll bet twenty pounds on it.'

'You're on,' Clive said. He sipped the bourbon, eyed the unruffled Patterson, who was perfectly relaxed in these surroundings. 'This is a dangerous part of the world, Harry, and one day you'll come up a loser. And I must say, I will regard that loss with mixed feelings.'

Patterson drank the water, studied him with cool and even eyes. 'You're still fretting about the past. I should have thought you would have moved beyond that.'

'I have the scar. You don't.' He put his glass down. 'There's a basic difference between us. You take life for granted and I don't. You see, Harry, one day I was walking down Wireless Road. For what reason I can't remember, but I'm certain it was something innocuous and totally unimportant. And then suddenly a car pulled up alongside me and two men climbed out, and before I knew it, I had been pushed into the back seat and the car was off. And even at that point I have to say that I couldn't really believe it was happening, not to me. I was certain it was some grand mistake. It was only when the torture began that I realized there had been no mistake, that they wanted me and they had me. From that moment on my life was changed. I have taken nothing for granted.'

'They sent a special team to retrieve you. I had orders not to interfere,' Patterson said without a trace of feeling. 'We all follow the same orders.'

'You were probably the one man who could have found me and you did nothing. Rules or not, you did nothing,' Clive said. 'But that's beside the point now, isn't it?'

'I wanted to make my position clear.'

'You've done so. Now to business. I put in a request for a record trace on the Cathay Pacific flight that brought Marston here. What did they find?'

'We have seating charts on that flight,' Patterson said. 'We have perhaps two dozen pairings of the kinds of names you suggest. We have been able to trace only a dozen so far, none of the others.'

'Do you believe Marston is in Bangkok?'

'No.'

'Then any effort you make will be a fart in the wind.'

'Listen, old chap, I know you're deliberately trying to provoke me,' Patterson said. 'But I am quite unflappable. You will get my best effort, but I don't believe Marston is here. I have the most sensitive net in the Far East. If he had come in, I would have had some rumors, some trembling of the web, as it were.'

'How about the daughter?'

'Ross is running a backcheck. She was abducted, flown out of Prague, only a guess as to destination. Vietnam would be my best estimate. Why Thailand? No sense at all to that.' He fell silent just as the orchestra finished a piece. In that moment of silence Clive could hear the frogs, omnipresent in this city of monsoon rains and sluggish canals flowing into the meandering Chao Phraya River, a galumphing of bass croaks and high-pitched reedy sounds.

'Ah, the frogs,' Clive said. 'One of my more pleasant memories.'

Patterson removed a cigarette from a case, and when he lit it, Clive smelled the pungent odor of cloves. Patterson imported his cigarettes from Indonesia, not as an affectation but because he liked the bloody weeds. 'Are you responsible for this Charlie Excalibur business?' Patterson said.

'What are you talking about?'

'The chaps at home have the misbegotten idea he's in Thailand, out in the uplands someplace.'

'I have no idea where Charlie Excalibur is or what you're talking about,' Clive said. He did not want to discuss Charlie Excalibur with Patterson. He signaled a white-jacketed waiter, sent him scurrying for another bourbon and water, then lit a cigarette of his own as protection against the stench of Patterson's tobacco, which hung like a pall in the motionless air. The orchestra had begun to play 'Waltzing Matilda,' which meant that there were Australian guests here tonight among the others.

The waiter returned with his drink. Patterson was studying his empty glass. Ice disappeared almost immediately in this climate. 'This is my territory,' he said, looking directly at Clive. 'I don't want anything to go on in this country that I don't know about. It will be helpful if you understand that.'

'My God,' Clive said, snorting a laugh, 'you still think this is your private preserve, don't you? I can bloody well let pass what happened to me in your territory.' He caught himself at the beginning of an ironic diatribe, cut it off. 'Marston's here. I know that logically, and I know it in my bones. The poor bastard. I've been ordered to find him, and that I will do. And when I find him, I want your word that you will get him out.'

'All I need is orders.'

'You will have them.'

Patterson nodded in the semi-darkness, looked as if he were about to say something, said nothing, for at the same instant both of them saw Boris Ludov shaking hands with the ambassador.

Clive did not approach Boris immediately. He smoked a cigarette, had another drink, and watched Boris circulate through the crowd, shaking hands, being rather over-cordial. Boris had changed since the last time Clive had seen him. At one time Boris had been darkly handsome, and his presence at a party was sufficient to galvanize all the women of any age, for he exuded a confident and pervasive sexuality. But now he was older, thinner, lines deeper in his olive-skinned face, not quite so much fire in his coal black eyes. A bald spot showed through his thinning hair in the light of the string of Thai lanterns. His white dinner jacket was slightly off cut, ill-fitting.

Finally, when Boris was at the bar alone, Clive approached him. Boris was in profile, thick nose casting a shadow on his high cheekbones. When he turned and saw Clive, there was no surprise on his face, just a slow spread of a smile as he extended his hand to welcome an old friend.

'I am delighted to see you,' Boris said. 'I heard this afternoon that you were in town.'

Clive returned the smile, shook Boris's hand. He could tell it would be a long, slow game. 'I've been hearing about your disastrous flings here and there,' he said. 'I hope they've been worth it.'

Boris shrugged. 'It is my nature,' he said. 'It is of little consequence anyway. I shall be retiring soon, going home. But what are you doing here?'

'My drink is empty,' Clive said.

'The hazards of our trade,' Boris said. 'Boring lives and empty glasses. Please permit me.' He turned to the bartender and from his prodigious memory for detail ordered a bourbon and water for Clive. Boris gave off the scent of lavender pomade. The dewlap beneath his chin glistened with sweat. Boris had never done well in the tropics, and as he had once confided to Clive, he seemed destined to spend his life playing out some ethnic Russian drama in which he was meant by fate to endure all those things he most detested. Positively Chekhovian.

He ordered a vodka for himself, prompting Clive to remember that this pleasant little man was indeed the enemy, that there was a small flagged pin on Sir John's chart wall which had marked his movements over the years. Despite his personal preferences, any surface feelings would be suspended immediately with fresh orders from his superiors. If he were instructed to kill Clive, he would do it instantly, perhaps with regret, but not enough to cause him a moment's pause.

With a smile Boris raised his glass in Clive's direction, downed the vodka, then patted his lips with a napkin. 'I have been forbidden by the doctors to drink for the sake of my liver. I have been forbidden to smoke for the sake of my lungs. The doctors would have me trotting like a horse in an aimless direction for five kilometers each day.' He shrugged again. 'Do you happen to have any American cigarettes?'

Clive offered him a pack. Boris shook one out, held it unlit in his clenched teeth while he ordered another drink, and then followed Clive to a pair of isolated chairs. The formal entertainment for the evening had begun, a Thai orchestra providing a tinny, unpleasant music for the beautiful Thai girls and their stylized dances. Boris lit his cigarette, alternated between it and sips from the glass. He appeared to be very weary, slumping in the chair. 'I was distressed to hear of your trouble here. How long has it been? A year?'

'Yes.'

'I take it you are now recovered, back in the game again? They didn't damage you permanently then. I'm pleased for that.'

'Not "they,"' Clive said. 'They were your people.'

'We supported selected locals from time to time in their various rebellions, I believe,' Boris said. 'But I was personally sorry for your bad treatment.' The coal of his cigarette glowed in the semi-darkness as he inhaled. 'So you are back in the game?' he repeated softly.

Clive sipped his drink, his caution dissipating. His eyes followed the birdlike movements of the Thai dancers with their long, curved fingernails flashing in the light. 'Briefly,' Clive said. 'One assignment, and then I pop home again.'

'Enviable,' Boris said. 'I am condemned for another year, perhaps two. I don't like this country. I shall do what

113

I can to cut my stay here as short as possible.'

'Then perhaps we can help each other,' Clive said, making an effort to be careful of his wording. 'I think you know what I am doing here. God knows I've advertised it enough.'

'My dear friend,' Boris said with a bemused smile, 'how do I know that there are no wires in the bushes or recorders in the chairs?'

'Listening costs nothing,' Clive said.

Boris nodded. 'I'm always interested in what you have to say.'

'I know that you have Marston,' Clive said. 'I know he is in Thailand, and I would guess that one of your special units is working him over. We want him back alive.'

'Marston is the Queen's Messenger, I assume,' Boris said. 'The one who disappeared.'

'The one who was snatched by your marvelous sleight of hand,' Clive said, drinking again. 'You also have his daughter, I believe.'

'For the record, I am woefully ignorant of either,' Boris said. 'But for conversational purposes, what are you proposing?'

'I am prepared to bargain for his release,' Clive said. 'In money, goods, an exchange of high-level agents we currently have in storage in the U.K.'

Boris shrugged. 'I don't mean to sound callous,' he said, studying the tip of his cigarette, 'but why would you want him back? I would think that a man in his position would be considered expendable.'

'He's not an agent. He's a Queen's Messenger, a special breed of man, and he is English. He is not expendable.'

Boris was silent. The dancers had changed. The discordant music remained the same. He pulled the last smoke from the cigarette, rolled the dead filter between his thumb and forefinger, giving himself time to think. He finished his vodka, placed the glass on the grass, slumped back in his chair. 'After all, I am a cultural attaché here,' he said. 'I do have access to a great variety of people. I can make a few discreet inquiries. Not that they will come to anything, of course. But I always prefer to see amicable settlements to disputes.'

'Untrue, you bloody Bolshevik,' Clive said with a smile. 'Boris, the bomber, the great man for demolition and fireworks.'

'Only in my early days,' Boris said with mock sorrow. 'We all change with age.' He paused thoughtfully. 'Of course,' he said, 'if what you say is true, and I would have no idea whether it is or not, then it might help if I had a market list, as I think you call it, those people you might be willing to trade.'

Clive breathed more easily, all ambiguity removed. He stretched his long legs out in front of him, finished his drink, and laced his hands behind his head. 'That would be premature, don't you think? Until we know the identity of the group that has him.'

If Boris realized his mistake, he did not show it. 'Of course,' he said. 'I become dense at this time of night. It would be sufficient for me to relay information that you are willing to trade primaries.'

'We would allow the opposition to determine who was primary and who was not.'

'Very well.'

'One proviso,' Clive said. 'Marston and his daughter must be alive.'

Boris said nothing.

'Alive,' Clive repeated.

'I can do nothing more than spread the word,' Boris said. 'And please, my dear friend, don't overestimate my influence. There have been changes in my situation over the years. I was once a very ambitious man with a chance to climb, but as you will notice, all these years have passed and I am still out in the field. Not that I'm complaining, please understand, but at one time I could simply scowl my displeasure and cause men to tremble. I could lift my little finger and have men jumping to please me. And now the most I can tell you is that I will circulate the information you gave me, and if there is a response, I will let you know.'

'Alive,' Clive repeated.

'I'll be in touch,' Boris said. 'You're staying at the Intercontinental, of course. Such luxury there. It may take a day or two, but you can rely on me to be in touch.'

By the time the reception was over Clive realized that he was travel-weary and looking forward to bed and sleep. But before the driver started the engine, he looked back over the seat. 'Colonel Patterson wishes to know if you feel up to dropping by his place for a few minutes, sir,' he said.

'Certainly.' Clive leaned back against the seat. The car crossed the main bridge into the Wongwian Yai section of the city. He could smell the river, even through the filtered air conditioning of the car. Within minutes they were into the maze of streets and canals in the heavy woods. He checked his watch. It would be too late to call Katy by the time he finished with Patterson. He felt the keen need to hear her voice, to have a loving conversation in which nothing was more complex than winter weather, a cantankerous father, and the perambulations of her sisters.

The car pulled up a narrow lane, passed through an entry gate in a wooden wall, arrived at a guarded compound along one of the wider klongs. Clive told the driver to wait and then climbed out of the car, his legs rather stiff. He could see the flickering lightning off to the southwest. Another monsoon storm would be coming along directly. He pulled the bell cord, heard a tinkling of chimes. The gate opened almost immediately, and there stood Patterson's legendary Thai woman, exquisitely small, dressed in silk. She pressed her hands together in a *wai*, an attitude of respectful greeting, the tips of her fingers just below her nose, showing him the greatest honor.

Through the trees he saw the glow of kerosene lanterns in the house. His curiosity overcame his fatigue. Patterson had closed off this area of his life to his compatriots, who knew only that he spent some of his time in a Thai house on one of the canals, living with a Thai woman to whom he was either married or not, depending on which gossip one heard, a relationship which had lasted fifteen years. The woman led Clive through a garden of exotic flowers vining from the trees. He heard the chattering of a pet gibbon hanging in the tree closest to the door where Patterson appeared suddenly. Clive was startled.

Patterson was wearing nothing but a pair of khaki shorts cut in a frayed and ragged line at mid-thigh and a single gold coin on a chain around his neck. He was in perfect physical shape, lean as a whipcord, not an ounce of fat on him, his skin nut brown from the sun. *Gone native*, was Clive's first thought, but he balanced that judgment immediately with his mental picture of Patterson at the ambassador's reception, perfectly poised and socialized.

'Glad you could drop by,' Patterson said. 'Come in and have a drink.'

He led the way down the corridor into a large room with teak walls and floor, splashes of colour from batik prints on the walls, a few ancient Buddhas on shelves, massive beams overhead. On one of them a lizard sat perfectly motionless as if it were a carving. Patterson spoke softly to his woman, who disappeared into another room.

Patterson sprawled in a wicker chair, his back to the wall which was fully open to the canal. He rested his feet on the lid of a heavy closed basket. He lit one of his clove cigarettes. 'This is where I entertain my Thai army officers. You would be surprised at the difference it makes. They look on me as one of them because in many ways I am one of them. I understand them totally. Not only do I speak Thai, but I can think in Thai. Some of the more superstitious blokes believe I can read their minds, even the ones educated abroad.'

He picked up a ceramic cup, poured himself a drink from a bottle without a label. Clive realized that Patterson was so talkative only because he was half drunk. 'I'm having *mekong*,' he said. 'Will you join me?'

'*Mekong* it is,' Clive said. The woman reentered the

room soundlessly, and Clive had the chance to see her more closely. She was a beautiful woman in her early forties, coal black hair pulled back severely from a delicate porcelain face, classic bone structure. She did not look at Clive directly. She served his drink, withdrew. Clive looked after her admiringly. 'Exquisite,' he said.

'She was a classical dancer at one time,' Patterson said. 'Her appearance is deceptive. Like so many Thais who appear to be so fragile, she's tough as a boot.' He raised his glass, made a toast in Thai.

'Yes,' Clive said. 'To survival.'

'You haven't forgotten your Thai, I see.'

'No.' Clive tasted the drink. It was very strong. 'It seems to me you're living on the edge,' he said, looking toward the klong, which was briefly illuminated by the lightning. An old woman poled a boat through the muddy water not twenty feet from where they sat. 'Christ, what's to keep anyone who holds a grudge from having a go at you anytime he likes? You're a perfect target here.'

Patterson's lips pulled back from his teeth in a tight smile. He reached over to a shelf, picked up a pistol, small-caliber, make indiscernible from this distance, probably a Walther 9 mm. 'We had a go around three months ago. A revolutionary, nationalist, I believe, took a shot at me from a boat.' He waved vaguely toward the far wall. 'The bullet hole is still there. He had the time for only one shot. I drilled him right through the forehead. So no one has had a go since. The Thai officers respect a man who's willing to take risks.'

'You're creating your own legend,' Clive said. 'But that's your business. Now, if all you had in mind was a social chat and a drink, I think I'll be moving on.'

Patterson poured himself another drink. 'I'm aware of what you chaps in the hallowed halls of headquarters think. You would like to replace me with one of your mannerly little bores.' He grimaced. 'Behave yourself, you bloody Thai loving bugger. Report and file and follow instructions from someone who doesn't know a klong from a trickle of Whitehall piss.' He looked up briefly as the lightning flashed outside, closer now, followed momentarily by a muted rumble of thunder.

'I must be going,' Clive said. 'Thank you for your hospitality.'

'You can't leave. Not yet,' Patterson said. The lightning cracked again, and with the thunder came the deluge, a dump of rain so intense the roof seemed to vibrate with the force of it. Clive swore softly to himself. The flooded streets would certainly slow the car taking him back to the hotel.

A bolt of lightning struck nearby; the room shuddered. Patterson stood up, his bare feet padded over the straw mats. He opened a tin box and he took out a banknote. 'Twenty pounds was the wager, wasn't it?' He put it down on the table next to Clive's chair. 'Cover it.'

'Christ,' Clive said, horror-struck, knowing now why Patterson had invited him here. 'Not in this storm.'

Patterson's wide hand patted the money. 'Cover it.'

Clive took a twenty-pound note out of his wallet, put it on top of Patterson's money. 'Don't do anything you can't undo.'

'The wager is accepted,' Patterson said, ignoring Clive altogether. He faced the lightning-shrouded klong for a moment, taking deep breaths as if to ready himself. Then he took the basket in his two arms and in one swift motion removed the lid and dumped the writhing shape on the floor.

Clive froze, his breath suspended in his throat. Patterson knelt, facing the king cobra, which had not become oriented yet, a massive bastard, a full six feet. It sensed Patterson, the head coming around, tongue flickering. Patterson was perfectly motionless, his forearms resting on his knees, not one sinewy muscle moving, his eyes unblinking. The snake continued to face in his direction, tongue darting out to sense the air. It was distracted by another bolt of lightning. The snub head pivoted toward Clive, who did not move. Then from Patterson's throat came a low and gutteral clucking.

The snake responded instantly. The head snapped

around, raised. The hood inflated, and still Patterson squatted motionlessly, eyes unblinking as he stared at the head of the snake which had begun to weave now, ever so slightly, a slow, shifting movement. And then it struck, so suddenly that Clive jumped reflexively, not believing what he saw. For in that instant Patterson twisted away, the fangs of the snake missing his head by less than an inch, and his hand shot out and caught the snake just below the head, the tendons in his arm taut as wet leather, the bony fingers digging in, holding as the massive snake whipped in a frenzy, trying to free itself, the wide jaws open, the fangs extended. But Patterson's hand held.

He raised to his feet, arm extended with the snake still whipping at the end. There was not one sign of weakness in that outthrust arm. Clive grabbed the pistol from the table, placed it beneath the head of the snake and fired. The crack of the gun filled the room; a spray of blood and tissue speckled the ceiling. The bullet slammed into the wooden beam overhead, sending the lizard scampering away.

Patterson's woman appeared at the door, trembling until she saw what had happened, and then she withdrew as quickly as she had appeared. The body of the snake was still writhing as Patterson walked over to the open wall and heaved it out into the rain. It splashed into the sluggish, muddy current of the klong.

Without a word Patterson washed his hands very carefully in a tin basin of water, dried them on a towel. He sat down, not even breathing heavily as far as Clive could see. He lit another clove cigarette, poured himself another *mekong*, sipped it casually. 'I would like you to sign the banknote,' Patterson said. 'Also put down the date. Proof of the wager.'

Clive could say nothing for a moment. He put the pistol aside. He took out his pen, scrawled his name and the date.

'You see, old man, I'm not afraid of dying,' Patterson said. 'I have no fear of pain. If the snake had won, I would have been dead in eight minutes at the most. Not too bad a way to die, wouldn't you say?'

'There are worse ways,' Clive conceded.

'Particularly in this part of the world, as you have every reason to know,' Patterson said, sprawling in his chair. 'I'm not important in London, in the hierarchy, but I count for something out here, Clive. The Thai generals are mullet-brained. This small part of the world could very well bring down the rest in time. Do pass the word around when you get home, old chap. Patterson is alive and well and intends to stay put.'

Once he was in the car and on the way back to the hotel Clive felt as if he were in a submarine. A stiff wind had risen, and the car seemed to be submerged in water so that his view from the windows was obliterated. The driver himself was having trouble. The windshield wipers could not work fast enough; he was forced to lean forward and peer through the windshield to keep track of the streets.

'We may have to make a detour, sir,' he said to Clive. 'Stay to the high ground, so to speak. Some of the regular thoroughfares will be impassable.'

'Take your time,' Clive said. He leaned back, lit a cigarette. He wondered how Patterson would go about releasing the snake story. Perhaps he would mention it to a subordinate, just in passing, but more than likely it would be his woman who would recount the tale, wide-eyed, to another Thai. In any event, the story would spread like wildfire, and eventually Clive himself would have to confirm or deny it. It would serve Patterson right if Clive looked totally blank when that time came.

He became aware that the engine was sputtering, that the car had begun to develop a lurching motion. He leaned forward. 'Are we about to drown out?' he said.

The driver gave him a perplexed look. 'No, sir. Gear trouble, I believe. Maintenance is a terrible problem out here. The Thais have never gotten the hang of keeping up equipment.'

Clive sat back, wiped the condensation from the inside of the back window, peering out, trying to get his bearings. He had the impression of smeared neon lights, a small business district set in the trees against a canal, the seedier part of the city. It was apparent now that the car was not going to make it at all, for there was a grinding sound from somewhere beneath the chassis, and the car alternately slowed, almost to a stop, and then caught again briefly and jerked forward. The driver pulled over to a curb just as the car shuddered and stopped altogether.

'I'm sorry, sir,' the driver said, a stricken expression on his face. 'It appears that we've had it, so to speak. I'm terribly sorry.'

'No harm done,' Clive said. 'I suppose you'll be calling for a tow?'

'I'm afraid so. I'll see if I can't scrounge up a taxi for you while I'm at it. It may take a bit, sir.' He squinted his eyes through the windshield, which was awash with water now, no blades to wipe it away. 'I'll be back shortly.'

'Thank you,' Clive said.

The driver braced himself, opened the door, and plunged out into the rain. Clive saw his blurred shape against the lights, and then he disappeared. Clive sat back against the seat. He put out the cigarette, found the tendency to drowse. It would be quite late by the time he reached the hotel, but no matter. The time difference was such that he could still expect Sir John to be in his office in London.

Abruptly the rain stopped as the thunderstorm moved on, the lightning flickering in the distant trees. He checked the door locks, settled back, was half asleep when he heard the tapping on the window. He jerked awake, saw a Thai face grinning at him from the other side of the window glass, a thin man with a missing tooth and a protuberant nose, who rapped on the glass again with his gnarled knuckles.

'Open the door, please,' the man said in Thai, nodding obsequiously, pointing a dirty finger at the lock button, indicating that Clive should lift it up.

'What do you want?' Clive said in Thai. But now he saw the second man, standing not three feet behind the first, his head on a constant pivot, checking the deserted street in both directions, his image slightly blurred through the wet window. He held something in his right hand, a stick perhaps. No, Clive could see the glint of metal in the reflection of a neon sign. He stood pounding a length of pipe into the open palm of his left hand, nervous.

'Open the door,' the first man said, the smile becoming a scowl. 'Open the door.' He grabbed the door handle, shook the car as if to force it open by sheer strength. Suddenly the second man lurched forward and with all his power swung the pipe against the window glass. It popped like a rifle shot, the glass splintering into a thousand cracks radiating outward from the point of the blow. And in that instant, with a roar, Clive pulled the lock and with his full weight thrust the door open with a pop that knocked the first man sprawling into a pool of water on the street. Clive caught the man with the pipe in the middle of his spindly chest, carried him backward against a pole that bore a road sign, slammed his back into it so that the arm with the pipe whipped violently around and the pipe flew into the street.

Reflexively Clive's fingers clutched for the cartilage of the windpipe, dug into it, smashed the round head against the wooden post until the pain in his back wrenched him loose and he realized the second man had hit him. With a yell he turned, kicked blindly at the man's groin, his foot striking a glancing blow off the man's hip. Clive grabbed the metal pipe up off the pavement. It was cold in his hand.

He stood erect, holding the pipe in his right hand, away from his body, and with his left hand he beckoned, murderously angry now, cursing the men in Thai. 'Come on,' he said. 'I'll wipe my feet on your heads. Come on.'

Both men were on their feet, no more than six feet away from him. He felt the adrenaline pumping through him, a sudden rage he did not know he had, no fear at all, just the strong desire to kill these men who had attacked him. He could hear the frogs croaking a chorus in a distant canal. The defective neon sign on the decrepit hooch of the closed bar flickered a red wash into the street, and he could hear the buzz of electricity.

The man with the missing tooth nodded to his companion. A knife appeared in the man's hand as he began to move, very light on his feet, circling to get behind Clive. Clive lunged at the man who had remained in position, swung the pipe against the arm the man thrust out to try to grab it. There was the crack of bone breaking, and the man leaped back with a yowl of pain, just as a taxi turned the corner, bathing the men in light for a brief moment before they turned and ran.

The taxi stopped, and Clive turned toward it with the pipe until the driver climbed out, showed himself in the beam of his own headlights. He was a young Thai in his early twenties, the dark shadow of a mustache on his upper lip. He wore a white shirt and a tie.

'May I help you, sir?' he said in English.

Clive breathed deeply, felt the pain in his back. He dropped the pipe, which clattered against the pavement. 'As a matter of fact, you very well might,' he said. He limped toward the taxi, an older black Pontiac, freshly waxed, the water from the rain beading on the metallic surface. The driver moved to open the door for him. The upholstery was worn but clean. Clive climbed in, waiting for his racing heart to subside. He felt more comfortable as the taxi pulled away.

'Are you hurt? Do you require medical attention?' the driver said.

'No. I'm bruised but all right.'

'May I take you to a police station, sir?'

'You know exactly what would happen if I reported this to the police,' Clive said. 'I would receive enough official apologies to occupy an hour, and then I would spend another hour filling out reports. I would then receive excellent and courteous advice to avoid certain sections of the city at night. And neither of those two men would ever be found. Am I right?'

'I am afraid so, sir,' the driver said apologetically. 'What happened?'

I was set up, Clive thought. *I can never prove it, but I was delivered into the hands of two men who were supposed to kill me and make it look like a robbery.* Instead, he said, 'The car broke down, and the driver went for help. Were you called to pick me up?'

'No, sir. I was just delivering a fare. Where would you like to go?'

'First I need to make an overseas call, and then I want to go to the Siam Intercontinental.'

'It might be simpler if you made such a call from your hotel, sir.'

'I have my reasons,' Clive said. 'Take me to the Empress Hotel first. I'll make my call from there.'

'Yes, sir.'

In the next twenty minutes he discovered that the young man went by the English name of Sam, that he owned his own taxi, that he had been a linguistics student at a university in India for two years but had come back to Bangkok when his father died and was now the sole support of his mother and seven brothers and sisters, who lived in a small house in the Thonburi section. Clive saw nothing of the streets they traveled, being keenly tuned to the way Sam handled the car, his ability to squeeze into a cross stream of traffic with scarcely a pause, to bluff a truck to give him room, never with a trace of either animosity or anxiety.

They crossed the bridge, followed the east bank of the river toward the Empress. Clive lit a cigarette, made his decision. 'My name is Clive, and I will be here on business for a few days. I shall need a car and driver on call at any time of the day or night. I will pay you the equivalent of seventy-five pounds for each twenty-four-hour period. When you are not driving me, I would expect you to stay in a place with a telephone somewhere near the Siam Intercontinental.' He paused, giving Sam time to translate the amount from pounds sterling into bahts.

'I truly appreciate your offer, sir,' Sam said, after thinking it through. 'I would need to know, however, if you will forgive the frankness of the question, if you are involved in some illegal trade.'

'Would that make a difference? Would you up the price?'

'No, sir,' Sam said. 'The price is exorbitantly generous, as I am sure you are aware. But begging your forgiveness, sir, if you are in illegal trade, then I will refer you to someone who is as good a driver as I am. But as for myself, since my family depends on me, I think I should do nothing which might jeopardize my license.'

Clive smiled. 'Nothing illegal,' he said. 'Consider yourself hired. I will expect confidentiality. You do understand that term?'

'Yes, sir,' Sam said. 'And I am most grateful for the business.'

Sam pulled into the drive of the Empress Hotel, and Clive went into the ornate lobby, found an empty telephone cubicle with a red velvet seat. He contacted the overseas operator, put in a reverse-charges call to the number in London, asking for Mr. Groton, Sir John's code name. It was not a long call. He simply reported the contact, wished Sir John a good evening, and placed the telephone back on the cradle.

Back in the taxi he asked Sam whether he would prefer his money in pounds or bahts. In the dim light of the overhead bulb, he counted out 150 pounds and gave them to Sam, accepted a card with a telephone number hastily written on the back. Sam would be staying with a friend near the Siam Intercontinental and would be available within five minutes, at any time, day or night.

At the hotel Clive found a message waiting for him at the desk.

> *I'm in town for a few days on another assignment. Same hotel. Drink? Talk?*
>
> *Liz*

He folded the message, put it in his pocket. He went to his room, had another stiff drink, listening to the pounding of the rain outside. It was a long time before he fell asleep.

12

LONDON

It had been a long day. Sir John had been here since dawn, and now, through his office window, he watched the late-evening sunset gradually fading. In the distance he could see the parapeted silhouette of the Tower of London and closer at hand the ever-present face of Big Ben and the spires of Westminster Abbey. The stability of such visual continuity was a comfort to him as he watched the lights of the city come on. Hearing a rap, he opened the door for Ross, offered him a brandy, which Ross declined, then poured one for himself and sat down behind his desk. Ross was exhibiting the subtle effects of overwork. There were darkening hollows beneath his eyes.

'You've put yourself through quite a pounding,' Sir John said. He lit his pipe while Ross separated the papers in the red binding, put them into piles.

'Shall I begin?' Ross said.

'Of course. Please do.'

Ross proceeded with piles one and two, computer analyses of all the dispatches Charlie Excalibur had sent. All of the dispatches had been handwritten on varying kinds of paper, running from expensive watermarked bonds, twenty- to twenty-four pound, down to pressed-out paper bags, and he had used pencils, pens (both fountain and ball-point), all the same handwriting, a fact determined by expert graphologists not only from the firm's staff but from New Scotland Yard as well. So it had been established that Charlie Excalibur was indeed a single individual, probably male, indeterminate age, with a decent education, perhaps some university.

Here Sir John stopped him. 'And how do you ascertain that?'

'A good grasp of grammar. Few mistakes.'

'I've known men writing to correct grammar in the *Times* who have been self-taught,' Sir John said. 'No formal education at all.'

'I daresay such men are in the minority,' Ross said impatiently.

'Do go on.'

The man was reared in an English-speaking country. His script was close to Spencerian at times with a tendency to block his letters when hurried. The name Charlie Excalibur was his own self-appellation. The first communication carried the signature in full. Others simply bore the initials C.E., and later the name would be written in full again. Ross tended to think of him as English, but there were no idiomatic expressions to indicate exact origin.

'What about his couriers?' Sir John said.

'He used Po most of the time.' Ross checked a separate file. 'One man, indeterminate nationality, used in September 1975 and in October of the same year, then never seen again. No identification or even a description on that one. Another one in 1977, used only once. A Cambodian perhaps, Thai, Laotian.'

'How much money have we paid Charlie Excalibur?'

'Not a penny,' Ross said.

Sir John puffed on his pipe. 'Your estimate of the intelligence he has provided us?'

'Varies. From C to A grade. All in all, high-level material.'

'Accuracy?'

'Ninety-five percent.'

'Area covered?'

Sir John was upping the pace, and Ross felt vaguely uncomfortable. 'He has provided intelligence in the following areas,' Ross said without even consulting his papers. 'Hong Kong, Red China, heavy concentrate of

Vietnam, Laos, Cambodia, Singapore, Djakarta. I have a breakdown according to percentages.'

'Not necessary,' Sir John said, waving the stem of his pipe. 'Can you chart where he's been, where he is?'

'No,' Ross said frankly. 'Quite obviously he's been in these areas, perhaps on the constant move.'

'With an organization?'

'He must have his sources. The kinds of information are so disparate. No way of projecting the extent of his organization if he has one.'

'I had a call from Clive,' Sir John said. 'He has made contact with the Russians over Marston. He thinks there is the possibility of a trade.'

'Which Russian did he talk to?'

'Boris.'

'I'll go through and see who we have in cold storage. Maybe a KGB. I think we should start low level.'

'We'll see,' Sir John said. 'Give me a summary of the value of Charlie Excalibur as a source.'

'First-rate,' Ross said, the two words clipped.

'Charlie Excalibur has always troubled me. He's a first-rate source, as you say, and yet he has never wanted money from us, never been paid a pound. Strange, wouldn't you say?'

'Are you suggesting Charlie Excalibur is a double?' Ross said.

'Not at all,' Sir John said. 'We need to invent a new term to describe him, this unknown man who feeds us reliable information upon which we act or which we pass along to the Americans. A damned clever man. And then there's Mr. Po, his carrier. What do we really know about him?'

'Very little except he's on a slab in the morgue.'

Sir John leaned back in his chair, thoughtful. The sky had darkened outside the windows. He took the time to knock the ashes from his pipe, reload it. 'Always the odd pieces that won't fit,' he said almost to himself. 'Why, for instance, has this very wise informant always used Clive as his receiver? Why not Harry Patterson? Would you say, just offhand, that there might be some connection between Clive and Charlie Excalibur of which we're all unaware?'

'I doubt it,' Ross said. 'When an informant picks a receiver at random, he generally continues with that individual. Habit, perhaps, superstition, I don't know.'

'Still, it strikes me as damned odd.' He lit his pipe. 'Here we have an informant who doesn't want money, who sends a courier all the way to Mongolia to deliver a dispatch when there were a dozen closer drops. We also have a Queen's Messenger who has a chat with Boris in Mongolia, becomes frightened, is approached by a chap on a jet in Hong Kong who shows him pictures which we can only assume showed Marston's daughter in jeopardy and persuades him to abandon his impeccable record and trot along. We have the fact that the Marston girl was abducted from Europe, taken God knows where. You would agree with me that those are the facts we have, wouldn't you?'

'Yes, sir.'

Sir John puffed on his pipe, trying to keep the coal alive. 'What is that American expression? Yes, scenario. I'll be damned if I can summon up a scenario to fit the facts. Can you?'

'Not yet.'

'Then keep at it,' Sir John said, suddenly tired. 'When we finally have the missing pieces, the whole bloody thing is bound to make sense.'

BANGKOK

Clive had not slept well. His back was bruised and aching from the attack, and he dozed in fits and starts, coming awake at six in the morning with the full knowledge that sleep was a luxury reserved for the man who was safe, as no man in the field was ever safe. It was a lonely feeling, not in the sense that he was deprived of human contact but that he alone was responsible for the success of his mission, the lives of two people. Here there were no vast resources at his disposal, essentially no protection from things like last night, for as he represented the British Crown, he was also apart from it.

Once he was dressed, he took a tape recorder from his gear, set it on Record, and then made a painstaking search of his quarters, covering the bathroom first, the most unlikely site for a planted bug. He checked the fixtures, the exposed pipes, the walls of the shower, inch by inch, with a thorough patience. Then he turned off the recorder to preserve the batteries, examined the telephone and almost immediately found the bug attached to the base.

Carefully he returned the telephone to its customary position next to the bed, drank a bottle of sour orange juice from the minifridge, and smoked a cigarette before he launched into the search for the second bug. The Russians always worked electronic devices in pairs, in case one failed. Shortly he located the second bug on the bottom of the small table. He was satisfied there were no more, but he could not take it for granted and went over the walls and the baseboards of the room with the running tape recorder which would emit a slight squeal if it encountered a pickup device hidden behind the plaster. He found nothing. He left the bugs where they were. He would use them fully before he was through.

The telephone rang, a call from Liz, sweet Liz, so tempting, but he kept the conversation limited and agreed to meet her later.

He went downstairs and used a safe telephone to call Sam, explaining what he wanted. Clive would leave the hotel in five minutes and Sam would follow at a distance, keeping him in sight, making a note of anyone who appeared to be following him.

He stood near the news-stand for five minutes and then went out into the cool early-morning air. He had forgotten the ritual of the city until he saw the monks with their saffron-colored robes and shaved heads walking down the other side of the street with their wooden alms bowls. He passed one of them where the hotel drive emptied into

Rama I Road, a young man whose head had been shaved too closely, leaving a thin red line of a cut immediately above the left ear.

It had rained heavily only an hour earlier. There were standing puddles of water along the divided boulevard, the heavy traffic sending up a continual spray of water. On the chain-link fence in the middle of the concrete median sat an ornamental chicken, long tail feathers drooping, one brilliant spot of color. He had no idea how the chicken had arrived at that precarious position, but sooner or later the chicken would move and be smashed by one of the cars speeding along the inside lane.

He walked up the stairs onto the pedestrian overpass which traversed the boulevard, stood for a long time against the wire screen, out of the pedestrian flow, observing the street entrance to the hotel grounds, looking for any sign of the Watcher, the traditional Russian who would have been assigned to follow him. He saw no one who might fit the role. A busload of tourists pulled out onto the boulevard from the hotel, the diesel pipes sending spumes of black smoke into the air. They would be heading for Chaigmai perhaps, or the ruins of ancient temples in the jungle, or one of the beach resorts down near Pattaya.

He saw no sign of Sam, wondered whether he was in his car or on foot.

Beneath him, on the boulevard, an army truck with flashing lights cleared the way for a convoy of military vehicles. The cocky officers sat in open jeeps, the troops in olive drab lorries. From this vantage point he could see a vast jumble of buildings, many topped with billboards painted in garish yellows and reds, the messages printed in Thai one advertising a Bruce Lee movie, another depicting television sets. He watched a Thai truck roll by beneath him, covered with ornately carved decorations calculated to give the vehicle the appearance of a mechanical dragon.

Bangkok was a fascinating city, business buildings and asphalt jammed together with the dozens of temples and shrines, their spires piercing through toward the sky. Clive knew the buildings were air-conditioned, Westernized, and despite the muggy and enervating heat, he could see flocks of men in business suits, the sweat condensing on their faces. But within an hour of the capital the country would change, become almost as primitive as it had been a thousand years ago. The villages, the tribal people had no grasp of what was happening in the world beyond the natural cycles of the monsoons or the dry season, day and night, hunger and full bellies, life and death.

He felt a shiver as another piece of memory returned, nothing more significant than a remembered view of a rattan blind dropped against a blazing sun in one of the rare times they had left him alone in his pain and delirium. He could remember the sense of wonder at the contrast between the irregular slats of bamboo which appeared black against the glowing light. It had given him the illusion that he was in a physical cage when he knew that he was not, but he had believed he would never get beyond that blind, indeed did not want to, wanting nothing quite so much as to die quickly.

He deliberately blocked the memory, lit a cigarette, walked down the stairs on the other side, walked on into the streets lined with shops. The monks were thick here, moving through the streets, collecting alms from businesses, rice, vegetables, money from shopkeepers, who met them at the door, bowing with their palms pressed together in front of their faces, making *wais*, earning merit for the life to come. For this was the season of the Buddhist Lent, in which young men of the proper age shaved their heads and became monks for three months, living the monastic life, circulating through the morning streets to gather the necessities for the temple communities.

Clive stopped one of them, a *bhikkhu* whose skull was still white from a recent shaving. The boy peered at him with great surprise as Clive fumbled through his wallet and placed five hundred bahts into the wooden bowl. The young novitiate gave him a blessing and then moved on.

Clive knew what he was doing. He was moving through his own past despite himself, for in that time when he knew he was dying, after he had been rolled from the car into a gutter along a curb, still conscious in that lucid final point beyond pain, observing with detachment his own blood steaming down the concrete gutter and into the iron grating of a storm drain, he had looked up to find himself staring into the alarmed face of a young novitiate monk. His own powers of observation were too far gone to fix the face in his memory, remembering only the glint of reflected light on that shaved skull and a comfortable feeling of irony that he was dying in the grace of an alien religion.

Only that one glimpse, and then he had passed out. He had awakened in an hospital, heavily sedated. The man dispatched from London to conduct the debriefing already sat in a corner of the room.

Clive wondered where that young priest, a year older, was now. In business, perhaps, or in the army, hair grown back. What would be his memories of that morning and the dying *farang*? Clive had always meant to find that man someday, send him money if he was poor, render thanks if he was well off, but he had done neither, would not do it now. The past was past. He did not want to revive it or relive it. He simply wanted to complete his assignment here and leave, go back to the familiar, where there was no need for this sense of spurred alertness, the continuous trickle of adrenaline through his system.

He found a park, where he sat on a bench beneath a tree for half an hour, again waiting to pick up any sign of his Watcher. There was none. Another monk passed him, and suddenly he felt a glimpse of recognition which he could not immediately place, and then it occurred to him the ragged thin line of a scar over the left ear. This was the same man, an obvious tracker, and he was on his feet in an instant, but there was a whole procession of saffron-robed monks moving down the street back toward their wats. He would never be able to pick him out.

Sam's taxi pulled up to the curb, and Clive climbed in.

'Did you see the man?' Sam said.

'The monk. Not until it was too late.'

'A terrible thing for a man to do,' Sam said. 'If he is a monk or if he is just pretending, he will still lose much merit with Lord Buddha.'

'Let's go back to the hotel,' Clive said.

'Certainly, sir. And if you don't mind, I think I will ask one of my friends to join us from now on. He is a very efficient fellow, a professional boxer. He will cost you very little money.'

'Why should I need your friend?' Clive said.

'The monk was not alone,' Sam said. 'Do you see that Thai man leaning against the near post? And over there, sir, if you will notice, there is a boy selling fruit from a basket. You had more than one follower from the hotel.'

Clive leaned back in his seat with a sigh.

'If you will forgive my saying so,' Sam went on, 'any man who is attacked one night and then followed the next day by so many people needs a bodyguard. He will be yours.'

13

BANGKOK

Nikolai Borowsky considered himself a student of human nature, although in the slang of his profession he was now classified as a Watcher who had been assigned to keep tabs on the Englishman Clive. He had checked into the same garden wing of the Siam Intercontinental within an hour of Clive's arrival, had assigned one of the Thai recruits to follow Clive, and then had used a pass key to enter Clive's vacant room. He had planted an electronic device in the telephone and another under the small table that held a vase into which the maids put fresh flowers daily.

The devices were remote transmitters, voice-activated, which broadcast to a small receiver he had placed in a drawer in his room. His procedures had been practiced so long as to become automatic, a part of a daily ritual in which he looked forward to the hours of the night when Clive would be securely established in his room so Nikolai could settle down on his bed, earphones clamped to his skull, to scan the tapes and see if he had caught anything of interest.

It took a patience which he had developed over his fourteen years with the KGB. There would not be much on the tapes to begin with. He could count on one sequence each day of the Thai maids cleaning the room, occasionally singing as they worked, or the blare of the televison set as they followed a program from one room to the next. Those portions he would carefully edit from the tape with a pair of scissors, putting the excess pieces in a small paper bag which he would dump in a trash bin in another part of the city. Any conversations which included Clive would be sent by a runner each day to the Soviet

Embassy, where he was certain they would be transcribed for Boris, who was his control and whose spot he coveted and would eventually seize when Boris transgressed once too often or made an irrevocable mistake. In the meantime, Nikolai was careful to make no mistakes himself.

Nikolai spoke the kind of English so common among international travelers that he could pass as an Englishman reared in Malaysia or an American who had spent most of his life in the Far East. But this time he had a West German passport and letters identifying him as a photographer for the glossy German magazine *Geo*. He wore khaki shorts and a tattered khaki top which resembled old American army fatigues with the arms cut out to reveal his well-developed and sun-browned biceps. He was extended every courtesy by the hotel, which courted European tourists. It would be more than coincidental that two-thirds of his hotel pictures would include, somewhere in the frame, that tall and rumpled Englishman named Clive. Whoever Clive talked to, even in a random conversation, would be captured on film as well.

Nikolai had it in the back of his mind, once this assignment was finished, to put together his non-Clive pictures into a photographic features on Bangkok and sell it to *Geo* if he could. It was highly possible he would be allowed to keep the money, equally possible that *Geo* might sign him on legitimately, the perfect cover.

On the first day he had photographed Clive at the British ambassador's garden party, photographed him with Patterson, photographed him with Boris, taken two or three pictures of Clive talking with the bartender, knowing that the KGB would check out any communicant as a possible. Nikolai had enjoyed that assignment. For that occasion he was able to get out of the cutoffs and to wear a dinner jacket, formal clothing which enhanced his self-recognized good looks. He had trailed Clive as far as Patterson's house, had been unable to record that meeting. He had witnessed the attack on Clive, the rescue, the stop at the Empress and stayed with Clive back to the hotel, observing the reception of a message and Clive's passage to bed. He had duly reported all this by telephone.

Quite early the next morning Nikolai was awakened by the small red light which indicated that Clive was on the telephone. Once the light went out, Nikolai played the tape, a conversation between Clive and a stunning woman Nikolai had seen in the hotel. As a matter of fact, Nikolai played the tape three times to catch the nuances of the conversation which, to an untrained observer, would have appeared perhaps, to be of no more than minor interest. The telephone had been answered at precisely 6:17 in the morning, Clive's voice quite alert.

CLIVE: Clive here.

LIZ: Did I wake you up?

CLIVE: No.

LIZ: Did you get my note?

CLIVE: Yes.

LIZ: You don't sound too thrilled about it.

CLIVE *(after a long pause)*: It's a mistake. It's more than that. You know it's impossible.

LIZ: I'm here on an assignment and I need your help. Do you know a man named Sydney Garvin?

CLIVE: It's better if we don't talk.

LIZ: Just hear me out. He's an American, a rather nice man whose son was lost in the Vietnamese War. He believes his son defected and is still alive.

CLIVE: Liz ...

LIZ: You have contacts. I thought you might talk to him at least.

CLIVE: There's an American embassy.

LIZ: They won't help him. They can't help him. At least have a drink with us. The British have an embassy in Hanoi.

And here in the conversation was a long pause of an almost embarrassing length which represented an imponderable to Nikolai. On the surface he could not account for the duration of Clive's silence, as if it were a matter of extreme importance whether he met with this American or not. There should have been no hesitation at

138

all, not over such a minor matter. In the end, after a full nine seconds of silence, Clive indeed had agreed.

CLIVE: I don't think I can help him.
LIZ: But you will talk to him.
CLIVE: Say, this afternoon, two o'clock, at the pool.
LIZ: You can't make it before then?
CLIVE: No. (Another long pause.) Two o'clock.
LIZ: Then that will have to do. Two o'clock.

As Nikolai lay in bed, playing the conversation again and again, he recognized an undertone there which he could not interpret in the light of the limited information which he had been given. He took off his dressing gown, paused to admire himself in the mirror, the muscle tone he had worked so hard to achieve, the patina of success and power which women found irresistable. Then he took a shower.

He lathered himself, shampooed his thick black hair, inhaled the steam, thought over what he knew about Clive. Very little, amorphous rumors, bits of conversation he had overheard and picked up. At one time Clive had been a top agent for MI6, but he had cracked under pressure. Nikolai did not know the details. Neither did he know what assignment had brought Clive to Bangkok, but it had to be of sufficient importance that Nikolai would be assigned to watch him.

He turned off the water, toweled himself dry, drew on a black silk robe, and then sat on the bed and, as was his habit when he thought things through, took the knife from the top of the nightstand where he kept it while he slept. He pressed the button on the handle, watched the thin, long sharp blade spring alive. He sat in the flow of cold air from the air conditioner, the only way one could get truly dry in the high humidity of Bangkok, then took from the drawer a small rectangle of a sharpening stone and began to hone the edge of the blade, already razor-sharp, as if in the rhythmic whir of blade against stone there was an orderliness which was transferred to his thoughts.

139

He finished sharpening the knife, closed it with reverence, then placed the worn stone in the small drawer of the nightstand. He was suddenly restless. There was no great pride connected with his work. As a collector of information he was, in essence, no more important than the tape recorder which purred on and off in his room. He had not been educated at the university, could claim no more for himself than perhaps a thousand other men in his service grade. To inherit the mantle which would soon slide from Boris's shoulders would require something to call attention to himself.

He would give that some thought. He had qualified as an assassin, an expert with his knife, felt no qualms about accomplishing these acts of murder. He poured himself a glass of vodka, drank it as he lay on the bed, staring at the ceiling.

Clive, yes. This assignment to Clive had put Nikolai into precisely the right position. He did not know how yet, but it would be this assignment which would provide him the opportunity to make his long-overdue ascent.

He would take this morning off and then pick up the trail again this afternoon at the pool. Two o'clock.

At one o'clock Clive ordered a pot of coffee from room service and then sat drinking it in silence, studying the telephone as a hostile instrument which he would have to learn to use to his advantage. He placed a long-line call to Katy in Australia, was informed by the operator that it would take a few minutes to go through.

When the telephone rang, he snatched it up with a momentary resentment that his privacy was being invaded, that there was some unknown third party on the line who would be sharing the intimacy between him and his wife. When he heard her voice, his perspective returned and he had the keen desire to chuck it all and join her in Melbourne. Her voice was a combination of concern and relief.

'Where are you, dear?' she said.

'Bangkok,' he said. 'The Siam Intercontinental.'

'What in the bleeding hell are you doing in Bangkok?' she exploded.

'You've been around your father, I can tell that,' he said with a laugh. 'Your Aussie lilt is back again. How is he?'

And she was off and running into a description of her father's misadventures. He had broken his leg and was in the hospital, where he was giving the nurses fits with his salty language and outback manners. Her sisters were well, if nagging, and had thrown her into the breach to control Father, for Katy was his favorite and the only one who could stand up to his withering blasts. She had been to the theater once, a play which ended with somebody's placing a sexual organ on a crucifix, and it had been rainy, chilly. But she loved being in Melbourne and felt that the years of being a second-class Australian in London had simply melted away. Full circle, and she was back to him again.

'But you haven't told me what you're doing in Bangkok,' she said. 'You were supposed to be here by now.'

'It's all routine,' he said in an even voice, as much for the listener as for Katy. 'I don't expect my business here to take very long.'

'What does that mean?' she said, pinning him down.

'Three or four days.'

'And then where?'

'To Melbourne, of course. As soon as I can make it.' And he told her he loved her, and she told him she loved him, and then he severed the connection, knowing that she would cry for a half hour after the conversation. But he was surprised how quickly the sentiment faded in himself, how automatically he dismissed the thought of her. He had the sure knowledge that she was safe in Melbourne, out of play, so to speak, while he was entering into the second phase of what had become a familiar game.

He put on a loose shirt and a pair of khaki trousers and went downstairs. He found an isolated telephone and placed a call to Patterson at the embassy.

'I've been expecting a call from you,' Patterson said, his voice wryly amused. 'My driver witnessed your fine art of defense from three blocks away, tried to call the police without success. He said you were in good form.'

'Go to hell,' Clive said. 'I was set up.'

'That's your basic paranoia for you,' Patterson said. 'My driver has been with me ten years. There was a transmission failure. It was just a case of a couple of Thai thugs who were attracted by what they might be able to pick up from a Westerner in a disabled car. Are you feeling all right? Were you damaged?'

'No, I'm fine. I want you to get a full report from the mechanic. I want to know if the car was tampered with in any way.'

'I'll do that, old chap,' Patterson said. 'Glad you weren't banged up too badly.'

Clive hung up on him and went out into the pool area, where he saw Liz in a stunning white linen dress. She was sitting at one of the tables beneath an umbrella next to the bar. With her was the American, Sydney Garvin, and from the moment Clive shook hands with him and sat down, he felt wary.

Garvin was in his late fifties, impeccably dressed in a tropical suit. He was not what Clive had expected, not the insecure supplicant with an air of desperation about him. Indeed, he was tanned, fit, his sparse brown hair well combed, his exposed arms muscular and tanned. There was a cool quickness to his eyes, as if he overlooked nothing of importance. Clive had seen that expression too many times not to know what it represented. This man was in surveillance, probably CIA.

'I'm pleased to meet you, Mr. Clive,' he said. 'Miss Sullivan here says you might be able to help.' The accent was midwestern. He looked off into the bright reflection of the sun on the surface of the swimming pool.

'Tell me something about yourself,' Clive said.

'There's not a great deal to say,' Garvin said. 'I'm a lawyer in Fort Wayne, Indiana. My son is one of those soldiers who simply disappeared in the Vietnamese War. I went through all the usual procedures with the government. I can't say they were uncooperative. They

142

simply had no information. So I came out here to see for myself.'

'That's understandable,' Clive said. 'Why Bangkok?'

'It seems like a logical place to begin.' Garvin's eyes seemed to be making a constant sweep of the grounds. His manicured fingers drummed on the tabletop as if he were too restless to sit still. 'I had the good fortune to contact the *Far Eastern Economic Review*, and I'm delighted that they sent Miss Sullivan along.'

'Was it your idea to contact me?' Clive said.

Garvin looked at him directly now. 'You might say that,' he said. 'I have some friends in Washington who suggested I might get in touch with British officialdom in the Far East. You have an embassy in Hanoi. We don't. I've also been told that your country has made a concerted effort to keep tabs on American defectors who are still living in the area.'

Definitely CIA, Clive thought. 'That's not in my line, I'm afraid,' he said. 'I suggest that you contact the British Embassy here and see what they can do for you.'

'He's already done that,' Liz said. 'He's been told that officially the British can't intervene in a matter like this. But it occurred to me that you might know a way around the rules.'

Clive snapped his fingers at a passing barboy, ordered a cold beer. He wanted to ask Garvin what in the hell he was doing here and what he was after. But he did not. 'Do you have any papers, Mr. Garvin?'

Garvin retrieved a plastic folder next to his chair, handed it to Clive. 'I have the usual assortment,' he said. 'Letters from all the proper officials, expressing concern but doing nothing.'

The beer was delivered and Clive was about to start sorting through the plastic folder when he saw a man on the far side of the pool, young, tanned, muscular, coal black hair. He was dressed in cutoff khaki shorts, wearing a gold medallion on a chain around his neck along with assorted camera gear hanging from straps. At the moment the man had a Nikon with a long lens focused

143

ostensibly on a Eurasian girl in a bikini who was floating, breasts up, in the blue water.

Clive had seen the man around the hotel. He remembered him from the ambassador's garden party, an omnipresent background figure who had now moved into the foreground. So this young man with the flashing teeth would be the number one Russian Watcher in charge of the delegation of Thai floaters.

Clive leafed through the papers with embossed seals and printed military logos, answers to letters requesting information, answers which contained no hard facts. Then he came across a photograph, an eight-by-ten glossy of a tall young man in fatigues, corporal's stripes on his shoulders, holding an M-16 rifle in the crook of his arm. The picture was grainy, obviously a snapshot which had been enlarged. The young man was tall and gangly, a rather lopsided grin on his face.

Corporal William C. Garvin had simply disappeared from Danang, exact date of disappearance unknown; that was the only solid information contained in all these sheets. He returned to the photograph again. Why would the CIA be interested in this particular ex-GI?

'When did you last see your son, Mr. Garvin?' Clive said.

'He was home for Easter in 1972,' Garvin said. 'He returned to Vietnam just as the marines were being withdrawn. He was transferred to the unit left behind to aid in the evacuation.'

'Which unit was that?'

'The Third Marine Amphibious Force.'

'And you know nothing about how he disappeared?'

'I've talked with officers in his brigade,' Garvin said. 'Record keeping was very loose during 1973. He was absent at a morning roll call one day. They have no idea what happened to him. They think he may just have walked away.' Garvin had been well briefed.

Garvin continued to talk about his son, about the efforts made to locate him. Clive nodded, made sounds of interest while he only half listened. His eyes followed the man who was moving around the pool with the grace of an

144

athlete, coaxing the girl into the shallow end of the pool, where she stood up, golden brown flesh exposed, posing, sensual. Clive would lay money that if the girl appeared on that exposed film at all, she would be to one side of the frame, out of focus, with a clear shot of Clive, Liz, and Garvin. By tonight there would be grainy enlargements of that midwestern face cast on a screen, the Russians seeking identification and connection. If Garvin was indeed CIA, the odds were good the Russians would make a fix by morning unless he was virgin to this territory.

'If he's dead, we can understand that,' Garvin said while Clive sipped his beer, eyes flicking back to the Watcher, who was changing his lens for an extreme Telephoto. He was a cautious, thorough man.

Clive took another look at the papers. The girl in the pool was giggling as the Watcher extended his hand, helped her out of the water, retreated with her to a pair of chaise longues on the other side of the pool, where he cased his cameras, ordered drinks.

On the face of it the case of Corporal William C. Garvin was a hopeless one, Clive concluded. The young man had undoubtedly died a long time ago. 'I don't know what I can do for you, Mr. Garvin,' he said.

'Perhaps you can give it some thought and come up with something,' Garvin said. 'I think it's appropriate that we should be working together. The English and the Americans, I mean. Now, if you'll excuse me, I feel I have taken quite enough of your time.'

Clive stood up, shook hands with him again. Garvin walked around the pool on the way to his room.

Liz put her hand on his arm. 'Will you take this up with the ambassador?'

'Don't touch me, Liz,' he said calmly. 'We're being watched. This conversation has to be strictly professional.'

'Watched?' she said, startled. 'By whom?'

'The young man across the pool, the one who fancies himself quite as much as the girl he's with.' He sipped his beer.

She removed her hand from his arm.

'Trust me.' He seemed to pay attention to the papers again. 'We'll talk about it later. Are you really here on this Garvin story?'

'Partially. There are so many MIAs still. The *Review* thought it might be a good idea to follow this one.'

The man across the pool was talking to the girl. She was laughing. Through her sunglasses Liz studied them. 'Have you come any closer to finding your Queen's Messenger?'

'We'll talk about that later as well.'

'I worry about you,' she said. 'I've never seen you so cautious before, so on edge.'

'I was jumped last night,' he said. 'It could have been thieves. It could have been because someone doesn't want me to find Marston. If the latter is true, they will use anything, anybody. Now you take that bloody preening man over there. He is keenly tuned to us all the time he's chatting with his bird. He's watching us like a hawk, trying to figure out our relationship. If it ever becomes necessary to apply pressure on me and they think there is anything between us, they would snatch you in the blink of an eye and send me one of your lovely fingers with the ring still attached.'

'Wouldn't you say you're dramatizing a bit?' she said.

'No,' he said. 'I have the scars to prove it.'

She was immediately silent. 'You have to forgive me, darling.' Her eyes were on the Watcher and his woman now, being served a drink, tall, orange-colored, in frosted glasses.

He finished the beer, ordered another. 'I'm not being capricious,' he said. 'I loved you a great deal once. And I don't want to take even the most remote chance of seeing you hurt.'

She started to touch his arm, remembered his warning, withdrew her hand, and smiled instead. 'And to be close to you is to be in danger? That's what you're saying, isn't it?'

'Yes, in a nutshell. That's it.' To explain it to her, that was the problem, and of course, he could not.

'I've had a lot of time to think about you in the past year,' she said, 'but I never really asked why we didn't get together after they sent you back to London. It just happened, and I could accept that. And I've had liaisons, if you want to call them that, with half a dozen men since then. But it wasn't the same. The feelings were not even remotely similar.'

'Liz –'

'Don't interrupt. When you showed up in Hong Kong again, I made my decision. I loved you then and I still love you and I think you love me. I know you're married to a fine woman and have a child on the way, but I'm shameless enough to say I want you anyway. I didn't come here to help a man whose son doesn't have the chance of a snowball in hell of being alive, and Marston is just an assignment.'

'Are you finished?'

'No.' She did not look at him directly. 'Now, with all these things taken for granted, I want you to do something for me, love. I can understand about your business. I saw you almost dead before and I don't want that to happen again. You care for me and I care for you. So we strike a bargain. You go on to Australia tomorrow, call everything off, live a good life with your wife and your new child. In turn, I'll catch the first flight for Hong Kong.' She stood up, began to fish through her purse. 'Give it some thought.'

'I'll get the check.'

'I'll pay my own.' She placed the baht notes on the table. 'I'd rather know you're safe. I do love you that much.'

'That doesn't change anything,' he said. 'I can't leave. You know that.'

'Then we'll take it a day at a time.' He could hear the clicking of her heels as she walked away. He did not look after her. Instead, he went through the papers without seeing any of them. He was aware that the man across the pool had put on a pair of mirrored sunglasses, the lenses reflecting the sunlight as if his eyes were on fire. He was still watching Clive. He had not been diverted by Liz. She was of no interest to him, Clive realized, because he had not made any connection beyond her as reporter and Clive as source. For the time being, Liz was safe.

14

BANGKOK

Nikolai was gleeful. The girl was spread-eagled on the bed, her legs and arms tied straight out to the bed corners. From the expression on her face she was obviously pleased that she could cause such euphoria in him because she was a professional and a happy man always gave her more money than one who was solemn in his pleasures.

Nikolai knew this, and it only increased his enjoyment as he sat on the edge of the bed and ran one hand over the golden brown breasts until the nipples hardened. She had nothing to do with the way he felt and would not understand if he explained it to her.

For early this morning he had been included, made heir apparent, sitting across from Boris in a safe house over a steaming glass of hot tea. Boris had been open, reflective, addressing him as an equal.

'I think you have been overlooked, Nikolai,' Boris said, sipping his tea. 'You have been so efficient at your work and made so few demands that you have been taken for granted.'

'I'm pleased that you have noticed my work.'

Boris smiled. 'That's not all I have noticed, of course. It occurs to me that there must be a dissatisfaction growing within you.' He waved his hand as if to stifle Nikolai's protests to the contrary. 'No, I understand what it is to be young and ambitious, frustrated because your advancement seems to have stopped. Would you like something to eat?'

'No, thank you, sir,' Nikolai said, absorbing every word like parched ground in a light rain.

'I will be out here no more than a few more months, and then it's retirement for me. Back to Moscow and perhaps a desk job. I must say it's time for that. But I must be sure that the man who takes my place is not only capable but dedicated. There are some jobs that no man likes to undertake, but revulsion is something which a man in our business must overcome, as a sailor overcomes sea-sickness.'

'I am ready for any responsibility you care to give me.'

'I know you are. But what I am going to propose will require all your skills.' He proceeded to describe what he had in mind in great detail while Nikolai sat spellbound, not with the task itself (which he would handle with no feelings at all) but with the implications. For he was being included in a top-level operation, something he knew about only from the periphery.

'I believe in you, of course,' Boris went on, 'or I would not be suggesting this, but I must tell you that among some of the others, your vanity is suspect. They believe that your vanity denotes a certain lack of profession-alism.'

And Nikolai, sitting across from Boris, was filled with an incredible frenzy to prove, to demonstrate, to meet any challenge, to deface himself if necessary. Such was the strength of his ambition, but he suppressed it, responding in a calm and dignified manner.

'I have no vanity, Comrade Boris,' he said. 'I have confidence in myself, but that is not the same thing. I look forward to the chance to prove myself. When do you want me to do it?'

'Shortly,' Boris said. 'The next day or two. I should add, purely as an aside, because duty is the important element here, that you will be receiving a considerable raise in pay to meet the requirements of your new position. I'll be in touch with you very soon.'

Nikolai had spent the rest of the day in a blissful state of anticipation he had not known before, even while he took pictures of Clive and his two major contacts for the day, even while he collected data from the hotel clerk on this sentimental American on his vain mission and the woman from the *Far Eastern Economic Review*. He had sent the data along with the film, allowing himself the luxury of adding his personal analysis for the first time, his observation that neither the reporter nor the American was important here, neither connected with Clive's mission.

He had hired the girl whose body had been a front for his pictures of the afternoon. Now she was on the bed, filled with what he interpreted as a growing impatience, clearly uncomfortable but forced by her profession to convert discomfort into something sexual.

His hand explored her flat stomach, the strip of lighter flesh which had been covered by the bikini in the hot sunlight, a triangular pattern. Soft, yes, and his skillful fingers located the promontories of the hipbones and moved back to the mons Veneris, the thatch of pubic hair beneath which he could feel the pelvis.

'I want you,' she said. 'Make love to me.'

'You're being paid.'

'But you arouse me.' She squirmed as if to confirm his effect on her. 'Please now.'

He poured himself another glass of vodka, downed it. Expensive vodka. Nothing cheap for him again. 'You miss the point,' he said with a low, throaty laugh, knowing she would not understand what he was saying, even if she understood enough English to grasp the words. 'I have you here for study purposes, primarily to learn how you are put together, how you are assembled. I have you here for practice. We will make love soon enough when I have finished my study.'

'I just want you to love me now,' she said. He was right. She had no idea what he was talking about. 'Untie me and I will show you one good time. The best time.'

He laughed aloud, continuing to probe with his fingers, working up her stomach again to the softness just below the rib cage. He had only a rudimentary knowledge of anatomy, but he knew the approximate location of the heart, probably upward from where his fingers pressed, at

150

an angle, perhaps thirty degrees. There were no impeding bones or muscles that he could detect.

He held his arm straight out, laughed to himself. Steady, by God, with enough vodka in him now to fell a workhorse and yet that rigid, outstretched arm was rock-steady, not a tremble in the tendons or the muscles, no unsteadiness at all in his fingers, which he moved, one by one.

On impulse he went into the bathroom and, having dumped the ice from the plastic ice bucket, waited until the water from the hot tap was steaming and then held the bucket beneath it. Once it was full, he took one of the small bars of soap and crushed it into the container, whipping up a weak lather. Not good enough. He unwrapped another bar of soap, carried it and the container back to the bed, a towel draped over his arm as if he were a waiter.

Now the girl had dropped all pretense of passion. Her eyes were openly curious, a little alarmed. 'What are you doing?' she said. 'What's going on?'

He said nothing. He sat down on the bed between her spread legs, humming tunelessly, regarding her with an objective smile. He put his hand into the soapy water and began to massage the thin lather into her pubic hair, down between her legs, into the delicate clefts of the labia, using a soft force which caused a shudder to run through her. Then he took the bar of soap and making tiny circles with it, rubbed it into the hair and down between her legs, aware now that the twitches in her body, the involuntary tightening of the tendons in those exquisite inner thighs, were not feigned. She moaned slightly. He continued to work, circles, circles, pressing, kneading, until to his surprise there was a convulsive movement in her loins and he could feel with his fingers the spasms of her climax. But still, he worked until the lather was the consistency of whipped cream.

Then he dried his hands on the towel, one finger at a time, until there was no moisture on his hands at all and the tips of his fingers were perfectly sensitive. He opened

151

the drawer of the nightstand, took out the knife. He pressed the button, and the blade sprang out with a snap which attracted her attention. She turned her face, peering through a tangle of long black hair, her eyes still half glazed until she saw the blade glittering in the lamplight. She spoke in alarmed Thai. He did not speak the language, but he knew what she was saying, and he held a finger to his lips, half smiled, made a soothing noise as a father would use to comfort a child.

'Please,' she said, a prayer in English.

'Nikolai won't hurt you,' he said. 'Not if you hold perfectly still. That's important. If you move, you will hurt yourself, and Nikolai won't be able to help you.' He examined the blade against the light, the razor-sharp edge perfect, as if he could see it through magnification, the one perfect thing in the world, that unblemished cutting edge. He sat down again between her legs, began with the pubis, stretching the skin tight with the index and middle fingers of his left hand. Then, with the blade held delicately in the fingers of his right, he ran the edge through the lathered hair, which seemed to melt away from the skin.

'Please, we talk,' she said, petrified. 'Men don't want me if you do that. I lose money.'

'Be very quiet,' he said gently. 'The blade is perfect. I have no desire to hurt you.'

She became desperately still, not a movement. He dipped the blade into the container of water, rinsed away the soap and the hair, resumed his shaving until the mons veneris was shining, bald. More delicately now, aware of the vulnerability of sweet tissue, he held the fold of the left labia firmly between thumb and forefinger, ran the blade transversely up the thigh and over the stretched skin. The knife was an extension of his hand, the blade perfectly controlled. Shave, rinse. Shave again, a slithery sound, no rasp.

She was weeping quietly, and he hummed a little louder, growing more aroused himself, his delicacy an act of love. Finally, when he was finished, he emptied his container of water, soap, and hair and, with a washcloth, came back and rinsed her clean, not a shred of hair left. He dried the knife, polished it with the towel, left it open in case there was some hidden hint of water still clinging to it. He placed it on the nightstand, to lie on its steel spine.

He took off his trousers and hung them neatly across the back of a chair, aware in his new position of the demands of tidiness and order. She was terrified as he lowered himself onto her, brushing the hair away from her tear-streaked eyes, murmuring endearments as he guided himself into position with his hand and entered her. The feeling engulfed him until he was out of control and she was threshing beneath him, whether from re-newed desire or a terror-stricken attempt to escape, he would never know, for he had such power within him, such a blind desire to reach that point of absolute blankness, that little death, he did not care. Eventually the snap occurred, the ultimate release. He spent himself and then, with athletic grace, pushed himself up with his arms and landed on his feet.

He untied her. She lay motionless and spent for a moment; then she went to the bathroom. When she returned, she was dressed except for her shoes, her hair neatly combed. But she was still aware of the open knife, sharp edge up, lying on the table.

'You have ruined me,' she said not too assertively.

He laughed. 'You can charge more. You're different now. Men pay more for the different.' He removed the money clip from the trousers draped on the chair, lifted out two thousand-baht notes. 'You see? I am paying you a great deal more. But this also means you will not speak to anyone about me. No one. Because I would know. I would find out.'

He held the notes casually in front of her face. With great respect she reached out and took them. She carried her shoes in her hand as if she did not want to take the time to put them on.

When she was gone, he took a shower, made one final examination of the recording equipment to make certain it was still functioning. Then he went to bed. He did not sleep immediately. Instead, he concentrated on what he had observed about the woman's body, the pulses which marked the surfacing of arteries, the contours of upper stomach, and that most vulnerable of hollows overshadowed by breasts. He made no philosophical observations. He would be quite up to it when the time came.

The whole practice had gone quite well. He was now ready for the real thing.

LAOS

Charlie Excalibur began to see the signs along the jungle path, the bleached skulls of various unrecognizable animals stuck in the clefts of trees, left in the center of the track. He came across an elephant skull propped up against a rock, the huge eye sockets empty, the tusks gone because they represented money. The village people were superstitious. They believed in ghosts and demons and the terror of the hours before dawn when malignant spirits were free to roam the world. And they respected these assortment of marker skulls enough to stay clear of the area.

Up ahead someplace would be a community of renegades who were in effect telling the locals to keep the hell out of this area or suffer the consequences. And the locals would pay attention and keep their collective mouths shut. When the authorities asked, they would say nothing because they feared the renegade camp and retaliation on their own villages.

Charlie Excalibur did not like the renegades and avoided them whenever possible. They were the true scum of both armies, the North Vietnamese defectors, the American defectors, equally outcast now, with no place to go and no real desire to go there, potheads who had shot their systems a long time ago and had banded together to survive.

But now he needed food and a place to rest without one

eye open all the time, and the renegades could provide that. Occasionally they would put together a squad and make a running attack on the edges of some town, robbing shopkeepers and hauling away the cases of beer and whiskey and canned foods they could not get otherwise. And they always carried magazines and newspapers as well, because they needed to keep up with the outside world.

He did not leave the path, did not try to take to the jungle now because he was certain he had already been spotted, undoubtedly by one of the gook renegades set out as pickets. They were good at it because they were willing to sit perfectly motionless in a tree all day long, waiting until an intruder had passed beyond earshot before they radioed the information back to the base camp. If Charlie Excalibur took to the bush, they would think he was up to something and he would just have time to hear the shot before he was drilled by a rifle bullet or cut in two by an automatic weapon.

When he caught the first whiff of the cook fires somewhere in the distance, he stopped in the middle of the path and let out a yell. 'My name is Charlie Excalibur,' he shouted. 'I've been snake-bit, leech-drained, shot at, knifed, doubled over by the running trots, and the last man who crossed me got his throat cut. Now, if any of you sons of bitches have anything against me, then you sure as hell better get your butts tight because I'm coming in.'

He waited for a minute, lit a cigarette to allow any gook picket who might have missed him to get a fix on him, and then he pushed straight ahead. The monkeys were chatting in the trees, and he could hear birds calling someplace in the lost foliage, but there were no dogs barking.

He came into the clearing, the settlement which had been deserted to allow the renegades to occupy it, a couple of small house hooches standing on stilts and a half dozen areas with tarps extending from trees to cover cook fires and provide shelter from the monsoon rains. He figured the total population here at fifteen, maybe sixteen men.

He could count a half dozen Americans with long hair and beards, wearing tattered remnants of uniforms. They gave him a glance, nothing more. He walked past a squatting group of North Vietnamese who were smoking, shooting dice. Some strange Oriental game which brought out a lot of high-pitched bickering. There were a couple of men with automatic weapons sitting beneath trees at the edge of the camp, but one of them was asleep and the other was nodding.

He walked up to one of the cook fires where a small animal was roasting on a wooden spit and a pan bubbled with assorted greens. The man who was turning the spit looked no more than twenty-five years old. 'That you yelling out there?' he said.

'The same. Can you spare some of that chow?'

'Do you want to know what we're eating?'

'No.'

The cook laughed, cut off a piece of the meat, and put it in an old mess kit with some greens. Charlie Excalibur retired to one corner of the tarp area, sat down with his back against a tree to eat.

Two men were sitting opposite him, going through a pile of newspapers and magazines. '"Corporal Sammy Jack Willard, please come home,"' one of them read aloud. '"Your mama and your two sisters miss you."'

'I got a better one than that,' the second man said. '"Sergeant Ardmore Holding, from Chicago, Illinois. You are forgiven everything and Dad will provide legal counsel. Your sister, Adrienne, is ill. Please contact the nearest American consulate."'

Charlie Excalibur continued to eat, watched them. One of them was in his thirties, with a tattooed dragon on his arm, and the other was a little younger, a baby-faced ex-grunt with a stoned smile. They would eventually be brought down by somebody's roving patrol if they didn't kill each other. But they were none of his business.

He finished eating, wiped his fingers on the grass. The mess kit, once laid by, was immediately covered with flies. He stood up and approached the two men. 'You got anything less than a month old?' he said, indicating the stack of newspapers. The man with the tattoo yawned, kicked some in his direction. He picked up a copy of the *Far Eastern Economic Review*, sat down again, and flipped through the pages halfheartedly, stories of refugees and swindles and cities like Singapore and Hong Kong which seemed so far in his past that he felt he had dreamed them.

He only half listened to the litany of names in the background, the gentle mockery of the advertisements for men never accounted for in the Vietnamese War, and he wondered if these men were not hoping against hope that they would run across their own names, proof that somebody cared, proof that they were not forgotten.

His eye fell on a story concerning the disappearance of a Queen's Messenger from Hong Kong, and it took a moment for the significance of that story to sink in, the connection of dates and times. He backtracked in his mind, figuring approximately how long it would have taken Mr. Po to reach Ulan Bator, and then with a rush the possibility hit him. His message could have been in the bags carried by that Queen's Messenger, in which case his enemies would know his proposal and Clive would not. If Charlie Excalibur went to the village he had proposed as a meeting place, he could run straight into the center of an ambush. If he did not go, and if Clive indeed had received the message, then he would miss his one chance.

He looked around. In the doorway of one of the hooches he saw a Vietnamese girl with a half-white baby on her outthrust hip. Life went on, if you could call it that, and a man had to take gambles beyond the secure or nothing could possibly get better. He lay back on the grass, putting the magazine over his eyes, keeping one hand on the pistol, in case anybody tried to lift it from him while he slept.

He did not like the odds, but he would never end up like this, existing with some girl in a hooch in the jungle, sitting around stoned and reading the appeals from people who still grieved for dead men to come home. Not for him. He would take the gamble, and if he was wrong, he would at least die quickly.

Charlie Excalibur slept.

BANGKOK

Sam was pleased to have the illustrious Tiger Man visiting his house. At one time Tiger Man had been at the top rank of Thai boxers, and to see him in the ring was to marvel at the perfection of the human body and his uncommon sense of timing, the flashing of arms and legs which eventually saw his opponent down before he knew what had struck him.

But Tiger Man was now in his late thirties, and he had been injured in a *samlor* accident which would have killed a lesser man. Tiger Man did not die, but his right leg had been broken, and he walked with a limp. He had not gone back into the ring again. He now sat in a wicker chair in the small front garden of Sam's house, a cup of *mekong* in his hand, while Sam sat near the miniature spirit house. They had gone through all of the proper greetings in Thai, but now Tiger Man wanted to practice his English.

'I work for English-speaking peoples sometimes,' Tiger Man said. 'It is important that I am speaking it.'

'I will be honored to help you,' Sam said. 'I wish to offer you a job. It is far beneath you, of course, but it is something which is of great importance.'

'If I can be helping you ...'

They were interrupted by Sam's mother, a delicate, graceful woman, who brought a tray of fruit and placed it on a small wicker table, making a proper *wai* to the esteemed Tiger Man, who was gracious enough to return it as she backed her way into the house. Sam could hear the laughter of his sisters someplace in the background.

'I have been hired to be a driver for an Englishman who is in much trouble,' Sam said, sipping the *mekong*. 'His name is Clive. It is possible he is a British intelligence agent, but that is none of my business.'

'How can I be helping?' Tiger Man said.

'He is followed all of the time,' Sam said. 'There is a Russian named Nikolai Borowsky who stays at the Siam Intercontinental Hotel. There is also a young monk whose name I do not know but who profanes himself by working for the Russians. There is also another man whose name is Kriang, who sells fruit sometimes, flowers at other times.'

'I know him,' Tiger Man said.

'I think he belongs to Colonel Patterson. Is that so?'

'Of course,' Tiger Man said with a rare smile. 'He works for the Thai soldier who is not a Thai.'

'He may be friendly, what is known to the English as a backup. Do you know that word?'

'No.'

'He may be there to observe the Russians who are following Mr. Clive.'

'I see.'

'I wish to hire you to protect Mr. Clive, to serve as a bodyguard.'

Tiger Man thought it over. He stared off at the thatched roof of the house, listened to the roar of a water taxi on the nearby klong. 'I do not wish to be insulting,' he said. 'Are those the proper English words?'

'Yes.'

'I do not wish to be insulting,' Tiger Man repeated, 'but is Mr. Clive a worthy man?'

'Most worthy, I believe.'

Tiger Man nodded. 'Then, of course, I am honored to be of help.'

They did not discuss money. That would be done at a separate time. Sam knew what Tiger Man received for his services and would make the figure considerably higher, out of respect.

'I am very pleased,' Sam said. 'If it is not inconvenient for you, you will begin as of this moment.'

Tiger Man nodded, finished his drink. 'Yes,' he said. 'That will be fine.'

*

Clive met his new bodyguard for the first time while Sam was driving him to the embassy. Tiger Man sat in the front passenger seat, saying little, while Sam revealed the identity of the two Thai men who had been watching Clive on the street. The fact that Patterson had assigned a man did not bother Clive much; he simply made a mental note to inquire why Patterson had not told him about the backup. But he was more intrigued with Tiger Man, who seemed to have a perpetual frowning intensity about him and who was constantly watching the cars that passed or the ones which followed, the crowds of people on the street, as if he were prepared to counter an attack at any time.

At the embassy Clive asked Sam to pick him up in a couple of hours and then entered the compound and went directly to reception, where he found that Patterson had arranged an office for his use while he was there, a pleasant enough room in one of the older buildings, with whitewashed walls and a ceiling fan which stirred the air.

Clive had been assigned a young clerk named Tremlett, who reflected the atmosphere here. There was about any British embassy a sense of orderliness, of things in their place, and Tremlett, in his spotless tropical suit, embodied those virtues. Tremlett brought him tea and then delivered a dispatch folder addressed to him which had been delivered by the Queen's Messenger. 'Is there anything else I can do for you at the moment?' Tremlett said.

'Yes,' Clive said. 'Do we have a file on our American cousins stationed in Bangkok?'

'Are you referring to the CIA, sir?'

'Yes.'

'There's no file as such. We know who they are because we maintain complete cooperation with them. That's not precisely correct, sir. It's not complete as such, but there is cooperation.'

Clive described Garvin to him while Tremlett absorbed

160

the information with a concentrated frown. 'Does he sound familiar?'

'I must say he doesn't. But he could be assigned here on special duty, a temporary.'

'See what you can find out. Send a signal to London and fill them in. See if they have any information.'

'Shall I have photographs made?'

'That would take too long.' He leaned back in the chair, which creaked with age. 'Also, if Colonel Patterson is around, tell him I would like to see him.'

'Yes, sir.'

Tremlett departed. Clive drank his tea and opened the large envelope which was full of research on Iris Marston, a thorough dossier which included a series of eight-by-ten glossy photographs. One of them showed a pretty and lively lass astride a white horse at an equestrian class; another caught her dressed in a gown for a ball. There was also a formal photograph designed to make her attractively demure. But her irrepressibility shone through all the pictures, a mischievous expression of great vitality. She was blonde, her hair long, her face bearing a strong resemblance to her father's. She was not exactly beautiful, certainly not a stunner, but she was full of a lively grace. He was touched by the pictures.

There was an accompanying profile which Clive only partially read before he sent it spinning across the office to dissemble in a shower of paper. Useless trivia, the name of her horse, her preference in foods, the rather untamed streak in her which had seen her sneaking away to a disco in Soho at the age of seventeen.

At that moment the door opened without a knock and Patterson came in, dressed in a tailored uniform, carrying a leather swagger stick. He smiled at the scattered papers. 'The high wind of frustration,' he said. 'A usual climate about this place.' He sat down, propped his polished leather Wellingtons on the edge of the desk, then thought better of it and poured himself a cup of tea. 'I just flew back from Aranyaprathet,' he said, adding cream to the cup. 'The Thai Fourth Cavalry keeps expecting an

161

invasion of Vietnamese troops, so they have a major force at the border. I keep telling them that the danger lies from within, that they should be about the business of putting down the bush rebels. But they have a different military philosophy.'

'And what do you hear about Marston and his daughter?' Clive said.

Patterson nodded, sipped his tea. 'I haven't been neglecting the home front, old chap,' he said sympathetically. 'I have been running a fine meshed net over the whole of Bangkok. I have double the usual number in the field. They have come up with absolutely nothing. I must say Ross has had a field day with unlimited electronic surveillance in cooperation with our American friends, and there has been absolutely no signal anywhere to indicate that the Russians have the Marstons, even that they are in Bangkok. Whatever the Reds are doing, they are doing bloody well.'

'Did Tremlett ask you about Garvin?'

'I've already called the chief of station here. In typical Yank fashion he pledged complete cooperation and told me absolutely nothing. They may have something going that they want to work by themselves. In any event it's bound to be uncovered or leaked.'

Clive put down his teacup. 'I want you to issue me a Walther and a silencer.'

Patterson looked momentarily surprised. 'I don't think you're going to be in a shooting match, do you?'

'Who knows?' Clive said. 'By the way, why did you assign me a backup without letting me know?'

Patterson was startled. 'Routine,' he said, recovering. He removed his black beret, smoothed the fabric with his fingers. 'I will have to give this weapon business considerable thought,' he went on. 'This is my territory, old chap. I've pissed the boundaries, so to speak. I don't want anything going on here which is not cleared through me first.'

'I am clearing through you. That's why I'm asking for the pistol. Since we are using metaphors so freely, this

162

watched pot is not only going to boil, it's going to explode,' Clive said. 'When it does, I intend to be ready. Now either you issue me a pistol or I'll pick one up on the street.'

Patterson thought about it a moment, then nodded. 'Very well,' he said. 'Then I shall issue you one, of course.' He stood up. 'We should have a signal from London on Mr. Garvin sometime today. In the meantime, if you need anything, Tremlett's a good man and entirely at your disposal.' He scratched his chin. 'You're entirely right, old chap. When things are this quiet with our Russian friends, they're certainly up to something. But we'll see.'

He left the office. Clive looked after him. The thought was already in his head. He had requested the pistol on impulse, without knowing why until this moment. If none of the elaborate systems, the entrenched bureaucracies, the government organizations could solve this problem, then he would take it on himself.

He picked up one of the pictures of Iris Marston from the floor. He found that happy smile unbearable.

15

LONDON

'Do come in, Mr. Pymm,' Sir John said. 'Ross should be along shortly.'

'Delighted to be here,' Pymm said, having a look at the slide projector set up on the table, at the screen on the far wall. He was an immense man, close to three hundred pounds, but he carried himself well for a man of seventy. Pymm prided himself on having every one of his own teeth and remarkable eyesight that still had no need of glasses. He had been retired for seven years now, but he was still called in occasionally to demonstrate his expertise on the CIA. He had spent years in Washington, and when it came to the identification of American agents, he had no peer. He described them as his walking collectibles, and his flat in Soho had turned into something of a private museum of memorabilia, photographs, and great stacks of papers from which it was his intention to write his memoirs.

'May I offer you a drink while we're waiting?' Sir John said.

Pymm eased his immense bulk into a chair, settling in. 'Some tea and a jelly bun, if you would be so kind,' he said. Sir John summoned Staff, passed the order while Pymm looked over the room. 'Remarkable how little this place has changed,' he said. 'Now, while we're waiting, what is old Pymm going to be able to do for his chaps?'

'We need identification on a cousin in Bangkok.'

'Bangkok, is it? An interesting place, that.'

Ross arrived at the same time as the tea and the jelly bun. He went through the formality of shaking hands with Pymm, but it was evident to Sir John that Ross was steaming. Ross was carrying the carrousel of slides, which he slammed into the viewer with a gruff precision.

'Bloody Yanks,' he said.

'Then you got nowhere,' Sir John said.

'They had the attitude that I was popping by to offer them help and they don't need any,' Ross said. 'I explained to them that they were stepping on our operation, and they pretended absolute and total ignorance.'

Pymm leaned over his plate, took a bite of the jelly bun, smiled. 'You will develop a tolerance for them as you grow older, Mr. Ross,' he said with a smile. 'After all, they have a lot to put up with. Dreadful political situation, you know. One president wants this; the next wants that. They are forced to do some terribly silly things.' A few crumbs fell onto his ample lap. He brushed them off. 'Now kindly fill me in. The source of the photographs.'

'An intercept,' Ross said. 'A minor source in the Russian Embassy in Bangkok. Sent by facsimile.'

'How very clever,' Pymm said. 'I could have used that technology in my time.' He consumed the rest of the jelly bun, washed it down with tea, nodded to Sir John. 'Shall we have a look?'

Sir John clicked out the lights and Ross projected an image onto the screen. It showed Clive, a woman, and the American sitting at a table. Pymm leaned forward, pursed his lips in concentration. 'There's our Mr. Clive, of course, and an absolute stunner of a woman,' he said almost to himself, ruminating, 'and so the third person must be the gentleman in question.' He scratched his chin. 'So familiar-looking, quite like a relative you know belongs to you but can't quite place.' He looked to Ross. 'Do you have a closer angle?'

Ross clicked the next picture into place, a grainy enlargement of the man's face. Pymm studied it intently, then leaned back. 'The thinning hair. That's what threw me. Also, he wore a mustache when he was younger. Looks fit now, don't you think?'

'You recognize him then?' Sir John said.

'Of course. Charles Edwin Randolph. Born in Muncie, Indiana, sometime about 1930. Far Eastern desk in Washington during the early sixties. Sent into the field on special assignment at least three times that I know of. During the Vietnamese War.'

'Specialist?' Sir John said, turning on the lights.

'General utility man,' Pymm said. 'Used to organize counter resistance among the hill tribes in Southeast Asia. Thought up insurgency projects with terrible names. What's his cover in Bangkok?'

'An American father looking for his MIA son.'

'That effort sounds a wee bit tardy if you know my meaning,' Pymm said. 'But any pot's a good one if it holds the water and can stand the heat. Is he alone? Does he have a team?'

'Alone, as far as we know,' Ross said.

Pymm scratched his ample chin. 'That's surprising, but don't be fooled,' he said. 'He wouldn't be there unless it's terribly important.' He reflected a moment. 'Americans, an interesting lot. Well, if there's nothing more that old Pymm can do for you, I'll be on my way.'

'We appreciate your effort, Mr. Pymm,' Sir John said.

Once Pymm was gone, Sir John tapped his fingertips together, almost an attitude of attentive prayer. Ross was still maintaining his glum petulance as he took the slides from the machine and put them into a small slotted box. 'So we add another element, do we?' Sir John said. 'The cousins have joined the game. But they could not be interested in our errant Queen's Messenger, could they, Mr. Ross? The age of chivalry is past. They wouldn't be interested in the damsel in distress. So it is up to us to determine whether their game has simply crossed ours by coincidence or whether, like Hamlet, we have a play within a play.'

'Whatever it is, they're not saying.'

'For the moment,' Sir John said. 'But that's only because our communications with them have been on the wrong level.' He glanced down at the crumbs of the jelly bun which Pymm had left strewn across the carpet. Everything had its minor drawbacks, requiring tidying up. 'Get a signal off to Harry Patterson with the identification. I'll make a personal call on the American chief of station,' Sir John said with pleasant determination. 'If theirs is a private game, then we'll not interfere. But if they're playing along with us, then we shall want to have the rules crystal clear.'

BANGKOK

Clive spent the afternoon at the hotel. He saw Liz only briefly when she stopped by his room to report on the progress of her story about Mr. Garvin. She was quite impressed with Garvin's sincerity, was convinced that he was exactly what he seemed to be, took the time to make a date for dinner, and then was off.

At two o'clock there was a call from Boris suggesting a meeting at Wat Po at three, when he would be there playing his role of cultural attaché and conducting a group of Russian doctors on a tour of the city. Within two minutes of Boris's call there was a telephone message from the embassy asking him to get in touch with Mr. Grayson, a code summoning him to contact Patterson for a message.

Clive went to the lobby and from a safe telephone first put in a call to Sam, telling him to bring the car around. Then he rang the embassy, and Patterson was on the line within thirty seconds.

'We have a positive identification from London,' Patterson said. 'Your hunch was ratified. We have a visitor from Washington whose name is Charles Edwin Randolph. Specialist in counterinsurgency, hill tribes.'

'I'll follow up.'

'Not for the moment, old chap. The high factotum himself wishes to do a bit of conferring in London to set the rules straight. It will provide us a bit of one-upmanship if Mr. Randolph is instructed to introduce himself to you.'

'I'll give him twenty-four hours,' Clive said.

He went outside to wait for Sam and was embarrassed to see Tiger Man occupying a chair over near the transportation desk. The car pulled up almost immediately, and Tiger Man moved to open the back door for him and then climbed into the passenger seat.

'I have an appointment at Wat Po,' Clive said.

'Yes, sir,' Sam said. 'Which gate, sir?'

'I have no idea,' Clive said. 'We'll try the main gate and go from there.' He looked to Tiger Man, who once again was devoting all his efforts to a survey of the bewildering traffic. Only now did he notice the effects of all of Tiger Man's years in the ring. A small piece of his left earlobe was missing, and there was a thin scar that ran from his temple all the way down to his jawbone where the side of a foot had caught him unaware.

'I suggest we rethink this bodyguard business,' Clive said. 'I appreciate your efforts, but the danger is simply not that great while I'm at the hotel.'

Tiger Man's expression did not change, and Clive realized that his English was not good enough to allow him to understand.

'We can change that, of course, if you wish,' Sam said, covering, pretending that the words were meant for him. 'We will simply provide protection when you're outside the hotel.'

'That would be best,' Clive said, and let it go.

When they reached the main Wat Po gate on Maharat Road, Clive groaned inwardly that he had not arranged a specific meeting place within the spacious grounds and the rambling complex of buildings. There were four black limousines parked along the street, the liveried chauffeurs all standing beneath the shade of a banyan tree. They were all tall, stout men with ramrod spines, certainly Russians. They stood smoking cigarettes and chatting. Boris and his visiting delegates would be someplace inside, somewhere in the crowds of saffron-robed monks, students, and people on crutches here to be healed.

Clive was about to get out when Sam said something to Tiger Man in Thai. Tiger Man popped out of the car and began to move very quickly. His right leg appeared to be slightly bent, as if a bone had been broken and then reset incorrectly. He disappeared into a crowd of Japanese tourists led by a girl with a malfunctioning green bullhorn which gave her a mechanical stutter as she led her civilian troops with a small green flag tied to the end of a stick.

'Tiger Man will locate the Russians for you,' Sam said. 'He knows the appearance of Mr. Ludov.'

'I didn't tell you I was going to meet Boris here.'

'That is just my sense of logic,' Sam said. 'I apologize if I am too presuming, but it is my business to know what goes on in Bangkok. That way it saves much time.'

'Much time,' Clive echoed with a sigh. He saw Tiger Man limping back through the gate, moving very quickly. He opened Clive's door.

'It is all much safe,' he said with a slight bow. 'The man you wish with which to speak is . . .' He paused, could not think of the English words, spoke to Sam in a flood of colloquial Thai which Clive could not follow.

'Mr. Ludov is at the X-ray tree,' Sam said. 'Do you wish me to conduct you?'

'I can find it,' Clive said. He made a slight bow to Tiger Man. 'Thank you.'

Clive was sweating profusely by the time he passed a building decorated with chips of multicolored porcelain and went into a cobblestoned courtyard with a bell tower. There was always a distinctive smell to the old wats, the lingering fragrance of the millions of joss sticks burned here over the centuries which seemed to permeate the stone and concrete and plaster which exuded its own damp smell of decay. Finally, he spotted the Russians, a group of nine or ten men dressed in business suits gathered around the massive tangled trunks of a single sacred banyan tree decorated with X-ray films hanging from wires, put there by desperately ill Thais in the hope of miraculous healing. One doctor had removed an X-ray from the tree and was holding it up to the light, his fingers probing the shadows of some unknown man's chest cavity while he carried on an animated conversation with a colleague.

Boris was standing to one side, impeccably dressed in a dark suit he wore out of respect for the visiting doctors. When he spotted Clive, he appeared to brighten. He spoke to one of the doctors, excused himself, walked over to Clive, and grasped him by the elbow.

'If you don't mind, we'll talk elsewhere,' he said with a smile.

They walked toward the main building with its ornate roof. They passed a line of Thai people on crutches and pallets waiting for the ministrations of a robed priest standing on a stone step, pouring a tin dipper full of water from a green plastic bucket onto the prostrate form of a woman who lay on the sidewalk. The priest was chanting. He seemed bored. Water and words, and the woman's relatives picked her up and moved her on while a man with withered legs took her place.

Boris stepped to one side to avoid the splash of water. He laughed slightly. 'Perhaps I should let the monk pour water on me,' he said. 'They would do as well as those doctors under the banyan tree. They think of the body as a machine put together with plumbing and wiring. You should listen to them talk sometime. If it's not wiring and plumbing, then it's dachas and automobiles.'

A Thai girl approached Boris with an accordion fold of picture postcards which rippled open in a long string of garish colors. Boris ignored her. 'And they all insist on wearing business suits, even in this roasting climate. So I am forced to do the same.'

They entered the building which housed the enormous reclining Buddha, 169 feet of him, the huge face carved in what was supposed to be a beatific expression. There were small altars down the length of the figure, in front of the railing where a few Thai worshippers were kneeling, burning joss sticks, clapping their hands to attract Buddha's attention.

'I have respect for the Buddhist religion,' Boris said. 'Even if their statuary is not to my taste.' They passed an old woman rattling a long, thin box full of fortune sticks until one slid out through a hole. 'Nirvana,' Boris said. 'Not a bad idea when one considers it. To lie down and enter a blissful state of nothingness.'

They reached the far end of the reclining Buddha, the soles of the huge feet serving as a wall for a private alcove.

'You're being sent home then,' Clive said. 'That accounts for the philosophical mood.'

Boris nodded, mopped his sweating face with a handkerchief. 'In a month. But to be honest, I am not sure where home is. I've spent most of my adult life in the field. You are my enemy, and yet I'm more comfortable with you than I am with my supposed countrymen out there. It's a true dilemma.'

'Are you prepared to deal for the Marstons?' Clive said.

'You see?' Boris said, as if the question had proved something. 'You move straight to the point. No indirection.' He frowned slightly, peered around the massive carved feet. The aisle in front of the Buddha was empty for at least fifty feet. There were no pilgrims or tourists moving in his direction. He lit a cigarette and inhaled it with a great sense of relief. 'The doctors I'm with won't permit smoking. They drink enough to riddle their livers and lecture me about my lungs.' He took another drag on the cigarette. 'I'm prepared to deal for the Marstons.'

'A trade then. Whom do we have that you want?'

'No trade,' Boris said. 'A private transaction, no questions, no explanations. Let's just say I can arrange for you to have them.'

'How much do you want?'

'My pension will be terrible,' Boris said. 'If I had stayed at a desk in Moscow, I could have lined my pockets. But a field man is at a disadvantage.' He squinted against the sting of the smoke, peered around the edge of the feet again. 'I want a hundred thousand pounds.'

'That's a bit steep.'

Boris smiled a patient, knowing smile. 'I know to the pence what you have in your contingency funds, just as you know how much we have in ours. That amount can come out of Hong Kong. You will be required to signal London, of course, but the payment will be routine.'

'Then you also know the requirements. Either Patterson or I will have to see them, both of them. Alive.'

'I would prefer to have you do it, my friend. The colonel is too impulsive. He might decide to bring his troops and make a small war out of it.' He sucked the last bit of smoke

171

out of the cigarette, ground it out beneath his shoe. 'I will appreciate it if you deposit fifty thousand pounds in a Swiss account for me. I shall give you the number and the bank later. Then I will need fifty thousand pounds in any size notes you like. I shall also expect your bookkeeping to show that only fifty thousand pounds were paid.' He sighed. 'This will have to be done within twenty-four hours, I'm afraid.'

'The sooner the better,' Clive said. 'When I have the approval, I'll send the message through Nikolai.'

Boris barked a laugh despite himself. 'He is pretty obvious,' he said. 'He is also too ambitious and will come to no good end. But do send the message through him. It will alarm him to know that he was spotted.' He rolled his wrist, checked his watch. 'I must be getting back,' he said. 'I'll walk you to your car.'

As they walked back through the courtyard of the wat, Boris took a deep breath. 'I shall miss all this,' he said with a note of sadness. 'It stinks like all the countries in this part of the world, but it is a familiar stink.'

They reached the gate, where Sam had pulled the car up to the curb. Boris nodded at him, smiled. 'You are in good hands, my friend,' he said to Clive. 'Sam is the best driver around.' He looked to Sam again. 'You should be careful whom you drive for,' he said with mock sternness. 'The English are noted for underpaying.'

'I take care of myself and my family,' Sam said. 'I find the English very generous.'

'I hope for your sake that is true,' Boris said, smiling. 'Nevertheless, be careful.' He turned to Clive. 'I shall look forward to hearing from you,' he said. 'Tomorrow noon?'

'At the latest.'

Clive watched Boris saunter back through the gates of the wat. What Boris said was quite true. He would be going back to Russia, but he would not be going home. It was only after Boris had disappeared in the crowds that Tiger Man came out of the grounds.

'Nobody follow,' he said to Clive with great seriousness. 'You are in the clearing.'

16

BANGKOK

It was not an easy thing to know if a man was faking, Boris realized. He sat in the back of the limousine with Marston sitting on the far side of the car, inert as far as Boris could see, except for the eyes. There was something very disturbing about Marston's eyes. The pupils were flat and steel-colored with a life of their own. He sat with his hands folded in his lap, freshly shaved, his coarse blond hair rather raggedly trimmed, dressed in a fresh tropical suit which was slightly too large for him. But then Marston was not the same man now as he had been when Boris encountered him on the train platform in Mongolia. He had lost weight. In that context he was slightly too small for the suit.

'Are you comfortable, Captain Marston?' Boris said. 'I can set the air conditioning to make it cooler if you wish.'

Marston said nothing.

Boris looked out the window. They were approaching the dock area, a spot on the Chao Phraya River where a lumberyard had burned and not yet been rebuilt, affording privacy for the old rice barge tied up at the pier. Boris took a packet of cigarettes out of his pocket. He held it out to Marston. 'You might enjoy a smoke, Captain Marston,' he said. Marston did not move. Boris shrugged. 'I'm sure you won't mind if I have one.' He lit one, inhaled the smoke, replaced the pack in his pocket. 'I know that you understand every word that I'm saying to you. You have been abused, traumatized. You are a proud man, and it is that pride which has kept you from telling us what we want to know thus far.' He inhaled the smoke again. 'I do not like for these things to happen to you. I am a civilized

173

man, but you must realize how important this is to us. There is something even more painful ahead. I would like to spare you. If you decide now to tell me what I want to know, nobody can blame you. You can be back in England in a matter of days. That would be very pleasant for you, wouldn't it?'

Marston remained motionless.

Finally, the car drew up to the pier and Boris could see the dim rounded shape of the top of the barge. He sighed. It was a shame that Nikolai was going to be the man for this unfortunate chore. He did not like Nikolai. The man took too much personal pleasure in inflicting pain. The car stopped, and the driver came around to Marston's door, opened it. Boris helped the driver lift Marston from the car, put him on his feet. He did not like the feel of the man. All of Marston's muscles were rigid, hard as stone, but as they started moving him toward the barge, his legs began to work, automatically bearing his own weight.

They took him up the gangplank and down into the cargo hold, where bamboo curtains had been dropped from the edge of the rounded roof to the hull to ensure privacy. Nikolai was already there, and the Marston girl had been readied. She lay naked on a table, spread-eagled, her hands and feet tied to the corners. Boris was startled to see how pale her flesh was in the light of the single kerosene lantern, how young she was.

She stirred on the table, testing the ropes that bound her arms. *Now they are finally going to kill me,* she thought. *I'm only nineteen years old, and I don't want to die.* She pulled at the ropes on her legs. *I'll never be married. I'll never have children.*

In her terror she began to breathe too quickly. She couldn't get enough oxygen. She felt as she had done when she was eight years old and her parents had taken her sailing off the coast of Naples. A sudden sweep of the boom in a freak gust of wind had struck her on the head, and she had found herself, in the next moment, deep in the water with no air to breathe and darkness everywhere. And in that darkness someone was waiting for her. Her lungs were bursting. Panic filled her. Fighting blindly, she threshed her arms and legs to keep the presence away from her, for she knew it must be the Angel of Death. At the last moment she broke free of the water and was amazed at the wash of blinding light around her head as she sucked the air into her lungs greedily.

Now she was submerged again, could not breathe, filled with terror at the two men who had come to watch her die.

She heard the voice of the athletic man who was whipping a lather of soap in a small bucket of hot water. 'I am ready to proceed at any time,' he said.

'I have no doubt of that,' one of the new men said. 'But I hope there will be no need for your services.' A warm hand touched her bare shoulder, and she flinched involuntarily. 'Open your eyes, my dear. I think you have a pleasant surprise in store.'

She kept them closed. From her nightmares as a child she remembered the appearance of the Angel of Death, who was a skeletal man dressed in a black robe. There was a picture of him on the wall in Miss Penrose's Bible class. She had studied that picture, and she had imagined he had icicles for fingers and dark hollows where the eyes should have been, and if she opened her eyes now, she would see him over her.

'Come, dear,' the man's voice said, a soft purr like the vicar at church. 'Do open your eyes. See for yourself.'

And against her better judgment she opened her eyes to a narrow slit and at first could see nothing more than the light of the kerosene lantern catching on the fine golden strands of hair across her eyes and beyond that the silhouettes of two heads. And one was familiar, but in the dark she could not see clearly. The second man had a soft middle-aged face with a melancholy smile. He reached out and held up a kerosene lantern next to the familiar head, and suddenly she began to laugh, with the same pain as the moment she had broken free of the strangling water, the light so intense her eyes ached with it.

'Daddy,' she said. 'Oh, my God, Daddy.'

But her father did not speak, did not move, only stood

there while the smaller man studied her father's face, patted him on the arm. 'It's your daughter, Marston. You see her, don't you? You see your little girl.'

Her father did not speak. She struggled against the ropes. 'Daddy, you're not going to let them do this to me. Daddy, for God's sake.'

'Your father is having trouble remembering you,' Boris said. His eyes were fixed on Marston's face. Was there some dim flicker of recognition in those eyes?

'What have you done to him?' Iris said, fighting the tears, the mounting terror from those eyes which looked right through her. 'Daddy, haven't you come to save me? Don't you know me? Please, oh, my God, please.'

The smaller man leaned over the table and cupped her face in his two hands so she could not avoid looking at him. There was a vague sadness on his face. 'Listen to me carefully, dear,' he said. 'Your father will not talk to us. He has information which we must have, and he insists on keeping it to himself. I wish you to tell him to cooperate with me. The moment he does, I will release both of you. You can be on a plane and on your way home by tomorrow.'

'Untie me and I will.'

'Persuade him.'

'You're not going to untie me?'

The face shook a negative smile. 'Words will untie you.'

'Please, Daddy,' she said, the tears rolling down the side of her face. 'Please tell them what they want.' She looked at her father and saw the grim set to his mouth, the way he had looked after her mother's death, withdrawn from the world. 'Don't go away from me again, Daddy,' she said. 'We'll be together and I'll go to university if you want and I'll cook and we won't need a housekeeper anymore. I'm sorry for the trouble I've caused you. But please be with me now. Don't let them hurt me. Tell them and take me home.'

Marston's face did not change expression, but something was different, something in the eyes. Boris felt the stirring of a great relief. He had come to respect this man

and certainly did not want the girl to suffer. He lit a
cigarette, put his hand on Marston's shoulder. He could
feel no stir of life, but there was some change. He knew it.
He motioned to the driver, and between them they moved
Marston to a straight-backed chair facing the table.
Marston sat down rigidly, put his hands in his lap,
staring straight ahead.

'Shall I begin?' Nikolai said.

'Reluctantly I give you permission.'

Carrying the bucket, Nikolai approached the girl with a
smile on his face. She closed her eyes against it,
shuddered at the touch of his hand running over her
breasts, the nipples, the ribs and the flat stomach. She felt
his mouth kiss her stomach, and she pulled away from
him, beyond coherence. 'Beautiful, beautiful,' the man
was saying. She could feel the soapy water on her pubic
hair, the violating hands, and she heard the throaty little
sounds the man was making. She felt so tired, so heavy.

Boris pulled up a chair at a right angle next to Marston,
leaning over to talk to him in a confidential tone. 'You can
stop pretending,' he said in a lulling voice. 'It is time for
you to realize that you are permitted to stop pretending.
This is your daughter, your little girl. I know how much
you love her. You don't want to see her suffer for the sake
of your pride.' Boris cupped the cigarette in his fingers,
took another drag. 'She is important to you, this daughter
of yours.'

There was a sudden intake of breath from the table.
Boris glanced at Nikolai. The knife had just been opened.
The blade had an obscene glint to it.

'You can stop him,' Boris whispered to Marston. 'At any
moment you can stop him.'

Marston did not move.

'Hold perfectly still, my darling,' Nikolai said to the
girl. He lowered the blade to the mons Veneris, made the
first scrape. The girl made a feeble attempt to jerk away. A
red tinge appeared in the lather. 'See what you did?'
Nikolai chided. 'You made me cut you. Now I am telling
you, you must be perfectly motionless. Not a move.'

She felt the hand between her legs, and her mind began to dim. *Oh, Daddy,* she said, weeping, in words that would not make it out of her mouth. *Please help me, Daddy.* All she saw in the darkness was that grim-set mouth and that expressionless face and those eyes that looked through her without seeing. Suddenly she threshed with all her might, and one hand came free. With a total consuming terror she grabbed the man's hair and yanked his head around. She'd hurt him. She could see it on his face. Then there was the pain, the terrible, wrenching pain, and in that fraction of a second she ceased struggling, filled her lungs with air one last time, and slowly surrendered to the dark.

Before Boris could make a move, the knife in Nikolai's hand had flashed upward, plunged into the white flesh immediately below the rib cage with a great gout of blood. The girl fell back, her body still twitching slightly, the fingers still entangled in Nikolai's hair. Cursing to himself, Nikolai pried her fingers loose, and her hand fell backward, the arm dangling off the table.

A waste, Boris thought. *A tragic waste.* He thought he would be sick to his stomach. He waited a moment and took a deep breath. He finished the cigarette, turned to Marston. Marston's face was dead white. His hands were passive in his lap. His eyes closed. Boris reached out, slapped him on the cheek, not a hard blow but a stinging one.

Marston fell forward, slumping out of the chair onto the floor, unconscious.

'She left me no choice. You saw it yourself,' Nikolai said, demanding, his face flushing.

Boris did not speak for a long moment. He was thinking through the possibilities. 'She was our last chance of breaking him if anything could break him.' He looked at the table. Too much blood. It seemed impossible that such a small woman could contain so much. 'You will clean everything up,' Boris said. 'You will scrub the deck and the table until your back aches with it. Then you will arrange to take the body and dump it into a klong. No place near here.'

Nikolai had put the bloody knife into the bucket. He was scrubbing at the blood which had covered his arm and flecked his shirt. 'You will never be able to convince anyone it was my fault.'

That was to be expected, Boris thought. The men like Nikolai could be counted on to defend themselves, even in the face of gross stupidity. But Nikolai would never climb in the ranks, Boris would see to that. Later. But now there were other things to be considered. For the intelligent man there was no final failure, only the opportunity to find a viable alternative. 'There is still another possibility,' Boris said. The plan was forming in his mind as he spoke it. 'If we can't bring him around, then perhaps his friends can.'

'You're suggesting that we turn him loose?'

'It's not this man himself I'm interested in,' Boris said. 'I want what he has in his mind.' He lit another cigarette, looking down at the unconscious Marston sprawled on the wooden floor. 'He won't tell me, but it's always possible he will confide in Clive.' He paused. 'And if he tells Clive, then the information will be available to us. Clive is a bright man and a loyal one, but as has been demonstrated before, Clive has no tolerance for pain.'

He stood up, spoke to the driver. 'Find a place for Captain Marston somewhere in this stinking barge. It won't even be necessary to bind him.' He turned back to Nikolai. 'You have made a most serious mistake in judgment,' he said. 'But while I am deciding what will happen to you, you will finish the work you have been assigned. A little humility might do you a world of good.'

At seven o'clock, Clive stopped by Liz's room to take her to dinner, only to find that she was sitting at her typewriter, wearing a dressing gown, pounding away, muttering oaths under her breath and Xing out whole sentences. 'Have yourself a drink,' she said almost unintelligibly, a pencil clutched in her teeth. 'I'm about through.'

'A fine thing,' he said. 'I invite you out to dinner and here you are, still hard at it.'

179

'The problems of the working girl,' she said. 'I won't be long.'

He mixed a drink from the minifridge, sat down in a comfortable chair in a loose sprawl, feeling relieved for the first time in days. His work was almost finished. Liz stood up, ripped the sheet of paper from the typewriter, read it with a frown. 'A damned good story if I say so myself,' she said. She folded the paper, stuck it in an envelope. 'Fix me a drink, love, just soda water for the moment while I call and see if a messenger is available.'

He searched through the minifridge while she made a brief call, and by the time he had put ice in the soda water, she was sitting on the couch. She smiled as he handed her the drink. 'A free evening?'

'God, yes,' he said. 'I've had enough of business. I want light conversation, any new jokes you've heard, and a good dinner.'

'I think we should have something of a celebration,' she said. 'You won't be dining with just any ordinary stringer, no standard ill-paid writer. I got a raise today, two hundred Hong Kong dollars a week.'

He leaned over and kissed her lightly. 'Then we'll do something special tonight. What would you like? Chinese food?'

'We'll see,' she said. 'I have a new outfit. And now, if you will excuse me for a few minutes, I'll get into it.'

He watched her go into the bathroom, lit a cigarette, feeling quite content to be there. There was a knock on the door, and Liz called to him from the bathroom.

'Would you get that, darling?' she said. 'And turn out the room lights, if you please.'

'What?'

'Don't ask questions.'

He shrugged, turned out the room lights and opened the door, and immediately could see why she had wanted the room dark. For there stood a Thai waiter with a beaming smile and a dinner cart decorated with flaming sparklers. He laughed aloud, stood aside as the waiter trundled the cart into the room. Only then did Liz come out of the bathroom, wearing a pink gossamer gown with a brilliant red feather boa wrapped around her neck and trailing down her back, as radiant as he had ever seen her.

'Surprise,' she said.

'Oh, it's that all right,' he said, delighted. 'Where in the hell did you find the sparklers?'

'It wasn't easy,' she said. 'Try to find the Thai word for sparklers sometime. Or simply try to explain to somebody who doesn't speak English what a sparkler is.' She turned to the waiter. 'Did you bring the martinis?'

'Yes, madame,' the waiter said. 'Very special. Do you wish me to pour, madame?'

'Absolutely,' she said. When the glasses were full, she handed one to Clive. 'Do you remember the first time we had martinis together?'

'How could I forget?' he said with a laugh. 'The day you took a swim off the Star Ferry, just to win a bet.'

'A ten-pound bet,' she said. 'A not inconsiderable sum for a little impromptu swim.'

He touched her glass, drank. 'Ah, the nonsense of those days,' he said. 'Marvelous.'

'And here's to the present as well,' she said. 'A whole free night. No soul-searching, no analysis.'

'I'll drink to that.'

The waiter had laid out the table with a linen cloth, steaks, a platter of fruit, vegetables, and bread, even a fresh rose in a stem vase. 'Shall I serve the dinner, madame?' the waiter said.

'No, thanks,' Liz said. This time she poured three martinis, one of which she handed to the waiter quite solemnly. 'To the King of Thailand,' she said, raising her glass. The waiter downed the martini, poured another round himself, proposed a toast to the Queen of England and a third round to the President of the United States. He was all smiles and giggling by the time he left the room.

'One further touch,' she said, rummaging around in the drawer of the small table for two disparate, awkward-looking candles, which she placed in ceramic holders on the table. She lit them with a match.

'You've thought of everything,' he said.

'I tried.'

He seated her and then attacked his steak with much relish, suddenly ravenous. They talked about the old days with a great deal of laughter, the richness of life they had shared in their days together, people they had known who had not come to his mind for what seemed forever. And finally, when they had finished dinner, they came into each other's arms without a word and he made love to her on the bed, marveling at the feel of her until the time came when he was carried out of himself and they came together in a frantic rush and then continued to lie together, still embracing. 'Ah, you bloody Yank,' she breathed with delight into his ear.

'You make it sound like a blessing for once,' he said, his nose against her ear.

'It is,' she said. 'It's the Englishman in you who does the thinking,' she said. 'But it's the Yank who makes love.'

'Love it is,' he said. 'Nothing more, nothing less.'

There was a comfort in the pale, inconstant glow of the candles. He ran his hand across the luminous flesh of breasts and stomach, feeling very proprietary. 'Would you like another drink?'

'Do we still have martinis?'

'I believe so, yes.' He left the bed, poured the drinks, touched her glass with his. 'To life,' he said.

'To life.'

He lay back on the bed, his head propped on his hand. He drank the martini. 'Tell me how things really are with you, Liz.'

'Fine, on the whole,' she said thoughtfully, her fingers tracing the outline of his jaw, his lips. 'I don't know what the future holds. I don't plan ahead anymore because when I do, life piles up on me. There's a Chinese proverb in there someplace, but I don't have the slightest idea where.' Slowly she drew a line down his chest. 'I don't want to be serious anymore if I can help it. I have a dark side, you know. Doubts, fears, terrors, but when I work it right, I can always put them off until tomorrow.' Her fingers traced the thin scar that ran across his abdomen. 'A clear line of demarcation,' she said.

'What?'

'It's quite obvious,' she said. 'Above the line, English. Below the line, American.'

He laughed aloud, the first time he had been able to regard the scar lightly. 'All American tonight.'

She finished the drink, handed it to him to be placed on the bedside table. 'I think,' she said, 'that I will call a holy man and arrange to have tonight transformed into a three-day holiday.'

He felt a tender stirring, leaned down and kissed her on the mouth, and they made love again, this time languidly, with no great sense of urgency, as if indeed, their time together would last forever. And when they were through, lying side by side in the candlelight, he thought what a marvelous combination of contradictions this woman was, tender, tough, able to experience the moment fully. He thought of Katy, who belonged to a totally different world. It was as if he were now in unexplored territory while she remained in a familiar world in which every square foot of surface was mapped, clocked, timed, so that one always knew how long it would take to get from here to there and what 'there' would be like. No great surprises, annoyances perhaps, predictable difficulties, as if the main solution to all problems had been solved long ago and one had but to look up the answers in the back of the book. But here, of course, in this metaphorical dark side of the moon, dealing with men like Boris, each problem was unique, with no reference points, and solutions were improvised.

To hell with philosophizing. He settled against Liz, her head resting on his arm, caught up in the sweet, fresh smell of her hair and the natural, wild fragrances of her body. He thought she was asleep, she lay so still. But when one of the candles guttered out, she shifted slightly. 'An omen,' she said.

'Good or bad?'

'It's bound to be a good one.'

The telephone rang. Neither of them moved for the longest time until it became apparent that the telephone would not stop ringing until it was answered. 'We might as well bet on it,' she said. 'A hundred bahts says it's for me.'

'You have to give me odds. Two to one. It's your room, after all.'

'It's a deal,' she said.

He picked up the telephone. It was Garvin, and from the moment Clive heard the tone to his voice, all frivolity fled.

'This is Garvin, Mr. Clive.'

'Yes?'

'I don't like disturbing you, but the two of us need to talk.'

'In the morning then.'

'Afraid not. It has to be now. Something has happened I think you're going to have to take care of. I'll meet you in the lobby. Ten minutes.'

Clive considered a moment, then agreed. 'Ten minutes.' He put the telephone back on the hook, inwardly disturbed, letting none of it show.

'Apparently I lost my bet,' Liz said.

'Right,' he said. 'It was Garvin, and he wanted to speak to me.'

'Why in the hell would he want to talk to you at this time of night?' she said, curious.

'I have no idea,' he said. 'But I'll let you know. And you can pay me later.'

17

BANGKOK

Before Clive met Garvin in the lobby, he put in a call to
have Sam bring the car around, determined to have his
own transportation. He was not in the best of moods when
he met Garvin, but he set aside his irritation almost
immediately. Garvin had changed both his clothes and
his personality. He was no longer a man searching for his
son. He was now dressed in a tropical suit, and as he
shook hands, his eyes were making a sweep of the lobby
automatically.

'I'm sorry to disturb you, Clive,' he said, 'but there's
something going on that I think you should see.' He led
the way outside. 'I have a car waiting.'

'I've called for my car,' Clive said. He could see the
headlights of the Pontiac turning into the long driveway
from Rama I Road.

'What I have to say to you is confidential,' Garvin said.
'I don't like the idea of talking in the presence of your
driver.'

'He's reliable,' Clive said.

Garvin shrugged, conceding. 'I've been instructed to
identify myself to you,' he said, his midwestern accent
less pronounced, his voice flat and unemotional. 'I'm
Randolph, CIA. But you already knew that, didn't you?'

'We checked you out,' Clive said. 'What are you doing
here, Randolph?'

'We'll get to that later. In the meantime, I would
appreciate it if you continued to call me Garvin.'

The car pulled up at the circular turnaround, and Sam
popped out to open the doors to the back seat. Clive could
see the omnipresent shape of Tiger Man occupying the

front, on the passenger side. Garvin frowned. 'I don't like this arrangement,' he said.

'It will have to do,' Clive said.

'Where would you like to go, sir?' Sam said.

'This is Mr. Garvin, Sam. He will give you directions.'

'We'll cross the Phraphuthayotfar Bridge,' Garvin said. 'Continue down Pracha Tipok Road until you make the circle at the statue. Then down Tak Sin Road. I'll direct you from there.'

'Very good, sir,' Sam said, using his best manners. Once the car was under way, he turned on the radio as if to provide privacy for the conversation in the back seat. Clive lit a cigarette, looked out at the lights as Sam whipped the car around the turn, and shot out into the congested traffic on Rama I Road, his horn blaring.

'It's obvious you know Bangkok very well,' Clive said.

'I've been here often enough,' Garvin said, with a tone of weariness in his voice. 'After the war I was sent in to help democratize the goddamned country. That lasted all of a couple of years. But it was worth trying, I suppose.'

'You're not following protocol, Mr. Garvin,' Clive said. 'You should have made yourself known to Colonel Patterson. This is his territory.'

'I don't like your Colonel Patterson,' Garvin said bluntly. 'I have a basic distrust of Westerners who go native. They have a tendency to make their own rules.' He braced himself as the car shot around a truck and Sam tucked the car into a break in the fast lane. 'But more to the point, you have the information I want.'

'And what would that be?'

'We'll come to that after a while,' Garvin said. 'A favor for a favor. I'm not even sure it's what you're after, but I suspect it may be.' And for the next twenty minutes he would provide no more specifics and Clive abandoned the effort to pin him down. Garvin had spent much of his adult life in this part of the world, and he chatted about Vietnam and Laos and the sorry state of the world while Clive smoked his cigarette and tried to reconcile this man with the stories Clive had heard about him. Somehow

Clive could not see Garvin back in the bush, bare-armed, sitting around a campfire with the wiry tribesmen while he put together his counterinsurgency teams. For Garvin looked like the traditional deskman who would be more at home with theoretical situations than the real.

After they had crossed the bridge and gone as far as the equestrial statue, Garvin leaned forward and tapped Sam on the shoulder. 'When you hit Soi Wat Sutha Road, turn to your left,' Garvin said. He leaned back, lit a cigarette for himself. 'If this is what I think it is, then what you do with it is your own business. You can notify your Colonel Patterson or follow up on your own. We don't care what you do.' He inhaled the smoke, peered out the window as they approached a bridge over the Bang Saikai Klong, leaned forward to speak to Sam again. 'A hard left at the next alleyway,' he said.

The car bounced down a narrow lane, the backside of the rickety wooden buildings fronting on the klong itself. And now Clive became aware of the commotion ahead, mobs of people gathered around a Thai police car with a light spinning on the top. And through the narrow space between two buildings, Clive could see the police boats on the klong, their spotlights sweeping a panorama of boats packed in so solidly that the water taxis had difficulty threading their way through.

'Stop here,' Garvin said suddenly as the car approached the edge of the crowd. He did not get out immediately. 'This may not be what you're looking for at all,' Garvin said. 'I really hope to hell it isn't.'

'You'd better fill me in,' Clive said. 'What's going on here?'

'They just fished the body of a young Caucasian woman out of the klong,' Garvin said soberly.

'My God.' Clive was out of the car in an instant, his heart racing, moving through the crowd, which parted to let him through. He ran down the narrow boardwalk alongside the rickety house which extended on poles out over the muddy water. He dashed up some wooden steps to a porch overlooking the water, so heavily laden with

187

earthenware pots full of flowers that the boards groaned beneath his feet. A half dozen Buddhist monks in saffron robes stood near the slanted plank pier which led to a flat-bottomed wooden boat rocking in the water. The monks were chanting, a droning sound, like reedy flutes. Out on the water a man on the police boat was shouting at the crowds of small boats to disperse, go home. But nobody was moving, for there was the smell of death in the air, a drama being played out with the monks here to exorcise the evil spirits.

Clive heard the wailing of a woman inside the room which fronted the water. He pushed his way through the policemen until he saw an old Thai woman sitting on the wooden floor, her betel-stained mouth uttering low, plaintive moans as she rocked back and forth, hugging herself with frail arms. An army officer stood in front of her, high rank, and it took Clive a moment to recognize him as General Thrup himself, the Mongoose, as he was called. Normal procedure. The death of a *farang* was always serious business, a threat to tourism. It would require diplomacy, a subsequent trail of paper work, letters of condolence and apology and explanation and the fixing of responsibility, the punishment of offenders before the balance could be restored.

The bloody balance.

The general was questioning the woman, but Clive did not hear either the questions or the answers. He approached a police captain, a thin middle-aged man with a mustache, and, introducing himself in Thai, asked to see the body. The captain pointed to a flight of ladder stairs and followed Clive up to the second floor, a shallow room full of debris. The body lay beneath a piece of stained cloth on the floor, and a Thai in a business suit stood nearby, writing on a clipboard. For a moment Clive knew he could not lift that cloth. He had the strong desire to turn around and walk away, to catch the next plane for Australia, never to inquire about what had happened in this old wooden building which groaned and creaked around him. He lit a cigarette, inhaled, nodded to the captain.

'Would you remove the cloth please?'

The captain uncovered the body. Something turned off in Clive at that moment, as if an electrical switch had been thrown, cutting off all his feelings. Iris Marston, yes, certainly, no doubt at all. The girl-woman's body was pale white, bloodless, with small areas which had been eaten away by animals and fish in the muddy waters of the klong. There was one puncture in the area immediately below the rib cage, the skin puckered in now around the edges of the wound. On the soft roundness of the mons Veneris. one area of the pubic hair had been shaved away and there was a slight cut. The face itself was more parody than actual, a distortion of the features he had seen in so many photographs. He experienced the oddest feeling of vacancy, as if the soul of the girl who inhabited this body had simply, at some point, deserted and left it behind.

Clive turned to the detective. 'I have some questions to ask if you would be so kind as to answer,' he said in Thai.

The detective did not look up from his clipboard. 'Who are you?'

Clive produced his diplomatic passport. 'My name is Gordon Clive. I'm with the British Foreign Service.' The detective's eyes flicked up over the edge of the clipboard to examine him. 'Can you determine the time of death?' Clive said.

'I would say she's been dead no more than four or five hours, in the water for perhaps two of those hours.'

'The cause of death?'

'She was stabbed in the heart,' the detective said. 'That would have killed her instantly.'

'Then she wasn't alive when she was dumped into the klong?'

'No. The knife did its work.'

'Can you estimate the type of knife?'

'Not scientifically. I probed the wound. Thin blade, sharp on one edge, perhaps five, six inches long.'

Clive drew in on his cigarette. 'Was she dressed? Was there any jewelry, any ornaments at all?'

'She was fished from the water just as you see her,' the

detective said, his tone of voice suddenly defensive. 'We are very reverential toward the dead. There has never been any question of the honesty of the Thai police.'

'The cut on the mons Veneris, the shaved area. Can you explain that?'

'I cannot,' the detective said. 'I have no idea how or why that came about.' He lit a cigarette.

'May I see where she was found?'

The detective spoke to the captain, then turned back to Clive. 'He will show you.'

Clive followed the captain down the stairs and out onto the dock, the air heavy with the smell of joss sticks. He felt detached, as if he were walking through a surrealistic scene, past the monks and down the gangplank to the boat, while in the background, the frail old woman wailed her story for what must have been the fifth time.

The old woman was a flower seller who lived on a klong and loaded her boat every morning with fresh flowers and occasionally fruit, which she sold to the tourists who came to see the floating market. She had been unable to sleep. Her skin had prickled and crawled, and there was a strange smell to the air, the chill of the presence of evil spirits. She had arisen in the middle of the night, lighted a joss stick, and made a *wai* to the small shrine in her house; then she went outside to make sure her boat had not been stolen. In the light of her lantern she had seen the body of the young woman floating just below the surface of the water, her hair feathered out like bleached water grass, one hand caught in the rope the old woman left dangling from the bow of the boat.

The captain flashed a light onto the surface of the water, and Clive could see the end of that frayed rope in the murky water as it moved to and fro, very slowly, caught in the sluggish current. Clive felt a chill.

The old woman continued to wail her story. She had been frightened out of her wits and had fled immediately to a nearby wat to summon a monk, convinced that the apparition which had seized her boat was an evil water spirit. The monk in turn had sent her to a fortune-teller,

190

who had accompanied the old woman back to her house, observed the body, and after various chants and magic spells had failed to make the body disappear. Only then did the fortune-teller suggest that the old woman call the police, and she did.

'You will leave the body here until we send for it,' Clive said.

'That is not our procedure,' the captain said.

'I don't care about your procedure,' Clive said, abandoning the politeness of the language, his voice very stern. 'She belongs to us. We will take care of her. Do you understand?'

'Yes,' the captain said.

Clive walked back up the plank onto the porch, and only now did he notice that Garvin was waiting patiently near the stairs. Clive went into the room where the Mongoose was bombarding the old woman with quiet questions, trying to pry from her some stray shred of memory concerning a boat she had not seen before or the sound of a motor which was not familiar. He was hoping to glean from her torrent of fearful words some clue as to how the young woman's body had been dumped in the klong. Clive knew he would not get it, for the old woman was obsessed now, convinced that the spirit of the dead girl would inhabit the boat and bring calamity upon anyone who touched it.

He looked around, realized he was wasting his time looking for a telephone in a house where there was no electricity. He joined Garvin on the porch, looked out over the water as a third police boat began to disperse the smaller crafts. The monks were still chanting. The old woman was still wailing.

'Was she yours?' Garvin said.

'Yes,' Clive said.

'I was afraid she was. Sorry.'

Clive led the way back to the car. Neither Sam nor Tiger Man was in evidence, but he had no sooner lit a cigarette than Sam came out of the crowd from one direction and Tiger Man from another. Sam had a strange expression

191

on his face, as if there were something he had to say which could not be voiced in Garvin's presence.

'I offer my apology for the person who did this,' Sam said respectfully. 'I offer an apology that it happened in my country. I am affronted by it.'

Clive nodded. 'It's an evil business. Now I need a place with two things,' Clive said. 'I want a telephone and a drink, in that order.'

'There is a place not five minutes from here,' Sam said.

Once the car had moved away from the crowds, backing around, making its way to the smooth surface of the street, Clive took a deep breath. 'How did you know about this?' he said to Garvin.

'We have our sources in the police department,' Garvin said.

Clive shrugged, did not press him. Momentarily, it seemed, the car came to a stop in front of a low building with an English sign which read 'Hotel.' Clive left Sam and Tiger Man in the car, Garvin in the small bar, and then found an old telephone off the lobby.

He called Patterson at home. He told Patterson that Iris Marston had been found dead, gave him the location where Patterson should send an ambulance to pick up the body, said he would be in touch in the morning. Then, before Patterson had the chance to begin his blustering questions, Clive severed the connection.

He called the Soviet Embassy, asked to speak to Boris Ludov, was informed that Boris Ludov had retired for the night and could not be disturbed. Clive left no message.

The small bar was all but deserted at this time of night. Garvin had picked a table in the far corner of the room and ordered a bottle of bourbon, a pitcher of water, and two glasses.

He poured a stiff drink for Clive and one for himself. Clive downed his without a word, poured himself another. 'All right,' Clive said wearily. 'It's been a long night and more than a shocking one. You have my attention, Mr. Garvin. Now just what in the bloody hell do you want?'

'Charlie Excalibur,' Garvin said simply.

192

'Christ,' Clive said with a snort. 'You and how many others? Why do you want him?'

'We believe he's the key.'

'To what?'

Garvin drank, poured himself another. The whiskey did not relax him. He gave the appearance of being less on guard, but there was a tightness to his words which did not pass Clive unnoticed. Garvin was one determined man.

He leaned back in his chair and began to talk about Vietnam, about the war. The Great Confusion he called it, because nobody knew what the hell was going on at any particular time, not even the commanders in the field, not the American people, for God's sake, who were fed so much contradictory propaganda that they eventually lost faith in any reliable explanation. Even the grunts, the poor sons of bitches who had to fight the war, never had a clear view of why they were there or who the enemy was or what the end result was supposed to be. And some of them smoked dope and some threatened to frag their officers, but for the most part they were just American kids, young men who were doing what they were told to do to the best of their abilities.

'Hell,' Garvin said, 'I spent years up in the hills, organizing groups of good tribesmen who were supposed to go blow the heads off other tribesmen. I had some damn good men who were pulling off raids for us and getting wasted in the process. And if you asked them why they were doing it, they wouldn't have any coherent answer that would make any sense.' He drank again. 'The war was a terrible, tragic waste.'

'Which still doesn't explain why you want Charlie Excalibur.'

'It gets pretty damn close to explaining it,' Garvin said. 'There are still some of us who refuse to forget the war in Vietnam. There were as many betrayals as there were battles. I could give you a dozen examples of strikes in force that were made against an enemy that suddenly vanished. Somebody was letting them know the strikes were coming, not Vietcong observers, not Vietnamese turncoats, but our own men.'

'And you think that Charlie Excalibur can shed light on these betrayals?'

'Yes, I believe that,' Garvin said forcefully. 'I've talked to too many deserters we've picked up over the years. They know all about Charlie Excalibur. He keeps a notebook on the strikes that were called and betrayed before they were completed. He had the information. I know it.'

'You also know about his dispatches over the years.'

'Of course.'

'I sympathize with your efforts,' Clive said. 'But I don't have any unique information about him.'

'You know considerably more than you think. Why do you think his dispatches have been directed to you?'

'He picked up my name from some old diplomatic register. Believe me, Mr. Garvin, this subject has been through thorough analysis. There is no connection.'

'I didn't pick the name Garvin by chance,' Garvin said. 'Charlie Excalibur's real name is William Charles Garvin. He was a marine corporal, and we have his complete history, including the date he decided to walk away from the war for his own reasons. He wrote to you because he knows you personally. You went to school together at Boston University in the sixties.'

'William Garvin?' Clive said, startled. 'I don't remember anybody with that name.'

'Apparently he remembers you. Perhaps you knew him as Bill or Willie.'

Clive shook his head. 'Are you sure this isn't a mistake?'

'Positive.'

'Assuming you're right, assuming that this man does know me, what bloody difference does it make?'

'I'm doing my best to make contact with him,' Garvin said. 'There's a chance that this father business might work. He does have a father, and they were apparently quite close. If he thinks his father is here looking for him, he may make contact. At that point, of course, he would discover the truth, and we would like to have you to shove into the breach. Apparently he trusts you.'

'Christ,' Clive said, his control gone, suddenly angry, 'what in the hell are you talking about? You want me to concern myself with some stinking forgotten operation in a war that's over and better forgotten? There's a girl dead on a dirty floor back on that klong, and it's highly likely her father will end up the same way, out of his head with a knife in his stomach. I don't give a damn about your operation, and that's the truth of it.'

'There are some of us who haven't forgotten,' Garvin said, his voice steely. 'Now it very well may be that this former classmate of yours is responsible himself for the deaths of thousands of men, that he himself is the betrayer. If he is, I want him. And I want your help.'

Clive took another drink. 'That would be pretty damned untidy, wouldn't it?' he said. 'I forget sometimes how bloody wrapped up the cousins get in conspiracy theories, in who shot whom and why, even if the victims are long dead.' He drank again, stood up. 'I'll tell you what I'm going to do,' he said. 'I am going to spend twenty-four hours a day until I find Marston and get him out of here. And if and when that happens, then there's a fifty percent chance that I will give a stray thought or two to all this business of digging up the past. But not until. Now I'm going back to my hotel.'

'Just consider it,' Garvin said. 'I realize you have other things on your mind that you need to take care of, but I think when these other matters are resolved, you'll see how important this is.'

Clive said nothing. He paid the bill and went back out to the car. He left Garvin at the Empress Hotel and then directed Sam to drive back to the Siam Intercontinental. Sam moved the car onto the street and then turned off the radio.

'I wish to discuss something with you,' Sam said. 'But it concerns the dead woman. If that is too distressful to you now, then I can wait until tomorrow.'

'No, it's all right,' Clive said.

'I talked with some of the policemen who told me of the condition of the body. Now I do not wish you to think less of me, sir, but in my business I come into contact with all kinds of people, sometimes with whores and prostitutes.'

'Please come to the point,' Clive said.

'Yesterday I was talking to one who considers me a brother. She told me that her business was ruined because a client tied her to a bed and then with a knife shaved off the body hair from her private parts. He frightened her most severely.'

Something quickened in Clive, and when the word came out, it was almost an oath. 'Who?' he said.

'The Russian who has been following you,' Sam said. 'The one named Nikolai.'

18

BANGKOK

It was shortly before three in the morning by the time they reached the hotel. He sent Sam to talk to the desk clerk, to see if Nikolai was in his room. He left Tiger Man sitting in a corner of the lobby, in case Nikolai came in and headed for the bar. Then he went to his own room. The fatigue had spread through him now, and with it came the lessening of his defenses against the pain. The lovely child-woman face of Iris Marston was stamped on the inside of his eyelids. He was outraged; he put all restrain behind him.

He took the time to shave, to wash his face, to put on a fresh shirt. He took the wooden case from his closet and lifted out the Walther to go through the routine of filling the clip. He screwed the silencer on the muzzle, then slipped it into his belt before he put on his jacket. The telephone rang, and he picked it up. He was aware that whatever was said would be recorded, but the odds were that there was no live monitor on his telephone at this hour of the night. He did not need to worry. Sam was very circumspect.

'I was correct, sir,' Sam said.

'Very good,' Clive said. 'I'll be in the lobby in a moment.'

When he started down the corridor, he found Sam waiting for him at the point where the corridor entered the lobby. 'He has been in his room since one o'clock,' Sam said. 'The desk clerk said he had been drinking when he came in and he was carrying a bottle in a paper bag. He left instructions that he was not to be disturbed for any reason.'

'Where's Tiger Man?'

'I sent him outside to cover Nikolai's glass door, which leads to the pool.'

'You're a good man,' Clive said. 'Now do you think you can find a passkey?'

Sam held up a key ring, a lone key dangling from it. 'It cost me a hundred bahts.'

Clive moved back down the corridor toward Nikolai's room. 'I don't expect any trouble,' he said. 'But if there is, I want you to be careful. Do you understand? I don't want you hurt.'

'I have been trained in the martial arts,' Sam said. 'I can take care of myself.'

Clive was touched by Sam and his 'trained in the martial arts.' Sam, in his *naïveté,* had no notion of the real violence to be defended against. Clive would just have to see that he came to no harm.

They moved to the door. Clive took the key and carefully inserted it in the lock, making no sound. Slowly he turned it, feeling the dead bolt drawing back. Then, just as soundlessly, he withdrew the key and handed it to Sam. He took the pistol out of his belt, clicked off the safety. The corridor was empty, silent. He could not even hear the sound of radios playing in any of the rooms. That would be a handicap. He nodded to Sam, then slowly turned the doorknob until it was free and silently pushed the door open, pulling the pistol up at the same time.

Nikolai was sprawled on the bed, wearing nothing but his ragged pair of khaki shorts. There was an empty bottle on the nightstand, and the knife lay there as well, closed. A low light was burning in the lamp. Clive brought the gun up to Nikolai's head, hard against the skull. Nikolai came instantly awake, his hand reaching out for the knife. He blinked. His hand came back to rest on his tanned chest.

Without taking his eyes off Nikolai for a second, Clive spoke to Sam. 'Get a washcloth from the bathroom and wrap up the knife,' he said. 'Then check the camera bags for a pistol. The son of a bitch is bound to be armed.'

'Yes, sir,' Sam said. Clive moved closer to the bed.

'What are you doing in my room?' Nikolai said. There was no fear in his eyes. 'You are making a mistake.'

Clive said nothing.

'There is a pistol in the camera bag,' Sam said.

'Fine,' Clive said. 'We'll take that.' He reached for the nightstand, the muzzle staying at Nikolai's head like a compass needle following north. Inside the drawer was the recorder, compact, red light blinking, showing that the power was on. 'Open the outside door. We'll need some help.'

When Sam slid back the door, the moist, warm air rushed in, stirring the drapes. Methodically Tiger Man proceeded to remove the machinery from the drawer, unplugged it, wrapped the cords around the rectangular shapes, very neatly. Nikolai watched them with an odd detachment. He ran his hand over his coal black hair, as if to smooth down stray wisps, his vanity innate, and Clive could see his mind working, feel the choice-making process taking place. Would he pick the easy route of denial, the pretense of a victim being accosted by thieves? Nothing to be gained there, no point in stalling for time.

He raised himself on his elbow, turned his slightly blurred vision toward Clive. 'So what is it that you want, Clive?'

'You do speak English well,' Clive said.

'I speak perfect English,' Nikolai said.

'Then you can understand my simple instructions,' Clive said evenly. 'Any deviation from what I tell you to do, even the slightest, and I'll drill a hole in the middle of your forehead.'

Clive found a pullover shirt draped over a chair. He threw it to him. 'Put it on,' he said.

Nikolai sat up, sucking his stomach muscles in. He pulled the shirt over his head, paid great attention to smoothing the wrinkles from the short sleeves over his biceps. There was a coolness about him which Clive found unbearable. 'I don't think you will want to set a precedent here,' Nikolai said. 'There is an unwritten rule that neither side kills Watchers.'

Clive looked to Sam. 'Find me a quiet, remote place.'

Sam nodded, picked up the telephone, asked for a number, and then spoke a few words in Thai and put the telephone back on the cradle. 'It is done, sir.'

'Very good. Your car is outside?'

'Yes, sir.'

'Take Tiger Man. Load the camera case and the recording equipment in the trunk. Go out through the lobby, everything above-board. Return the key. Let me have his pistol.'

Sam handed the pistol to him, and Clive put it in his jacket pocket. Nikolai shrugged as if what was happening were of no consequence to him. 'I suggest you call the Russian Embassy,' he said. 'Or if you will tell me what you want, then we can terminate this business without spending all night at it.'

Enough time had passed. Clive gestured with the pistol. 'Now, on your feet. We're going down the corridor and out to the car. If the slightest thing goes awry, I'll kill you.'

'Your meaning is quite clear,' Nikolai muttered almost to himself. His head was clear now, and despite the possible danger, he felt no fear. As a matter of fact, he could turn this to his advantage. Clive wanted to know where Marston was, and Boris wanted him to know where Marston was. Nikolai would give him that information, not easily, of course. It was possible he might have to endure some pain in the process to make it look convincing, but he could already see ahead to the moment when he would tell Boris Ludov what he had done, watch the scowl disappear from that saturnine face. This could easily be the turning point in his career, all because he was able to turn a debit into a credit.

They reached the car without incident. Nikolai padding down the corridor and across the sidewalk in his bare feet, carrying himself with the grace of an athlete. He took his place in the back seat with an air of resignation.

It was only after the car had crossed the river and headed for the northwest part of the city, running into the heavy forest, that Clive began to have an idea where Sam was heading. Finally, the car pulled into a lane, and Clive could see the small house in the trees, on the edge of a narrow klong. Sam stopped the car, and Clive handed the pistol to Tiger Man, who leveled it across the top of the seat at the seemingly incredulous Nikolai, who made a small groan and rolled his eyes heavenward. 'If he moves, kill him.'

'I am understanding very well,' Tiger Man said.

Clive climbed out of the car with Sam, looked toward the house, where he could see a light in the window. 'Is this your house?'

'Yes, sir,' Sam said proudly. 'My mother has taken my brothers and sisters and gone to stay with another family for the night.'

'It's time for a chat,' Clive said, 'an understanding.'

'Have I done something to offend you, sir? Are you dissatisfied?'

'No,' Clive said. 'On the contrary, I think you're a fine man, extraordinary. And that's the problem. I don't want to involve you or your family in anything that might endanger you, and things have reached the point where they might. What do you think is going on here, Sam? What business do you think I'm in?'

Sam thought a long moment. 'A dangerous business, I think,' he said. 'I say that with all respect.'

'We had an agreement at the beginning if you'll remember. I promised I would involve you in nothing unlawful. Well, the moment has arrived when I have now fully committed myself to something unlawful. The man in the back seat is my enemy, a murderer. I intend to have a confession from him. It occurs to me that using your house is not such a smashing idea. I may already have put you at risk as it is.'

Sam was silent a long time. 'Thais are very polite people,' he said. 'We usually do not express ourselves in negative ways because the things which happen to us are predestined. But I have been away from Thailand, and I have seen how other people act, other ways of thinking.' He looked toward the house. 'A man who drives for the *farang* has to accept people the way they are. I have had people who called me a cheat and refused to pay my fare. I have had other people who have laughed at the monks and the wats, and one drunk Japanese who pissed on the wall of a holy place. But with you I feel respect and generosity. I see you now according me great respect by telling me the truth. So you are most welcome to my house.'

'I have doubts.'

'You are meant to take him to my house,' Sam said. 'And obviously he is meant to go there or he wouldn't be here now.'

Clive nodded. 'Thank you,' he said.

'You are most welcome.'

Clive relieved Tiger Man of the pistol, waved it slightly at Nikolai, and told him to get out of the car. Something about the Russian had changed now. It was almost imperceptible, a difference in his eyes, perhaps, the compression of the muscles around the eyes. He was squinting slightly as if he had now settled on a course of action and had not yet decided how to accomplish it.

Sam led the way through a courtyard full of flowers, a small and delicately wrought spirit house on a stand, and then into a traditional Thai room. Clive was startled to see an ornately carved coffin sitting on a pedestal, banks of flowers against the base of it. The pungent smell of the joss sticks smoldering at the base stung his nostrils. On the wall behind the coffin was an oversize portrait of an elderly man with a solemn expression on his face, very dignified, posed against a drape. Inside the coffin would be a large ceremonial urn, and inside the urn would be the body of the man in the portrait, kept here a year so his relatives could say prayers and earn merit with Buddha.

'Who was he?' Clive said.

'This is my father,' Sam said cheerfully. 'We will be having the cremation ceremony in another month.'

'I have no desire to dishonor your father,' Clive said.

'He was a soldier for many years,' Sam said. He pressed his hands together, holding them high against his face,

202

bowed to the portrait, made a *wai*. 'I am sure this would please him, a confrontation between my friend and his enemy. He often talked of his days in the army. In his later years he drove a *samlor*.'

'Is there another room?' Clive said.

Sam led the way into a room bare of furniture except for a television set in one corner and two chairs. Clive was dubious, for none of the windows had glass or screens, and although none of them opened toward another house, he could hear the motor of a small boat on a klong just beyond a distant clump of trees. Sam showed him the Coleman lanterns and the candles which could be lighted when the electricity failed and the old French telephone with which there were certain problems at different times during the day. As an afterthought, he pointed out the rolls of bamboo shades which could be lowered over the windows in case of rain. 'But to do that makes the house terribly hot,' Sam confessed. 'It does away with the ventilation.'

'I would like you to lower them anyway,' Clive said. 'I would like the privacy. If you have any *mekong*, I would like a bottle and two glasses. Then I would like you and Tiger Man to wait in the car.'

'Certainly,' Sam said.

The setting was everything, the bamboo blinds lowered, a bottle of *mekong* on a small table Sam had placed between the two chairs, the only light that from a dim bulb suspended from an overhead cord. Nikolai sat in the one chair, muscled legs sprawled out in front of him, the poseur who had nothing to fear. Clive took out his own pistol, put Nikolai's away. Nothing was going as he would have predicted it would, for the resistance in the Russian had simply melted away, evaporated, and then it occurred to Clive why this was happening. Things had gone awry between Nikolai and Boris; it had not been planned that the girl should be killed, for with her death the Russians would lose leverage. But this son of a bitch had slipped, gone too far, and that smooth hand with the large-knuckled fingers which now scratched that classic chin had committed an unforgivable error.

Clive poured himself a drink, sat down in the chair facing Nikolai. He kept one hand on his knee, the pistol pointed at Nikolai's midsection. 'All right,' Clive said. 'Tell me about the girl.'

'What?'

'You made a colossal blunder when you killed the girl. I know it. You know it. And most important, Boris knows it as well. He was dealing, you know, with a rather large amount of money. You cost him that. And you won't be permitted to walk away from that scot-free.'

Nikolai was trying to read Clive's face, to determine what would happen if he admitted the killing, what would happen if he did not. Nikolai rubbed his hand over his mouth. 'What did the girl mean to you?'

'I didn't know her,' Clive said noncommittally.

Nikolai shrugged. 'It was an accident,' he said. 'One of those things.'

'You do realize how tenuous your position is now?' Clive said.

'You must not believe that simply because I am in difficulty, my country will not stand behind me. I am very good at what I do.'

Clive snorted a laugh. 'Nonsense. You're a very poor Watcher. I had you made from the moment I saw you at the pool. You're so bloody vain you stick out like a red flag. And the mistake you made tonight is hardly a recommendation for your skill.' He sipped the *mekong*.

'May I have a cigarette?'

'It will ruin your physical condition,' Clive said. He flipped him one, along with a matchbook. Nikolai lit the cigarette, leaned his head back against the top of the chair, blew the smoke toward the ceiling.

'What's your offer? You do have an offer to make?'

Clive smiled. 'I have your knife. It is impossible to remove all the bloodstains without using acid, and you've had no time for that. So I could ship you through the Thai courts and have you spend a year or two in a Thai prison before they finally execute you. You have no diplomatic status. You're registered as West German, but they won't claim you. The Russians can't without admitting complicity. Why should I offer you anything?'

'You're forgetting the information I can provide you,' Nikolai said. 'I can be of great value. I'm liaison with the Communist Party of Thailand now. I can provide names, locations.'

'Very well, let's have them.'

Clive listened to Nikolai's recital, names, places, and he stored them away in his memory to be used another time. He lit a cigarette of his own. He imagined he could smell the body in the urn, and the smoke obliterated it, real or imagined. 'I want Marston.'

Nikolai relaxed against the chair, pleased with himself. 'Five thousand pounds, in advance,' Nikolai said. 'I know where he is.'

'I'm sure at this point you could tell me the location of the Second Coming if you thought I'd swallow it.'

'All right, I'll tell you where Marston is.'

'I want him alive.'

'He was alive earlier tonight. That's all I can tell you.' He began to give directions to the barge anchored on the river, ten miles downstream. He described the barge, the color of the bamboo cover, Marston's location in a cabin used only for storage, only slight ventilation. There was only one guard, for Marston was out of his mind, catatonic, no trouble to keep in place. He inhaled the smoke, let it trickle out through flared nostrils. 'I want to go to my embassy. That must be a part of the bargain.'

Clive reached out, picked up the French telephone. The line was dead. He proceeded to dial anyway, talking to an imaginary man in Thai, making elaborate arrangements which would reassure Nikolai if he spoke any Thai at all. And while he talked, Clive felt unreal, as if the coffin he could partially glimpse through the door to the other room were a stage prop. The call of a parrot from the garden was a recorded sound, Nikolai himself a projection, sitting there relaxed, convinced of his invulnerability like a trapeze performer who had just bounced into a protective net and landed on his feet. Vanity, the cardinal sin in this business, youth its companion, the cockiness of inexperience. And yet there was something about this whole process of revelation which disturbed Clive, for there was a sense of inconsistent relief in this man who prided himself on his toughness. He had bargained the information too cheaply, been too willing to tell Clive where Marston was. Clive did not think he was lying, and in the end he would have no choice but to believe him. Clive muttered a few more words, put the telephone back on the high cradle.

'A boat will pick you up on the klong in ten minutes.' Clive stood up, his joints stiff. 'We'll go out and wait.'

He kept Nikolai in front of him as they left through the rear door of the house, through the back garden in the general direction of the klong. He could see the water through the trees. Clive followed Nikolai on a path which ran beside the klong, perhaps 150 yards before they came to a deserted and rotting pier. The boards groaned under their weight. A boat poled by in the darkness, crossed the path of light from a distant house – an old man carrying a load of vegetables in his canoe to sell at the floating market. The chorus of frogs grew louder, incessant.

'May I have another cigarette?' Nikolai said.

Clive handed him one, this time flicked his lighter to provide a flame, allowing Nikolai to see that Clive had withdrawn the Russian pistol from his pocket, Nikolai's own pistol. It was important in this moment that he should see the gun and the cold rage on Clive's face so he would not pitch into death blindly, easily. A single fragmented, intense moment of terror dilated Nikolai's eyes as he realized what was going to happen to him. He began to babble, the panic garbling his words. 'Wait. A trade. Life for life. Something you should know.' His voice rose, turned shrill.

Clive pushed the pistol into the center of his chest and pulled the trigger. The explosion was muffled, no louder than the pop of a firecracker. Nikolai clutched reflexively at his chest, his eyes still alive in the flare of the lighter, startled. He took one step backward and then seemed to fold all at once, toppling to the edge of the pier, one arm dangling down toward the black water. Clive stood motionless for a moment. Christ, it was not enough, no, and the anger dissipated and drained out of him with the cold realization that there was no balance here. One Nikolai for one Iris Marston. Never. He turned and rammed his fist into a post. A chunk of the rotted wood splashed into the klong. He became aware of the night noises, the cry of a distant bird, the incessant croaking of the frogs. The house downstream did not come ablaze with lights.

He had deliberately executed a man and would have to live with that. He took out his handkerchief, wiped the butt of the pistol. He leaned down, forced the dead fingers of Nikolai's right hand over the grip, then tucked the pistol into Nikolai's waistband. He gave the body a nudge with his foot. It resisted momentarily, then gave way all at once, rolling into the water. By morning the body would have drifted downstream, far from this spot, safely away from Sam's house.

Clive walked back to the house, examined the rooms for any sign that Nikolai had ever been here. There was nothing except a few ashes on the floor near Nikolai's chair. Carefully Clive removed them.

He passed through the front room, looked up, saw the picture of the old man above the coffin. Without knowing quite why, he pressed his hands together and made a respectful *wai* to the coffin, then went outside to the car, ready for the last move which would end his business here and give him time for rest.

Half dozing in the back seat of the car, Clive remembered the eyes of the first interrogator he had faced after he had been properly stitched up and pronounced fit enough for debriefing. The man's name was Pembroke, and he seemed to spend all his time fiddling with his pipe, ramming cleaners up the stem, banging the bowl against the side of a crystal ashtray, either blowing through the airway or sucking, as if the perfect draft were foremost on his mind, which it wasn't, of course. He was out to know why Clive had broken under pain and what he had revealed as a result of that pain.

That was his goal, and the evenness of his voice implied the detachment of a mathematician (one could hardly feel emotional about 4 + 4), but even while his voice prattled on about other men who had broken, giving out a practiced reassurance, those gray-hazel eyes of his were as hard as a mineral and spoke his true feelings, asking with a silent glitter, *Why didn't you die first, old chap? Rotten bad form, you know, that you should have lived while the others got sliced up or blown away. Should have kept your bloody mouth shut.*

He stirred. Odd to remember Pembroke now, but he could see the determinant chain. He thought of Nikolai dead in the klong and Marston hoping to be delivered and he wondered why he simply didn't call Patterson and turn this whole thing over to him. Patterson would love it. He could put together his small special team, and they would all be dressed in uniforms and use a mufti Land-Rover. It would be a swift, bold move, and it was probable Marston would be plucked out with a minimum effort.

Instead, Clive had the good-hearted Sam and the unknown skills of Tiger Man in the front seat and the Walther in his own hand. He himself was tired now to the point that he was talking to Pembroke in his mind, not using actual words but trying to explain the general sense of things, that he had not died for any reason except that he had not died, that he had certainly willed to die. The body had been too strong for the mind, that was certainly part of it, and the great rip in his body had been insufficient to kill him. Or he could explain in religious terms that God (take your choice, Pembroke: Christ or Buddha) had predestined this, saving him from a merciful death at one point so he could rescue a soul in the same jeopardy at another. An avenger, first, the instrument of God to put Nikolai into the klong, for Nikolai had violated the Unnumbered Commandment and killed an innocent.

208

He came fully awake. They were approaching the burned-out lumberyard Nikolai had described. The rain had begun to fall, and the metronome of the windshield wiper was clicking back and forth. Clive saw the rectangular form of a single standing wall, charred at the top, irregular, looking like a piece of modern sculpture, and once beyond it, the smeared lights from the opposite side of the river. He tapped Sam on the shoulder, told him to stop the car, turn out the lights. He squinted through the curtain of rain, trying to make out the barge, which should be there at the edge of the river. He thought he could see the cylindrical shape of the bamboo roof above the straight line of a wooden pier.

'I'm going to scout this out,' Clive said. 'If there's only one guard, then we'll have no trouble. If there are two or more, then we'll find another way.'

'Begging your pardon, sir,' Sam said, 'but Tiger Man knows about these things. Let him go first.'

Clive patted him on the shoulder. 'Give me five minutes and then come along.' Sam handed him a flashlight, and Clive slipped out into the rain. He was immediately drenched. The shock of the water brought him alert, and he set off through the ruins, charred timbers now stacked and awaiting removal, surprised that the smell of the fire still persisted, that the rain had not washed it away. He moved slowly toward the dock, which, as he drew closer, he could see had been partially burned as well, with a series of gangplanks threading across gaps in the boards.

He could not see well, so he took his time, followed a cleared area through the ruins until he had a better view of the stern of the barge, the overhang of the arched roof which protected a projection of deck. If there were a guard, he would be there, protected from the rain, certainly not asleep, for if his employers found him dozing, things would go very badly for him.

So Clive stood, the rain soaking him through, peering into the shadows of that overhang, waiting for even the slightest shift of grays which would indicate movement. Presently he was rewarded. He saw the flare of a match and immediately thereafter the glow of a cigarette coal.

He found a charred crossbar of a timber still standing, extended his arm to rest upon it to steady the pistol, sighted along the barrel, knowing full well he could squeeze three shots away before that shape could move, knowing that at least one of the shots would do the job.

He did not fire. Supposing that Nikolai, even in the last minutes of his life, was lying. Suppose, then, that this person on the barge had no connection with Marston, that the barge itself was no prison but simply a boat waiting for cargo. He could not kill capriciously.

He pulled the pistol back, circled through the ruins to meet Sam and Tiger Man, who loomed like shadows in the rain. 'There is a person on the aft deck,' he said. 'We have to check this out. I don't want anyone hurt if Marston is not on that boat.' It would be a matter of logistics now. Tiger Man would approach the boat directly, a night watchman for the derelict lumberyard, and Clive would provide backup from the shadows while Sam stayed clear. At the most, if indeed the person on board were a guard, Tiger Man would be told to go away.

Clive waited while Tiger Man walked toward the series of gangplanks in his awkward limping gait, making plenty of noise to alert whoever was on board that he was coming while Clive again took to his vantage point where he could observe that glowing cigarette coal.

Clive heard Tiger Man hailing the boat, announcing himself as a night watchman. And then, abruptly, from the back of the barge came the sharp, piercing beam of a searchlight, focused first on Tiger Man, who, squat and sodden, looked to be exactly what he said he was. But then the searchlight began to move, making a slow sweep of the burned-out ruins. It caught Sam just as he ducked behind a piling. There was gunfire from the barge, the chatter of an automatic weapon.

Clive's chest tightened, and he held his breath while he squeezed off a flurry of shots, the Walther bucking against his hand, a deliberate pattern which arced to either side of the searchlight to down the invisible man before the final shot popped the light with a shatter of glass and brought immediate darkness.

There was no more firing from the barge, no sound at all, and Clive yelled to Sam and Tiger Man to stay put. He flipped on the flashlight, began a ragged, zigzag run toward the barge, holding his pistol at the ready to answer the fire, but there were no more shots.

The beam of his flashlight picked up Sam on one of the gangplanks, kneeling by the impassive Tiger Man, who sat upright, his left leg stretched out in front of him, the fabric of the pants leg torn to shreds, the blood pouring out. Sam was applying a tourniquet to Tiger Man's thigh, but Tiger Man waved Clive on.

'*Mai pen rai,*' Tiger Man was yelling, his voice almost drowned out by the rain. '*Mai pen rai.* It doesn't matter.' And Clive kept moving, balancing on the swaying planks until he came close enough to the barge to grasp the teak rail and swing on board. The circular wash of light fell on the body of the Thai man who lay sprawled on the deck, one side of his skull bloodied. The automatic carbine lay up against the leg of a chair next to the shattered searchlight.

Clive leaned against the support of a bulkhead, listening, waiting. But the barge continued to rock slowly back and forth in the sluggish current, the timbers moaning with the stress. The rain continued to drum down on the bamboo cover. He moved cautiously to a door in the bulkhead, edged it open with his extended foot. He flashed his light into the darkness. The barge was empty of cargo, riding high in the water. Below the platform of the cargo deck he could hear the bilge sloshing back and forth. The boat stank, an ancient, rotting smell.

He climbed down the shallow ladder, found the door to a compartment already open, flashed his light inside. The beam fixed on a man crouched against the bulkhead, emaciated, with hollow, vacant eyes.

'Christ,' Clive said. 'Marston? Is that you?'

He approached the man, who remained motionless, frozen as a wild animal in cover, the eyes unblinking. Clive put his pistol in his belt. 'It's finished, Marston,' he said. 'I've come to take you out.' He touched Marston's shoulder, and suddenly Marston's fist lashed out and hit Clive in the stomach with great force, knocking the breath out of him. Sam came down the stairs, stopped short when he saw what was happening.

Clive stood for a moment to get his breath. 'He's gone around the bend,' Clive said. 'We'll carry him out. Watch yourself.'

They advanced on Marston from either side. But with the one act of defiance Marston had exhausted himself. He neither fought nor helped them as they lifted him up, one on either side of him and guided him up the ladder. They steered him along the gangplank and left him sitting beside Tiger Man while Sam ran to bring the car around. Tiger Man was placed in the front passenger seat, still not complaining, expressing no pain. It was a struggle to get Marston into the back. He offered no resistance, but it was necessary to shape him into the posture of sitting, to bend his back to place him on the seat, to lift his legs one at a time and put them inside the car. And then he sat perfectly rigid, as if he had forgotten how to use his body.

Once they had closed the door, they stood in the rain for a moment, Sam with a questioning expression on his face. 'Have you now accomplished your mission, sir? Do you have what you want?'

'We have him back,' Clive said, quietly. 'But I think it may be bloody nothing we're taking with us.' He stirred. 'We'll take both of them to hospital immediately. How is Tiger Man?'

'Very brave, I think. Indestructible.'

'Yes, he is,' Clive said. 'Very brave.' He climbed into the car, and in a moment the Pontiac lurched ahead. Clive looked at Marston, who stared straight ahead, expressionless, off in some silent, impenetrable world of his own.

PART THREE

19

LONDON

A current of electricity flowed through the building, carrying the rumour, not yet confirmed, that Marston had been retrieved in a glorious bit of derring-do in which the details were sketchy. The decoder of the long cable from Sir John to Clive, a young sandy-haired man named Pinkston, was besieged with questions, to which he displayed an impervious expression except for a rather jubilant gleam in his eyes.

It was noted that a bottle of Mumm's had been ordered by Sir John and that he and Ross had lunched together, a meeting from which Ross emerged with a troubled expression as he went back to the computer section. Moorhouse, never one for tact, had blurted out the question 'So Marston is back in the fold, is he?' Later, reporting on Ross's response, he could say that he had received nothing more than a grunt which could be interpreted as either a positive or a negative.

Sir John himself was caught between jubilance and a more cautious view of what was happening. For every action in the service seemed to provoke (contrary to the laws of physics) an accelerated reaction which was always out of proportion. He sat at his desk and pored with mixed feelings over the decoded cables. The first was from Clive, two simple words: 'MARSTON RETRIEVED'. The second was from Patterson, all the more puzzling because it contained neither indignation nor judgment, both of which Sir John would expect from an authoritarian man who had been bypassed in the operation. But his cable was no more than a collection of facts, nondescriptive, a narrative which proceeded from Clive's cooperative discovery of the Marston girl's body with the CIA cousin to the death of Nikolai and the storming of the barge which had resulted in Marston's retrieval.

Marston had currently been installed in a bungalow at a Thai hospital, where the combination of adequate security and proper medical treatment was maintained. The hospital was generally reserved for Thai royalty. It was now guarded twenty-four hours a day by the Thai police, with a cover story identifying Marston as a Mr. Burroughs, a visiting English businessman who had come down with a highly infectious tropical disease.

Marston was in a critical state from exhaustion, malnutrition, dehydration, and traumatic shock. The bones in the fingers of his left hand had methodically been snapped. There were burn marks on his testicles from electrical shocks. There was a festering wound across his stomach where an incision had been made and then imperfectly sutured. Marston did not speak at all. An English psychiatrist, currently teaching at Chulalongkorn University, had ventured an opinion that Marston was currently catatonic and the prognosis was not a sanguine one. The embassy physician was feeding Marston intravenously, keeping him sedated.

Bloody useless in the end, Sir John thought, a Pyrrhic victory which would do wonders for his men but perhaps accomplish little else. The Foreign Office would certainly be buzzing this morning, and as usual he would have to tie up the loose ends. He might screw the lid on tight or admit all and in doing so reveal that all proper procedure and protocol had been abandoned and that Marston had been rescued in an improvised operation by an ex-agent with the cooperation of a Thai taxi driver and an over-the-hill Thai boxer, an informal attack which had resulted in the deaths of a photographer with a West German passport and a Thai barge captain. He would have to admit that this action had not been cleared through the embassy or the Foreign Office or by him. Whatever else came of this action of Clive's, it would certainly go a long way toward wiping off what was an unspoken blemish on Clive's record.

The champagne, meant to cheer, had only bloated him. He walked around the room, finally making up his mind to take the initiative. He called the superintendent of the Queen's Messengers, arranging for a strictly private meeting with him in the ambassadors' reception room at the Foreign Office. Then he dispatched a man to make certain the room was not only available but private. Finally, he gave Ross a ring.

'We will be inundated shortly with calls,' he said. 'I want the word passed that there will be no comment from anyone except myself. As deputy you will state simply that I will be available sometime later this afternoon.'

'Yes, sir.'

Sir John took a car to the Foreign Office, climbed the gloomy red-carpeted stairs to the hallway leading to the reception room. He passed his man in the corridor who reported that Colonel Evans was already on hand. Sir John opened the heavy door and saw the colonel standing at the far end of the splendid room, staring out the window. He turned with a frown as Sir John entered. Sir John moved forward, shook his hand, then sat down on one of the Victorian divans. Abandoning all preliminary small talk, he moved directly to the point.

'We have retrieved Marston,' he said.

'Thank God,' the colonel said. 'How is he?'

'Not good, I'm afraid. They've bashed him around, put him through the grinder. He will not talk to anyone. That's not surprising. They've undoubtedly used every trick in the book to break him.'

'The dispatch bags?'

'Not found,' Sir John said, not startled by the question. The Queen's Messengers had an absolute passion for duty.

'A grisly business,' Colonel Evans said. 'When will he be returned to us?'

'When he's in shape to move. Right now, I want a favor from you. What Queen's Messenger do you have scheduled anyplace close to Bangkok in the next twenty-four hours? It would have to be someone Marston would recognize instantly.'

Colonel Evans scratched his chin. 'I have Major Ashton-Croft in Singapore. He was on Journey Twenty-six with Marston on that fatal last run.'

'Are they close personal friends?'

'I should say no,' Evans said. 'But Marston would recognize him immediately. That's one thing my chaps have, if I have to say so myself, complete trust in one another.'

'All right, then have him catch the next flight to Bangkok. He's to contact Colonel Patterson at the embassy, and Patterson will take it from there.' He stood up.

'Our discussion's not over,' Colonel Evans said in protest. 'I want all the details you have. I want to know how he was captured. In short, everything.'

'Not for the moment,' Sir John said firmly. 'The Fleet Street moles would have the whole business in the *Express* the moment security was breached by so much as a centimeter. You will have to wait.'

'I think my chaps deserve more than this,' Colonel Evans said. 'This may be routine to you, but if my Queen's Messengers are vulnerable in any way, it is my duty to take immediate steps to correct the situation.'

'Your chaps are human after all,' Sir John said. 'In that sense, it's impossible to guarantee invulnerability. As for the details, you shall have them complete before they are released to anybody else.'

Colonel Evans nodded, absorbing. 'Very well, I can let my men know that Marston is all right, can't I? I must say, the rumor is already circulating that he's been found. I can say that much.'

'Yes,' Sir John said. 'All right' is a loose term, signifying that the man is breathing and his bowels are working, but it does not mean that there is any mind left in that physically functioning skull. 'Yes, you can tell them that much. And I will be in touch, Colonel, as soon as there is definite information.'

LAOS

Charlie Excalibur saw the thin snaking of the telephone line through the trees a few miles outside Vientiane. It had been recently strung, running from a skinny peeled pole to a tree and then off through the high foliage in a general easterly direction, a thin black line etched against the patches of open blue sky. Only as he saw the line did the idea occur to him, and he knew it was foolishness, for the odds were a thousand to one against his being able to bring it off. For wherever the line led, at the end there would be people, probably Laotian military, and he knew goddamn well that American grunts were a valuable commodity here. The Laotians traded in them, bargaining them back and forth as prisoners who were able to translate or operate machinery.

He sat down on a rock, smoked a cigarette, tired, not wanting to gamble now that he was this close to the end. He had set everything up, and pretty soon all of this would be behind him, if his luck held. He exhaled the smoke into the hot afternoon air, raised his eyes to the thin telephone line against a sky so bright that it gave him a headache. In all likelihood that goddamn line only connected two army posts and did not go through the Vientiane exchange at all and would therefore be useless to him.

He shrugged. What the hell. He could always check it out and see what was going on, and then, if the line terminated in a military camp, he would just fade back into the jungle and go on his way. He crushed out the cigarette and began to follow the line through the trees. The crazy damn Orientals had just strung the line anyplace it happened to be convenient, and at one point it rested unattached in the crotch of two branches.

Laboriously he climbed a hill, his ears picking up the whining of machinery in the distance, his nose detecting the smell of scorched wood. When he reached the crest, he could see where the telephone line led, to a recently erected sawmill in the middle of a thick growth of jungle trees, near the bank of a sluggish river where the finished lumber could be loaded onto barges in the muddy water.

He could make out perhaps a dozen Laotians, naked except for loincloths and headbands, dragging the logs into a shed where the large wheel of the saw screamed with the effort of cutting them into boards. He could see no military at all, but that did not mean that there were no soldiers in the vicinity. He checked the pistol in his pack, thought about sticking it in his belt but decided against it. To show that he was armed would be asking for trouble.

He left the cover of the trees and sauntered down the path, nodding with a forced smile to a gaunt man who was trundling sawdust out of the shed and adding it to a high pile. The man glanced at him, moved on. Charlie Excalibur made his way to a small shack where the telephone line terminated. There was no door on the building, and inside, he could see a diminutive Laotian man sitting at a table, scribbling figures on a piece of paper. He was wearing a short-sleeved cotton shirt, and that meant he would be the head man here.

Charlie Excalibur rapped on the raw wood doorjamb and grinned widely. 'Hello there,' he said. 'Do you speak English?'

The man looked at him, startled, sitting upright in his chair. It was obvious he was more irritated than threatened. 'Some English,' he said. 'What you want?'

'Business, maybe,' Charlie Excalibur said. His eyes had spotted the telephone now, an old French instrument with a brass filigree on its base. It sat on a corner of the table, and he eyed it with a desire that took the breath out of him. 'May I look at your telephone?'

'Who you belong?' the man said with suspicious eyes.

'The colonel,' Charlie Excalibur said, keeping his smile in place. 'Little fellow, very mean. All the time yelling. Very angry man. All the time, hop, hop.' He had reached the telephone now, and he picked it up, the metal warm against his sweating palm. 'All time, yelling at me, check this. Do that. Very mean.' He put the telephone to his ear and heard the sweet droning of a dial tone. Ah, Jesus, it was possible, and he put his index finger in the circle and dialed and in a moment heard the high nasal voice of a Laotian operator. 'English operator,' Charlie Excalibur said. 'I need someone who speaks English.'

There was a moment's pause, and he heard a voice say, 'Hello,' before the line went dead. The man's finger had depressed the cradle. He was standing by the table, a full head shorter than Charlie Excalibur, but he was clearly dominant here. For a moment Charlie Excalibur remembered the pistol in the pack, but one look at the man's eyes told him he was not going to need it. For the expression was shrewd, bargaining, not angry.

'Much money,' the little man said. 'You use, cost much.'

'I have no money,' Charlie Excalibur said. 'Colonel one hard man. No money.'

The man did not understand all of it. His eyes fell on the watch on Charlie Excalibur's arm, the old and faithful Rolex with its combination of gold and stainless steel. 'You give watch, make call,' the man said.

'That goddamn watch is worth hundreds of American dollars,' Charlie Excalibur said, but he knew in advance he was not going to be able to bargain. He wanted to use that telephone, would die to use it, and the shrewd sons of bitches over here could smell the want in a man. He shrugged, slipped the watch off his arm, and handed it to the man, who examined the tiny jerking movement of the second hand and held it to his ear to listen for the ticking.

Charlie Excalibur picked up the telephone, dialed zero, asked for someone who spoke English and then an international operator. His mouth was dry, and his heart had accelerated to pound against his chest. 'I want to call a number in the United States,' he said. And the number was suddenly there in his memory, as if he had just called it yesterday, and he gave it to the operator, expecting her to say that there would be a three-hour delay or that it was impossible for her to put through his call, but Christ, she just asked him to wait a moment, and then he could hear the strange beeps on the line as linkages were established and the excitement was so strong within him he thought it would tear him apart.

He could hear the telephone ringing, and suddenly he could see the bedroom and pots of African violets arranged on the windowsill to catch the light, and he could smell summer through the screen door. And then the miracle occurred, and he heard his father's voice, raspy, full of sleep, that deep, resonant voice of his childhood.

'Hello?'

Papa, oh, sweet Jesus, Papa, it's me and a miracle has just happened and I'm hearing your voice and I want to tell you that I'm coming home and I have it all arranged. And he wanted to ask about the people he knew and the neighborhood, but his mind stuck on the fact that his father was alive, breathing, his voice forming a word on the other end of a line thousands of miles long. *How are you, Papa? I love you and I've worried about you and your ulcers and there are a thousand things I want to say, to ask you about.*

'Hello? Hello? Is anybody there?'

It's your son, Papa the one you gave up on and I'm still alive and you'll be proud of me when you find out what I've done. Jesus, Papa, it's me. He wanted to speak, but the rush of memories was too great, the lawn dazzling green, the smell of the stew his mama was cooking in the kitchen, the purr of the Ford engine his father was always tuning on a Saturday morning.

A woman's voice in the background. His mother. 'What is it, dear? Who's on the line?'

'I don't know.'

It's me, Papa, and I want to speak to Mama and ask her how things are and if she misses me and I want to tell her how much I love her. I'm coming home, Mama, soon now, because I've made things all right. I've missed you so much that I've ached with it.

And suddenly he was weeping, the tears streaming down his face, so overcome with homesickness that his heart was breaking with it. And he listened to his father

222

say, 'Hello?' one more time, and then he put the receiver back on the cradle and covered his face with his hands, the pain so great within him he could not bear it. He wept until he had exhausted himself and only then became aware of the little Laotian sitting in the chair, adjusting the watchband to fit his wrist.

'Americans very soft,' the Laotian said. 'Which colonel?'

'What?'

'To which colonel you belong?'

'I can't pronounce his name,' Charlie Excalibur said. 'Very mean man.' He felt tired, depleted, but he had to get himself together, to move back into the here and now if he hoped to survive. 'I better get back.' And he went out the door into the harsh sunlight and went back up the hill at a quickened pace. He had achieved a miracle. For a moment he had been there, at home, and he had heard their voices, and that was worth the price of the watch and the pain.

When he reached the top of the crest, he walked past the point where the telephone line lay in the crotch of a tree. And he had the feeling that at this very moment the impulses were going through that line, the voice of the sawmill boss calling to check up on him. He crawled up the tree with ease, no more than ten feet to the wire. He took out his knife and with one clean stroke cut it in two. The link severed. No more voices.

BANGKOK

Clive had expected difficulty with Patterson because he had not consulted him before he retrieved Marston. Patterson had been specific about his territorial imperatives, and he had made quite clear, in his own words, that he had 'pissed the boundaries'. But when Clive called him from the hospital to send his own cable and to ask Patterson to report the details, Patterson was quietly amiable. Within an hour he showed himself at the hospital, wearing his quasi uniform, the black beret tilted

223

at a slight angle over one ear. He came into the sitting room of the cottage where Clive was leaned back in a chair, thrust out his hand, and said. 'Good show, old chap. I meant to congratulate you earlier.' He lit one of his clove cigarettes, glanced toward the door to the bedroom. 'How is our errant Queen's Messenger this morning?'

'Alive but absent,' Clive said.

Patterson pushed open the bedroom door with the back of his hand just enough to see inside. He saw a short, rather fat doctor in a white coat who was currently leaning over Marston's head, pulling back the rims of the eyelids and flashing a penlight inside, as if trying to locate the man's sensibilities. Patterson closed the door. 'Who's that?' he said to Clive.

'The psychiatrist who teaches at Chula,' Clive said. 'His name is Wadley.'

'Has Marston spoken?'

'No.'

Patterson shook his head, rolled his wrist to check his watch, as if even caught up in concern, one had to keep track of the time. 'You may be worrying about repercussions, but you needn't. The Thais are secretly delighted. They were aware of Nikolai and will write his death off as suicide. The man on the barge was a member of the CPT, in possession of an automatic weapon. The police will probably claim credit for the raid on the barge.'

'Fine,' Clive said, not in full possession of his wits now, only half awake, not even certain what time it was. Noon, perhaps. The sunlight was flooding through the airy sitting room.

The door opened from the bedroom, and Wadley came out. Clive saw him not so much as short but as having a low center of gravity with short legs beneath a normal, if fat, torso. He took off his white examination smock, folded it neatly, and placed it on a rack before he put on his regular tropical jacket. He would have made a fine American football player, Clive thought. It would take tremendous leverage to knock him off his feet.

'How is he?' Patterson said.

'Normal for his condition,' Wadley said enigmatically, his chubby fingers vigorously polishing the round lenses of his wire-rimmed glasses while his eyes squinted. He did not describe Marston's condition as much as he lectured. Marston's condition was typical of a military syndrome which had afflicted soldiers in battle as well as prisoners of war who had been exposed to too much pain, both mental as well as physical. Marston felt guilty as well, for he had betrayed what he considered a sacred trust and had survived when his subconscious beliefs insisted that he should have died.

Patterson asked a couple of questions which Clive only half heard, questions concerning the duration of this condition (indeterminate, Wadley said) and the possibility of complete recovery (a poor prognosis, Wadley said). Clive believed none of it. For on that barge, in that single sudden moment of Marston's attack, his fist hitting Clive's stomach, he had suddenly declared at least a momentary cognizance, bursting into a rage which pronounced that he would never surrender his silence to the trickery of his enemies.

Wadley floated off, and after a few minutes of proper sympathy, wrapping up loose ends, Patterson departed as well, leaving behind the scent of cloves. Clive stirred himself, caught one of the butterfly nurses, and in Thai told her to bring him a pot of coffee, hot, and to see that it remained both hot and full. He went into the bedroom where Marston lay rigid against the white linens of the bed, a single sheet covering him, tubes drooping like vines to feed into his arm. In preparation Clive pulled a chair up next to the bed. Then he went back into the sitting room and used the telephone.

First he called Sam, found that Tiger Man was being taken care of in another hospital. He had two bullet wounds in the calf of his leg, was currently the center of attention because he refused to speak about how these terrible inflictions had occurred, and he was also anxious that both wounds would leave a proper scar which he could later exhibit with pride.

Clive called Liz and, from the moment that she was on the line, realized that no deception was possible. He could feel the excitement of her curiosity flowing through the line. 'There are all kinds of stories afoot, darling,' she said. 'Can you tell me what's happened?'

'Marston has been retrieved.'

'No,' she said, an exhalation not of disbelief but of wonder. 'What does he say? How did it come about? Was his daughter rescued, too?'

'The daughter is dead, but we have the father. That's all I can tell you now.'

'Can I attribute?'

'Yes.'

'Does anyone else have the story?'

'Not here. They may put a D Notice on it in London, but it will leak anyway. I'll give you the details later.'

'How are you? Are you all right?'

'Yes, I'm all right.'

'I love you.'

He put down the telephone. The nurse had arrived with a Thermos of coffee. He drank a cup. It helped only slightly to lessen the fatigue which had begun to settle in over his mind like a comfortable blanket. Then he went in to sit beside Marston and to begin his vigil.

He sat in silence for the first hour, perhaps dozed off, although later he would not be able to say whether he had or not. And then he talked to the man who lay like stone on the bed, staring straight ahead out the open window at a green paddock in the center of the hospital grounds, seeing nothing. Clive chatted about himself and his Katy, about plays he had seen in London recently, about anything which came to mind which was connected with home, with the familiar, the pastries at Harrods, the reconstruction of the Old Bailey, cricket matches.

There was a purpose to the monologue. It was designed to reassure the man on the bed and let him know, in some vague way, that he was now among his own kind.

Clive regarded the man on the bad as a puzzle to be

226

solved, as if Marston were now an alien being with whom communication had to be established, some new and presently unknown syntax developed, some key words understood. Marston was not lying in a stupor. Those cold blue eyes did not see because Marston willed them not to see. The long fingers of his one unsplinted hand were knotted into such a tight fist that the prominent knuckles were white with the strain. His body was braced, taut, hardened to withstand anything while his mind had scurried away to some hidden and remote place where it had burrowed in.

So Clive continued to talk, weaving elaborate sentences, whatever came to mind, the royal family and Princess Margaret frolicking. 'Ah, Christ,' Clive said with a smile, 'now that would be the life, wouldn't it? To go where you want and do what you want, with all the money in the world and aides to do those things for you which you wouldn't want to do. The built-in respect, and if royalty slips and becomes human, there's always a wink and a nod and forgiveness.'

The doctors came, examined, went. The nurses floated in to exchange the hanging bottles, to secure the tubes, to sponge-bathe that body bound up by inner ropes, and Clive finished one Thermos of coffee, saw it replaced, sat, dozed, talked. He saw Patterson at the door, and he stood up and went into the sitting room, but he only half listened to what Patterson had to say and did not know why he was not really interested.

Patterson stalked the room, hands clasped behind his back. He was wearing a fresh uniform, puffing on the incessant clove cigarette, looking at Clive in quick, peripheral, assessing glances. 'Are you all right, old chap?' he said.

'Never better,' Clive said, Patterson something of a blur. 'I must get back.'

'He's not speaking, is he? The doctors say there's no change. He could be this way for months.'

'He's not talking because he doesn't want to talk,' Clive said. 'But he's there all right.'

'There's a Queen's Messenger on the way from Singapore, a man Marston knows well.'

'Fine,' Clive said softly, nodding, standing, moving back toward the room, closing the door behind him. He sat down again, lit a cigarette for himself, slumped back in the chair, regarding the finely chiseled features of the profiled face on the bed which had not moved so much as a twitch. Clive slumped back in the chair, knowing fully for the first time why he was here, the reasons no longer tilted toward that squirreled-away mind.

'Ah, you poor buggered-up bastard,' Clive said. 'We have both been through it, and they can't understand what it is because they haven't been there. I went through the same thing for a time, you know. They tell me that after I was in the hospital, I didn't speak for days. But it wasn't for any reason they could understand, no physical traumas, because I could stand that, had stood that, with the pain of Christ on the cross. A damn good thing they weren't Christian or perhaps they would have thought of that as well, nails through the hands and feet, barbaric.' He sucked on the cigarette. 'Guilt, guilt, guilt,' he said. 'Do you know what I did? Possibly not. Not in your area.' The smoke stung his eyes. His eyes watered. The pain began, one sharp jolt which left him curious because he could not locate it in his body.

'Five good men. Can you understand that? Not just five men, not just a number, but five good ones. Rare. They looked up to me because I was running them with a cool wisdom, and I remember taking care of them like children, pulling them out of spots when the risk was too high, providing money for their families. One was in love. Wanchai, Chinese, early twenties. In love with the tiniest woman I ever saw, a perfect miniature, a porcelain.'

The water was running freely from his eyes, not the smoke, no, crying. It surprised him. The tears did not come from a surface hurt, not even current. It was stored up, from a reservoir of insufferable agony he did not know existed. 'Christ,' he said. 'You hear me, you bastard. I know you hear me. Do you know what my runners collected for me? Bits and pieces, just bits and pieces. Incredible. I used to collect their findings like honey from a hive, put all the pieces of information together, and send it back to London once a week. The list of names from a Russian trade delegation coming into Chiangmai. Where the Russians were getting their automobiles repaired. A description of the new treads the Russians were putting on their tanks for use in rocky desert. The movement of spies that was no secret. God, there's a column in the *Far Eastern Economic Review* that spells that out weekly. Chinks in the wall, they used to call it in London. Pieces of old jigsaw puzzles which they filed away against the day that they might need an odd hole filled. How did the Russian diesel engines bought in East Germany end up in Laos? The search for significance, meaning, grand extrapolations from little clues.'

He blew his nose, the gorge rising in him, the bitter taste of bile. Was there a connection between tears and bile? The inner pain made it difficult to breathe. 'So I was picked up by a whole party of little men who smelled of garlic and betel nut, and they worked me over, just like they worked you over. Christ, the places on the human body where pain can be inflicted. All endurable. I didn't die. I floated out of my mind, and the mind deserted the body for a while, but I didn't die. There was another figure there, standing in the doorway once or twice, a large man. It may have been God or the devil, I don't know. I prayed to him for deliverance, whoever he was, whichever. But there was no deliverance, of course.'

He smiled, laughed sharply. 'You see the joke. You know it, don't you? As I was spending my days and nights running a net of men looking for significance, these bloody little bastards were cutting me up, looking for significance, too. I've never known a great secret, can you understand that? I've never known the date of an invasion or the particulars of a plot to destroy the world.' He stared at the man in the bed, tears streaming down his cheeks. He could feel them, and he thought helplessly that he could not stop them. They might never stop.

'So,' he said, a long exhalation of breath. He put the flat of his hand against the drape of the cool sheet on the bed. 'So,' he said again. 'In the end I gave them the names of my men. I thought, you see, that once they saw these men, once they talked to them, they would see that they had nothing significant either. No, that's a lie. I didn't even think at all. There was no rationalization. I traded words, little combinations of syllables, for an absence of pain. And they didn't even bother to talk to any of my men, not one, not a word. They just eliminated them, pistols, knives. Efficient deaths. But the joke, you see' – and here he laid his hand on the rigid flesh of Marston's upper arm – 'but the joke is that the moment my men were killed, every speck of intelligence they had provided for weeks was reexamined, reevaluated, like a bunch of Indian fakirs sorting through cow dung for an augury. Nothing there, of course. Nothing. All a part of the game. I was grabbed and my men were killed because there might have been something there. A possibility.'

He slumped back in the chair. The tears ceased almost instantly. The pain began to lessen. He was surprised. Had the reservoir been emptied? Perhaps. 'Your guilt will pass, whatever it is. There's nothing you could have told them that will make any great difference in the long run. The dispatches you were carrying were just words.' He leaned his head back, drifted off so suddenly he was briefly alarmed, jerked upright before he put his head back again and allowed the darkness to come.

He was awakened by a tap on the door. He was not aware of how long he had slept. He had not kept track of the time. Still daylight. He went to the door, into the sitting room. It was the Queen's Messenger who introduced himself as Major Ashton-Croft and was on first glance the most imperious civilian Clive had ever seen. He had popped out of the car from Don Muang Airport in a totally pristine shape, his blue blazer and gray trousers showing not a wrinkle from the Singapore flight, his Queen's Messenger tie perfectly knotted over a crisp white shirt, his black shoes gleaming, unblemished. He held himself ramrod straight, shook hands with Clive firmly and formally. 'I'll see him alone if you don't mind.'

'I do,' Clive said.

'Do what?'

'I do mind. He's in my care.'

Ashton-Croft shrugged. Clive opened the door, and Ashton-Croft pushed into the room just as a Thai nurse entered with another bottle. He glared at her. 'Finish your bloody work, woman, and get out,' he said.

The nurse understood no English, but she scurried to hook up the bottle and adjust the drip and then fled. Clive looked at Ashton-Croft with wonderment. There was not a trace of compassion on his face as he strutted around the bed, hands on his hips, as if he were having a closer look at this miserable specimen of a man who lay on the clean white sheets, hollowed eyes glaring out of a sallow face. Finally, Ashton-Croft stood at the foot of the bed and looked straight into those vacant eyes.

'You are a rotting son of a bitch,' he said in a loud, angry voice. 'You are a disgrace to the service, Captain Marston, and if it was up to me, I would nail your bloody hide to the wall. Where are your diplomatic bags, you son of a bitch? Not one bloody time in three centuries has any cowardly bastard like you come along.' His voice rose until he was shouting, yelling, bellowing so that the whole room vibrated with the noise. Ashton-Croft's face turned a vivid red, the sweat pouring down his scalp despite the current of cold air from the air conditioner.

Clive stood spellbound, fascinated by the torrent of abuse, and there was an instant when he considered grabbing Ashton-Croft by the scruff of his neck and throwing him out of the room. Then Ashton-Croft suddenly reached out and, with all his force, slapped Marston's face with a ringing blow.

The head nurse appeared at the door, prepared to do battle, but Clive waved her away, quietly, his eyes on Marston's face, the skin dead white except for the flushed imprint of a hand across his cheek. There was a subtle change in Marston's eyes, a slight reflection of a quizzical gleam appearing. The mouth which had been so tightly closed now gaped slightly. Was Marston coming out of his hiding place? Was he about to surface?

'Now, you bloody faker,' Ashton-Croft yelled at him, 'I am going to give you one chance to redeem your miserable soul. You choose to stay in that bloody stupid pose of yours, and when I get back to London, I will personally see that your name is removed from all the records, that as far as this service is concerned, you cease to exist.'

Ashton-Croft fell silent. Then, miraculously, Marston's gaping mouth formed a word, with just enough breath to expel it but not enough to form a sound.

'Speak up, you bloody traitor,' Ashton-Croft commanded. 'I can't hear you.'

Again the mouth formed, and no word came forth.

'I expected as much from you,' Ashton-Croft said with great contempt. 'On our last journey together I found your manners insufferable. So speak up now and admit that you are a miserable bastard or be damned to hell forever as far as I'm concerned.'

The mouth formed the word again, pushed it out. 'Bastard,' Marston said with a hoarse rasp of air. 'Bastard.'

Ashton-Croft appeared to relax. He removed a handkerchief from his pocket, wiped his face. 'You know me then?'

Marston nodded slowly.

'And what is my name, you bloody derelict?'

'Ashton-Croft,' Marston said with great effort.

'Do you know this gentleman here?' Ashton-Croft said, glancing toward Clive. Marston studied Clive with curious eyes.

'No.'

'His name is Clive. He's with the Foreign Office. Can you grasp that?'

Marston nodded.

'He can be trusted,' Ashton-Croft said. 'I don't have the time to waste with you. You will cooperate with him or you'll answer to me.'

232

'Go to hell,' Marston said.

Ashton-Croft stalked from the room. Once they were in the small sitting room, Clive could see that Ashton-Croft's hand was trembling. The major sat down, wiped his face with his handkerchief.

'You gave a fantastic performance,' Clive said.

'May I have a cigarette?' Clive gave him one, and Ashton-Croft smoked in silence for a while. 'I was not so sure that would work,' he said finally. 'I am writing a history of my regiment, and a sergeant major described the method he used to communicate with one of his chaps who had been put in a pit by the Japanese and left for six weeks. Actually the sergeant major used a cane on him. Rather brutal, but it was effective.' He held the cigarette delicately, horizontally, gingerly. 'It's not easy to see one of your chaps go around the bend. I have never been particularly close to Marston, but he's one of us, after all, isn't he?' He stood up, looked for an ashtray, snuffed out the cigarette. 'I have to make a connection to Hong Kong. If I'm needed again, I shall be available.'

Another brisk handshake and he was gone. The nurses returned, chattering in Thai, rushing in to examine what they were certain would be the remains of their patient. Clive took his time. His work was now to begin. He stopped one of the nurses, told her to bring two cold glasses of orange juice. They were brought to him on a small circle of a silver tray. He carried them into the room, aware of the fragility of the situation, as if a slight crack had opened into Marston's psyche, a narrow opening which could close at any time. He pulled a chair close to Marston's bed, put the tray on a table, handed one of the glasses of orange juice to Marston. The unsplinted hand moved to receive it, the fingers stiff around it, the knuckles knoblike, purple, bruised. He finished the first glass, spilling part of it on the hospital gown. Then he reached out for the second glass and drank it greedily.

'Do you know your name?' Clive said.

'Yes.' Marston cleared his throat, but his voice was still a raspy whisper. 'Where am I?'

'In hospital.'

'Bangkok?'

'Yes.'

'Is there more orange juice? Do you happen to have a cigarette?'

Clive summoned the nurse, sent her for orange juice, a pitcher this time. He lit a cigarette, handed it to Marston. 'What do you remember?' Clive said.

'Your name again?' Marston asked.

'Clive.'

'Yes. And Ashton-Croft was here?'

'Yes.'

'Ashton-Croft. He's a bloody bastard, but he tells the truth, you know. By the book.' He inhaled the cigarette, laid his head back against the pillow. 'They had me and you rescued me. Is that right?'

'You don't remember then?'

'Only bits. Small pieces. Nightmarish.'

'Yes,' Clive said. 'I know.'

'My daughter,' Marston said. 'They had her.'

'Yes.'

'Did you get her back as well?'

'Yes.'

'How is she? Is she in this hospital? I would like to see her.'

Clive blinked. The blanks were there. Marston did not remember. 'We found her a few days ago, sent her home. We didn't know whether we would find you or not.'

The pitcher of orange juice arrived. Marston drank another glass, his face screwed up in a frown. 'Don't ring her up,' he said.

'Who?'

'My daughter. Not just yet anyway. Not until I write my official report. The dispatches?'

'Which despatches?'

'From the diplomatic pouches. Recovered?'

'Don't worry about them.'

He removed the cigarette from his mouth. His hand trembled so that the ashes showered all over him. 'Bloody damned fingers.'

'They put you through it.'

'Inexcusable,' Marston said. 'A Queen's Messenger should have no attachments. There are rules, you know. I just couldn't follow them. Bloody inexcusable.'

'We're all human,' Clive said. 'The man who boarded the aircraft. He showed you pictures of your daughter.'

'Bastards.'

'He showed you pictures.'

'Yes. Wretched, wretched.'

'The welfare of your daughter had to come first.'

Marston gave him an oblique, wondering look. 'Gordon Clive, yes. You're he?'

'Yes.'

'They wanted the dispatch that was addressed to you. Boris Ludov told me that in Mongolia.'

'I see.'

'The other man didn't know that.'

'Which other man?'

'On the aircraft,' Marston said. He took another cigarette and talked in fragments, little snippets of sights and smells. On the aircraft, the appearance of the balding man with the stink of cabbage about him and the obsequious air of a rug salesman, opening a packet of instant pictures as if displaying his wares. The color uneven, an improper flash, skin tones bluish, pictures of Iris, a man holding a pistol to her head, another of a man with a knife to her throat. He was grimacing at the camera, posing, and on the daughter's face a spacy, dopey look the father had never seen before, did not know how to interpret.

The bloody scum of a cabbage breath sighs a lot as if his sympathy is all with Marston while Marston himself has grown stone-cold with a rage he dare not let seep out. The messenger is detached from the message. It is all 'they say' and 'they will', but the text is made plain none-theless. If Marston does not cooperate, then another set of pictures will reach him in the mail, this time far less pleasant, the man says with a knitting of his thick eyebrows together, a great belch of cabbage sympathy.

Marston considers, balances, responds, that pictured bluish flesh making the final tilt. He rises on stiff legs, follows the man to the men's rest room, brain suddenly racing with trickery when he realizes that this man, never known to him by name, has not been instructed as to which document they consider important, has no list, is a simple carrier, who, if shot down on this cold tile floor, taken captive by the authorities, would have nothing to tell them except a repetition of his instructions.

So Marston cooperates, enters the stinking lavatory stall to change clothes, opens the diplomatic bags himself while the slow-witted cabbagehead remains outside. Marston finds the Po dispatch, light onionskin, rips it open, glances at the message, wads it, flushes it down the toilet, puts the rest of the dispatches into a zipped nylon bag, together with the folded diplomatic bags and his clothes. He dresses in the suit that cabbagehead has provided for him. The material is scratchy against his legs, light wool, northern European, ill-fitting. He darkens his hair.

Back onto the same flight, through the economy door. The cramped journey. Forced to take a tablet in orange juice. The vain hope that it will be lethal. Death before dishonor. His daughter. Flights of angels protect her. Just drowsy. No death. A car at the airport. Off to a bloody nest of men. Questions. No answers. Endless. Darkness and light. Terrible pain, release from pain, worse pain to come.

The cigarette had gone out, the filter clinging to Marston's lip. He asked for another cigarette, which Clive lit for him. A Thai nurse came in with an assortment of pills in a small paper cup, gave Marston a dazzling, gentle smile.

Clive waved her away. He wanted no pills to interfere, not yet. He pressed the tips of his fingers together contemplatively. 'They were interested only in the letter addressed to me,' he said, reminding.

'Yes.'

'I have been through this,' Clive said. 'Any man would have told them. You have to realize that.'

236

'Told them what?'

'What they wanted to know. You said you read the letter.'

'Yes.'

'And you told them what was in it.'

Marston shook his head. 'It was important to them. I wouldn't give them that satisfaction. I destroyed it so they wouldn't have it.'

'But you read it.'

'So I could pass on the information. I was determined to complete Journey Twenty-six to the best of my ability.'

Clive was light-headed. He felt as if he were drifting. No guilt here in this man. He was left with his own, unshared, unabated. 'And they did not force it out of you. You didn't give it to them under the influence of drugs so that now you simply don't remember.'

'I did not give it to them.'

'I see.'

'I was able to do away with words altogether after a while,' Marston said with a small glow of pride. 'Not just words, but the thought of words, the conceptualization of words, so that directly, without words, there were no objects, and finally, you see, I could conceptualize them all out of existence.' He winked at Clive as if he were making a joke. 'I could cause you to cease to be, in my mind, if I wished. I didn't know I had the gift.'

'The message,' Clive said. 'You can deliver it now.'

'Send my daughter roses, after all. Let her know I'm alive. Apologize.'

'Yes. Now the letter from Charlie Excalibur.'

Marston looked at him shrewdly. 'You are the addressee. I suppose it's all right.'

'Believe me, it is.'

Marston concentrated, closed his eyes. 'Meet me at three-two-eight on June twenty nine. I will trade vital information for asylum. This is very important and I will meet with you only. Don't let me down. Remember the buzz.' He opened his eyes. 'Then there was just the simple signature, "Charlie Excalibur".'

'Christ,' Clive said, suddenly sick to his stomach. *You held that message back when who knows what it means? It had better mean a hell of a lot because they killed your daughter for it right in front of your eyes.* 'Are you sure that's accurate? He did not explain what three-two-eight refers to?'

'No.'

'Or "remember the buzz"?'

'That was the whole letter. Word for word.'

Clive searched Marston's face. He had not broken, and Clive admired him for that. There was something noble about him. Tired, he lifted a hand, scratched his chin, then stood up. 'You had better rest,' he said because he did not know what else to say.

'Inform my superintendent.'

'Of what?'

'That the message was delivered to you. That I completed Journey Twenty-six as best I could.'

'Yes.'

'And remember the roses. Most important.'

'Yes, the roses.'

20

BANGKOK

The hotel lobby was crowded. A new tour from the States had just arrived, and there were mountains of stacked baggage, a flustered tour guide trying to assign room numbers and schedules to a party of senior citizens who had difficulty making out what he wanted them to do. Clive pushed his way through the crowd to the bar, in need of the cool, dark isolation and a drink. He coaxed the waiter into bringing him a bourbon and water first with a sandwich to follow later; before he settled down to think, he called Garvin's room, asked him to drop by the bar.

It was only then that he settled in, allowed himself the drink. His mind continued to work. He had realized the meaning of the numerical reference in Charlie Excalibur's message, but for the specifics it would be faster to deal with Garvin.

Garvin arrived at the same time the waiter delivered the sandwich from the dining room. He sat down, ordered a drink, and studied Clive with sympathetic eyes. 'You look awful,' he said. 'Hard day?'

'Very,' Clive said. He bit into the sandwich, realized he had no idea what the ingredients were, ate anyway. 'I need your cooperation.'

'What kind of cooperation?' Garvin's drink was served. He sipped it.

'During the Vietnamese War your military worked on a numerical grid system. Different villages were assigned different numbers. Right?'

'Yes.'

'Was Thailand included in that numerical system?'

'It was.'

239

Clive finished half the sandwich, pushed back from the table, signaled the waiter, and ordered another drink. 'Do you know the numbers assigned to the villages?'

'Certainly.'

'Marston gave me his message,' Clive said. 'I know the time when Charlie Excalibur will be at a particular village. He wants a meeting with me, an exchange of information in return for asylum. Unless I'm there on a certain day, by myself, then neither you nor I get what we want.'

'An interesting dilemma,' Garvin said. His eyes roved the room. 'The question is: At this point are you in a position to strike any bargains?'

'What in the bloody hell are talking about?' Clive said. 'I'm the only one who can strike a bargain, as you put it. I know the location and I know the time.'

'I'm thinking beyond that,' Garvin said, evenly. 'If Charlie Excalibur is the man we want, we will expect you to hand him over.'

'If we get him, he goes to London first. From that point he's negotiable. But that decision will be made on a higher level.'

'You don't seem to understand,' Garvin said, running an index finger around the wet rim of his glass. 'It's a difference in philosophy perhaps. As far as you're concerned, I am the United States. If he's the traitor I think he is, then I will have him. So this will be settled between the two of us. Or if you wish, bring Patterson into it. But in the end I will have Charlie Excalibur.'

The second drink arrived, but Clive did not touch it. He stood up, put the baht notes on the table. 'I'll let you know what I decide.'

'Do that,' Garvin said.

Clive went down the corridor to his room. He needed sleep, time to think. But when he opened his door, he saw Liz sitting at the table by the window, her hair glowing golden in the sunshine, intent on penciling a manuscript which lay before her. He kissed her on the top of her head, then began to take off his clothes without a word, after placing the pistol on the nightstand.

'In advance, I love you,' he said before she had a chance to speak. 'I adore you, and I like nothing better than making love to you, except perhaps talking with you. But at the moment I intend to sleep.'

'You look like you need it,' she said. 'But you can talk while you're getting ready for bed.'

He took off his shoes, then his trousers. 'I am ready for bed,' he said. 'But you can do something for me. You have sources that are faster than mine. Get in touch with BBC Worldwide. Have them run a story about me.' He pulled back the coverlet on the bed, plumped the pillow. 'The story should have to do with my making a tour of the backcountry on behalf of the American government, looking for Americans still listed as Missing in Action.' He slid between the sheets.

'Is that true?' she said.

'Partly.' He pulled up the sheets, settled back against the pillow. 'Now go away like the good girl you are.'

'How long do you intend to sleep?'

'Until I wake up.' He closed his eyes. 'Out with you,' he said.

'I don't forget rebuffs,' she said. 'You'll get yours, Henry Higgins.'

'I hope so,' he said. He heard the door close behind her.

He rolled over, expecting to fall asleep immediately, waited for it, and, in doing so, made it impossible. There were too many burrs on which his thoughts caught instead of flowing through. There were too many idiosyncrasies which made no sense at all. He should have accepted Garvin's offer immediately, not postponed it out of some stubbornness which even he himself could not rationalize as sensible.

He did not even know Charlie Excalibur, owed him nothing. And then he recognized the burr, the catching point, the nagging sense of guilt which would not be quieted, the terrible comparison between himself and the man lying on the hospital bed, who, as a matter of course, against all the requirements of expediency, had honored his word when it had cost him everything. And Clive, of course, had not.

He dozed off, his mind still tumbling the words of Charlie Excalibur's message, the single word 'buzz' sticking out. Half asleep, he remembered. A university class, a nameless professor of semantics who spent much of his time attacking his students in the name of enlightenment, a spare, bony, Socratic man who used his long, pointing index finger like a pistol to bring down his muddleheaded quarry.

Buzz.

Buzz with a capital *B*, a name under attack, the shrill, pedantic voice making sport of it and the boy whose nickname it was. 'What does it mean?' that lean predator's face demanded. 'What is the significance of calling yourself by a sound made by insects? Do you think it distinguishes your intellect? A "buzz" word. Do you think it stimulates thought in the people around you? Do you think it enhances you? "Buzz" is also a sound made by machines. Do you consider yourself a machine?' Arms outspread now to the rest of the class. 'A man's name influences his self-concept. He shapes himself to his name. He becomes it.'

'Do you know, sir, what your nickname is among the students?' the young man asked.

Clive blocked the voice, trying to remember the face of the young man who sat at the seminar table. He could not visualize it, but he could remember the shrewd smile that had persisted all through the diatribe, that cunning, pervasive grin. Now he could see the eyes, open, blue, never wavering from the professor for a single moment, never backing away. Clive could remember the young man's voice, firm, funny. 'We call you Bullshit Jones.'

No laughter at the end. Dead, hushed, appreciative silence. The young man had not been intimidated for a moment. End of scene. Clive could remember no more. He had a beer with Buzz that afternoon. Blurred, much laughter, a checkered oilcloth on the table of a student bar. Was this Charlie Excalibur? Large hands. Tall. A basketball player? He could not summon up the last name. Garvin? He did not know.

He fell into a deep and dreamless sleep.

Marston was dreaming. He was on the train crossing the Mongolian plain, looking out the window, when suddenly he saw the riders on horseback who appeared out of nowhere, yelling, waving, raising clouds of grayish dust. They raced the train on their ponies, dashing ahead, out of sight, only to fall back again, laughing, raising their arms to salute a temporary victory and the inevitable defeat of flesh against machines.

He saw the single proud uniformed rider, with the scarlet banner streaming from a pole in the wind, whose duty it was to ride ahead of the train and signal that the track was clear. And at the end of the journey civilization ended and gave way to the tribesmen with their herds of ponies and their untrammeled freedom.

Journey 26, the ultimate pilgrimage.

He was excited, for only miles ahead, beyond that point of infinity where the parallel tracks, gleaming in the thin sunlight, came together, was the platform at Ulan Bator where Margaret would be waiting. She would be stalking back and forth impatiently now, wiping back a strand of brown hair from her forehead, squinting down the track for the first sign of the train, listening for the first faint thunder of wheels, the far-distant wail of the whistle.

He awoke in a cold sweat, not wanting to awaken at all. For Margaret was dead, gone, and the ache in him for her had not diminished. It was stronger than the pain he felt in the bones of his hand, in the flesh of his body. For he had learned to control those, to remove his mind to a safe place where that pain did not exist. But there was no secret place where he could hide from the aching emptiness and the fact of Margaret's death.

He brought himself around. He must face facts. Facts. Such a harsh word, and he could see 'facts' as little, spiny, prickly creatures which insisted on self-recognition. He reached out with his right hand and picked up the glass of

243

cold orange juice. He drank it slowly, swallowing in small gulps as if his throat would not accept too much at one time.

Plans. He would have to retire. He would like to go back to Dorking, where he and Margaret were married and lived the first years of their life together, the sweet smell of the country. A small flower garden, perhaps, where he could move among the blooms and give himself time to mend. That would not be possible for a while, of course, for there was Iris to consider, the headstrong, delightful willfulness of youth which sought the lights and the excitement. It was a pity Margaret was not here, for she had always had a gift with the child, a close communication, sometimes unspoken, sometimes conveyed in the warmth of a glance which said, *You and I share the same flesh, the same sex, and although you do not realize it yet, I understand you.* Without her mother, Iris was blooming too fast.

Where are you, Margaret? I need you. Iris needs you.

He drained the glass. He must embrace the spiny little facts to stay rational and practical. He could not remember something which he knew was very important, a specific memory with sharp edges which existed somewhere just beyond his grasp. He tried to seize it, pull it into view, but he could not.

He looked around as the door opened, and the head nurse appeared, eyes slightly wary. He had given her a hard time, but then he had been given a hard time.

'Yes?' he said. 'What is it?'

The head nurse bowed, smiled, obviously impressed with what she had to say. 'A lady has come from the embassy,' she said. 'She brings you flowers and wishes to present them to you. A ceremony, I think.'

The formalities, yes. He rubbed his hand across his face, felt the faint rasp of stubble. It would have to do. 'Send her in, please.'

The woman entered in a rustle of cloth. 'I am Adrienne Hudson,' she said softly. She was a smiling, cherubic lady in her mid-sixties, paisley print and perfume which reminded him of lilacs. He had not seen a hat like the one she wore since the forties, the wide brim matching the dress, and she carried a bouquet of mixed flowers cradled in one arm, as if she were carrying an infant.

She looks like the Queen Mother, he said to Margaret, *come to cheer up the troops.*

She means well, Margaret said, gently chiding. *I think she's dear. Keep an open mind.*

Mrs. Hudson was speaking in a small, charming voice, and he realized he was not listening, had to make a conscious effort to listen to what he recognized as a speech which she had rehearsed well in advance. The head nurse was right. Indeed, this was a ceremony.

'... and on behalf of the grateful members of the embassy in Bangkok as well as the whole of the diplomatic community, which you have served so faithfully...

I have an idea, Margaret. The girl is talented. You said that yourself many times. She simply is unchanneled, you might say, all that energy going off in sparks. But my idea is this: I'll put her in professional school for training as a dancer. She has the grace for it, something she inherited from you. Not that she'll make it as a profession, but then again, she might in the end. She has the perseverance.

'... not from any single individual, but from a collection representing every member of the Bangkok staff, including the ambassador himself, Sir George, who personally asked me to express to you the heartfelt appreciation for your service and devotion to your country and to express to you his personal condolence and sincere sympathy for the loss of your beloved daughter.'

There the words registered. Stopped. Her mouth continued to move as she went on speaking. He wanted to roll back the tape, hear those words again.

Did you hear her, Margaret?

Margaret was not there. Nobody there. Condolence... loss. He heard a scream, a high-pitched wail of agony. He looked around. Not here. Not in this room. An image. Iris prone. The glitter of something in a man's hand.

Fragments. His heart stopped and started again. He would not put them together, refused.

Mrs. Hudson was not speaking now. The head nurse had given Mrs. Hudson a vase, and she was sticking the stems of the flowers into it, standing by the window, stabbing the flowers into the heart of a white vase.

In a chair, the slow rocking of the deck beneath his feet. The girl tied to the table, arms outstretched, screaming to him to save her. His heart stopped. He willed it to stop. It missed only two beats, began again, knocking against his ribs.

Daddy, help me, please.

He willed it, insisted upon it, concentrated on the pattern of veins and arteries coursing through him, the red grid, ordering that it close down. Another heartbeat. Only one. *I have done it, Margaret.*

Mrs. Hudson saw him convulsing on the bed, called in panic for the nurse, who took one look and struck an emergency button. He knew that she was ripping away the hospital gown which covered his chest.

Please do not upset yourself, but I have finished my work, and the message has been passed on. He passed through a red darkness, feeling as if he were hurtling at great speed. And then suddenly he was on the train again. He looked out the window as the train rounded a bend. He saw the man on horseback with the scarlet banner streaming in the wind, dipping in salute as Marston swept past him. The journey was over.

He could see the platform now. Margaret was there, jumping up and down, laughing, waving, her cheeks wet with tears of joy, and beside her, glowing with pleasure, alight with forgiveness, stood his daughter.

Infinity.

21

BANGKOK

When Clive awakened, he was disoriented. The room was dark. Night had fallen, and the monsoon rain was pouring down outside. The room was illuminated by an occasional flicker of lightning. It took him a moment to realize that the telephone was ringing. He groped for it with his right hand and picked it up.

'Johnson here,' the voice came, and he had trouble placing it. One of Marston's doctors. 'I'm terribly sorry to disturb you, Mr. Clive.'

'Hold on.' Clive clicked on the lamp, glanced at his watch. It was three minutes after nine. 'What can I do for you, Mr. Johnson?'

'It was just one of those unfortunate occurrences,' Johnson said. 'It's nobody's fault that I can tell. Of course, considering his psychological state, one could have been more cautious, I suppose.'

'Please come to the point,' Clive said.

'Captain Marston is dead.'

Clive sat speechless, stunned.

'He died this afternoon. A massive coronary.' He paused for a moment. 'I say,' Johnson said, 'are you there, old man?'

'Yes.' He cleared his throat. 'You're sure of the cause?'

'It was the shock, don't you see?' Johnson said. 'A pity, but not to be helped now.'

'What shock?'

'He found out his daughter was dead.'

'Who told him?'

'It was one of those things we couldn't have foreseen.' The voice droned on with the details, filled with a professional commiseration. Clive sat overwhelmed with

247

misery. He had retrieved this splendid man, and now he was dead. 'I realize that there is a form to be followed here, so I shall leave it up to you chaps. I trust you will notify Colonel Patterson.'

'Yes,' Clive said. And slowly he replaced the telephone on the cradle.

Christ, you poor bastard, and what were those last noble thoughts that floated through your brain before you blotted yourself out? You did it yourself, that implacable will of yours, as surely as if you put a gun to your head. You just finally gave up. Didn't you know that in the end survival is what counts?

He picked up the telephone, called Liz, told her to come. He had to go out. He needed her. Then he rang Sam's number, told him to bring the car around.

He was half dressed by the time Liz let herself into his room with her key. 'What's wrong?' she said. 'What happened?'

'Marston is dead,' he said with an anger which came upon him unaware. 'He discovered his daughter had been killed, and so he just quit living.'

'Marston?' She sank into a chair as if the wind had been taken out of her. 'Jesus.'

'Yes,' he said. He told Liz the whole story while he buttoned his shirt. 'I've met Mrs. Hudson,' he said. 'A cheery sort of woman, not an ounce of malevolence in her. Natural causes. Nothing to be done. But I'll have to get around to the hospital.'

'What can I do to help?' Liz said.

'I have to notify London right away,' he said. 'No time for codes, for proper routings. I want you to send a telex for me, even if you have to raise holy hell with the desk clerk to get a dispatcher. This is urgent.'

He grabbed a piece of hotel stationery and a ball-point pen and began to block out the message.

GROTON/WHITEHALL/TELEX: 263563/4/5 (A/B PRO-DROME LONDON)

THE KNIGHT ERRANT IS DEAD. NATURAL CAUSES. I HAVE

A LOCATION FOR OUR PERIPATETIC CORRESPONDENT AND
AM DEALING WITH OUR COUSIN OUT OF NECESSITY. I
REGRET THAT THERE IS INSUFFICIENT TIME FOR CONSEN-
SUS FROM YOUR END.

CLIVE

He handed her the paper, slipped on his jacket, tucked
the pistol into his waistband. She gave him a curious,
disheveled look, pulled her dressing gown tighter about
her.

'Oh, hell,' she said, disgusted. 'Say it isn't so.'

'What?'

'That I have not been naïve, that this very skeptical
woman correspondent has not been had. I know the
terms, the phrases. I know what "cousin" means. My Mr.
Garvin is CIA, isn't he?'

'Yes,' he said.

'You bastard.'

He kissed her briefly. 'I couldn't let you know, old girl.
But things are coming to a head now. Stay put and we'll
talk when I get back from the hospital.'

She held out an umbrella to him. 'You'll need this.'

Outside, beneath the *porte-cochère*, he found himself in
a freakish calm as one edge of the curtain of falling rain
swept past across the boulevard and the banks of neon
lights. He could see another solid wall of rain approaching. In a few minutes it would crawl across the four
lanes of traffic and engulf the hotel again. He did not have
to unfurl the umbrella after all. A black Mercedes pulled
into the circular drive to receive a tuxedoed Thai
gentleman and his exquisite formally gowned lady. As it
pulled away, he saw Sam's car pulling down the long
driveway. He did not wait for Sam to climb out and open
the door for him, but instead took the front passenger seat.

As they drove to the hospital, he told Sam what had
happened, but to his surprise Sam was not shocked. 'It
was his karma,' Sam said gravely. 'He had finished what
he was supposed to do in this life, and so he has moved on.
It was meant that it should be this way for him or it would
not be so.'

They drove to the hospital gate, where a Thai policeman directed Sam to park his car on down the street, to clear the entrance for emergency vehicles. Sam was about to argue, but Clive stopped him. 'It's all right,' he said. 'I'll be only a few minutes.' He unfurled the umbrella as he left the car, the rain coming down in sheets.

The lights were blazing in the cottage, and as he reached the porch, he furled the umbrella and leaned it against the wall. He wiped his feet on a rattan mat and went inside. From the permeating smell of cloves he knew instantly that Patterson was here, even before he saw him at the small desk in the sitting room, glowering at a sheaf of papers he was attacking with a ball-point pen. The ashtray was full of cigarette butts, and a lighted cigarette dangled from the corner of his tight-lipped mouth. He glanced up at Clive, turned his eyes to the papers again.

'Is the body still here?' Clive said.

Patterson nodded, spilling ashes down the front of his uniform. 'We have an ambulance standing by to take him to the embassy as soon as I complete these bloody forms.'

Clive let himself into the bedroom, closed the door behind him. There was something to be said for Thai ceremony, their reverence for the dead, for English hands had not been at work here. No lumpish remains beneath a sheet drawn over the head to conceal the fact of death. Instead, Marston's head lay on a pillow and his arms had been crossed over his chest. The electric lamps had been replaced by a bank of candles, and there were three joss sticks smoking from a small urn of sand.

He pulled up the chair in which he had sat for such a long time, coaxing the mind of this man from its hiding place, reassuring him that it was safe in the outer world. But it was not safe, no, and so Marston had retreated to a place from which he could not be pulled back.

Clive cradled his chin on his hand and studied the profile of the man who lay on the bed, the mystery of him which now was beyond solving.

When I was captured and tortured, he said to Marston

without speaking, *when they had me in that hut with the tin roof, I prayed for deliverance, for someone to come bursting in and carry me out and to kill my tormentors. And when no one came and I survived anyway, I lived past the bitterness and the shame.*

The candles flickered unsteadily on the dead, waxen face which looked more peaceful now than it had in life.

And yet, Clive went on, *I came for you, and I killed the man who savaged your daughter. In a way I gave you back your life, you know, and you decided that you didn't want it. Why?*

There were no answers. There would be no answers. He stood up. Marston was not here. Long since departed. Beyond recall.

He went back into the sitting room, sat down without a word. Patterson scribbled something on a line, leaned back. 'These ladies with the bloody Women's Institute mentality,' he said. 'Mrs. Hudson should never have been allowed in.'

'He would have known some other way. The memory would have come back to him,' Clive said. 'There will be a postmortem?'

'Yes.'

'Who is the next of kin?'

'None to speak of,' Patterson said. 'London says there is a great-aunt in a nursing home in Canada. She's eighty-six years old.'

'No one to survive him then.'

'No.'

'Burial?'

'Somewhere in Sussex, I suppose.' He added another cigarette to the clutter in the ashtray. 'I hear you and our American cousin had an animated conversation at the hotel restaurant. Is there anything you would like to confide to your pagan superior?'

The Watchers, and Clive had forgotten them. Even now, as they were brought to mind, he did not rankle. 'From time to time I forget how organized you are,' Clive said. 'Do you know the numerical grid system the

Americans used for the classification of Thai villages?'

'I know of it,' Patterson said with quickened interest. 'I don't know the specifics.'

'We'll talk tomorrow,' Clive said.

'We'll talk now,' Patterson said. 'No bloody secrets from the chief, that's the rule.'

Clive stood up. 'Tomorrow,' he said. He walked out onto the porch. The rain had let up again but only temporarily. He did not unfurl the umbrella but tucked it under his arm as he passed the administration building and reached the main gate. There was no guard now. The policeman had evidently decided to have a drink or go to the urinal. But there was no need for him, for the street was deserted except for Sam's car, which sat at the curb, perhaps a hundred yards away. The lights were on. The engine was running. He could see the plume of steam from the exhaust.

He raised his hand to signal. The car did not move. He lit a cigarette and stood expelling the smoke into the damp night air. He found himself smelling the air, surveying the empty street and the park beyond it. No movement at all, a dead calm, but in the distance lightning. It would rain again soon. He felt the tension, the sharp suspicion which had become a sixth sense, the dreadful significance of that car which did not move.

Using the umbrella as a walking stick, he approached the car. The windows were steamy, semi-opaque. He could see the figure of a man behind the wheel, heard the muted discordant sounds of Thai music from the car radio. Through the window of the driver's side he saw Sam, his head tilted back against the headrest of the seat at an unnatural angle. There was a dark hole in the center of his forehead, the flesh peppered with dark specks. Point-blank range. He stood where he was, momentarily paralyzed, refusing to make the connection between the tableau in the front seat of the car and the living Sam.

He saw the limousine turn into the street fronting the hospital, and he began to walk back toward the administration building, not forcing himself, falling back on his early conditioning. Timing was everything at this point. That limousine was certainly here for him, and he could not outrun it. He shifted his grip on the umbrella, holding it slightly below the center of the shaft in his left hand. He was twenty yards from the building as the limousine caught up with him, a black Mercedes. As it drew abreast of him, the rear window rolled down and he saw Boris's smiling face, innocuous. But at the same moment the doors opened on the other side of the limousine and two men got out, large, square, bulky men, one sauntering around the rear of the car to stand by the rear bumper, the other standing between Clive and the building, his massive arms folded across his chest.

'We need to have a chat, you and I,' Boris said.

And everything was suddenly clear, Nikolai's last words, the ease with which Marston was taken, everything. The message had passed on to Clive. Marston would not talk, but old Clive would. That had been demonstrated. His breath caught in his throat, the rage in him so suddenly intense he thought he would explode with it.

'Marston,' he said.

'What?'

'Dead, you son of a bitch. And now my driver.'

'For Nikolai,' Boris said, still smiling.

'Sam? For that bastard?'

'Nikolai was a bastard, but he was our bastard. We're even now. Too bad about Marston. Come. Get in, my friend. It's going to be raining in another few moments.'

With an ease which struck him as a natural movement, like an intake of breath, Clive's right hand drew the pistol from his waistband, swung it up, the finger squeezing the trigger. The explosion, square in Boris's face, which fell away into the blackness of the car. And at the same moment the man at the rear of the car shot forward, arms outstretched, as if to embrace him, and Clive jabbed the point of the umbrella tip into the middle of his chest, just below the sternum, with such force he could feel it stick into the flesh. And as quickly as he jabbed, he withdrew it, just as the second man came running from the front of the car. As Clive swung the umbrella, it popped open and one of the curved metal staves caught the man in the center of his eye. With a howl of pain the man fell back against the side of the car, clutching his face.

Clive abandoned the umbrella, ran across the street and into the park, slogging through the rain-soaked grass. He could hear the voices behind him, the shouts and cries, men calling to one another. How many others had there been in the limousine? Two? Three? He couldn't tell. They had had him before. Never again. He'd die first.

He ran past a fountain and a statue of a Thai warrior on a bronze horse just as the wall of rain caught him, engulfing him with such force that he gasped for air. He made it across a decorative bridge and into the shelter of a grove of trees, the darkness broken only by the reflected light from a distant boulevard. He fell against a tree trunk, the water streaming down his face. He looked back toward the hospital, which was an abstract smear of lights in the darkness. Above the drumming roar of the rain he could hear the yelling voices. He saw the stabbing beams of the flashlights, at least half a dozen men spilling into the park.

Christ, they had been clever, and the neatly constructed trap they had prepared for him had now been sprung. He took the long silencer from his pocket, screwed it into the muzzle. He waited. A man ran by, not ten yards from where he stood, the flashlight all but useless, the beam diminished by the density of the rain. He waited for the voice, heard only inflections. Thai. He let the man pass.

He ran on through the bushes and abruptly ran into a high chain-link fence which separated the park from a busy street. He clawed with his fingers at the chain link, beginning to climb. Somewhere to his left he heard a man shouting in Russian and the awful whine of the bullet as it missed his head and ricocheted off the metal post.

He let go of the fence, fell to the ground, and brought his pistol up, holding it in both hands, steadying it against his knee. In a few moments he could see the man's shape, no features, only a silhouette. Still, Clive waited, until he heard the man shout again, definitely Russian. The man was looking at him, raising his pistol for another shot. Only then did Clive sight into the center of that shadow, holding his breath as he squeezed the trigger.

The pistol jerked against his hand, no noise at all in the rain. The blocky silhouette fell away, a target in a shooting gallery. Clive returned the pistol to his waistband. He clawed with his fingers at the chain link and scrambled up it. He slipped twice, reached the top, where his jacket caught on the top barbs, ripped as he half climbed, half fell down the other side. He blinked against the cataract of rain, made out the shapes of heavy machinery against the smeared lights of a shopping arcade across the street. He was in a construction zone, a vacant lot, torn-up concrete, piles of dirt, holes in the ground already half filled with water, cratered as a battle zone.

He collected himself, only half aware of the sounds of traffic from the street ahead of him. He threaded his way on fragmented pieces of stone to the street, passing a heavy earthmover.

The street itself was a river, flowing curb-deep, the cars moving very slowly, sending out waves like the wakes of powerboats. He waded the street, dodging a three-wheeled *samlor* intent on running him down. When he reached the other side, he paused beneath the sheltering canopy of a variety tourist store with a rack of umbrellas showing through the window.

He went inside, where the walls were covered with framed batik, patterns of gaudy sunsets and an abstract tiger peering out with burning eyes from a grove of bamboo stalks. He stood on the plastic runner, dripping water. A small woman bowed to him, making a formal *wai*.

'I would much appreciate it if I could use your telephone,' he said in Thai. 'I will pay you for the call.'

The woman led him to the rear of the shop, indicated the telephone on its own teak table. 'I will be most pleased if it works,' she said.

'Thank you.'

He dialed the hotel, had Liz on the line in a minute. The moment she heard the tenor of his voice, she was concerned. 'What's going on?' she said. 'You sound like you've been running. Are you all right?'

'Yes, for now,' he said. 'But I'm in an untenable situation. I want you to do something for me. It may be bloody impossible, but give it a try.'

'What do you want me to do?'

'First, get Garvin in tow. Leave the hotel. Then find a taxi and pick me up.'

'Where are you?'

He spotted a piece of shop stationery on a desk, read it upside down. 'It's a shop called Beautiful Batik.' He read her the address, spelled out the street name.

'I'll be there.'

'One more thing. When you get here, if you see that I'm in custody, pass on by. Go to the British Embassy straightaway, and let them know what's happened. But under no circumstances are you to play tigress rushing to the aid of her wounded mate. And don't let Garvin play this his way. You go to the British Embassy.'

'I love you,' she said.

He severed the connection, turned to the woman who stood behind the counter at the front of the shop. He would need time now. She was leafing through a catalogue written in Chinese. 'How much do I owe you for the telephone call?' he said in Thai.

'*Mai pen rai.*'

'Thank you then. But I do need an umbrella or, come to think of it, a matching pair. One for myself, a larger one, and then a smaller one for a friend.' He had left Liz's umbrella back on the pavement where he had been attacked.

The woman began to go through the rack, an apologetic frown on her face, chattering in Thai about the poor quality of fabrics in umbrellas anymore. He listened and nodded and looked out the front window, across the street

256

into the construction yard. The rain had begun to slacken, and he could see a flash of lights. The cordon of men would be spreading out soon.

He turned his attention to the umbrellas, chatting it up with the Thai woman, narrowing his interest to the two pairs of matching umbrellas she had laid out on the counter before him, weighing the ivory handles of one set against the polished teak of the second, trying to demonstrate a proper concern while his eyes monitored the construction site. There were multiple lights at the point where he had crossed the fence. A matter of minutes now, no more than that.

He made his choice, the ivory-handled pair, haggled politely over the price, as was expected of him, finally agreed to a price of which he was only dimly aware. Two Thai policemen on motorcycles roared down the river of a street, turning into the construction site. The motorcycles wound through the earthmoving equipment and the muddy craters. Clive counted out the money from his wallet, the paper baht notes so wet he had to peel them apart. Lights were fanning out, tracking from the point where he had crossed the fence.

His view was blocked by the shape of the taxi pulling up to the curb in front of the shop. He saw Liz's face peering through the rain-streaked window and, beyond her, Gavin. Clive opened the larger of the umbrellas, held it low to cover his face and strolled to the waiting car, where he furled it and climbed into the comfortable darkness. Liz clutched his arm. 'You're drenched,' she said.

'Let's get out of here,' Clive said. He spoke to the driver in Thai, told him to drive on. As the taxi pulled away, he looked out through the rear window as one of the Russians in a dark suit, gun in hand, waded through the water, crossing the street toward the batik shop.

He settled against the seat, wiped his face with a handkerchief, remembering Sam, the naïveté of that sincere and vulnerable face – 'I have been trained in the martial arts, sir' – and Christ, he had wanted to keep Sam safe. Sam's voice, remembered: 'He had finished what he

257

was supposed to do in this life, and so he has moved on.'
Untrue. His life had been cut short for no reason except to
balance the score between enemies. Too many deaths,
Clive thought. Far too many.

22

BANGKOK

Lloyd Jenkins was the night duty officer at the British Embassy in Bangkok, a conscientious young man who took himself and his duties very seriously. He was a short, stocky young man with coal black hair and round spectacles with thick corrective lenses, and at the moment he found himself faced with a dilemma. For not ten minutes before, he had been confronted by Gordon Clive, drenched and bedraggled, looking for all the world as if he had been in a street brawl, immediately issuing orders that he wanted use of the small reception room to which Jenkins was to see that hot tea and sandwiches would be brought. Not for himself alone but for the two people he had in tow, the very pretty woman, whom, despite her obvious charms, Jenkins recognized as a magazine correspondent, and a cool, detached American of indeterminate middle age who was bound to be American intelligence.

'And ring Colonel Patterson at the hospital and get him here straightaway,' Clive had said, almost as an afterthought, as he stood dripping on the expensive carpet. 'If you receive any inquiries, none of us is here. And keep this to yourself.'

That was all very well and good, Jenkins thought, all this ordering about and catering to, and he had made the call to Colonel Patterson all right. And he had rung the kitchen and endured the complaints of the night staff about such refreshments after hours, and not on the say-so of the ambassador, but that of the night duty officer, who could not say why they should go to this trouble. But there were rules to be observed, and Sir George had made them quite clear in an all-embracing memo posted on all the bulletin boards when he had taken over here. A clean sweep. No mucking about. With everything to be cleared through a higher officer, no delegated duties that his lordship did not clear personally.

But the Ormsby-Fletchers were in Chiangmai, another ribbon to be cut, another hospital to be graced by the presence of, and the counselor and head of chancery, Henry Phillips, OBE, old No. 2, had been in something of a pet when he retired to quarters with a miserable head cold, leaving instructions that he was not to be disturbed short of a national disaster. So Jenkins stayed at his desk and fretted.

Within half an hour Colonel Patterson arrived, stalking through, his uniform damp, his temper miserable. 'I want you to make a call for me,' he informed Jenkins without even looking at him. 'Call the Bangkok police and inquire after a shooting of one Boris Ludov. I want to know if he's dead. But be circumspect. This is not an official call. Do you understand me?'

'Quite,' Jenkins said.

'Where are the others?'

'The small reception hall.' And then the obligatory question, just tossed off but full of implications for Jenkins: 'It is all right, I assume, for them to have the use of the facilities?'

'Certainly,' Colonel Patterson said on his way down the corridor, and that was quite sufficient for Jenkins. He jotted it down in his night log, authorizing the meeting under Patterson's name. He felt quite better about it once it was on paper. The colonel was considered something of an eccentric anyway.

The Thai waiter came up from the kitchen, pushing a tea cart. Jenkins jerked a manicured thumb down the hall toward the reception room. 'Get on with it,' he said a little more abruptly than he needed to. 'Colonel Patterson is waiting.'

The tea cart trundled on. Jenkins picked up the telephone to make the call.

*

The tea was hot, strong, and Clive sipped it, not in the mood for this meeting at all, finding himself in the position of intermediary between two men whose dislike of each other was like a polite electricity in the air. He did not like the room itself, a long rectangle with an unfortunate combination of Thai and Victorian furnishings and a lazy overhead fan which squeaked slightly as it turned. He was drenched, uncomfortable, and yet he sat on a satin sofa with complete disregard for what his soggy clothes would do to it. Liz sat next to him, being very quiet as if to make herself invisible, knowing that at any moment Colonel Patterson might decide to ask her to remove herself from what was to be a private conversation.

At the moment Patterson was standing by the corner of a teak table, rocking back and forth on his heels while he smoked a cigarette and studied with a sidelong glance the sitting Garvin, who was sprawled in a teak armchair, his legs crossed like an American cowboy, with the ankle of one leg resting on the knee of the other.

'With all due respect, Mr. Garvin,' Patterson said in a tone of voice in which there was no respect at all, 'you can understand that this is strictly a British operation, always has been. The dispatches from Charlie Excalibur were directed to us, after all, not to you.'

Garvin stifled a yawn. 'We're talking about an American deserter, Colonel,' he said. 'This is an American boy we're talking about.'

'Jurisdiction here is a matter of principle with me,' Patterson said.

'Principle, hell,' Garvin said with a smile. 'You're afraid the ball will get out of your court.'

'Don't push this too bloody far,' Patterson said.

Clive leaned forward, slapped the flat of his hand against the table. The sharpness of the sound startled even him. 'All right,' he said evenly. 'I have had quite enough.'

'This is out of your hands,' Patterson said.

'The hell it is,' Clive said. 'I am outranked here. I am

261

well aware of that. On the one hand, there's a colonel who thinks that the fate of Asia rests in his grip, and on the other, an American who has let me know that he is the whole bloody United States. But you are both forgetting that I am the only one with any solid information here, and if I bloody well decide to leave you and go home with it, then you have absolutely nothing.'

'You're forgetting yourself,' Patterson cautioned.

Clive sipped his tea. 'Not bloody likely. I am tired and sore, banged up mentally and physically. I've seen two fine men die today, for no good reason that I can see, and my own life has been in danger as well. I've had quite enough of power plays and international balances that end up in corpses. So I am going to dictate a compromise which the two of you will bloody well accept or you'll go it without me.'

Garvin was quietly contemplative. Patterson was fuming.

'I'll hear what you have to say,' Garvin said, lacing his fingers beneath his chin. He shifted his eyes to Liz. 'But I would feel more comfortable without the presence of the press.'

'She stays,' Clive said adamantly. 'If this whole thing falls apart because two intelligent men refuse to compromise, then I certainly need an objective witness.'

Garvin shrugged, looked to Patterson. The colonel sat down. He picked up his teacup, used the fine china saucer as an ashtray, and waited.

'All right,' Clive said. 'I have the number of the village and Garvin knows the number code. The meeting is to take place the day after tomorrow. I want an indication of your good faith, Garvin. The three hundred series refers to what part of Thailand?'

'Northeast,' Garvin said, 'along the Laotian border.'

'Fine. Then you, Colonel Patterson, will provide a lorry with one driver and an aide. You, Garvin, will be permitted a car and two aides. The meeting time is the day after tomorrow.'

'That soon?' Garvin said. 'What's the number of the village?'

262

'Hear me out,' Clive said. 'We leave tomorrow night, seven o'clock. Once we're on the road, and only then, will I give you the number of the village. There is to be no radio equipment in either vehicle. Is that agreed?'

'I'll go with that,' Garvin said. 'Colonel?'

Patterson leaned back in his chair as if he were playing cards and had not yet decided how he would play the hand. 'But once he is taken, he is our property.'

'I can't agree to that,' Garvin said.

'Neither of you will decide that,' Clive said. 'I intend to cable London tonight and tell them what we plan to do. Our chaps will meet with the American CIA in London and work out what will happen to Charlie Excalibur, if and when we do have him.'

'I can give you the American position now,' Garvin said.

'If you're right and London accepts it, then I'll go along.' He finished the tea. 'And that ends the discussion. It's up to you gentlemen. Either accept or reject.'

'I accept,' Garvin said.

Patterson finally nodded assent. 'Tomorrow then.'

The telephone rang. Patterson picked it up, listened, nodded, then grunted and replaced it on the cradle. 'You might be interested to know that Boris Ludov is in critical condition, but he is still alive,' he said to Clive. 'You managed to mess up the side of his face and his left ear.'

'So be it,' Clive said. He shrugged, tired, sorting through the situation in which he found himself. They would be all over the streets tonight, the Russians and their Watchers, with a vengeance. He stood up. 'Have the night duty officer prepare a guest room. Miss Sullivan and I will be spending the night here.'

'Two rooms, I assume,' Patterson said.

Clive laughed, genuinely amused. 'One room. And right away. Also, send someone around to my hotel to fetch my clothes. And Miss Sullivan may need a few things as well.'

In the corridor, on the way to the guest cottage, Liz took his arm. 'You would really have walked away if they hadn't accepted, wouldn't you?'

'Yes.'

'Just like that.'

'Yes. Just like that. From here on out I make my own decisions.'

1/1/1.   07605/A-B. PRODROME TO BANGKOK-CLIVE
CODED/POWELL 9144. DECODED/TREMLETT 5448. 6/27/
79 OPEN.

AFTER CONSULTATION WITH CIA CHIEF OF STATION,
LONDON, THE FOLLOWING AGREEMENT HAS BEEN
REACHED.

YOU ARE HEREBY AUTHORIZED TO OFFER THE SUBJECT
SANCTUARY IN THE UNITED KINGDOM IN RETURN FOR HIS
UNCONTESTED SURRENDER AND HIS UNQUALIFIED CO-
OPERATION IN PROVIDING SUCH INFORMATION AS HE MAY
HAVE WITHIN HIS POSSESSION. ON SURRENDER, PRIVATE
TRANSPORTATION WILL BE PROVIDED FOR HIS RETURN TO
LONDON UPON NOTIFICATION OF THIS OFFICE.

FOR YOUR INFORMATION AND FOR THE INFORMATION OF
THE CIA REPRESENTATIVE ONLY, THE SUBJECT WILL BE
DETAINED IN THE UNITED KINGDOM FOR A PERIOD NOT TO
EXCEED NINETY (90) DAYS, AT WHICH TIME THE DECISION
WILL BE MADE WHETHER TO OFFER HIM PERMANENT
SANCTUARY OR TO RETURN HIM TO THE UNITED STATES.

NONE OF THE ABOVE SHALL BE CONSTRUED, IN ANY WAY,
TO DETRACT FROM THE AUTHORITY OF COLONEL PATTER-
SON, WHO WILL SERVE IN A CONSULTANT CAPACITY TO
EXPEDITE THE OPERATION.

ROSS. CLOSE.

When Clive received the cable from the orderly, he retired to a chair by the window in the guest cottage. He read the carefully calculated wording for the second time and then initialed the sheets before he handed them back to the orderly, who, being ex-military, clicked his leather heels together before he made his exit.

'Your breakfast is getting cold, love,' Liz called from the

table where breakfast had been laid out and was awaiting him. He took his place at the small table, cut into the fine piece of gammon, discovered he was hungry. She buttered the overly dry toast from the ceramic rack. She frowned. 'Are you going to tell me what was in the cable?'

He smiled, genuinely amused not only by her response to his silence but by the cable itself. 'Not specifically, no,' he said, opening an egg. 'Sometimes at the most serious of times things turn bloody funny. You know what I mean.'

'Not exactly, I must say.'

He ate hungrily, interspersing his bites with fragments of sentences. 'The Russians are dying to get hold of me at this point.' He sipped his tea. 'I'm getting ready to mount a bloody expedition into the jungle to pick up a man who may or may not be there, may or may not be a traitor, may or may not have information which will be of use to us. And so here comes a cable from London, top echelon, negotiated rules with a little something for everybody thrown in, about what will be done with the subject, that's what Charlie Excalibur is being called, if we catch him and if he turns out to be what we think he might or might not be. It's rather like detailing a zoological order for a unicorn. Nobody's sure he exists, but they want to make damn sure what's done with him if he does.'

He finished his breakfast with a hearty appetite while she picked around at a single egg on her plate. 'You're avoiding the main question, you know,' she said, a slight, querulous edge to her voice that was always there when she was having to skirt a subject instead of dealing with it straight out.

'I don't see that I am.'

'Then you're dense.'

'Undoubtedly,' he said. 'Perhaps you had better enlighten me.'

'You're patronizing me.'

'Sometimes you need it.' He reached across the table, put his hand on hers. 'Out with it, old girl. It's not your way to hold back with anything.'

She sat back in her chair as if preparing either to meet

an attack or to mount one. 'I intend to go along for the meeting,' she said darkly. 'If you don't make provisions for me, then I'll follow you. Now you must give that some thought.'

He was not to have the opportunity to think about it, for through the window he saw Patterson stalking across the compound, and from the way he held his head back, as if he were marching to a drumbeat, it was apparent he was in quite a pet. In a moment he was rapping sharply on the door. Clive let him in, and Patterson stood just inside the door, flexing a leather swagger stick in his two lean hands, dour-faced.

'You're in time for tea,' Clive said. 'Breakfast, if you wish.'

'I don't care for any,' he said, eyeing Liz. 'I'd like a private conversation if you please.'

'Certainly,' Liz said, and taking her teacup, she disappeared into the bedroom, closing the door behind her. Only then did Patterson decide to sit, perching in one of the wing chairs next to the window.

'I have read the cable from London,' he said rather absently, as if what he was about to say should be taken as fact, beyond question. 'It simply won't do, you know. I have dispatched a return signal to that effect, but it's highly unlikely that we will have a reply by this evening. You know what night dispatch is like back there.'

Clive took the time to pour himself a fresh cup of tea and then settled in the chair facing Patterson. 'I don't see what you're upset about,' he said.

'Then you're not thinking straight,' Patterson said. He moved restlessly about the room. 'Take the larger view. We are mounting a joint operation to go back into the bush against God knows what odds. Garvin's men will certainly be armed, and I won't allow my chaps to go into a situation like that bare-assed. Now what that amounts to is a foreign military operation on Thai soil.'

Clive nodded, sipped his tea, and for a moment felt a great sympathy for this lean, tanned man with his hawk-like face and restless eyes. Patterson was a born leader of

266

men, would have liked nothing better than to test himself against enemy troops, leading his chaps into a fight, exhorting their courage in the face of death. But there were no current wars, not even the prospect of one. An anachronism, Patterson was born a hundred years too late.

'What did you have in mind?' Clive said.

'I can see very well why it would not occur either to you or to Garvin. This isn't your country, after all, and you'll bloody well be moving on. But were we to undertake something like this without the full cooperation of the Thai authoriies, General Kriangsak would know about it within twenty-four hours and I would be persona non grata here. It simply won't do.'

Clive sipped his tea, said nothing, waiting.

'I intend to notify General Sem of the problem, ask for their cooperation. They are a very understanding lot and certain to comply. They can have units of the Thai Fourth Army moved into position today. They can establish a cordon, pick up Charlie Excalibur, and have him here by tomorrow afternoon.'

'And you would be going along, I suppose?'

'As liaison. To protect our interests.'

Clive smiled, shook his head. The sunlight fell across him like a blanket. He felt relaxed, but the recalcitrance within him was like steel. 'I'm sorry,' he said, 'but we will be going ahead according to plan. Now, if you wish, you can cover yourself in the matter by withdrawing from the operation. You can leave it to Garvin and me.'

'I wouldn't think of it.'

'You've made my point. Garvin would never consider your proposal seriously, nor would I.'

Patterson jabbed his cigarette toward Clive, and a perfect smoke ring rolled from it, hanging in the bright shaft of sunlight. 'You can't do this,' he said. He was trying to project menace, Clive realized, but there was a poignant appeal to his voice. 'With one telephone call I can make the whole thing impossible.'

'But you won't,' Clive said. He tasted the tea again. It

had gone cold, and he set the cup and saucer aside and lit a cigarette for himself. 'I know you consider yourself to be in an impossible position. Damned if you do and damned if you don't. But there's always the possibility that what we've planned will work, that the Thais will know nothing about it. And there's no chance that you can abort this without swift retribution from London.'

'So finally you get your revenge,' Patterson said sourly.

'Revenge?'

'My orders kept me from retrieving you, and now you will use the standing orders to bring me down. That's your bloody idea of revenge.'

Clive examined the idea to see if there was any truth in it, then shook his head. 'I was bitter toward you for a while,' he said. 'But that passed a long time ago. What I did was very difficult to live with, so I tried to spread the guilt around, I think. But I have finally accepted my own responsibility for my actions. You did what you had to do. I respect that. So this current operation has no connection with the past.'

Patterson ground out his cigarette in a ceramic ashtray shaped like a flower. The swagger stick twitched in his hands like the tail of a restless lion. 'Nevertheless, I can still make the decision to scrub, if I choose.'

'Yes.'

'I'll let you know what I decide directly.'

Clive watched him stalking away across the lawn. Liz came out of the bedroom, a thoughtful expression on her face. 'He's in a real crack, isn't he?'

'You listened through the door.'

'Of course.' She poured herself another cup of tea. 'What will he do?'

'He will brood awhile, and then he will go along,' Clive said. 'He knows that to go against orders at this point would be the end of him here. They'd yank him out in a minute, and he would shrivel up and blow away without this country to keep him occupied.' He drew on his cigarette. 'No, he will have to compromise here long enough to retire, and then he'll build a house on the beach down at Pattaya and write his memoirs, a scathing indictment of the way the Western countries have screwed up this paradise of his.'

The telephone rang. He picked it up to find Garvin on the line. Garvin was in the embassy compound and clearly unhappy. 'We have to talk,' Garvin said.

'Yes.' Clive looked out through the window, saw a bench on the lawn beneath a bank of white frangipani flowers. 'Come back toward the guest cottage. I'll be waiting for you on a bench.'

'You've missed your calling,' Liz said as he put the telephone back on the cradle. 'You should have been a labor negotiator.'

'Salving wounded egos is not my specialty,' he said. 'In this case it has to be done. But much of this and I would turn into a bloody tyrant, an absolute dictator.' He kissed her lightly, went out into the steaming heat of the morning. By the time he reached the bench he saw Garvin steaming around the corner of the main building.

Garvin sat down, got directly to the point. 'I hear that the esteemed colonel has his nose out of joint and is trying to play soldier.'

'Everybody would like to run the show his own way,' Clive said.

'And it appears that you have that opportunity,' Garvin said. 'I had a cable from my chief of station in London. You managed to pull this off pretty well, didn't you?'

'I don't feel any sense of victory,' Clive said calmly. 'Personally I'll be pleased when this whole bloody thing is behind me.'

Garvin shrugged, twisting his large hands together as if he were restless and needed some physical movement to drain off the tension. 'I don't like Patterson, but he does have a point. I know the Thai military. It might be a good idea to let them know what we're up to. I have some good contacts.'

'No,' Clive said firmly. 'I will tell you the same thing I told Patterson. If you can't see your way clear to going along with the specified orders, then you're free to drop out and Patterson and I will do it.'

'That's not acceptable.' Garvin stood up. 'I'll carry through with this, but in my opinion you're courting disaster.'

Clive went back to the cottage, deep in thought. He sank down into a chair by the window while Liz respected his mood and occupied herself by making notes on a piece of stationery. There was no certainty in this life, Clive realized, and he could count on both Patterson and Garvin to issue protests to the hierarchy, pointing out in advance all of the things that could go wrong. So if the scheme did go awry, they could point, Cassandra-like, at their preregistered portents of doom and prove themselves right in the end.

He had his own doubts as well. He had no desire to go off into the jungle, to place himself in jeopardy toward a goal which perhaps was unattainable and, if reached, could prove to be worthless. Too, at the back of his mind lay the foundation of violence which had already been established by the Russians, for from the moment he left the embassy compound he was fair game again.

Quite suddenly he had the overwhelming desire to be back in London, back in the safe and predictable routine, the quick breakfast before the rush to the tube to get to work on time, the time-consuming minutiae of the day, the noncritical overlay of concern about a leaking water tap or what to name the baby. The desire became an almost irresistible keening, a sharp pain, and he cut it off. He picked up the telephone, asked the embassy operator to connect him with Patterson.

'Clive here,' he said, giving Patterson no opportunity for argument or rebuttal or the voicing of doubts. 'I want you to contact the appropriate Thai government official and give him the following information. Official representatives of the government of Great Britain and the United States of America are going to make a fact-finding tour of refugee camps along the border. We will be taking along Miss Elizabeth Sullivan, a correspondent for the *Far Eastern Economic Review*. The purpose of the visit is to help determine the amount of money which will be appropriated by our respective countries toward the overwhelming burden which the Thai government has been forced to assume.'

There was a silence on the other end of the line while Patterson was thinking it through. 'I don't know,' Patterson said finally.

'If this is beyond you, Colonel, I'll have the economic counselor make the appropriate notification.'

'No,' Patterson said, withholding any comment as to whether he thought it was a good idea or not. 'I'll make the contact.'

'Fine,' Clive said. He put down the telephone, suddenly drained. He felt Liz's arms come around his neck from behind.

'I appreciate this,' she said, elated. 'You found a way to make room for me after all.'

He took her hands in his, found her fingers warm, comforting. 'Dear Liz, you have it all backwards,' he said. 'I included you to make what we're doing seem legitimate. But if I had my choice, I would have left you behind, hurt feelings and all. Because what we're about to do is to make a blindfolded walk across a minefield in which everything can blow up at any point.'

'I take my risks, too,' she said, kissing him on the top of the head. 'When it comes right down to it, I'm a pretty tough cookie. I can take care of myself.'

Sam said the same, Clive thought. *We all believe in a personal invulnerability because we exist now, at this moment, and we cannot conceive of not existing.* But Sam was in the morgue and soon would be in a ceramic urn, not Sam himself but his mortal remains, preserved for a year before the fires released the corruptible elements and left the residue of fine ash. Clive voiced none of this, did not put it into words. Instead, he patted her hands, gave her a smile which was meant to be reassuring, and then he went to take his morning shower.

23

VILLAGE 328

Charlie Excalibur liked the idea of numbers. There was an impersonality to be found in digits. It made life simpler to be known as a number because numbers could be shifted around and lost. He had the feeling that once he walked away from the marines, it was the number they searched for and not the man.

And it was easier in battle to destroy a village which had no name but was known only as a number, as grid coordinates, for in writing reports, '098 OBLITERATED', it was as if something nonhuman, something arithmetical, had been erased. And if it had been done by artillery, from a distance, it was possible to believe that no people had been involved, that there was just a target with a label off on the side of a distant mountain, obscured by trees, and the billowing black smoke that arose from the barrage was little more than a test of accuracy, a score.

The last time Charlie Excalibur had been at Village 328 he had been with Epstein. Funny that he should think of Epstein now, Charlie Excalibur thought, except that he was now climbing the brushy trail through the rocks which led to Village 328 and that was where he had first run into Epstein, who had let his hair and his beard grow long and was living like an Old Testament prophet, except for the fatigue jacket with the death's-head patch which he still wore. They had made plans to go home together, and now Epstein was dead, and here he was, carrying out the plan alone.

Charlie Excalibur remembered Village 328 as a small hamlet, a collection of hooches and one single Quonset hut, donated by the Americans, he supposed, on which the curved metal sheets had begun to rust from too many monsoon rains and to pop loose from their bolted positions. But as he reached the top of a ridge, shading his eyes with his hand against the burning sunlight, his heart sank. The whole goddamned place had changed, and to one side of the valley there appeared to be a refugee camp teeming with half-naked, brown-skinned, emaciated people, surrounded by barbed wire, a scattering of Thai army trucks here and there. A few permanent houses had been built of wood. There were dozens of temporary hooches scattered through the trees and off to the left, almost obscured by a thick growth of trees, a makeshift steeple with a Christian cross on the top of it.

He had seen this place as a perfect meeting ground because it had been small enough that he could monitor the approach of any vehicles, know when Clive arrived, make sure he was by himself. Not only had that possibility now evaporated, but he could find himself trapped if he did not exercise extreme caution. For where there were Thai troops, you could know in advance that they would be continually on the move, foraging for food around the countryside.

He squatted down and had a drink of brackish water from his canteen while he made up his mind what he was going to do. If Clive had received the message, Clive would be here tomorrow. To make other arrangements, to send another message and pick another time and place would be impossible. Time was running out for him. He could feel it in his bones. He would simply have to risk it.

He decided on the church spire as a point of reference because it was somewhat away from the center of the village. He picked his way along the path, heard a babble of voices, and melted into the brush. He watched a group of Cambodian refugees straggle past him, old men and women with babies for the most part, for Pol Pot had made a point of massacring the able-bodied young males. He stayed off the path from that point, for wherever there were new refugees, there would be Thai soldiers to round them up and herd them behind the barbed wire before they were shipped back to Cambodia.

It took him the better part of three hours to survey the entire camp, the street markets of farmers under sunshades with rice and vegetables spread out in front of them, the strings of dried fish glinting silver in the harsh glare of sunlight. The stench of the refugee camp permeated the hot, still air. Too many people, too close together.

He made his way down into the valley close to the church, which proved not to be a church building at all but a makeshift Western-style house with a steeple perched on the roof. The windows were without screens and glass. To the south of the building was a clearing with ancient American GI tarps stretched on poles, so thin in spots that shafts of green sunlight poured down on what appeared to be dozens of children, most of them quite young, many naked with bloated bellies, skinny arms.

One group under the tarp was singing 'Jesus Loves Me' in a cacophony of different dialects. Another group, the children slightly larger, were collecting carrots and cabbages from a weedy garden. He saw a Thai woman cooking something in a large pot, stirring it with a wooden stick, the smoke from the fire rising straight up. He could smell the aroma, and his stomach growled with hunger. He stayed in the bush behind the irregular compound, squatting motionlessly, the sweat running in rivulets down his back. A swarm of gnats congested the air around his head. He did not move.

After a while the singing stopped, and he saw a woman come out the back door of the house. She was a white woman, heavyset, in her early sixties perhaps, her gray hair gathered in a bun at the back of her head. She was wearing a cotton dress with a subdued floral pattern, and she carried herself heavily, with great effort, as she approached the wooden platform of a covered well. She lifted the lid and lowered a bucket on a rope. Her broad back was to him, and while she waited, she rested one hand on her hip. He approached within ten feet of her before she turned, fixed him with questioning brown eyes.

274

She had no business out here in this tropical country, her face told him that. For her skin was normally dead white and now it was a splotchy red, sunburned and peeling. But her mouth was compressed into one tight line, and her eyes told him she was not easily frightened.

'Don't be afraid of me,' he said calmly. 'I'm American.'

'I'm not afraid of you,' she said, her accent American southern. 'Who are you? What do you want?'

'Well, first, I'm hungry.'

'Around here everybody's hungry.'

'I'm sorry for that, but I need food. I would appreciate some food if you can spare it.'

Her eyes examined him closely. 'If you're American, then you're a deserter.'

'Yes, ma'am. And I need food and a place to wash up and rest a little. That's all. I'm not going to hurt you.'

'If they catch you here, they'll burn us down and turn us out,' she said. 'Wait here.' And without retrieving the bucket from the well, she limped back into the house. He felt a moment of panic, for she could be summoning the Thai troops. If that happened, he could, of course, pull his pistol and fight it out, knowing that he would be dead in the end, but not without cost to the men who tried to take him.

But the woman reappeared again, this time accompanied by a man about the same age, a thin, wiry man with a fringe of stubbly gray hair around a sunburned scalp. There was not an excess pound on him anywhere. His exposed arms were all tendons and bones with stringy muscle, and his T-shirt was drenched with sweat. He stood in front of his wife, as if to protect her. 'We're ministers in the Assembly of God Church,' he said. 'I can understand what you're going through, but we have over seventy children to take care of, and we're not going to risk them to help you. We don't want any trouble, but that's the way it is.'

'We all have troubles,' Charlie Excalibur said. 'Now I'm supposed to meet a representative of the British government here tomorrow, and I'm going to turn myself in. You

275

just happen to have the only place in town where I can keep from running into Thai troops.'

'I'm sorry,' the man said. 'The answer still has to be no.'

Charlie Excalibur licked his cracked lips. He could smell the uncertainty in this man, and it had nothing at all to do with the risk of dying. No, there was another vulnerable area, and Charlie Excalibur picked it up immediately. 'I mean you no harm,' he said. 'But I need some food and a place to rest. Can you call yourself a Christian and turn me away?'

The man's thin face grew more uncertain. He bit his underlip. 'Just food and a bed?'

'Food, a place to rest, water to wash with. One night. I'll be gone tomorrow.'

The man gave it thought, rubbed his chin. 'All right. You can come inside. But you leave your pistol outside. We insist on the peace of God inside our place.'

'As long as I have my pistol, I know the peace of God is going to be maintained. Believe me, I'm not out to rob you or hurt you in any way. Here today, gone tomorrow.'

The old man nodded his assent. The woman went back to the well, ignoring Charlie Excalibur altogether as he walked past her. She had the smell of soap about her. He followed the man into the house, through a large room with a small altar and a picture on the wall of Jesus and some sheep, into a back room which served as their bedroom, and then down a short hallway to an even smaller room. There were boxes of medical supplies along one wall and an old army cot.

'You can stay here,' the old man said. 'We'll bring you something to eat directly. After dark we'll get a shower rigged up. Do you read?'

'Yes.'

The old man nodded, the patience of years of things gone awry etched on his face. He left Charlie Excalibur to the room, switched on a radio in the bedroom, the distorted sounds of music coming from the BBC World-wide. In a few minutes the old man was back with a tin plate full of a thick vegetable stew, no meat, and a pile of magazines, which he put on top of a box of medical supplies. He stood in the doorway while Charlie Excalibur wolfed down the food.

'I suppose you got your reasons,' the old man said.

'For what?'

'For walking away.'

'I thought I was doing a good thing at the time.'

The man took the plate when it was empty. 'I don't want to know your name,' he said.

'All right.'

'I had a son killed in Vietnam,' the old man said. 'Maybe it would have been better if he had walked away. But he didn't. I don't think I can forgive the fact that you did. So I don't want to know your name.'

He left the room, pulled a curtain over the door. Charlie Excalibur put his small knapsack on the cot, picked up the stack of magazines. They were mostly religious tracts and magazines about missionaries and where they were and what they were doing.

He scouted the room. It was hot, ventilated by one small high window which overlooked a road. But he would be safe here. He lay down on the cot, unsnapping the holster and fitting his hand around it so that if he fell asleep, he would be ready to protect himself on the instant of awakening.

He drowsed, listening to the sounds of children playing. As he relaxed, the doubt hit him. Suppose that the message had not been delivered and suppose that Clive did not come. Suppose that tomorrow came and went, the sun burning across the sky with no news one way or the other. He shook his head and thought about the here and now. It was all he had, a full stomach and a bed and the protection of the old man and his wife. It was enough. It was more than Epstein had had. Tomorrow would take care of itself.

Something within him let go, relaxed for the first time in years. His head listed back against the knapsack. He fell into a dreamless sleep.

24

BANGKOK

In the end Clive was surprised that the exit from the city
went so well, but he knew it was only because Patterson
had settled in and put himself to the task at hand. He was
a professional, after all, and did not do things halfway.
Clive had helped Liz into the back of a closed panel lorry
at precisely seven o'clock and had found himself in the
company of one of Patterson's two men, a large, bluff ex-
soldier named Mullins, who was sprawled out on one of
the two wooden benches. He nodded to the lady, gave
Clive a grunt of greeting, and then settled back with one
hand resting on the rack of automatic weapons and used
the other to light a cigarette.

Patterson had chosen to drive, sliding under the
steering wheel without a word. His second man sat with
him in the front seat. His name was Owenby, and
although he was smaller than Mullins, with the wiriness
of a long-distance runner, he was his psychological twin,
taciturn, closemouthed, not given to any conversation.

Through the single slot window in the back Clive
observed the traffic on the way out of Bangkok trying to
spot the Watchers, for he could not believe that Patterson
would not be followed everywhere he went. He thought for
a while that the Russians were represented here by an
ornately decorated Thai truck with a garish dragon
decorating the grille. It seemed to stick fairly close,
staying two vehicles behind, whipping around slower
vehicles to maintain both the pace and the interval, but
after a half hour on Mittaphap Road it turned off.

Christ, was there a second one? It was always possible
that the tracking was being handed off, with one Watcher
turning off and passing it on to the next, but Clive saw no

evidence of it. If they were there, he could do nothing about it. He realized he was fretting over something he could not control.

The brief twilight set in. The sun plummeted like a stone in the west. The car lights came on and, as the lorry pulled farther away from the city, the traffic dwindled, disappeared. Clive gave up looking, leaned back against the hard wooden seat, rested his hand on Liz's leg without a word.

Finally, Patterson pulled off the road and stopped, and Clive checked the luminous dial of his watch. They were on time. He opened the back door and helped Liz out of the lorry. In the darkness he could smell the distant smoke of burning rice straw, the heavy odor of manure, but he could see nothing except a pinprick of light in the far distance. A farmhouse perhaps.

He saw Garvin's car waiting some twenty meters ahead, and he waited for Patterson before he went to meet Garvin, who stood by the side of his car, taking the opportunity to polish the exterior rearview mirror with his handkerchief.

'Were you followed?' Clive said.

'Not that I could tell,' Garvin said.

Clive took the road map out of his pocket, spread it against the side of the car. It was fixed in the small circular beam of Garvin's penlight.

'The number of the village is three-two-eight,' Clive said.

Garvin sucked the air in between his teeth in a whistling sound. 'Charlie Excalibur's picked himself a hell of a meeting ground,' he said. He traced a road on the map with the tip of an index finger. 'Village Three-two-eight is here. It's currently a refugee camp, Thai troops all over it. Fourth Army if I'm not mistaken.'

'Yes,' Patterson said in the darkness. A flat affirmation. Clive studied the map, put his finger on a small red dot which represented a rural hamlet. 'How far is this community from Village Three-two-eight? Four or five kilometers, wouldn't you say?'

'About that,' Garvin said.

'Very well. Then that's where we'll set up,' Clive said. 'Miss Sullivan and I will ride with you, Garvin. One of the colonel's men will take your front seat. Your two men will ride with the colonel. This is a joint operation. We will operate strictly by the rules, and I intend to be the man who sets those rules. If either of you disagree, then let me know it now.'

'All right,' Garvin said. 'I'll go with that. Colonel?'

Clive could not see Patterson's face in the darkness, but he could tell that Patterson was having difficulties with this. 'I agree,' he said finally.

'Then let's get on with it,' Clive said. He walked back to Liz, who was waiting for him in the warm darkness, leaving it to Garvin and Patterson to make their own arrangements.

'Trouble with the troops?' Liz said quietly.

He shook his head, took her by the arm. 'We're in the car from here on,' he said.

'Thank God for little favors,' she said wearily.

The transfer of men was made. Mullins took his place in the front seat of Garvin's car, now carrying an automatic weapon, which he carefully placed on the floor, the muzzle pointed toward the door.

'You take the lead,' Clive said to Garvin. 'Keep your speed down so Patterson can maintain a proper interval. How long do you think it will take us to reach this hamlet?'

'Three hours. Maybe four.'

'Carry on then.' He sank back into the seat, lit a cigarette to stay awake. Within fifteen minutes Liz was asleep, her head resting on his shoulder. Clive sat observing the back of Garvin's head, silhouetted against the reflection of the headlights and Mullins's Anglo-Saxon profile, a stoic face which remained speechless and seemed to hold an impassive expression of waiting.

Eventually Clive put out his cigarette and fell asleep, awakening sufficiently to realize they had left the highway for a two-lane macadamized road with scarcely any traffic at all except for an occasional truck. He tried to sleep again, could not. He could smell the jungle rather than see it, smell the rich, pungent smoke of a smoldering teak tree trunk which was being burned out somewhere in the undergrowth. Finally, the car jolted onto a dirt track which had been turned to mud by the monsoon rains, crusted over by the hot afternoon sun. He was aware that Garvin had shifted into low. The car slowed but continued to move.

Through the rear window Clive could see the lorry, keeping pace. He checked his watch. They should be reaching the hamlet soon. His fingers touched the darkness of the pistol tucked in his waistband. Through the front windshield he could see the clearing taking shape in the high beams of the headlights, the shadowy shapes of perhaps half a dozen stilt houses scattered through the thick trees adjacent to the narrow track of the road. There was a light showing in one house, the dim glow of a kerosene lamp, and Garvin stopped the car to one side of the house and killed the engine.

'It's my guess this is the head man's house,' Garvin said. 'We'll get better cooperation if we talk to him and give him a vague idea what we're doing and request permission to spend the night.'

'We should have brought some *mekong* with us,' Clive said.

'I come prepared,' Garvin said. 'There's a case in the trunk.'

Clive nodded. He left Liz sleeping in the car and climbed out. He stretched his legs, coming fully alert. Patterson had parked the lorry and had joined them by the time Garvin opened the trunk and took two bottles of *mekong* from the case. Another light went on as a small Thai man came out out of the house onto the porch. He was an old man, and he wore a loose-fitting robe with great dignity. Behind him was a young man, perhaps a relative. His hair was cropped very short, just beginning to grow back. He had obviously just finished his religious duties as a monk.

Clive made a respectful *wai* to the old man, who returned it, and then the polite conversation began, the wandering observations on the weather and the crops, a proper admiring of the lorry and the car on the part of the old man, a proper compliment on the beauty of the community from Clive, the introductions of himself and Garvin, the old man's presentation of his son, who had just left the priesthood and come home to the community where shortly he would take his father's place.

Garvin presented the old man with the two bottles of *mekong*, and the son immediately went into the house to get drinking glasses. There was a ceremony involved in the drinking of the *mekong*, and Clive was pleased to see that Garvin did it well, making pleasant conversation which only slowly encompassed the request and the response.

'If you would be so kind as to permit it,' Clive said, 'we would appreciate permission for our vehicles to remain here until dawn. We are going to the village, and the road is treacherous in the darkness.'

The old man smiled, loosened by the *mekong*, holding out his glass so his son could pour it half full again. 'Unfortunately your vehicles, as fine as they are, would get bogged down in the mud on this road,' he said. 'Our village would be pleased to offer you the poor facilities we possess. Then tomorrow, if you wish, you can go back to the main highway, which offers you a good but winding road for perhaps twenty kilometers to the village. Or if you prefer to walk, it is very close to here.'

More than I hoped, Clive thought, heady from the *mekong* on an empty stomach. For the head man proceeded to issue orders, and in what seemed like moments a family was moving out of one of the Thai houses, a woman shepherding her sleepy children to a neighboring house to make her home available to the *farangs*. Clive went back to the lorry where Patterson was waiting.

'We have been given a house for the night,' he said. 'Your men and Garvin's will stay with the vehicles. The weapons are to be kept out of sight.'

Patterson lit a cigarette. 'I would suggest, old chap, that you give the situation another look. I would suggest that you are being bloody naïve if you're taken in by the impeccable Thai manners. Now what is to keep that old man, the moment we're accounted for, from sending his own runner to the Thai Fourth and explaining that there's something bloody peculiar going on and inviting them to come around and have a look in on us?'

'What are you suggesting?'

'I've taken the liberty of having a look around,' Patterson said, blowing smoke into the damp night air. 'There's this road to the village and there's a path over there ... you can't see it from here... that goes the same direction. It wouldn't hurt to post a couple of pickets to make sure no stray villager decides to take a stroll in the middle of the night. It's just good strategy.'

'Then you would admit to them that we are a military force.'

'They already know it,' Patterson said. 'My God, man, don't you suppose that the head man realizes how many people we have with us, that we're not tourists out for a lark?'

Clive nodded. 'All right,' he said. 'You will wait until everybody is settled and then post your men. Teams of two, one of Garvin's and one of yours on each.'

Patterson nodded. 'There's hope for you after all, old chap,' he said. 'You are open to suggestion.'

'Just as long as you recognize the limits,' Clive said.

'Oh, I do that,' Patterson said. 'There will be no need for violence or threats. Even if everybody in this whole bloody village appears to be asleep, they will know that the exits are blocked. They do respect men who watch out for themselves.'

Clive walked away to get Liz from the car and to settle in for the night.

VILLAGE 328

Charlie Excalibur awoke to the sound of singing, a hymn. He sat up instantly, startled but not alarmed, for there were scarcely two mornings in a row when he came awake in the same place, and he was always prepared to defend himself until he realized that he was, for the moment, safe. The sunlight filtered into the room through the small window. It was early morning, perhaps shortly after dawn. He could hear a rooster crowing somewhere in the distance, the sound of truck engines. He stood on one of the boxes, looked out toward the road where Thai trucks were rolling past, packed with refugees who would be taken back to the Cambodian border and turned loose.

He pushed back the door curtain with the back of his hand and saw that the bedroom was empty. He could hear the old man's voice outside, praying in his southern drawl, while a Thai woman interpreted in a low, melodic voice. Through the crack in the outside door he saw all of the children sitting in rows beneath the tarps while the old man prayed, with his head back, face raised to heaven, eyes squeezed shut as if he wished to minister to this heathen place but not to see it.

The old woman was supervising the preparation of a morning meal off to a side of the clearing, with three large pots steaming over cook fires, the smoke rising to hang in a level stratum just below the top of the trees, a pale blue in the soft dawnlight. Her eyes caught him through the crack in the door. In a moment she had dished a mound of rice from one of the pots and was limping toward the house with a tin plate in one hand and a cup in the other.

She came into the main room, put the cup and the plate on a table. 'We only have rice in the mornings and a weak tea,' she said.

'I appreciate it,' he said. He sat down to eat, aware that she was standing at the door, watching him.

'Did you know Sam Palmer?' she said.

'Beg your pardon?'

'Did you ever happen to run across a Corporal Sam Palmer? He was a clerk typist in Saigon.'

Her son, of course. 'No, ma'am. I wasn't in Saigon much.'

She picked at the frayed hem of her sleeve. 'You'd think

that would be a safe job, working in an office. But then one day, just like that...' She blinked, long past tears, still caught in the strange wonderment of bereavement which was beyond sorrow. 'A bomb through the window. Not a big one. You'd thing it was safe, working in an office.'

'There was no safe place,' Charlie Excalibur said.

'How old are you?'

He had to think. He had not kept track. The question had not been asked in a long time. 'Thirty-five,' he said.

'Sam would have been thirty-three.' She nodded, blinked again, bringing things back into perspective again. 'You said you want to take a shower, clean up.'

'Yes, please.'

She showed him the makeshift stall in back of the house where a fifty-five gallon can was raised on stilts, a shower head attached to the bottom of it, the water turned on by a valve. She had been thoughtful enough to have the can filled with water during the night. She provided him with a worn bar of soap, a threadbare towel, a pair of scissors with which to trim his hair and his beard, a mirror.

She was offering him thoughtfulness and a kind of caring, and he was so unused to it that his whole body was taut with wariness, waiting for the catch, as if he were being set up for something. It had been a long time since he had been anything but defensive, so prepared to kill or be killed at any moment that he did not know how to accept a simple kindness.

He went out to the stall and took his shower, having hung his shorts, his shirt, his pistol, and his knapsack on a wooden peg inside the makeshift cubicle. The water was lukewarm, and he soaped himself all over and was startled at the sight of his own naked body, at the scars he bore, the cuts and scrapes on his legs and arms which had wealed over, the leathery quality of his skin that seemed more hidelike than human. He washed himself; then he turned off the water and propped the mirror against a cross support. A stranger stared back at him from the reflective surface, a man with a scraggly brown beard and long, matted hair falling down around a gaunt, tough face with a thin blade of a nose, shrewd and wary eyes. He reached out a hand to the man in the mirror. He did not recognize himself. He would have to trim the beard, and he worked at it, clipping until it was short and neat, then cut his own hair as best he could until it was chopped off at the midpoint of his stringy brown neck. He turned on the water again, rinsed the loose hair off him, and with his foot pushed it between the cracks of the wooden platform on which he stood, not wanting to leave a mess behind him. He dried with the towel, stepped into the dirty pair of shorts, buttoned the shirt, buckled the pistol into place, and carried the towel and the soap back to the house. The old man and woman were sitting at a table under the picture of Jesus and the sheep, talking with a young Thai man who was having trouble speaking English.

The old man looked up at Charlie Excalibur, held up an envelope. 'This fellow lives in a community five kilometers south of here,' he said. 'Maybe you'd better read this.'

Charlie Excalibur took the envelope, hunkered down with his back to the wall from long habit. On the outside of the envelope was written in English script 'To the American Missionaries', and inside was a brief note: 'I have a reason to believe that an American soldier will be in your community today. If you can possibly make contact with him, would you be so kind as to give him the message contained in the second envelope? It is extremely important that we contact him.' It was signed 'Gordon Clive, Her Britannic Majesty's Diplomatic Service.'

For a moment Charlie Excalibur was stunned. Clive was here. The message had been received and he would be going home and he could not believe it.

You should have hung in there, Epstein. You should have hung in there.

He had to steady his hands before he examined the second envelope, marked simply 'William Garvin'. He was being addressed by his real name, and there was a strange and unfamiliar excitement in that. The last time he had received an envelope with nothing but his name written on it, it had been an invitation to some formal function at the university. He could not remember what kind of party it was or even whether he accepted it, but that was not important. For this envelope was his invitation to go back to the world.

He savored the anticipation; then he ripped open the envelope and devoured the brief contents. Clive was in the hamlet five kilometers south. He would not come into the village itself because of the heavy presence of Thai troops. Instead, he would meet Garvin on the trail between Village 328 and the hamlet. The time would have to be indeterminate since Clive was unsure of when the word would reach Garvin, but he would be there all day. He added that he had representatives of the British and American governments with him but that they would in no way interfere with any negotiated agreement between Garvin and Clive.

He folded the letter, put it in his knapsack, looked to the young Thai man. '*Sawadee*,' he said in Thai. 'How many *farang* men are in your living place?'

The Thai rolled his eyes, not knowing what to say. 'There are six men, sir, I believe. And there is also a *farang* lady.'

'Do the men have weapons?'

'I believe that is true.'

'Automatic weapons? Rifles?'

'Yes, sir. I believe that is true.'

'You would honor me if you return to your living place and tell the man who sent this message that it has been received. I will meet him halfway along the trail in the next two or three hours.'

'Yes, sir, I will do that,' the young man said. He stood up, made a *wai* to Charlie Excalibur and then to each of the missionaries in turn.

The old man stirred, ran a bony hand across the stubble of his hair. He had caught enough of the conversation to be aware of what was going on. 'It might be best if we tell this young man to bring your contact here,' he said. 'This would be safer maybe than meeting him out in the bush.'

Again Charlie Excalibur was touched and it made him feel awkward. He did not know what to do with the feeling, how to respond. 'I appreciate that,' he said. 'But I think it's better if I meet him in the open.' On impulse he took his worn checkbook out of the knapsack, found a ball-point pen, and carefully wrote out a check. He stood up and placed it in the old woman's hand. She looked at it with incredulous eyes, handed it to her husband. 'It's real,' Charlie Excalibur said. 'It's good. You just send it to a Bangkok bank and they'll check it out and you'll get the money.'

'Twenty thousand Hong Kong dollars?' the old man said. 'You really have that much money?'

'Yes, I really have that much money,' Charlie Excalibur said.

'You'll need it when you get back home,' the old woman said.

'No, believe me. It's all right. And now I got to be going. I appreciate what you've done. And I'm sorry about your son. I really am.'

When he left, the old woman was crying, and he did not like that. He did not trust the softness he was feeling inside. He had learned a long time ago that you couldn't trust anyone, and here he was giving away a lot of money just because an old couple had put him up for the night and fed him and let him have a shower.

And as he padded along the path, winding down through an outcropping of rocks toward the deep green of the rain forest which lay in the valley below him, he thought about God and wondered if there really was one. In the past few years he had not really seen much evidence of one, not in all the villagers who lit joss sticks and prostrated themselves in front of crumbling idols in a hundred different villages only to have their families blown away or starve to death. Jesus, he was going soft in the head. He had given away four thousand American dollars.

He passed through a bamboo grove and was engulfed

by the heat. The hot air seemed to be trapped in the low places where there was not a stir of a breeze. But overhead he could see a fringe of gathering clouds and there would be another monsoon rain before too long, a couple of hours maybe. When he emerged from the walls of bamboo, he could breathe more easily. The oxygen seemed to flow down from the tiers and banks of leaves overhead which were so thick they all but blocked the sun, allowing only a few shafts of light to penetrate to the forest floor. He increased his pace until he had covered a kilometer, and then his caution returned and he left the path and made his way quietly through the brush, his sixth sense telling him that he was close to people again. It was not that he could hear them or smell them, but he knew they were there all right. He followed an old Vietcong trick and soundlessly pulled himself up into a tree, ascending into the higher branches like a monkey until he had a clear view of the path and yet was himself hidden.

Then he saw the two men, dressed in coveralls with the sleeves cut out. They were carrying automatic weapons and coming down the trail. But they passed on by, and then he saw a man who looked familiar, and he parted the leaves with the back of his hand to have a better look. Clive all right, good old Clive, looking fifteen years older but still the same, plodding along a jungle path, fit as he always was, light on his feet.

'Clive,' Charlie Excalibur called out, the single word sounding muffled by the heavy trees which seemed to soak up sound. Clive stopped dead in his tracks, looked around, eyes squinting as if to see through the heavy foliage.

'Garvin?' Clive said. 'Is that you? Where are you?'

'That's beside the point. Get rid of your gun bearers.'

Clive called ahead, and the two men returned. Charlie Excalibur watched them conferring, and the two men were looking around, but they couldn't spot him either, and finally, they went on back down the trail toward the hamlet.

'It's safe,' Clive said. 'You can come out.'

'You wouldn't fool your old buddy?'

'No, I wouldn't fool you.'

Charlie Excalibur stayed where he was for a moment longer; then slowly he began to climb down the tree.

Clive waited, his hand resting on the pistol in his waistband, and then suddenly the man seemed to materialize by the side of the trail. It took Clive a moment to realize that the wild apparition with the bush of hair and beard was indeed Garvin, that the bright and skeptical eyes were those of the young man at the university, now fifteen years older, and the lopsided grin had not changed.

'Goddamn, I'm glad to see you,' Charlie Excalibur said as he thrust out his hand while all the time his eyes continued to watch the trail. His hand was gristle and calluses. 'I didn't know until today that you had my message,' he said. 'How's my man Po? Do you know about him? He must have gotten through or you wouldn't be here.'

'He's dead,' Clive said.

'Dead,' Charlie Excalibur said with a wistful acceptance. 'So, dead then. He was a good man.' His deep sigh reflected his sadness. 'What happened to him?'

'It's a long story,' Clive said.

Charlie Excalibur's eyes probed the trail again, his hesitancy almost palpable, as if he did not know what to do with himself now that he was here. 'You got my message,' he said. 'You were supposed to come by yourself. What's the deal? Who do you have with you?'

'A whole bloody delegation. My chief, a man from the CIA, a woman correspondent from the *Far Eastern Economic Review*.'

'And four gun bearers,' Charlie Excalibur said grimly. He moved restlessly. 'I don't feel comfortable talking out here in the open,' he said. He moved away from the trail, Clive following, until he reached the protection of a large banyan tree with massive gnarled roots. He settled himself on the ground in the shelter of a cleft in the tangled roots. 'Do you have any cigarettes?'

Clive handed him the pack, and Charlie Excalibur shook one out and lighted it. He was not as secure as he sounded, Clive realized. There was a tremor to his fingers as they carried the cigarette to his mouth. 'That's good,' he said, inhaling. 'It's a long time between good cigarettes out here. You've been getting my messages all along?'

'Yes,' Clive said. 'Why didn't you identify yourself? Why did you use Charlie Excalibur?'

Charlie Excalibur smiled. 'That's a long story,' he said. 'I used the name Charlie because that's what the American troops called the Vietcong. And Excalibur was King Arthur's sword, and that pleased me somehow.'

Christ, this man was really strung-out, Clive realized, as Charlie Excalibur sucked on the cigarette, looked around, testing the air, alert to any danger. 'What's going to happen to me?' he said. 'I mean, you got the CIA here. They're going to want my ass.'

'They will question you,' Clive said. 'After all, they have you listed as a deserter.'

'I never intended to desert.' It was as simple as that. He hadn't meant to desert. He had gone on leave in a little Vietnamese village, got high on a combination of things, and he had stayed out too long, past the point where he could go back. Too, he didn't want to go back to fight battles there wasn't a chance in hell of winning because regardless of where his unit was, the enemy always seemed to be someplace else. It was as if they knew in advance what the Americans were going to do.

And then he had heard about this master guns, a Sergeant Epstein, who had deserted to track down some leads. 'So I thought, what the hell,' Charlie Excalibur said, 'I'd look him up and see what he had.'

'You found him?'

'Sure. It took a while.' Epstein had collected some material, but he was already so spaced-out he didn't know what he was doing half the time. Charlie Excalibur had picked up where Epstein left off and drifted in with the Communists, who offered him protection in return for his services as a translator. And Charlie Excalibur made

291

money on the black market, stealing supplies from the North Vietnamese and selling them in Laos or Cambodia or Thailand, all the time building his own file on how the American positions had been compromised.

Occasionally one of the big men would come through on his way to Hanoi and get drunk and brag about something they were planning to do in Hong Kong or Singapore, and Charlie Excalibur would remember the details. One day he decided to do something about it. He had heard that there was a Gordon Clive with the British Embassy in Bangkok, and he figured there wouldn't be two Gordon Clives in the world, so he wrote his first dispatch addressed to Clive and paid some of his black-market money to have it delivered.

'Hell,' he said with a grin, 'I didn't even know the damn letters were getting through until this Hanoi hot-shot came through one day and his ass was in a sling because one of his plans didn't go through, and I knew the letter I wrote about it had gotten through okay. I didn't even crack a smile, but I went on a private drunk that lasted three days.'

Ah, Clive thought with a sense of irony, all the projections in London that had gone into a psychological profile of Charlie Excalibur, the grizzled Brit Watcher in the bush, the noble patriot, and now here the real man sat, a college boy turned soldier, grown into manhood, playing a dangerous and whimsical game. 'Go on,' he said.

'While I was wandering around Cambodia, I heard of a Soviet agent named King. That was his code name. He was supposed to be the guy who knew every move the American military was going to make, right down to the small operations. Hell, the North Vietnamese, when they were holed up in Laos and Cambodia, they'd get messages relayed from King, calling the next day's shots on the Ho Chi Minh Trail, letting them know exactly what was coming off. And the gooks would be ready. Jesus, I collected enough stories about King to fill a book. He was a real operator, something every day.' He opened his knapsack, fished out a battered notebook, which he handed to Clive.

Clive thumbed through it. There were long lists of dates, each with grid coordinates which designated the locations.

'There's over fifty of them listed there,' Charlie Excalibur said. 'The dates, where they happened, every one of them a disaster, big or small.'

'Where did King operate from?'

'I didn't know that at first, but it became a hobby with me to find out. I thought maybe he was in Saigon, somebody making an extra buck selling information like some other guy would sell parts off a truck. So I made buddies with the radio operator and got him drunk.' He looked up. The atmosphere had begun to darken; the dim rays of sunlight had disappeared. 'I hate this weather,' he said. He held his right palm up to catch the first drop of rain. It had already begun to rustle the leaves high overhead. 'Look, why don't you get the man from the CIA up here? I can give him the information directly and see what he's willing to do.'

Clive handed the notebook back to him, and he tucked it away in the protective safety of the knapsack. Clive retrieved the pack of cigarettes as the downpour began, penetrating the multitiered layers of branches. If the service had taught him anything, it was patience and the ability not to push an informant too heavily when he was close to revelation. He shook a cigarette out of the pack and sheltered it with a cupped hand while he lit it. He turned the pack upside down in his pocket to protect it.

'We'll get him up here after a while,' Clive said.

Charlie Excalibur stared up at the rain. 'Do you think I can make it, Clive?'

'What do you mean?'

'Well, look at me, man. Do I look like your average man on the street? I've been in the bush so long I don't know how I can make it back there.' He looked away, blinking back tears. 'Sometimes I think I'm more animal than human.' He shook his head. 'I used to think my father was crazy as hell because all he did was go to work in the morning and come home at night and have dinner and watch television. Jesus, that sounds good to me. You think I can make that?'

Moved by his sudden vulnerability, Clive reached out and touched his arm in reassurance. For a moment Charlie Excalibur held onto his hand and then let go.

'You've survived here,' Clive said. 'You're still alive, and that takes a hell of a lot of courage. You'll make it.'

'I hope so. God, how I hope so. I'm sure as hell going to finish up here as fast as I can and give it a try.'

'Our people are very interested in you,' Clive said. 'You've given us some first-class information over the years. We owe you. What can we do to help you now?'

'I trust you,' Charlie Excalibur said. 'I'll give you the rest of what I have, and you make a deal with the Americans to let me go home and drop any charges against me. If they don't agree, then you arrange it so I can live in England. I don't expect charity, just a work permit. I have plenty of money. I'm just tired of being around people who don't speak English. I never want to see another plate of rice. I'm tired of being on the run. There's no safe place for me anymore.' He looked up, his eyes squinting against the rain.

'What do you mean, "the rest"?'

'The part that affects you.'

'How?' Clive said. And as he said it, he had the awful feeling that he really didn't want to know.

'Well, I found that King wasn't in Saigon. He was in Bangkok with the Americans, with the big boys who co-ordinated air cover for all the strikes. He'd get the fresh stuff every evening at the high-level briefings, even before the flights were dispatched the next day.'

Clive sucked smoke from the sheltered cigarette, but he could not preserve the lighted coal. The rain washed over his hand, penetrated the cupped fingers. The cigarette disintegrated even as he held it.

'Anyway,' Charlie Excalibur said, 'I figured he was American until after the war was over. Then the

American forces pulled out of Saigon and Bangkok, and I moved on into Cambodia, back and forth across the Thai border. I ran into some of the Communist Party boys from Thailand, and I was curious as hell because the Thai troops were out to get them, and I mean in force. But just before there was to be a Thai raid, the CPT boys would pack up and be long gone before any troops arrived. When I asked how they knew they were going to be raided, one of them told me King sent them a message before each raid. So you see, I knew King was still sending, that he was still in business.'

'Did you ever get a physical description of him?' Clive said, above the drumming of the rain.

'Better than that, I saw him once,' Charlie Excalibur said reflectively. 'He had warned a group of a raid and told them to get the hell out because he was going to be along and if the Thai troops caught any CPT son of a bitch who didn't hop to, he'd kill him personally. So I stuck around, not too close, of course. He was riding in a jeep with a Thai captain.' He examined his dead cigarette, turned to pulp by the rain. 'That would be worth trading for, wouldn't it? I mean, I got the proof after all.'

'Yes,' Clive said.

'I don't think I really started with the idea of trading,' Charlie Excalibur said. 'But after I sent a couple dozen messages to you, it came to me what I was doing. I was building up merits the same way the Thais do by bowing to Buddha. I figured by helping you, you'd help me. And then I found the information I was looking for, and I was ready.' Charlie Excalibur flipped the cigarette away. 'About a year ago I was going to come into Bangkok to talk to you, and then you had your bad luck.'

Clive shook his head. 'It wasn't bad luck,' he said, 'I broke under torture, and five of my men were killed.'

'Shit,' Charlie Excalibur said with a gleam in his eye, snorting a laugh, 'you know better than that.'

'No, I don't know better than that. What are you talking about?'

Charlie Excalibur's face grew serious. 'You really don't

know, do you? Hell, everybody in the CPT camps knew.'

Clive grew suddenly cold. 'Then you bloody well had better let me in on it, don't you think?'

'Your men were all dead by the time you had spent your first night in captivity,' Charlie Excalibur said. 'Somebody else put the finger on them, wanted them gone, and they were dead before you were picked up. I think one of Epstein's men betrayed us, and the CPT didn't know whether we'd gotten to you or not. So they wiped out your men and tortured you. But you didn't kill anybody, old buddy.'

All the breath had left Clive. He could not speak.

'I'm letting you know that was King's doing, too,' Charlie Excalibur said. 'Everybody in the CPT knew that. I asked the boys what language he was sending in, and they said sometimes English and sometimes Thai. And I don't mean pidgin Thai, but the real language.'

'The name,' Clive said. 'Do you know King's real name?'

'Hell, I wouldn't have anything to trade if I didn't.'

'God damn it, man,' Clive said, 'I want his name.'

'I heard him chattering with the Thai captain, and the gook called him by name.'

'Which was?'

'Patterson.'

Clive was stunned. A feeling of unreality settled over him, and he felt unsteady on his feet. The earth had shifted beneath him. 'Do you know what you're saying?' he said. 'Perhaps they were talking about Patterson, and you misunderstood. Perhaps you're mistaken.'

'Hell, it's no mistake.' Charlie Excalibur tapped the side of his canvas knapsack. 'All those dates. You check them against the briefings, and you'll find Patterson was in on every one of them. Hell, man, I wouldn't risk my life unless I was sure. I want to get out of here. I want to go home.'

Christ, he did not want to believe, and yet there it was, the corroboration that Charlie Excalibur could not know about. For the Russians had not followed when Patterson left the compound, and now the reason showed bright as pure silver. There was no need to follow if Patterson was one of them. Clive was chilled to the bone. He would have to move thoughtfully, carefully, from this point.

'You'll have your bargain,' he said. 'But you have to do exactly as I say, follow my instructions to the letter. Patterson's here. He's one of the men who came along.'

'Jesus,' Charlie Excalibur said. 'He knows that I know about him. He's chased me from village to village.'

Clive could see the sudden panic in his eyes. 'In any event he can't do anything about it, not in the presence of witnesses. We'll go into the hamlet together. As far as he's concerned, you haven't told me anything.'

Charlie Excalibur stood up, miserable, drenched. The rain diminished, became a mist. 'Can I trust you, old buddy?'

'You can trust me,' Clive said. 'Now I want your pistol.'

'Why?'

'I want nothing to go wrong when we go into camp, no excuses for gunning you down because you're armed. Now listen carefully. You have turned yourself over to me, but you're American after all. You want to be questioned by the CIA. You want to deal directly with your own people. Do you understand?'

Charlie Excalibur nodded. 'But our deal still holds. Right?'

'Yes.'

Charlie Excalibur unsnapped the flap on the holster. And in that moment there was the sound of a pistol being cocked, and then that familiar voice, as casual in tone as if Patterson were just ordering himself a drink. 'Just leave the pistol where it is,' he said. Clive saw him, standing in the deep shade of a tree, a cigarette dangling from his lips, his own pistol quite steady in his hand, the muzzle pointing in Charlie Excalibur's direction. Patterson leaned back against the tree in the mist, a relaxed expression on his face, but Clive was not deceived. The son of a bitch was wound as tight as a clock spring.

'This man is an American,' Clive said. 'He wants the

protection of his government.'

'Man?' Patterson said, amused, his smile broadening. 'I don't recognize a man here. Scum, maybe. An American deserter that no one really cares about anymore, except perhaps for myself. Garbage like this contaminates Thailand.'

Charlie Excalibur was frozen where he was. *For God's sake*, Clive thought, *don't provoke him. Don't give him an excuse. Leave him to me*.

Patterson did not look at Charlie Excalibur at all, but the pistol stayed centered on him nonetheless. 'He's a deserter, old man, a coward.' Patterson tapped the ash from his cigarette. 'I'm sure he's an embarrassment to his family. Why open old wounds for them?'

'Put your pistol away, Harry. You've seen the orders from London.'

'No old chap. London's a long way from here.' Patterson seemed to sigh, as if whatever he was being forced to do carried with it a certain regret. 'Now I shall want the notebook.'

In the flicker of an eyelid Charlie Excalibur grabbed for the pistol in his holster and managed to get it free before Patterson squeezed the trigger. The explosion of the shot was muffled by the jungle, but the impact of the bullet caught Charlie Excalibur in the chest and slammed him against the tree and seemed to hold him there while the pistol fell from his paralyzed fingers, bounced off a root, and went into the mud. The expression in his eyes was one of sadness, no room for words or clear thoughts. He slumped back against the trunk, slid halfway down before a root caught beneath his right arm, held him there.

Patterson stood where he was, the calm smile still intact on his face. 'My timing was perfect, old chap,' he said. 'He was obviously drawing his pistol to shoot you down. But I got him first.'

Clive said nothing. He dropped on his knees beside Charlie Excalibur, felt for the pulse in the stringy neck. Still beating. The blood still pulsing through him. The shot had been high, in the shoulder, well above the heart, a gaping wound from which the blood was flowing. He took out his handkerchief and stuffed it under the ragged shirt to stop the flow of blood.

Only then did Clive stand up, turning to face Patterson, who stood sucking the last wisp of smoke from the cigarette before he dropped it and ground it out beneath his boot. The pistol was still in his hand.

'Go ahead, finish it, you son of a bitch,' Clive said.

'Finish what?' Patterson said.

'Me. Shoot me. You can't leave me alive,' Clive said, the anger pumping through him, everything clear to him now. 'You've gone to too much trouble to keep his message from reaching me. My God, you've left a trail of death halfway across this continent. And now, you bloody bastard, you'll have to kill me as well.'

'Don't be foolish,' Patterson said. He returned the pistol to his holster, unsnapped his canteen, had a drink. 'It's *mekong*,' he said. 'It takes a considerable amount of it to make this weather bearable. Would you care for a nip?'

Clive stood for a moment, in awe of such audacity; then he pulled the Walther from his waistband, leveled it at Patterson. Patterson shook his head, not intimidated in the least. 'Come off it, old chap,' he said quietly. 'You're not going to shoot me any more than I am going to shoot you. We're both in Her Majesty's service. We don't kill our own. Things aren't done that way, and you know it.'

'Just how are things done, old chap?' Clive said. 'Tell me about it.'

Patterson capped his canteen. 'Certainly,' he said. 'But let's see precisely where you stand, shall we? I heard what he said to you, an unsubstantiated accusation by a man who under any circumstances would be considered unreliable. All hearsay.'

'Why in the bloody hell would you betray your country?'

'I did not betray my country. The Vietnamese War was an American expansionist intervention. The French had gone, and here were the Americans. There should have been no foreign intrusion in this part of the world at all.

299

Peaceful trade interchanges, perhaps, but no military action. In that way it could be shown, I think, that I only warned native populations of planned military actions.'

'Christ,' Clive said. Charlie Excalibur lay half dead on the ground, perhaps would die soon without help. Thousands of men were dead because of this man, and here he stood, talking politics. Still, Clive had to know, despite the risks, had to take another minute. 'And how do you explain the warnings to the CPT?'

'Foolishness, a small harmless favor to the Russians. The Communist Party in Thailand is dwindling instead of growing. The government has things firmly in hand. Soon the Communists will have no influence in Thailand.' Patterson shook his head, perfectly at ease. 'I'm really home free, old chap.' He looked down at Charlie Excalibur, who was showing signs of movement, the long fingers twitching. 'Can you see him as a witness in the dock? The prosecution will undoubtedly try to clean him up, cut his hair, clean up his language, buy him a suit of clothes off a rack which will only make him look worse. And I shall be there in my full-dress uniform with my ribbons. And the most he can prove is circumstantial, that I was present at meetings with dozens of other chaps from which information was leaked. It will be demonstrated that all he has is hearsay from other deserters, from Communists in the field. And what about you, old chap? Will the service look lightly on a man who brings charges against a covert operator, exposing all the secrets in a case from which I will be vindicated? The Foreign Office will be standing by, wringing their hands, slapping a D Notice on anything which comes close to compromising security.'

Abruptly the rain stopped. Patterson looked up cheerfully. The edge of the cloud passed over, and a shaft of sunlight broke through the trees behind him, a solid column of light, making him a dark silhouette. And suddenly Clive remembered the moment in the hut when in his delirium he had seen the silhouette at the door, black against the blinding light. Not imagined, no, neither Christ nor the devil. Patterson, come to look in on him, to see how things were going.

'You were there then,' Clive said, his voice hushed. 'You didn't just plan it, set it in motion. You were there. Christ, you watched them cut me open.'

Patterson nodded. 'They would have killed you, old chap. It was necessary to break you, but I was adamant about keeping you alive. I am truly sorry you had to go through it, but you see, I had to be sure.'

Patterson's eyes checked the sky. 'It appears we're in for fair weather,' he said. He looked toward Clive, his voice even, his thoughts cool and collected. 'Now, as to a resolution,' he said. 'I would suggest that you put the past behind you. I would think of myself if I were you. It just might be better for all concerned if this poor man were allowed to die.'

'That's absurd,' Clive said. 'Better for you, perhaps.'

'I shall take care of his papers,' Patterson said, ignoring him. 'It will save a lot of embarrassment for all concerned in the end. That's really the only solution I can see to all this.'

'No,' Clive said. 'There's one other.' He stared at him for a long moment, the truth of what Patterson was saying washing over him like a wave, dissolving the rationality, the dispassion.

The pistol went off in his hand, the bullet grazing Patterson's left arm and thudding into the tree. 'That's for Mr. Po.'

'I see I have underestimated you,' Patterson said.

The gun exploded again, and the bullet ripped through the very edge of his right arm while Patterson stood and looked at the blood seeping down, his expression more curious than concerned.

'For Iris Marston,' Clive said.

He fired again. Blood from the left ear. 'For Bill Marston, a far better man than you.'

Christ, Patterson was unfazed, standing there with his cold logic to protect him, feeding on the pain as if it offered him a chance to demonstrate his absolute control. 'This really isn't your style, but get it out of your system, old chap,' Patterson said. 'Then we'll clean up the mess with your deserter.'

Without a word Clive raised the pistol to level it at Patterson's head. And now, for the first time, there was a crack in Patterson's reserve, the first glimmer of realization that his coolness might not save him. His face turned ashen, and there was a spark of fear in his eyes that had ignited too late. His reflexes should have taken hold, moved to save him, but the instant of fear had thrown his timing off. This time he would lose to the metaphorical snake and he knew it.

'Now...' he said, as if he could launch a string of words that would save him, keep that finger from pulling the trigger, but he could not. Clive fired. The pistol made a thudding pop and the bullet caught Patterson in the center of his lean face, in the separation of his eyebrows. The horror of his own death hit him, and then the eyes went blank. Patterson continued to stand upright for a moment as if held by invisible strings which suddenly gave way. He fell headlong into the mud.

Sick and empty, Clive stared at him lying there. It was all over, ended. He threw the Walther into the bush and then moved to Charlie Excalibur. He knelt beside him to do what he could to keep the man alive.

Charlie Excalibur stirred and gave off a moan which sounded like a word. Clive leaned close and the sound came again and this time he could make it out.

'Home,' Charlie Excalibur said.

'Yes, home,' Clive said gently. 'You're going home.'

25

BANGKOK

A gray afternoon, fitful rains, and Clive could see the airport ahead through the front window of the taxi, a 747 rising to lose itself in the low clouds. Liz sat next to him, her arm linked through his possessively. Clive leaned forward, told the Thai driver to pull over to the shoulder for a few minutes before they reached the airport complex.

'We'll have no time at the airport, love,' he said. 'I guess we've covered everything. Is there anything we've missed?'

'We've missed a lot,' she said rather wistfully. 'I wish we could have had a lark, a few days like we used to have. Back when the world didn't seem so grim.'

'Yes,' he said. 'Back when there was time.'

'You'll be in Singapore tonight then?'

'I talked to Katy. I hate to cut her holiday short. But she'll be meeting me there. And then we'll have twenty minutes before the flight to England.'

'What will you tell her?'

'About what?'

'Us.'

'I'll tell her nothing except that I ran into an old friend named Liz Sullivan, a woman I admire very much.'

'And that's all I am to you, a woman you admire very much?'

'You know better.' He kissed her lightly. 'But we've said it before. We belong to the old days. We had a chance to relive a few of them, but they are the past.' He cleared his throat. 'Now, as to the practical matters, I have arranged that you can interview Charlie Excalibur in the hospital in Hong Kong when he is better. He'll be there three weeks before he's shipped back to England for a full debriefing. Garvin and I have come to an agreement on that, so you should have no trouble.'

'As to my story,' she said, 'I don't need your approval, mind, but damn it, you know I'll curb my journalistic instincts if you ask me to.'

'Just one small request,' he said. 'You can use the whole thing, Charlie's accusations against Patterson. You can even quote an unnamed high-level source that Patterson's actions were political in nature. Christ, that's the truth for sure; he was the true believer, Asia for the Asians, a man who had the misfortune not to be born Thai. He sold out Russia just the way he sold out his own country, all with the aim of getting both out of the Far East.' He watched another jet rising from the airport, a TriStar. 'But leave the details of his death purposely vague. Just write that he was shot to death by a stray bullet during a fire fight and that the authorities are investigating.'

'You wish me to remove you from it then.'

'For the time being, yes.' Silence now, and they both knew that time was passing and that the jet to Singapore would be leaving. He leaned forward, asked the driver to take him to departures. Clive put his hand on her arm, faced her. 'There's no way I can tell you what you've meant to me,' he said. 'And I doubt I shall be coming this way again.'

'I don't want to hear that,' she said, tears welling up in her eyes.

'I thought you were the realist, the pragmatist.'

'Not when it comes to you. So let's just say that you're leaving for now and the future will take care of itself.'

He took her in his arms, kissed her. 'I'll write to you from London, let you know what happens.'

'Will you be in trouble?'

'I don't know. I sent a long letter by Queen's Messenger this afternoon which should get there shortly before I do. It may raise a few hackles.'

'You might call me sometime,' she said, drying her eyes,

her emotions under control. 'You can call collect, you know. You're a prime source now. The *Review* will pick up the tab.'

The taxi drove around the loop, parked temporarily at departures. The driver got out to open the door for Clive. 'Well, pet,' Clive said, 'I'll never forget you. Keep yourself safe.' He kissed her again and was gone, moving as far as the door before he turned to watch the taxi driving off, one last glimpse of her wave and then her face through the rear window.

He turned and went into the terminal to seek out his jet to Singapore.

British Embassy
Wireless Road,
Bangkok, Thailand

DISPATCH BY QUEEN'S MESSENGER

Dear Sir,

You will by now have news of Charlie Excalibur and you will also know the bare skeletal facts of Colonel Patterson's death. You will receive, if you have not done so already, an account from the CIA man in the field which will be incomplete because I have purposely left it that way and he does not know to the contrary.

I do not know how you will regard the death of Colonel Patterson, what sense the Foreign Office and the embassy and the Thai government will make of it, and you must give me a plus for leaving that a blank, so you can fill it in as you wish, which will totally change the context of that death and give my colleagues considerable material for argument. It is quite a marvelous turn – isn't it – that simply by filling in any solution you like, you change the whole puzzle.

If you wish, you may release the information that Colonel Patterson was killed by a 'stray bullet' and let it go at that. If such you choose, then understand that there will never be any utterance from myself to the contrary. There will be a series of articles in the *Far*

Eastern Economic Review which will detail all the charges against Colonel Patterson, but then you may choose to deny them if you wish, to label them speculation, or to ignore them altogether.

There is a debt which I wish to have paid out of whatever contingency fund is available (and I know in advance that old Sampson will suffer apoplexy with this request). I had a friend, guide, employee, agent, call him what you will, who went by the Anglicized name of Sam. His full Thai name and address are on file at the Embassy Registry. He died in my service, and his death will work an extreme hardship on the surviving members of his family, a mother and a gaggle of smaller children, all of whom were solely dependent upon him for their support. I want a fund of twenty-five thousand pounds (25,000) set up for their maintenance, perhaps invested in trust for the family, the interest to be paid to them on a monthly basis. I want a further stipend of one thousand pounds (1,000) paid to a Thai known as Tiger Man who served me faithfully. His address is also on file at the Registry.

You know of my agreement with Charlie Excalibur. I shall expect it to be honored.

I am on my way to collect my wife and will return to London in time for Marston's funeral.

Yours aye,
Gordon Clive

LONDON

The article in the *Far Eastern Economic Review* had made all the wire services. The confessions of Charlie Excalibur, alias William Garvin, an American marine deserter, had included the accusation that a British colonel, highly decorated, singularly dedicated, had provided intelligence to the enemy in America's Vietnam War.

In the building at Queen Anne's Gate, Sir John had

become inaccessible, holed up except for one foray to meet with a minister, at which time he passed through the corridors like a silent wraith, grim-lipped, with that aura around him which implied that even to speak to him would result in a painful electric shock to the intruder.

Old Sampson was perhaps the most perplexed man in the building. His auditor's tidy mind was outraged by the request for the expenditure of sizable sums for unskilled men recruited, wounded, killed in Bangkok.

But the matter of Clive's status left him very perplexed, for there was no official pronouncement on whether he had resigned (as rumor had it) or was on leave, authorized, paid, unauthorized, his monthly pay suspended. And what of Colonel Patterson? There were death benefits which by law must be paid to his widow, unless the case against him were proved, and one could not simply suspend such matters for months when there were strict regulations to be observed.

In the hospital in Hong Kong Charlie Excalibur had recovered sufficiently to answer questions, and he was already in the safe and steady hands of Dunhill, who was sending hourly reports to Sir John. Charlie Excalibur (now officially listed as Garvin) had no resistance in him whatsoever and demonstrated a phenomenal memory for specific detail. It was Dunhill's duty to determine that this paragon of an informer was what he professed to be, but so far everything he said had checked out.

It was on the day of the joint funeral for Marston and his daughter that Sir John finally emerged. It had been decided by the Foreign Office, in consultation with the Queen's Messenger Service, that the ceremony would be held at a burial ground in Dorking, some forty miles south of London. Colonel Evans would be attending with all of the Queen's Messengers who could be released from duty. Since Marston's wife was already interred in the family plot and since the nearest surviving relative was an ancient aunt in Canada, there would be no bereaved family. The arrangements had been left to the members of Marston's old regiment.

On the morning of the funeral, which was to be held at two o'clock in the afternoon, Ross received a call from Staff with a request from Sir John that Ross join him in the drive down to Dorking. No formal clothes, simple business suit. So shortly after eleven Ross met Sir John at the rear exit to the building, where the Rolls was waiting, a vehicle which was hauled out only on special occasions when the drive was to be a comparatively long one and the glass partition between driver and passengers was needed to ensure privacy.

Ross concluded on first glance that Sir John looked positively awful, gray hollows around his eyes, a whitish pallor to the face. Overworked. Sir John offered him a smile and a firm handshake. They made small talk as the limousine pulled out and crossed the river to begin traversing the miles of industrial works and the sprawl of suburbs before it broke into the open green countryside.

'How would you handle the Patterson business?' Sir John said.

'That would depend on the Americans, wouldn't it?' Ross said.

'Make your judgment independent of their actions.'

'Impossible,' Ross said.

'The war in Vietnam is over. The Americans are not much inclined to be very concerned about a dead British traitor if it strains their relations with us.'

'Very well,' Ross said. 'First, I would bring Charlie Excalibur back to our favorite hamlet in the north of Yorkshire under strict surveillance. Then I would let our dubious hero know in no uncertain terms that if he opens his mouth about his exploits, so much as a peep, one stray note to the newspapers and the Americans will have him back and promptly hang him. That's the one great fear he's expressed to Dunhill.'

'Now address yourself to Patterson,' Sir John said.

'I've balanced the alternatives,' Ross said. 'On the one side, we have a detailed account of Patterson's treachery published in a prestigious and widely respected news-magazine. It has caused a stir because it is so specific. On first glance it would appear that for whatever reason, Patterson's treachery is undeniable. I believe it myself, by the way. Patterson was a rotter, no doubt of it, a bloody traitor. But you remember the Philby and Maclean controversies. Damned costly, I would say, in terms of not only image but credibility. Shook MI6 to the roots, so consider...' And his finger traced a geometric pattern on the space of leather seat between them as if to illustrate a geometric precision in his thinking. 'Just consider what Patterson can do to us if the current story is allowed to stand. Undermine our whole standing in the Far East, especially in Thailand. And what of the KGB? I can imagine the kind of propaganda use they could put this to.'

Sir John pivoted open a recessed ashtray, lit a cigarette. 'Have you read Clive's dispatch?'

'Yes, I have.'

Sir John smiled faintly. 'What did you think of it?'

'He made a serious mistake. By all rights, if he had brought Patterson in, all of this could have been contained, the publicity avoided. Word has it that the correspondent who wrote the story was an old flame rekindled.'

'So,' Sir John said noncommittally. 'Continue. The disposition of the Patterson business.'

'Here is the story. Patterson was conducting one of his routine intelligence gathering operations and the Communist guerrillas killed him. Who will contradict that? Charlie Excalibur? Not likely. Our intrepid wise owl Dunhill says he's a pragmatic bastard, shrewd enough to do anything to get himself out of the Far East. Clive? He purposely left a blank to be filled in. He will support any version we care to put out.'

'I see,' Sir John said. They were into the trees now, the south of England opening up to them, the leafy glades, the rolling hills.

'It will work quite well, I think,' Ross said, pursing his lips thoughtfully. 'I can find no holes in it. This version gives us enormous advantages. The Thais will go after

309

the pockets of CPT guerrillas with an absolute vengeance, and Mother Russia will suffer a grievous blow locally and internationally. We will allow the Thais to give Patterson a state funeral, trumpets, elephants, a whole bloody tattoo. We can even arrange, through Thai sources, of course, for them to put up a bronze statue of Colonel Patterson in his military gear, a Brit who lost his life doing his duty. It will give us enormous leverage – that is, if your idea of the American attitude is more than an hypothesis.'

'It is,' Sir John said. 'They are willing to let the whole business go by. They're having enough troubles of their own.'

Ross settled back in the seat as if the matter were settled. 'Where is Clive, by the way? When will he get in?'

'I've had him and his wife sequestered in Brighton until we make a disposition,' Sir John said. 'He'll be at the funeral.' With that Sir John turned to stare out the window, as if he had absorbed it all, then promptly fell asleep.

Clive sat in the old stone chapel at St. Martin's, Katy next to him, her hand on his arm all through the prayers and the eulogies. He was moved by the mounds of flowers banking the two bronze caskets, the men in uniform standing at attention, the crowd of dignitaries who filled the small chapel and overflowed into the courtyard outside. There was a prayer, and the middle-aged vicar made a final reference to the bravery of this man and the tragedy of his daughter's life cut short.

You would have liked this, Marston, Clive thought, *this final vindication from the people who admired you, this last tribute.*

The military band struck up a slow dirge, and the coffins were carried by strong young men in uniform out into the bright sunlight, out to the protection of the striped canopy over the two graves, side by side, the rawness of the earth covered with artificial green grass.

Clive stood in the sunshine, feeling the warmth of the day on his face. He was aware of the cerulean sky with only a few puffy clouds for a change. The cemetery itself was full of wild flowers bursting among the ancient fading tombstones. The band was playing as the pallbearers placed the bronze caskets on the transverse strips which would eventually lower them into the earth. Katy was crying softly and Clive put his arm around her and she drew close to him for comfort.

You have a beautiful day for it, Marston, Clive thought, *and you will be here forever, with your daughter to one side and your wife to the other, reunited at last, with the lovely valley falling away green to the rise of Box Hill in the distance. And here I am, with my arm around my wife, literally full of life.*

The regimental team raised their rifles, and the shots echoed across the valley. A lone bugle sounded and then died away, and the funeral was over.

Clive saw Sir John approaching, looking tired, under pressure. He made a slight and gallant bow to Katy and took her hand gently. 'I'm pleased to see you again, Mrs. Clive,' he said. 'I wish it could have been under more pleasant circumstances.'

'Thank you,' Katy said.

'I wonder if you would mind if I borrow your husband for a moment. It shouldn't take long.'

'Not at all,' she said. 'I have him back. That's the important thing.' She put her hand on Clive's arm. 'I'll be in the car.'

'A sad time,' Sir John said, looking toward the Queen's Messengers still gathered about the canopy. He cleared his throat. 'But decisions still must be made.' And briefly he told Clive of what was being considered. 'But if this is done, then you are deprived of your rightful due,' he said. 'Your part in the whole operation will be minimized, except for your rescue of Marston. And Patterson will end up being publicly lionized, at least in Thailand. We are proposing a statue to honor him. Ironic, isn't it? There will always be a few doubters, of course, because the stories

311

about him will have their effect, but in time they will die away.'

Clive paused, the line of thinking no surprise to him, for indeed, he had left it open. 'I don't care about the heroics, the way things are made to look. He put me through it, and in the end I killed him and that was that.'

'It will be recorded properly in the archives,' Sir John said. 'That's little comfort, I know, but the straight of it will exist somewhere.'

'That's not important,' Clive said. 'I found that I didn't kill my own men, and that makes life easier for me.' The Queen's Messengers had left the grave sites now, returning to their cars. 'As for Patterson, I know the larger policy has to prevail. But there will be no goddamned statue. That's going too far. I'll not have that bastard cast in bronze as a hero when this better man lies here dead because of him. And the others who died because of him. No, there won't be any goddamned bloody statue. I won't have that.'

Sir John nodded with understanding. 'Fair enough, no statue. I want you to consider something else. We're going to need a new man in Bangkok. It would be a considerable promotion. It's yours, if you want it.'

'Thank you, sir,' Clive said. 'Bangkok holds too many memories for me. Besides, I'm content here.'

'Very well. Take a day or two to rest yourself if you like. Things will be pretty hectic for a time, but it will all clear away in time for the next crisis. That's the nature of the business. I'll walk you to your car.'

'If you don't mind, sir, I think I'll stay here a bit longer.'

Sir John nodded, moved away toward his car, and Clive found himself alone at the side of the caskets, aware that the attendants were still standing by the chapel, waiting to finish the job of getting things in order.

I can't leave you yet, Marston, not without a final word. I came to retrieve you, and in the end you gave me back my life. Maybe you've finished your journey, I don't know, or maybe you are just beginning a new one, but God speed thee on thy way. Flights of angels, old man. Flights of angels.

312

He stood for a final moment, then reached out and placed his palm on the bronze of the casket, warm in the sun.

Good-bye, friend.

He turned and walked through the brilliant sunshine toward the waiting car.

A selection of bestsellers from SPHERE

FICTION

CROSSINGS	Danielle Steel	£1.95 ☐
THE SIRENS OF AUTUMN	Tom Barling	£1.95 ☐
THE GOLD SHIELD	Marie Castoire &	
	Richard Posner	£1.95 ☐
SPRING MOON	Bette Bao Lord	£2.25 ☐
CLOUD WARRIOR	Patrick Tilley	£1.95 ☐

FILM & TV TIE-INS

THE KILLING OF KAREN		
SILKWOOD	Richard Rashke	£1.95 ☐
SCARFACE	Paul Monette	£1.75 ☐
STAYING ALIVE	Leonore Fleischer	£1.75 ☐
BY THE SWORD DIVIDED	Mollie Hardwick	£1.75 ☐
AUF WIEDERSEHEN, PET	Fred Taylor	£1.75 ☐

NON-FICTION

THE GOEBBELS DIARIES	Fred Taylor (Ed)	£3.95 ☐
SHADOWS ON THE GRASS	Simon Raven	£1.95 ☐
THE BOOK OF		
ROYAL LISTS	Craig Brown & Lesley Cunliffe	£2.50 ☐
HOW TO MAKE A SECOND		
INCOME	Godfrey Golzen	£1.95 ☐
WHO'S WHO IN INTERNATIONAL		
WINTER SPORTS	David Emery	£2.95 ☐

All Sphere books are available at your local bookshop or newsagent, or can be ordered direct from the publisher. Just tick the titles you want and fill in the form below.

Name _____

Address _____

_____

Write to Sphere Books, Cash Sales Department, P.O. Box 11, Falmouth, Cornwall TR10 9EN

Please enclose a cheque or postal order to the value of the cover price plus:

UK: 45p for the first book, 20p for the second book and 14p for each additional book ordered to a maximum charge of £1.63.

OVERSEAS: 75p for the first book plus 21p per copy for each additional book.

BFPO & EIRE: 45p for the first book, 20p for the second book plus 14p per copy for the next 7 books, thereafter 8p per book.

Sphere Books reserve the right to show new retail prices on covers which may differ from those previously advertised in the text or elsewhere, and to increase postal rates in accordance with the PO.